ANDRÉ GIDE

TRAVELS IN THE CONGO

Translated by
Dorothy Bussy

PENGUIN BOOKS

Penguin Books Ltd, Harmondsworth, Middlesex, England
Viking Penguin Inc., 40 West 23rd Street, New York, New York 10010, U.S.A.
Penguin Books Australia Ltd, Ringwood, Victoria, Australia
Penguin Books Canada Limited, 2801 John Street, Markham, Ontario, Canada L3R 1B4
Penguin Books (N.Z.) Ltd, 182–190 Wairau Road, Auckland 10, New Zealand

First published in France as *Voyage au Congo* and *Le Retour du Tchad*
by Librairie Gallimard, 1927 and 1928
This translation first published in the United States of America
by Alfred A. Knopf, Inc., 1929
Published in Penguin Books 1986

Made and printed in Great Britain by
Cox & Wyman Ltd, Reading
Filmset in 10/12pt Linotron Aldus by
Rowland Phototypesetting Ltd
Bury St Edmunds, Suffolk

A10609.

Travels in the Congo

André Paul Guillaume Gide was born in Paris on 22 November 1869. His father, who died when he was eleven, was Professor of Law at the Sorbonne. An only child, Gide had an irregular and lonely upbringing and was educated in the Protestant secondary school in Paris, though his mother's family had recently become Catholic. He became devoted to literature and music, and began his literary career as an essayist, and then went on to poetry, biography, fiction, drama, criticism, reminiscence and translation. By 1917 he had emerged as a prophet to French youth and his unorthodox views were a source of endless debate and attack. In 1947 he was awarded the Nobel Prize for Literature and in 1948, as a distinguished foreigner, was given an honorary degree at Oxford. He married his cousin in 1895; he died in Paris in 1951 at the age of eighty-one. Gide's best-known works in England are *Strait is the Gate* (La Porte étroite), the first novel he wrote, which was published in France in 1909; *The Coiners* (Les Faux-Monnayeurs) published in 1926; and the famous *Journals* covering his life from 1889 to 1949.

To the Memory of
JOSEPH CONRAD

CONTENTS

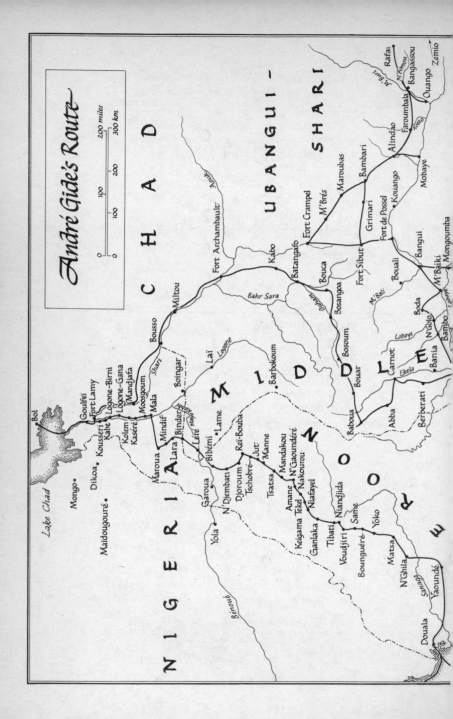

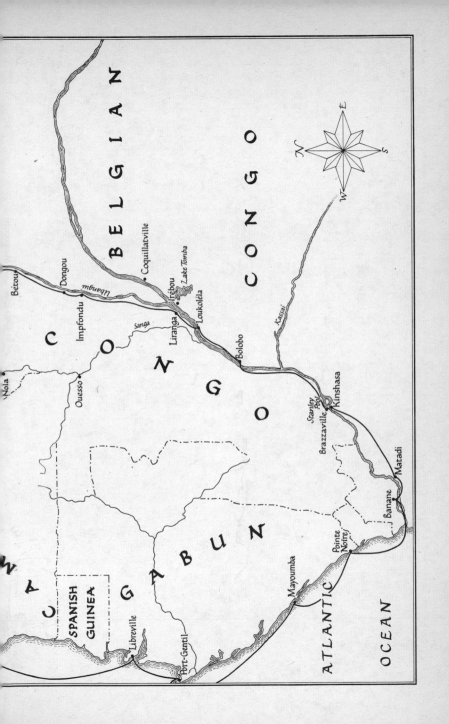

PART ONE

TO THE CONGO

Better be imprudent
moveables than prudent fixtures

Keats

❖❖

CHAPTER ONE

VOYAGE OUT – BRAZZAVILLE

21 July – third day of passage out

My state is one of inexpressible languor; the hours slip by empty and indistinguishable.

After two days of bad weather the sky has begun to turn blue; the sea is growing calmer; the air warmer. A flock of swallows is following the ship.

What a mistake it is not to rock children's cradles from their earliest babyhood! I even think it would be a good plan to calm them and send them to sleep by means of a special pitching-and-tossing apparatus. As for me, I was brought up according to rational methods and by my mother's orders never slept in beds that were not fixed; thanks to which, I am particularly liable to seasickness.

Nevertheless I am holding out; I do what I can to keep my swimming head in order and am glad to see that I am more successful than a good many of my fellow passengers. The recollection of my last six crossings (Morocco, Corsica, Tunis) reassures me.

Our travelling-companions are mostly officials and traders. I think we are the only ones travelling 'for pleasure'.

'What are you going out for?'

'I shall see when I get there.'

I have plunged into this journey like Curtius into the gulf. I feel already as if I had not so much willed it (though for many months past I have been stringing my will up to it) as had it imposed upon me by a sort of ineluctable fatality – like all the important events of my life. And I come near forgetting that it is nothing but a project made in youth and realized in maturity; I was barely twenty when I first made up my mind to make this journey to the Congo – thirty-six years ago.

I am re-reading with rapture all La Fontaine's fables, beginning with No. 1. I can hardly think of a single quality he does not possess. There is nothing one cannot find in him, provided one knows how to look; but the eye that looks must be a skilful one, his touch is often so light and so delicate. He is a miracle of culture – Montaigne's wisdom; Mozart's sensibility.

Yesterday my cabin was flooded in the early dawn, when the decks were being washed. I found my pretty little leather-bound Goethe, given me by Count Kessler (in which I am reading the *Elective Affinities*), floating lamentably in a swamp of dirty water.

25 July

The sky is of a uniform grey; strangely soft. This slow and constant descent southwards will bring us to Dakar this evening.

Flying fish yesterday. Today shoals of porpoise. The captain shot at them from the bridge. One of them turned up its white belly and showed a gush of blood flowing from it.

In sight of the African shore. This morning found a sea-swallow against the bulwarks. I admired its little webbed feet and queer beak. It did not attempt to struggle when I took hold of it. I kept it a few moments in my open hand; then it flew away and disappeared on the other side of the ship.

26 July

Dakar by night. A dreary, sleepy town, with narrow, deserted streets. Impossible to imagine anything less exotic or more ugly. There were a few groups in front of the hotels; the café terraces were glaringly lighted, with vulgar laughter coming from them. We followed a long avenue which soon led us out of the French town. What joy to find oneself among Negroes! We went into a little open-air cinema in one of the side streets. A number of black children were lying on the ground behind the screen at the foot of a gigantic tree – a silk-cotton tree no doubt. We sat down in the front row of the second-best seats. A big Negro behind me read aloud the

4

words on the screen. We went out again and wandered about for a long time till we were so tired that our one thought was bed. But the noise of a night fête underneath the windows of our room in the Metropole Hotel kept us awake for a long time.

At six o'clock in the morning we went back to the *Asie* to fetch a camera. Then we took a carriage to drive to the market place. The horses were like skeletons, with their sides scraped raw and their sores daubed with Prussian blue. We left this wretched conveyance for a motor-car, which drove us six kilometres outside the town, across a piece of waste ground haunted by hordes of carrion birds. Some of them, perching on the roofs, looked like huge bald-headed pigeons.

Visit to the Botanical Gardens. There were a great many trees I did not know. Hibiscus shrubs in flower. One plunges down the narrow paths in the hopes of getting a foretaste of the tropical forest. Some handsome butterflies, like big swallow-tails, but with a large splotch of mother-of-pearl on the under wings. I tried in vain to catch sight of the strange birds whose song we heard. A black serpent, very slender and rather long, slid by and disappeared.

We tried to go to a native village we saw some way off in the sands, by the sea-shore; but an impassable lagoon lay between it and us.

27 July

Incessant rain all day and rather a rough sea. A great many of the passengers were ill. The old colonials say complainingly: 'A dreadful day! You will have nothing worse' . . . On the whole I am bearing it very fairly well. It is hot, thundery, damp; but I have felt worse in Paris; and I am astonished at not perspiring more.

On the 29th we arrived off Konakry. We were to have landed at seven o'clock in the morning; but at dawn a thick fog closed down on the ship and we lost our bearings. The lead was dropped and re-dropped continually. Very low water; very little room between the coral-reefs and the sand-banks. The rain came down so heavily that we had almost given up the idea of landing, but the captain offered to take us in his petrol launch.

It was a long way from the boat to the wharf, but it gave the fog time to clear; the rain stopped.

The ship's officer who landed us warned us we had no more than half an hour and that the boat would not wait for us. We jumped into a *pousse-pousse* drawn by a young Negro *'mince et vigoureux'*. Beautiful trees and half-naked laughing children with languorous eyes. A low sky and an extraordinary stillness and softness in the air. Everything here seems to promise happiness, ease, forgetfulness.

31 July

Tabou. – A low lighthouse, looking like the funnel of a steamer; a few roofs hidden in greenery. Our ship lay up two kilometres off the shore. Not time enough to land; but two big boat-loads of Croumens were brought on board. The *Asie* has recruited seventy of them to supplement the crew. They will be brought back again on the return voyage. Admirable men for the most part; but we shall only see them again with their clothes on.

An isolated Negro in a minute canoe was jerking out the water that was threatening to swamp it, by slapping with his leg against the side of the boat.

1 August

The harbour-bar at Grand Bassam is like an illustration in an old picture-magazine. The landscape is long and low; the sea is tea-coloured, with long trails of stale yellowish foam floating on it. And though the sea looks almost calm, the swell is powerful enough to spread a wide fringe of surf along the sandy shore. The trees that make the setting of the scene look as if they had been drawn by a child and cut out of cardboard. A cloudy sky.

On the wharf a swarm of Negroes hurry about like black ants, pushing trucks before them. There are sheds at the back of the wharf; and right and left, low, squat houses, with red-tiled roofs, intersect the line of trees. The town is squeezed in between the lagoon and the sea. It seems impossible to imagine the great virgin forest – the real forest – there, close to us, just behind the lagoon . . .

To reach the wharf we had to take our places, five or six at a time, in a sort of swinging crate, attached by a hook from a sling; we were then hoisted up into the air by a crane and slung over the sea towards a huge barge, into which the windlass dropped us heavily.

One fancies toy sharks, toy wreckage for dolls' shipwrecks. Naked Negroes run about, shouting, laughing, quarrelling, and showing their cannibal teeth. Boats are floating about on the tea, and little red and green canoes, shaped like ducks' feet and reminding one of the little boats one sees at home at nautical fêtes, scratch and furrow its surface. Divers snap up the coins which are thrown them from the deck of the *Asie*, and stuff them into their cheeks. A long wait for the barge to fill; a long wait for the Grand Bassam doctor to make out sundry certificates – so long a wait that the passengers who had been too eager to get into the boats, and the Bassam officials, who had been in too great a hurry to welcome them, succumb to the swinging and shaking and tossing, and lean over the sides, right and left, to be seasick.

Grand Bassam. – A wide avenue paved with cement down the middle and bordered by low, detached houses. A quantity of grey lizards darted out at our approach and made for the nearest tree-trunk, as if they were playing puss-in-the-corner. Different kinds of strange trees with large leaves – very astonishing for the traveller.

The streets are transversal and lead from the sea to the lagoon, which is narrower at this part and crossed by a Japanese-looking bridge. We were attracted by the luxuriant vegetation on the farther shore; but time was lacking. The other end of the street loses itself in a sort of sand-dune; then comes a group of oil-palms, and then the sea, invisible, but with its place shown by the masts of a big ship.

Lomé, 2 August

Early this morning the sky threatened a downpour of rain. But no; as the sun rose, the greyness became paler and paler so that it turned at last into a milky, azure mist; and the softness of this profusion of silver is beyond words. The immensity of the light shed from the veiled sky is like the *pianissimo* of a full orchestra.

Cotonou, 2 August

Fight between a lizard and a snake. The snake was about a metre long, black, patterned with silver-white, very slim and agile, but so much engaged with its opponent that we were able to observe it at close quarters. The lizard, after a struggle, managed to escape, but at the cost of its tail, which it left behind and which continued to wriggle about aimlessly.

Conversations between passengers.

I should like to start a page in this notebook in the style of some newspapers, beginning: 'Is it true that . . . ?'

Is it true that an American company that has been set up at Grand Bassam buys up mahogany, which it afterwards sells as 'Honduras mahogany'?

Libreville, 6 August; Port-Gentil, 7 August

At Libreville, in this enchanting country,

> *ou la nature donne*
> *Des arbres singuliers et des fruits savoureux,*

people are dying of hunger. It seems impossible to cope with the famine. And inland, we are told, it is still more terrible.

The *Asie's* crane sets to work picking up packing-cases out of the hold in a wide-meshed net and then empties them into the landing-barge. The natives receive them with a great deal of shouting and bustling. It is a miracle that any of the cases get landed intact – squashed and banged and flung about as they are. Some of them burst open like pods and shed their contents of tins like seeds. I picked up one of these tins and showed it to F., the chief agent of a food-supply business, who recognized the trademark and assured me that it was one of a lot of damaged goods which it had been impossible to sell on the Bordeaux market.

8 August

Mayoumba. – The dangerous crossing of the bar was made to the accompaniment of the boatmen's lyrical chanting. The song and the refrain overlap each other.[1] Every time the boat dips, the boatman uses his bare thigh as leverage for the pole of his paddle. There was a

---

1. I afterwards met with this characteristic overlapping in the chants of the Chad region.

wild beauty in this half-plaintive chant; a joyous play of the muscles; a farouche enthusiasm. Three times the boat reared, standing almost on end out of the water; and when it fell again, an enormous packet of water drenched us; but we were soon dried again by the sun and the wind.

We started on foot together towards the forest. A shady path leads into it. What strangeness! We came upon some clearings dotted with reed huts. On our way back we were met by the administrator of the station in his *tipoye*. He kindly put two others at our disposal and made us turn back into the forest. If I had been twenty my pleasure would not have been keener. The porters shouted and leapt. We returned along the seashore. On the beach herds of crabs on tall legs and something like monstrous spiders fled frantically at our approach.

9 August, 7 a.m.

Pointe Noire[2] – A larva-like town, which has scarcely emerged from underground.

2. This spot on the coast is to be the terminus of the Brazzaville–Ocean railway, which is the sole means of obviating the difficult bottleneck that is so hampering to our commerce. The Congo would be a natural outlet for the riches of the interior if it were not that the river traverses a mountainous region not far from the coast and ceases to be navigable at Matadi; it only becomes so again at Stanley Pool (Brazzaville-Kinshassa). Matadi is connected with Kinshassa by the railway that King Leopold caused to be laid down in the Belgian Congo by the advice and under the management of Colonel Thys. This railway, which has been open since 1900, crosses the region that Joseph Conrad was obliged to cross on foot in 1890 and which he gives an account of in *Heart of Darkness*. This admirable book still remains profoundly true and I shall often have occasion to quote it. There is no exaggeration in his picture; it is cruelly exact; but what lightens its gloom is the success of the project which in his pages appears so vain. Costly as the establishment of this railroad may have been in money and human lives, its existence is now an immense benefit to the Belgian colony – and to our own. But at the present moment it has ceased to be adequate; how much so the following letter from the president of the Belgian Chamber of Commerce at Kinshassa will show:

'The situation, from the point of view of the warehousing of *general* cargo [that is to say, of commercial goods packed in cases] is more inextricable than it has ever been. On 1 January 1926 in the Manucongo warehouses at Matadi 6,089,200 kilos of merchandise were being held up. Among these stocks were included 694 tons lying on board the *Rogier*, which had left France in October. This steamer had been more than seventy days at Matadi and not a single case had been unloaded at the time I was there.

9 August, 5 p.m.

Today we entered the waters of the Congo. The captain's launch set us down at Banane. Every opportunity of going ashore finds us ready and eager. Returned at nightfall.

My joy is perhaps as keen; but it penetrates less deeply; it re-echoes in my heart less soundingly. Oh, if only I could forget that life's promises are closing in before me! . . . My heart beats as if I were twenty.

Night-time. We are slowly ascending the river. There are a few lights in the distance on the left bank; a bush fire on the horizon; at our feet the terrifying thickness of the waters.

10 August

An absurd contretemps prevented me from paying my respects to the Governor when we were at Bôma (the Belgian Congo). I cannot get it into my head that I am charged with a mission and therefore an official personage. I have the greatest difficulty in puffing myself out to fill this role.

Arrived at Matadi on the evening of the 10th and left on the 12th at 6 o'clock in the morning; arrived at Thysville at 6.30 in the evening.

We left again about seven in the morning and did not reach Kinshassa till night had set in.

Next day we crossed Stanley Pool. Arrived at Brazzaville on Friday the 14th at 9 a.m.

Brazzaville

Strange country, in which one suffers not so much from heat as from perspiration! . . .

I have caught a few fine tailed butterflies, sulphur-coloured, with black spots – very common – and one other, which is rather more rare, like a swallow-tail, but bigger, yellow, striped with black. (I had seen it before at the Dakar Botanical Gardens.)

---

footnote continued

'The cargoes of four French steamers – the *Alba*, the *Europe*, the *Tchad*, and the *Asie*, containing nearly 80,000 demijohns and a considerable number of cases of wine, were being held up in the Manucongo warehouses.'

This morning we revisited the confluence of the Congo and the Djoué, about six kilometres from Brazzaville. (We went there yesterday at sunset.) There was a little fishing village and a queer dry river-bed, traced by an incomprehensible accumulation of almost black boulders; it looks like the moraine of a glacier. We jumped from one to another of these rounded stones, till we reached the banks of the Congo. There was a little path, almost along the river's edge, and a shady creek where a canoe was lying moored; a great number of butterflies of a great many different kinds; but my butterfly-net had no handle and the finest got away. We then reached a place that was more wooded, on the banks of the tributary, the waters of which were much more limpid. There was an enormous silk-cotton tree, whose monstrous spreading base we skirted round; a spring came gushing from below the trunk. Near the silk-cotton tree was a reddish-purple amorpha growing on a thorny stem of about a metre long. I tore open the flower and found a crawling mass of little grubs at the base of the pistil. A few trees to which the natives had set fire were slowly burning from their base upwards.

I am writing this in the very pleasant hut which M. Alfassa, the acting Governor-General, has placed at our disposal. The night is warm; not a breath stirring; an incessant concert of crickets on an undertone of frogs.

23 August

Third visit to the Congo rapids. But this time we set about it better; and, besides, we and one or two others had the benefit of M. and Mme Chaumel's guidance. We crossed one of the branches of the Djoué in a canoe and came right up to the banks of the big river, where the height of the waves and the impetuosity of the current can be seen particularly well. The sky set its serene and radiant seal upon a spectacle that was more majestic than romantic. From time to time an eddy churns up the water; a jet of foam leaps up. There is no rhythm; and I cannot understand these irregularities in the current.

'And would you believe it,' said one of the guests, looking at me, 'a spectacle like this is still without its painter.' This was an invitation to which I shall not respond. The quality of temperance is an essential one in art, and enormity is repugnant to it. A description is none the more moving because ten is put instead of one. Conrad has been blamed in *Typhoon* for having shirked the climax of the storm. He seems to me, on the contrary, to have done admirably in cutting short his story just on the threshold of the horrible and in giving the reader's imagination full play, after having led him to a degree of dreadfulness that seemed unsurpassable. But it is a common mistake to suppose that the sublimity of a picture depends on the enormity of its subject. I read in No. 2 of the bulletin issued by the Société des Recherches Congolaises:

'These tornadoes, whose violence is so extreme, are in my opinion the most beautiful spectacles of intertropical nature. I end by expressing a regret that there had not been found among our colonials a musician gifted enough to transpose them into music.' A regret I do not share.

24 and 25 August

THE SAMBRY TRIAL

The less intelligent the white man is, the more stupid he thinks the black.

An unfortunate official is being tried who was sent out to the colonies too young and placed in a remote station without sufficient instructions. He needed a strength of character and a moral and intellectual quality that he was without. When these are lacking, a man tries to make the natives obey and respect him by the spasmodic, outrageous, and precarious use of brute force. He gets frightened; he loses his head; having no natural authority, he tries to reign by terror. He feels his hold slipping from him and soon it becomes impossible to quell the growing discontent of the natives, who, notwithstanding that they are often perfectly amenable, are goaded to fury by injustice, violent reprisals, and cruelty of all sorts.[3]

What seems to transpire more than anything from this trial is an insufficiency of supervision. Only tried and trusted officials should be sent to out-of-the-way stations in the wilds. Until a

---

3. However serious the misdeeds attributed to Sambry, those we came across later were, I regret to say, a great deal worse.

young man has proved his worth, he should be closely watched and guided . . .

I particularly noted the amazing incapacity of the two interpreters; though totally unable to understand the judge's questions, they always translated them with the utmost rapidity and no matter how, causing the most ludicrous blunders. When they were told to take the oath, they repeated stupidly, 'Say: "I swear",' so that the audience burst out laughing. And their transmitting of the witnesses' evidence was the merest guesswork.

The accused has got off with a year's imprisonment and been allowed to take advantage of the law which remits the punishment for first offences.

I cannot succeed in forming an opinion as to what the numerous natives who were present at the trial think of it. Does Sambry's condemnation satisfy their sense of justice? . . .

During the third and last hearing of this melancholy trial a very beautiful butterfly flew into the law-court, of which the windows were all open. After circling about for some time it settled most unexpectedly on the very desk at which I was sitting, and I managed to catch it without spoiling it.

The next day I had a visit from Mr X., one of the judges.

'Do you want to know the meaning of all this?' said he. 'Sambry used to go to bed with the wives of all the native soldiers under his command. Nothing could be more imprudent. As soon as they get out of hand, these native guards become terrible. Nearly all the cruelties that Sambry was accused of were committed by them. But they all gave evidence against him, as you saw.'

I am taking these notes too entirely for myself. I see now that I have said nothing about Brazzaville. At first I was delighted with everything; the novelty of the climate, of the light, of the vegetation, of the perfumes, of the birds' songs, and of my own self in the midst of all this was so great that I could find nothing to say from excess of astonishment. I did not know what to call things. I admired without distinction. It is impossible to write well when one is drunk. I was in a state of intoxication.

Now that the first surprise has worn off I take no pleasure in describing a place I am already wanting to leave. The town, which is enormously distended, owes its whole charm to the climate and to its position along the river shore. Kinshassa opposite looks hideous. But Kinshassa is intensely alive and Brazzaville seems asleep – too big for its small activities. Its charm consists in its indolence. And then I realize that it is impossible to get into contact with anything real; not that things here are factitious, but civilization interposes its film, so that everything is veiled and softened . . .[4]

We have engaged at random two *boys* and a cook. The latter, who answers to the ridiculous name of Zézé, is hideous. He comes from Fort Crampel. The two boys, Adoum and Outhman, are Arabs from the Ouadai; our journey northwards will take them part of their way home.

30 August

I recognize a numbness – perhaps a diminution. Eyes are less keen; ears duller; and they carry less far desires that are no doubt weaker. The important thing is that this equation between the urging of the soul and the obedience of the body should be maintained. Even when growing old, may I preserve within myself an undiminished harmony! I do not like the Stoic's proud stiffening of the lip; but the horror of death, of old age, of all that cannot be avoided, strikes me as impious. Whatever may be my fate, I should wish to return to God a grateful and enraptured soul.

---

4. I could not foresee that these questions of our dealings with the natives, which are so distressingly urgent and which I had then only caught a glimpse of, would soon engage my attention so much as to become the chief interest of my journey and that I should find in studying them the *raison d'être* of my presence in the country. But I was soon to learn.

A traveller who has just arrived in a country where everything is new to him is held up by the difficulty of making up his mind. How fortunate the sociologist is who is interested only in manners and customs; the painter who cares only for the country's aspect; the naturalist who occupies himself with insects or plants! How fortunate the specialist! His whole time is not too much to devote to his limited domain. If I had a second life, I could be happy spending it merely in the study of white ants. (It was at Brazzaville I first came across them; prepared though I was, they opened out to me astonishing vistas. I shall speak of them later.) Let me be forgiven, then, if I was only able to look at all the novelties before me with vague and hesitating eyes.

2 September

Belgian Congo. – To Leopoldville by car. Visit to Governor Engels. He has advised us to go as far as Coquillatville (Equateurville) and has offered to put a whale-boat at our disposal to take us back to Liranga, which we had at first meant to go to direct.

Our veranda is chock-full of packing-cases and parcels. The luggage has got to be divided up into loads weighing from twenty to twenty-five kilos. Forty-three cases, bags, or canteens, containing our provisions for the second part of the journey, are to be dispatched direct to Fort Archambault, where we have promised Marcel de Coppet to arrive in time for Christmas. For the detour into Belgian Congo we shall take with us only what is 'strictly necessary'; the rest will be sent on board the *Largeau* as far as Liranga, where we shall find it in ten days' time. Brazzaville has nothing new to show us; we are eager to be moving on.

CHAPTER TWO

UP-RIVER

5 September
Left Brazzaville this morning at daybreak. We crossed the Pool to Kinshassa, where we were to get on board the *Brabant*. The Duchesse de Trévise, who has been sent out here on a scientific mission by the Pasteur Institute, is coming with us as far as Bangui, where she has work.

The sky is grey. If there were a wind, we should be cold. The lower part of the Pool is choked with islands whose banks are hardly distinguishable from those of the river; some among these islands are covered with bushes and low trees; others are sandy and low lying, bristling with an unequal and meagre growth of reeds. In places the grey surface of the water is glossed by large circular eddies. Notwithstanding the violence of the current, the stream seems undecided. There are cross-currents, strange swirls, backwashes, which are made more noticeable by islands of floating weed. These islands are sometimes enormous; it is one of the colonists' jokes to call them 'Portuguese concessions'. We have been told over and over again that this interminable ascent of the Congo was unspeakably monotonous. We are making it a point of honour not to find it so. We have everything to learn and we set to work slowly spelling out the landscape. But we never cease to feel that this is merely the prologue to our journey, which will not really begin till we come into more direct contact with the country. As long as we only see it from the boat, it seems impossible to think of it except as a decorative background – almost without reality.

We are coasting close alongside the Belgian shore. The French shore in the distance opposite is almost out of sight. There are

enormous flat reaches which my eyes search in vain for hippopotamuses. Every now and then the vegetation on the banks grows
thicker; shrubs and trees take the place of reeds; but whether it be
shrubs or weeds, the vegetation is continually encroaching on the
river – or the river on the vegetation, as happens in times of flood.
(But a month from now the water will be much lower, we are told.)
Branches and leaves along the river edge dip and float in the water,
and the wash of the boat as it passes lifts them gently in a kind of
indirect caress.

On deck there are about twenty passengers dining at the common
table. Our three places are laid at another table, parallel to it.

A highish mountain stands across the end of the Pool, which at
this place grows wider. The eddies become larger and more powerful; then the *Brabant* enters the *'couloir'*. The shores become banks
and draw together. The Congo at this point flows between a
discontinuous chain of fairly high, wooded hills. The tops of the
hills are bare, or at least look as if they were covered with short grass
like the Vosges *chaumes* – one expects to see herds grazing on them.

At about two o'clock (I broke my watch last night) we stopped at a
wood station. A pleasant shade of mango trees; a few huts and an
indolent population in front of them. For the first time I saw
pineapples in flower. Some marvellous butterflies, which I tried to
catch, but in vain, for I lost the handle of my butterfly-net at
Kinshassa. The light was glorious; the temperature not too hot.

At nightfall the boat stopped at a miserable village on the French
shore, consisting of about twenty huts dotted round the wood
station, where we took in fuel. Every time the boat puts in to shore,
four huge Negroes, two fore and two aft, plunge into the river and
gain the shore so as to fasten the moorings. The gangway was
lowered, but it was too short and had to be lengthened by long
planks. We found our way to the village, guided by a little seller of
necklaces, who is travelling with us; an odd kind of blue netting,
veined with white, covers him from shoulders to waist and falls over
his nankeen breeches. He cannot understand a word of French, but
he smiles so charmingly when one looks at him that I look at him
often. We took advantage of the last gleams of light to go hastily

over the village. The natives had all got either the itch or the mange or the scab, or something of the sort; not one of them had a clean, wholesome skin. Saw for the first time the extraordinary fruit of the barbadine (passion-flower).

The moon, which is almost full, has been shining through the mist directly ahead of us, and our boat steamed forward straight in the path of her light. There was a gentle following breeze, and a marvellous shower of sparkles – like a swarm of fireflies – was blown back from the funnel. After gazing a long time, I had to resign myself to regaining my cabin, to sweat and stifle under my mosquito-net. Then the air grew slowly cooler and sleep came to me . . . I was wakened by curious noises; I got up and went down to the lower deck, which I found dimly lighted by the glimmering of an oven; the cooks were at work baking bread to an accompaniment of loud laughter and singing. I don't know how the others, who were lying close by, managed to sleep. Three big Negroes were gambling with dice in the shelter of a pile of packing-cases and by the light of a storm-lantern – a clandestine game, for playing for money is forbidden.

5 and 6 September

I have been re-reading Bossuet's funeral oration on Henrietta of France. Except for the admirable portrait of Cromwell and one particular sentence at the beginning on the limits set by God to the growth of schisms, there is nothing which, to my taste at any rate, seems very good. I note this phrase nevertheless: '. . . *parmi les plus mortelles douleurs, on est encore capable de joie*'; and this: '. . . *entreprise . . . dont le succès paraît infaillible, tant le concert en est juste.*' There is an abuse of flabby quotations in this oration.

The oration on Henrietta of England, which I read immediately after, seems to me much finer and more constantly so. I once more feel the liveliest admiration. But how specious the argument is! Imagine someone saying to the traveller: 'Don't look at that fleeting landscape; keep your eyes fixed on the partition of the railway carriage; that, at any rate, doesn't change.' 'What an idea!' I should answer, 'I shall have plenty of time to contemplate the immutable, since you assure me my soul is immortal; give me leave to make haste and love what is so soon to disappear.'

After a second day's somewhat monotonous steaming we lay up for the night in front of the American mission at Tchoumbiri, where we moored as early as six o'clock. (The night before, the *Brabant* did not stop.) The sun was setting as we walked through the village; we saw palm trees as we went, luxuriant bananas (the finest I have so far seen), pineapples, and the big arums that have edible rhizomes (taros).

After dinner we went on shore again in the dark and found ourselves escorted by a troop of provocative, ribald children. On the low ground beside the river innumerable fireflies were twinkling in the grass, but their light goes out as soon as one tries to take hold of them. I went on board again and lingered on the lower deck among the black crew, sitting on a table next to the little seller of necklaces, who dropped off to sleep, with his hand in mine and his head on my shoulder.

Monday morning, 7 September

The most magnificent spectacle greeted us on waking. The sun was rising as we entered the pool of Bolobo. Not a wrinkle was to be seen on the immense sheet of widening water, not even the slightest shiver to blur its surface; it lay, an intact and perfect shell, holding the pure and smiling reflection of the purest sky. In the east, the sun was crimsoning a few long, trailing clouds. Towards the west, sky and lake were the same pearl-colour, a delicate and tender grey; in this exquisite mother-of-pearl every blended colour lay dormant, yet already quivering with the promise of the day's glories. In the distance a few low-lying islands floated ethereally in a liquid haze . . . The enchantment of this mystic scene lasted only a few seconds; the outlines sharpened, grew definite; we were on common earth once more.

The air blows sometimes so light, so suave, so voluptuously soft, that one seems to be breathing deliciousness.

We have been cruising all day among the islands; some of them abundantly wooded and others covered with papyrus and reeds. A strange tangle of branches dips into the thickness of the black water. Sometimes one knows that a village is there because of the palm trees and bananas, though its huts may be barely distinguishable. And the landscape, in its varied monotony, is so fascinating that I hardly leave it for my siesta.

Tonight an admirable sunset was repeated impeccably in the smooth water. The horizon was dark with thick clouds, when a corner of the sky opened and showed an unknown star in the ineffable purity of its depths.

8 September

It is pleasing to think that the sacred orator owes the survival of his memory to those very qualities that are most profane and that he considers the vainest.

I expected the vegetation to be more oppressive. It is thick, indeed, but not very high, and neither the water nor the sky is overwhelmed by it. This morning the islands are disposed so harmoniously on the great mirror of the Congo that one feels as if one were viewing a water park.

At times some strange tree overtops the brushwood of the shores and plays a solo in the massing of the vegetable symphony. Not a single flower; not a note of any colour but green, a very dark, monotonous green, which gives the landscape the solemn tranquillity of the monochrome African oases, and makes an impression of dignity unapproached by our northern landscapes, with their diversity of tones and shades.[1]

Last night we stopped at N'Kounda, on the French shore – a strange and beautiful village, made still more beautiful by the imagination; for the night could hardly have been darker. The

1. Auguste Chevalier, who went up the Congo in August 1902, and has left an excellent account of his travels, describes this part of the forest, on the contrary, as being full of flowers. Even in the equatorial regions the flower season lasts only a short time.
When we crossed the Cameroon in the following spring, we found fields of big amaryllis, which we should not have seen if we had been a few days later or earlier.

sandy path along which we ventured glimmered faintly. The huts were set very far apart, but eventually nevertheless there came a kind of street or very long place; farther on, the ground broke up into a marsh or river, sheltered by a few huge trees of some unknown species; and suddenly, not far from the edge of this hidden water, we came upon a little enclosure, in which we made out three wooden crosses. We struck a match to read the inscriptions. They were the tombs of three French officers. Near the enclosure an enormous euphorbia candelabra was giving itself the airs of a cypress.

A colonist called 'Léonard' (a kind of short colossus, with plastered hair, *à la* Balzac, falling in locks over his flat face) made a terrific scene last night. He came on deck horribly drunk and began making the most frightful row about a boy whom one of the passengers had engaged and whom he wanted to get away. One would have been sorry for the boy if he had succeeded. Then it was some Portuguese or other who excited his fury and whom he covered with foul abuse. We followed him on shore in the dark, till he came opposite a little boat, which, as far as we could understand, the Portuguese had bought from him, but had not yet paid for.

'He owes me eighty-six thousand francs, the brute – the filthy devil – the P-p-portuguese. He's not even a real Portuguese. Real Portuguese stay at home. There are three kinds of Portuguese; real Portuguese – and filthy Portuguese – and Portuguese filth. He's Portuguese filth! Filth! Filth! You owe me eighty-six thousand francs . . .' And so he went on, repeating and shouting the same phrases, exactly the same, over and over again, in the same order, untiringly. A Negress was hanging on his arm; his 'housekeeper', no doubt. He pushed her away brutally and we thought he was going to hit her. His strength was evidently Herculean . . .

An hour later, back he came again on board the *Brabant*. He wanted to have a drink with the captain; but as the captain very firmly refused to give him the champagne he asked for, alleging the bylaw that forbids serving drinks after nine o'clock, he burst out again into a fury of abuse. At last he went off, but he continued his invectives from the shore, while the poor captain shrank away in the dark to the other end of the deck. There I went to keep him company. He was trembling all over, with tears in his eyes, swallowing the insults without uttering a word. He is a Russian, who was in the Tsar's entourage; after having been condemned to death by a revolutionary tribunal he took service in Belgium, leaving his wife and daughters at Leningrad.

After Léonard had at last taken himself off and disappeared into the dark, this poor wreck of a man began protesting: 'Admiral! He called me an admiral . . . I've never been an admiral . . .' He is afraid the Duchesse de Trévise may believe Léonard's malignant accusations. This morning he told us he had not been able to sleep a wink all night. And the passengers, who up till now have never called him anything but 'captain', are showing their sympathy and indignation by addressing him on every possible occasion as 'commander'.

The scenery is beginning to be more what I expected; it is becoming *like*. The abundance of extremely tall trees no longer balks the eye with a too impenetrable curtain; they stand a little farther apart from each other, so that deep gulfs of green and mysterious recesses open out between them; the creepers that wreathe them are festooned in such gentle curves that their embrace looks voluptuous – as if less for the sake of suffocation than of love.

8 September

But this orgy did not last long. This morning, as I write these lines, the islands among which we are steaming show nothing but tufts of uniform grey vegetation.

Yesterday we steamed all night. This evening, as the night was falling, we anchored in the middle of the stream, so as to start again with the first light of dawn.

Yesterday the halt at Loukolela was particularly thrilling. We took advantage of an hour's stop, and all three of us hurried up the fine wooden stair that connects the big saw-mill on the river shore with the village above it; then we followed a path that led into the forest, and with a feeling almost of fear plunged into the heart of an enchanted Broceliande. It was not yet the great dark forest, but it had a solemnity of its own, peopled with strange forms and smells and noises.

I brought back a few very fine butterflies; they flew across our path in great numbers, but their flight was so rapid and so capricious that it was with the greatest difficulty I managed to catch them. Some of them were blue and mother-of-pearl, like the *morphos*, but with deeply notched wings and a tail like our swallowtails.

At times there are narrow water-paths which lead into the depths under the branches and make one long to venture down them in a canoe; nothing can be more enticing than their sombre mystery. The most usual creeper here is a kind of flexible climbing palm, with an alternating and rhythmical arrangement of great girandoles of palm-leaves along its arching stem, which has a somewhat affected grace.

12 September

Reached Coquillatville on the 9th. My regularity has broken down. I am afraid I shall lose interest in my diary if I don't write in it day by day. The Governor has put a car at our disposal and kind M. Jadot (Procureur du Roi) is showing us round the different quarters of this vast and still shapeless town. It is not so much what it is that one admires, as what one hopes it will be in ten years' time. There is a remarkably fine native hospital, which, though it is not finished yet, is supplied with almost everything.[2]

The head of this hospital is French, an energetic-looking Algerian, and, it seems, a very able doctor, whose services it is most unfortunate the French Congo, where there is such a lack of medical assistance, were not able to retain, for want of sufficient remuneration.[3]

On the 11th we visited the Botanical Gardens at Eala, the real object of our detour into Belgian Congo. M. Goosens, the head of

2. In order not to feel too much distressed when one compares it to our wretched hospital at Brazzaville, one is obliged to remind oneself that the Belgians have only this one colony and that they are able to concentrate all their efforts upon it; that the Congo too is our poorest colony and that people in France are fortunately beginning to wake up to its wretched condition.

3. It is a French doctor too who is at the head of the model hospital at Kinshassa, and for the same pecuniary reasons.

the gardens, introduced us to his most interesting nurslings; we looked at them in amazement: cocoa palms, coffee trees, bread trees, milk trees, candle trees, loincloth trees, and the extraordinary Madagascar banana, the 'traveller's tree'; if the thirsty traveller slashes open the petiole at the base of the great wide leaves, there gushes forth a cupful of the purest water. We had already passed a few delightful hours at Eala on the preceding day. M. Goosens's science is inexhaustible and his kindness as untiring as our curiosity is insatiable.

13 September

The most interesting days are the very ones when there is no time to note anything. Yesterday I was interrupted by the car, which came early in the morning to take us to Eala; there we embarked in a whale-boat. A tornado during the night had cooled the air a little; nevertheless it was quite hot enough. We went some way up the Bousira and landed among the reeds opposite Bolombo, an annexe of the Eala gardens, where M. Goosens has established his most important nurseries and his orchards of oil palms. At my request, we took a two hours' walk in the forest, following a very narrow and almost invisible path, while a native armed with a stick preceded us to clear the way. Interesting as this walk was, amongst the unfamiliar vegetation, I must confess I am a little disappointed with the forest. I hope to find better elsewhere. The trees are not very high; I expected more shade, more mystery and strangeness. There are neither flowers nor tree-ferns; and when I asked for them, as if they were a number of the programme which the management had suppressed, I was told that 'this is not the region'.

Towards evening we went up by canoe as far as X, where the motor-cars were waiting for us. Great stretches of reeds coloured the banks of the river with a lighter, softer green. Our canoe glided along among white nymphaeas over a slab of ebony and then darted under the branches out into a flooded clearing; the tree-trunks were hanging over their reflections in the water, and slant rays of light pierced holes in their foliage. A long green snake slid from branch to branch; our boys pursued it, but it escaped into the thick of the brushwood.

14 September

We left Coquillatville at eight o'clock in a little oil-boat which was to have taken us to Lake Tomba; but we are limited as to time by the necessity of catching the *Largeau* at Liranga on the 17th. The lake is 'dangerous'; we might be delayed. We shall leave the *Ruby* at Irébou, where we shall pass the 15th, and from there a whale-boat will take us on to Liranga. The sky is very lowering. Yesterday evening it was illuminated by monstrous three-forked flashes of lightning, much bigger, it seemed to me, than in Europe, but silent or too far off for their thunder to be heard. At Coquillatville we were devoured by mosquitoes. We were stifled under our mosquito-curtains in the night and drenched with perspiration. Huge black beetles swarmed about over our toilet things.

Yesterday they had an open-air auction of hippopotamus meat in the market; the stench was unbearable; there was a seething, yelling crowd, a great deal of talking and quarrelling, especially among the women; but it always ended in laughter.

The *Ruby* is flanked on each side by two whale-boats as long as herself, laden with wood, packing-cases, and Negroes. The weather is cool, damp, and horribly close. As soon as the *Ruby* started, three Negroes began a deafening tamtam on a calabash and an enormous wooden drum, as long as a culverin, and roughly carved and painted.

I have been re-reading the funeral oration of Marie-Thérèse of Austria. There are admirable passages in it; I really think I prefer it to the two Henriettas.

15 September

The *Ruby* landed us at Irébou at nightfall. We were received by Commandant Mamet, who is at the head of the military camp, which is one of the oldest in the Belgian Congo. A fine avenue of thirty-year-old palm trees running alongside the river (the branch of it, that is, which flows into Lake Tomba) led to the hut that was reserved for us. Dined at the Commandant's. Devoured by mosquitoes.

This morning we made an excursion in a whale-boat in the direction of Lake Tomba. The boatmen's songs were admirable. The metal case in the stern of the whale-boat serves as a drum, on which one of the blacks thumps indefatigably with a large log of wood; and the whole whale-boat, which is entirely made of iron, vibrates; it was like the regular rhythm of a piston regulating the oarsmen at their work. Behind the man that beats the drum, there is a younger native, armed with a stick, who breaks this implacable rhythm by a regular system of syncopation between the beats.

We halted at Makoko (Boloko), a little village on the wide channel that connects the Congo with Lake Tomba. We had no time to go as far as the lake. It was excessively hot and the midday sun very fierce. I chased butterflies on the shore – big black ones, flecked with blue. Then, while our lunch was getting ready, I plunged with my two companions into the forest that adjoins the village. Great butterflies quite unknown to me darted up before us, preceding us along the winding path in a fantastically capricious flight and then vanishing in the tangle of the creepers. It was maddening not to be able to catch them. (I did, however, succeed in capturing a few, but the most astonishing escaped me.) This little corner of forest struck us as more beautiful than anything we had seen round Eala. We came upon a piece of flooded ground at the bottom of a slope; the vaulted depths above us lay repeated in its black waters; a monstrous tree-trunk spread its huge base; and as we drew near, a bird's song sprang up out of the depths of shadowy gloom, far away, itself charged with gloom – the whole shadowy gloom of the forest. Its long chirruping was drawn out in a strange chromatic descent.

16 September

We left Irébou this morning in a whale-boat. Liranga is almost opposite, a little way downstream; but the Congo at this place is extremely wide and choked with islands; the crossing takes about four hours. The boatmen rowed slackly. We went through great expanses where the water seems absolutely still; then, at moments, and particularly near the shores of the islands, the current suddenly becomes so rapid that the boatmen had the greatest difficulty in remounting it. For, for some reason or other, we had gone too far down; the boatmen, however, seemed to know the route, and no doubt the crossing farther up stream is not so safe.

A Portuguese, the only white man left at Liranga, who had been warned of our coming by telegram from Brazzaville, was there to meet us. The father in charge of the important mission of Liranga was obliged to leave his post last month in order to get medical advice at Brazzaville. He took with him several of the worst cases among the children of the district, which is being decimated by sleeping-sickness. The mission house, where we are to lodge, is about a mile from the landing-stage; it is on the river shore, but the banks are too rocky in this place to allow of boats of more than a certain tonnage putting in, at any rate when the waters are low. The village, which is intersected by orchards, lies along the shore.

After passing through a fine avenue of palm trees one comes to a brick church, beside the long, low building where we are to put up. A black 'catechist' opened the doors for us, and, as all the rooms are at our disposal, we shall be very comfortable. It is frightfully hot, damp, and thundery – stifling. Fortunately the dining-room is very airy. I rose from my after-lunch siesta streaming; then went out walking. The path began by leading through some big orchards of banana trees, with very wide leaves, quite different from those I have seen hitherto; it then grew narrower and plunged into the forest. One could easily walk for miles in this way, enticed on by a fresh surprise at every twenty steps. But the night began to fall. A terrific storm was brewing, and delight gave way to fear.

Three times a day there is an hour's catechism in the vernacular. Fifty-seven women and a few boys mechanically repeat the answers to the questions which the catechist instructor repeats as monotonously. One can sometimes make out words that no one has been able to translate, such as: 'Holy Sacrament'; 'Extreme Unction'; 'Eucharist' . . .

18 September

The temperature is not very high (not more than 90° Fahrenheit), but the air is heavy with electricity and moisture, and thick with tsetses and mosquitoes. The latter particularly like attacking one's ankles, which are left unprotected by one's shoes; they even venture up one's trousers and attack one's calves; even through the stuff one's knees are bitten. Siestas are impossible; besides, it is the hour for butterflies. I am beginning now to know them almost all. When a new one appears, it is all the more delightful.

The *Largeau*, which we have been awaiting in vain for the last two days, turned up early this morning. We hoisted a white flag in front of the mission house, and she put in at the little landing-stage, so that we were spared the difficulty of carrying our luggage on board in canoes. The mosquitoes and tsetses have been so harassing that we are not sorry to leave Liranga.

The *Largeau* is a boat of about fifty tons; she is extremely pleasant, with good cabins, a saloon, a big dining-saloon, and electricity everywhere. According to the custom of the country, she is flanked on either side by two whale-boat barges. Besides Captain Gazangel, we are the only whites on board; but one of the passengers, a rather good-looking and well-mannered mulatto, goes by the name of 'young Mélèze'. His father is one of the best-known colonists in the '*couloir*'.

We have left the Congo for the Ubangui. The water is thick with mud, and the colour of *café au lait*.

At about 2 p.m. a tornado forced us to lie up for an hour in the lee of an island. The scenery has a prehistoric look about it. Three superb blacks swam ashore; they searched the tanglewood of the flooded forest to cut long switches for taking soundings.

Towards evening we were hailed by a very narrow canoe. It was W, the owner of the next wood station, who wanted to know if we had brought him his mail. He is going to Coquillatville for medical treatment, for he has had, so he says, five or six 'good whacks on the head'. This is what people here call an attack of fever.

Stopped the night at Boubangui. The natives who crowded round us were neither handsome, attractive, nor curious. What 'young Mélèze' told us has been confirmed: the huts of this village, at the season when the river is high, are flooded for a period of about six weeks. The water comes up almost waist-high and the inhabitants have to perch their beds on piles. The cooking is done on little mounds of earth. The only way of getting about is in canoes. As the huts are made of mud, the water wears away the bottom of the walls.

The captain assures us that some villages remain flooded for three months.

I am in an excellent mood for working. The monotony of the landscape conduces to it. I have just finished a small book by Cresson: *Position actuelle des problèmes philosophiques*. His exposition of Bergson's philosophy convinces me that I have long been a Bergsonian without knowing it. There are no doubt pages in my *Cahiers d'André Walter* which might even be thought directly inspired by *L'Évolution créatrice*, if the dates allowed of it. I greatly mistrust a system that comes so pat in response to the tastes of the period and owes a great part of its success to flattering them.

Traité de la concupiscence. There is nothing noteworthy in this except the very quality that Bossuet considered the vainest, so that it is a refutation of his theory.

I know besides, from having often indulged in this amusement, that there is nothing in the life of a nation, as in the life of an individual, that may not lend itself to a mystical or teleological explanation . . . nothing in which one may not recognize, if one really wishes to, the opposing actions of God and the devil; and one is often inclined to think this interpretation the most satisfactory, simply because it is a striking image. My whole mind today rebels against the easiness of this attitude, which strikes me as not being very honest. For the rest, the style of the *Traité* is exceedingly fine and Bossuet has nowhere shown himself a better writer and a greater artist than in this work.

It has rained almost without interruption for the last two days. The *Largeau* lay up last night off Bolobo on the Belgian shore; a wood station and brick factory.

We arrived at Impfondo this morning at eight o'clock. There is a fine long avenue, widening out into a public garden on the river bank. Farther upstream and farther downstream are native villages – wretched dilapidated huts – but all the French part, at any rate, is cheerful, tidy, and prosperous-looking. It shows to a small degree what might be done with care and perseverance. M. Augias, the administrator, who is on a tour of inspection, is expected back tomorrow. The country surrounding Impfondo is fine; there are river creeks where canoes are lying moored, and unexpected views of the interplay of land and water. But it must be confessed that the ascent of the Ubangui is hopelessly monotonous.

The sky is covered, but the clouds are not low. During the last three days there has been frequent rain; a fine rain which drifts with the wind, and at moments a heavy shower. Nothing can be more melancholy than the dawn of one of these rainy days. The *Largeau*'s progress is desperately slow; we ought to have slept at Bétou; but, owing to the bad quality of the wood fuel, we shall no doubt not get there till about noon tomorrow. The wood stations, when there is no proper supervision, provide nothing but rotten wood. The insufficiency of personnel is everywhere felt. There ought to be more subordinates. There ought to be more labour. There ought to be more doctors. And first of all there ought to be more money to pay them. There is a lack of medicaments everywhere. Everywhere people suffer from the lamentable penury by which diseases that might be the most easily checked are allowed to hold their own and even to gain ground. The medical service, when it is asked for medicines, generally sends, after an immense delay, nothing but iodine, sulphate of soda and – boric acid![4]

In the villages along the river shores, one meets with hardly anyone who isn't scarred and disfigured by hideous sores (mostly due to *pian*). And all these resigned people laugh, amuse themselves, stagnate in a sort of precarious felicity, incapable, no doubt, of even imagining a better state of things.

We stopped at Dongou for the night. The government station of Impfondo has been removed to Dongou. We landed at nightfall. In front of the European houses, which are built so as to face each other, is a kind of public garden, which makes a separation between them, though without giving them sufficient isolation. There is an avenue of orange trees, which are bowed down by the weight of their green oranges (for here, even the oranges and lemons lose their colour and brightness and become indistinguishable from the uniform green around them). The trees are still young, but in a few years' time the garden will probably become a very fine one.

4. At least, so we were told.

Opposite the landing-stage is a signpost marked: 'Impfondo; 45 kilometres.' The same road leads in the opposite direction to a native village, which we visited after dark.

23 September

The forest is changing slightly in appearance; the trees are finer; their trunks, which are freed from creepers, are more distinct; their branches are hung with masses of light green lichen, like the larches in the Engadine; some of these trees are gigantic, far bigger than any of our trees in France; but as soon as one is at some distance from them (owing also to the immense width of the river), it is impossible to judge of their size. The creeper palm, which was so frequent a few days ago, has disappeared.

Towards evening the sky at last cleared; it was rapture to see the blue again! The open surface of the waters reflected a golden apotheosis, streaked with delicate tints of crimson and purple, not where the sun was setting, but in the east. We spent the night off Laenza. We went over the small, uninteresting village by twilight. In one of the huts a woman had just been confined. The child had not yet begun to cry; it was still fastened to the placenta. The midwife, in our presence, severed the cord with a wooden knife; she left a length on the child, which she carefully measured off as far as its neck, after having first passed it over the baby's head. The placenta was then wrapped up in a banana-leaf; it no doubt has to be buried according to certain rites. There were a crowd of curious spectators at the door, which was so low that one had to stoop one's head to go in. We gave a *pata* (five francs) to welcome little Veronica's entrance into the world, and went on board again, where we were very soon assailed by a horde of charming little green cicadas. The *Largeau* put off again at two in the morning. The moon was in her first quarter; the sky very pure; the air warm.

24 September

I have been re-reading the first three acts of the *Misanthrope*. At each fresh reading my judgement becomes more definite. The sentiments that form the mainspring of the action, the foibles that Molière satirizes, need a more delicate, a more finely shaded portrayal; they lend themselves ill to that broadness of line, to that 'erosion of the contours' that I admire so much in the *Bourgeois* or the *Malade* or the *Avare*. Alceste's character seems to me slightly artificial, and, just because he puts so much of himself in it, the author seems to me ill at ease. It is often difficult to grasp what or whom he is laughing at. The subject is better suited to a novel than to the stage, where there is too much need of exteriorization; Alceste's sentiments suffer from this enforced expression, by which his character is given a surface ridiculousness of a rather inferior quality. The best scenes are perhaps those in which he himself does not appear. Finally, except for his frankness (which is more often than not intolerable brutality), it is not very clear what those eminent qualities are which we are given to understand would fit him for the highest posts.

At ten o'clock we stopped opposite Bétou. The natives here, Mojembos by race, are healthier, more robust, handsomer; they seem freer and franker. While my two companions went along the river bank, I found my way to the Compagnie Forestière's station. A squad of very young girls were at work weeding the ground in front of the station. They were singing as they worked; they were dressed in a kind of ballet skirt made of plaited palm fibre; many of them had on brass anklets. Their faces were ugly, but their busts admirable. I took a long, solitary walk across fields of manioc, chasing extraordinary butterflies.

The village, which I visited afterwards, is enormous, but un-attractive. Farther on I came upon the church, half buried in the brushwood; it has been deserted for the last two years, for this particular race has always refused to listen to the missionaries' teaching or listen to their morals. The church, with its doors and windows wide open, is already overgrown with vegetation. A troop of children along the riverside were amusing themselves by diving from the top of the bank.

About two o'clock young Mélèze parted company with us. He crossed in a canoe to Boma-Matangué, on the Belgian shore, with his 'housekeeper' and a little 'boy' of twelve, whose business it is to spy on the woman and act as informant.

25 *September*

We moored for the night on the Belgian shore at the foot of a huge tree. We arrived at Mongoumba about eleven o'clock. A monumental wooden staircase, bordered by mango trees, leads up to the station. The banks are about fifty feet high.

The Ubangui has become more rapid, and the *Largeau*'s progress is slower. The fineness of the trees is not enough to break the monotony of the forest. We saw four black and white monkeys in the branches, of the kind which are, I believe, called 'capuchins'.

I am re-reading *The Master of Ballantrae.*

Every day between one and four o'clock there are a few rather trying hours; but we read in the packet of newspapers the captain has lent us that the thermometer was at 96° Fahrenheit in Paris at the end of July.

A beautiful half-moon, like a cup above the river, sheds its light on the waters. We have moored off the side of an island; the boat's searchlight is illuminating the jungle fantastically. The whole forest is vibrating with a continuous sound of shrill creaking. The air is warm. The lights of the *Largeau* have just been put out. All is quiet.

26 *September*

We are approaching Bangui. The idea of seeing a country again that is free from water fills us with joy. This morning the villages that are succeeding each other along the river banks are less melancholy, less dilapidated. The trees, whose bases are no longer hidden by undergrowth, look taller. Bangui, which has been in sight for the last hour, climbs half-way up a very high hill that stands across the stream and deflects it towards the east. The houses are gay, half hidden by greenery. But it is raining – rain that threatens to become a deluge. The luggage is packed, the canteens shut. In a quarter of an hour we shall have left the *Largeau*.

CHAPTER THREE

‹‹

BY CAR

M. Bouvet, the Governor's secretary, came on board to bring us his greetings and invite us to lunch. Leaving our luggage in charge of our boy Adoum, we got into two cars and drove through the rain, which was still pouring, to the two huts which are reserved for us. Mme de Trévise's is charming; ours is very pleasant, spacious and airy. I am writing these lines while Marc is gone to look after the luggage. I am sitting in a large cane armchair watching the shower drench the landscape; and then immersing myself again in *The Master of Ballantrae*.

28 September

I have had some very encouraging conversation with Governor Lamblin, who has invited us to take all our meals with him. I like him extremely; he is a man of great modesty, but the admirable work he has accomplished shows what might be achieved by an intelligent and consecutive administration.

Visited the villages on the bank of the river downstream from Bangui. Spent a long time watching the preparation of palm-oil, which is the first oil extracted from the ligneous pulp. Another oil[1] is afterwards extracted from the kernel, after the shell has been crushed. But the first operation is to separate this kernel from the surrounding pulp. To do this the grain is boiled, then ground in a mortar with the handle of a pestle, which offers so small a surface that the hard shell slips away to one side, and its torn envelope comes off on the other. This soon forms a kind of saffron-coloured

---

1. This oil, which is of superior quality, is what we properly call palm-oil. But it can be obtained only by means of special crushers.

tow, out of which the oil is squeezed by hand. The women who do this work reward themselves by chewing the residue. All this is not very interesting to tell (though highly interesting to observe). I leave the rest to the textbooks.

This morning, started at nine o'clock in a motor-car for the falls of M'Bali. A small lorry followed us with our sleeping-arrangements, for we are not to return till tomorrow. Mme de Trévise, who is due at Bambari on service, has obtained two days' leave to accompany us. The road is admirable; this word is always recurring under my pen, especially after a good night's sleep. I feel my heart and spirits as light as air, and my mind not over-stupid; everything I see enchants me. The road soon plunges into a spacious wood of very tall trees. The tree-trunks, no longer muffled in undergrowth, are visible in all their native nobility. They are extraordinarily bigger than our European trees. On a number of them, at the point where the branches begin to spread (for the tree shoots uninterruptedly up without a single break until its crowning summit of green), grow enormous epiphyte ferns, pure green in colour and resembling elephants' ears. All along the road, groups of natives, men and women, are seen hurrying to the town, carrying on their heads the produce of the distant villages – manioc, millet flour, and what not – in large baskets covered with leaves. As we pass, all these people stand at attention and salute; then, if there is the slightest response, they burst out into shouts and laughter. When I waved my hand to the children as we were going through one of the many villages, they were in a frenzy of delight, jumping and dancing about wildly in a kind of delirious rapture. For when the road emerges from the forest, it goes through a highly cultivated region, where everyone looks prosperous and the people seem happy.

We stopped for lunch at the farther end of one of the biggest villages, in the travellers' hut,[2] and soon a troop of children gathered all along the palings that surround the hut; I counted forty of them.

2. On all the roads of equatorial Africa the administration has been at pains to set up, about every fifteen miles or so, a shelter which makes it unnecessary to carry tents. These shelters consist as a rule of two vast huts whose doors face each other; a single roof connects them and projects sufficiently to form a veranda. They are almost always in close proximity to a village where food can be found for the porters. Other huts, in which the porters can shelter, surround the principal dwelling.

They stayed there watching us eat, just like the crowd at the Zoological Gardens that comes to see the seals fed. Then little by little, encouraged by us, they grew bolder, invaded the enclosure, and came close up to us. One of them who knelt down in front of my chair was wearing a great feather on the top of his head, in the style of the Mohicans.

Before lunch, in the baking sun, we went to see another village, belonging to the first and almost touching it, in a clearing of the forest – a village so strange and so beautiful that we felt we had found in it the very reason of our journey and its very core.

And a little time before we halted, there was a wonderful river-crossing. A tribe of blacks stood on the bank; on the opposite bank stood more tribes, waiting. Three big canoes fastened together made the ferry-boat; and our two cars were placed on the planks which joined them. A metal cable, which the ferrymen caught hold of, was stretched from shore to shore to enable the boat to stem the very violent current.

The falls of the M'Bali, if they were in Switzerland, would be surrounded by enormous hotels. Here all is solitude; a hut, two huts with straw roofs, in which we are to sleep, do not spoil the wild grandeur of the scene. Fifty yards from the table where I am writing this, the cascade falls in a great misty curtain, silvered by the light of the moon between the branches of the great trees.

Bouali, 29 September

My first night in a camp-bed, where one sleeps better than in any other. At sunrise the waterfall, looking golden in the slanting rays, was an exceedingly beautiful sight. An immense island of greenery divides the current, and the water falls into two cascades, disposed in such a way that it is impossible to see them both at once. And one learns with astonishment that the first fall that strikes one owes its majesty and fullness to only half the waters of the river. When one draws near the bank, one discovers the second, hidden in the shade by some jutting rocks, and half buried, as it were, under the abundance of vegetation. The shrubs and plants are not, it must be admitted, the least exotic in appearance, and if it were not for a strange little island of pandanus with its aerial roots, nothing would remind one that this is almost the heart of Africa.

By Car

Got back without encountering any other incident but a tornado, which surprised us while we were having lunch at the same station as yesterday and as agreeably. A sudden gust struck down a small tree beside us. During the deluge of rain, which lasted for about an hour, we occupied ourselves by organizing games for the tribe of children who had gathered round us – gymnastic exercises, songs, dances, ending up with a march past. I forgot to say that the children had begun by getting a good ducking in the rain that streamed from the roof, so that the object of the first exercises was to warm them up after their shower-bath.

Bangui, 30 September

Mme de Trévise has left with Dr Bossert. They are going into the Grimari region, in order to try the preventive action of '309 Fourneau' on sleeping-sickness. Governor Lamblin proposes we should make a motor tour of about a fortnight, through a highly cultivated region which we intend to traverse again later on foot, but he wishes us to see it before the harvest so that we may get an idea of its prosperity. He cannot accompany us himself, but M. Bouvet, his secretary, is to do the honours of the country for us.

1 October

The car that was to take us came back from Fort Sibut out of order. We had to wait at Bangui till six o'clock for it to be repaired. The lorry that follows us was so loaded with our luggage that our two boys had to sit beside the chauffeur in our car. The night fell quickly and we had no headlights; but the full moon soon rose in a cloudless sky and showed us our way. I am full of admiration for Mobaye, our excellent chauffeur, a native who has been trained by Lamblin. He had just returned from a very tiring trip and had to start off again without any rest. We asked him several times if he would not like us to stop for the night at the next stage, but he said no, he could 'hold out'. So at midnight we stopped only just long enough to devour a wretched little chicken and a bottle of wine, served on a table set up in a moment in the middle of the road by moonlight. We arrived at Fort Sibut at three o'clock in the morning, exhausted. Too tired to sleep.

2 October

By a lucky chance we have happened on Fort Sibut the day of the monthly market. There are swarms of natives bringing in their crop of rubber in great baskets. Thanks to Lamblin's initiative, the regions bordering the roads are covered with recent plantations of cearas. This rubber is in the form of yellowish strips, like swallows' nests or dried seaweed. Five traders, who have hurried up in their cars, were waiting for the market to open. The region here has not been conceded; the market is free[3] and the bidding began at once. We were surprised to see it stop almost immediately. But we soon understood that these five gentlemen were making a ring. The first carried off the whole crop for seven francs fifty a kilo, which probably seems a very fair price to the native, who only recently was selling his rubber at three francs; but at Kinshassa, where the traders resell it, it has fetched for some time past between thirty and forty francs, which leaves a very respectable margin. What about our gentlemen? As soon as the business is concluded with the native, they meet together privately in a little room, where another auction begins and they divide the spoil among them. The administrator is powerless against this secret auction, which, with every appearance of being illicit, does not, I am told, come within the power of the law.

These small traders, young men for the most part, often lead a hazardous and precarious existence, with no proper premises and consequently no overhead expenses. They have come out to the country with the fixed idea of making their fortune, and that quickly. Their advent is extremely harmful to the native and to the country.

From Fort Sibut to Grimari the country is a little monotonous; along the sides of the road there are almost continuous plantations of cearas; those that are more than four years old are already fine shady trees; it is only at this age that the periodical bleedings begin. This operation, which soon exhausts them, leaves long, slanting scars all down the trunk.

---

3. For that matter, the big concessionaire companies, of which I shall have much to say later on, have no right to plantation rubber, but only to what the natives get out of the forest from rhizomes or creepers.

By Car

Sometimes a little stream intersects the plain; then, in the valley that it forms, a narrow strip of forest springs up again and gives us a moment's delicious coolness. Very beautiful butterflies haunt the sunny places on the banks.

Bambari, 3 October

Bambari is situated on a piece of high ground, overlooking the whole country beyond the Ouaka, which we were ferried across yesterday and which flows past the station, less than a quarter of a mile away. This morning we visited the school and the dispensary. It is the monthly market day. We went in some curiosity to see whether yesterday's gentlemen would appear and whether the same scandal would be repeated. But today it is only the weighing that is done; the bidding is for tomorrow. Rubber, we are told, fetched sixteen francs fifty here last month.

Bambari market, 5 October

Rubber of the same quality as that which we saw sold the other day for 7 fr. 50, today fetched 18 fr. M. Brochet, the representative of the Kouango Company, who is an important trader settled at Bambari, bid against the traffickers. One of them, who knew that Brochet was after the whole crop, wanted at any rate to make him pay dear for it. But Brochet suddenly dropped off and the other man found himself let in for more than he could pay for; so that he had afterwards to sell the whole lot to Brochet.

Bangassou, 8 October

I have had no time to note anything for the last few days. The country has changed in appearance. Instead of being a plain, the ground is broken up by quantities of strange-looking hummocks; they are sorts of low hills with regularly rounded tops like domes, and M. Bouvet tells us they are old termitaries. I cannot see what else can explain these odd mounds. But what seems to me particularly curious is that in the whole country there is no sign of any recent termitary of the same monumental size; these, which are so immense, are in all likelihood several centuries old and must have been long ago abandoned; the rain must have taken a very long time to wear them away, if they were the same as those I admired so much in the forest near Eala – works like medieval castles or cathedrals with walls as hard as bricks and almost vertical. Or are these the work of a different race of termites? And have these termitaries always been rounded? And yet they all seem deserted. Why? It seems that another race of termites, whose buildings are on a small scale, now occupies the ground in place of the monumental ones. Some of these tumuli which I saw later had been cut straight through to make way for the road, and the mystery of their inside was displayed, with its passages, rooms, etc. I cursed the car for not letting me examine this matter more at leisure.

All along the road, for about fifty kilometres, there is an almost uninterrupted succession of villages and of crops of the most varied kinds: cearas, rice, millet, maize, castor oil, cotton, taro (a large arum with edible rhizomes), oil palms, and bananas. The road, which is bordered with small citron trees, looks like a road in a park. Every thirty yards or so, there is a reed hut, half hidden by the foliage, and shaped like a pointed helmet. These garden-cities that lie stretched along the sides of the road are nothing but the merest mask of prosperity. The race that inhabits and over-populates them is not a very fine one. Before it was subjected two years ago, its members lived scattered in the bush; the old people will not let themselves be tamed; they sit squatting on the ground like baboons and hardly glance up as the motor passes by, one never gets a salutation from them.[4] The women, on the contrary, run up, waving and shaking their bundles; their sex (they are shaved) is sometimes hidden by a bunch of leaves, the stalk of which passes backwards and up between the buttocks and is tied to the girdle, from which it either droops or stands up in a kind of ridiculous tail. There are quantities of children; some of them, when they see the motor coming, run up and either sit or lie down in the middle of the road. For fun? Out of devilry? Bouvet thinks from curiosity: 'They want to see how it works.'

On the 6th we slept twenty kilometres this side of Mobaye, so as to avoid arriving there by night. We were given an amazing tam-tam in front of the rest-house of Moussareu; they danced at

4. The young men of the Marouba tribe, who willingly accept the French rule, turn out of their villages the old irreconcilables, whose influence and advice they will neither submit nor listen to.

first by the light of our photophores, which our boys held up at arm's length, and later by the light of the full moon. Admirable alternating songs tempered the enthusiasm and frenzy of the pandemonium and gave it rhythm and support. I have never seen[5] anything more disconcerting, more savage. A kind of symphony was organized, consisting of a soloist and a chorus of children; the end of each of the soloist's phrases blended with the voices of the chorus as they took it up. Unfortunately our time here is counted. We must leave before daybreak.

We left this station on the 7th, early in the morning, hoping to return to it some months hence on our way back from Archambault. As we started, the silvery dawn was mingling with the moonlight. The scenery here becomes rugged, with rocky hills, between four and five hundred feet high, along which the road skirts. We arrived at Mobaye at about ten o'clock.

This station is admirably situated on the banks of the river which it overlooks. Upstream are the Ubangui rapids, whose waters, now that they are high, almost flood a charming little fishing village that stands on the Belgian shore in the shadow of a group of palm trees.

Dr Cacavelli showed us round his dispensary hospital. The patients come sometimes from distant villages to be operated on for elephantiasis of the genital organs, which is very common in these parts. He showed us a few monstrous cases that he was preparing to operate on; one is dumbfounded, without at first understanding what the huge bag can possibly be that the native is dragging along underneath him . . . Dr Cacavelli told us that the cases of elephantiasis before us probably weighed no more than thirty or forty kilos. The mass of hypertrophied conjunctive tissue of which he rids his patients sometimes (if we are to believe him) amounts to seventy kilos. He once, he says, operated on a case of eighty-two kilos. 'And,' he adds, 'these people manage in spite of it to make journeys of from fifteen to twenty kilometres on foot to come to be treated.' I accepted his statements, but gave up trying to understand them . . .

When the operation is properly performed, he says that it respects and saves the patient's virility, which lies buried in the mass of conjunctive tissue without being in any way harmed. And in this

5. Nor were we ever to see.

manner during the last three years he has restored the power of procreation to 236 impotents.

'Now, 237, come along!'

We hurried away, so as not to lose our appetites altogether.

Immediately after lunch we started for Foroumbala, a hilly but not very interesting place. The inhabitants of the villages we passed through are ugly. The car put a few guinea-hens to flight. A terrifying thunderstorm was threatening, but turned aside at the last moment. We arrived at Foroumbala about five o'clock. The station is unoccupied; it is finely situated on the Kotto; there are a few admirable trees. The schoolchildren were out on the shady place in front of the rest-house, and as they were being taught to spin, each of them was holding a little spindle, with the bobbin hanging from it like a spider from its thread. They were all drawn up in rows, a smile on their lips. One expected them to start singing one of Gounod's choruses. After this the native master gave them gymnastic drill. Then there was a very merry game of football, in which we joined. An orange served as ball. All these children talk a little French.

I saw them again after dinner, dancing by the light of a straw fire, with the wives of the absent native militia. One of these children, who was very wretched-looking, kept in the shade, apart from the others. As the night was chilly and he seemed to be shivering, I made him come near the fire. But the others at once drew away. He was a leper and had been cast out of his village,[6] which is three days' walk away. He knows no one here. Marc, who came up just then, said he had already met him and given him something to eat. He had even left enough with one of the native women to provide the little pariah with food for a week; the woman has promised to look after him. We shall be coming back here again and we shall know whether she has kept her word. But if the child is incurable, what is the use of prolonging his miserable existence?

On the 8th, as soon as we got out of Foroumbala, we crossed the Kotto, which is in flood, in a boat. In this region, there are biggish cotton fields interspersed with manioc fields, all square and regular,

6. Not so much, it seems, because he was a leper, as because he 'brought bad luck' to the village.

as in the cultivated parts of France. In places the ground was scattered with quantities of perfectly round gourds, like colocynths, of the size of an ostrich's egg; we are told that the natives eat its seeds.

As we got nearer Bangassou, we began to meet people whose heads were dressed in a very peculiar manner; one side is shaved, the other covered with little waving locks which they bring over to the front. They are N'Zakaras, one of the most interesting tribes of the sultanates.

Bangassou, 8 October

I am writing these lines in the veranda of our hut. I am a little disappointed by Bangassou. The town has no doubt been affected by the military occupation and lost much of its strangeness. I have had a bad day. I began by breaking a tooth; then I had to have a monster hookworm extracted, which has left my foot very sore. My head has been aching and the visit to the American mission, where M. Bouvet carried me off, exhausted me. We had an interminable lunch at M. Eboué's. He is the *chef de circonscription*, originates from Guiana, and is the author of a little Sango grammar that I have been studying for the last week; a man of remarkable ability and with a very sympathetic personality . . . But my headache became worse and worse and I came in shivering and went to bed with an attack of fever; Marc went without me to the tamtam, which was broken up early by a tremendous tornado.

9 October

I was able to sleep and felt well enough this morning to go with my companions to Ouango, a picturesque station, situated on a height overlooking a bend of the M'Bomou (the name by which the Ubangui is known in its upper reaches). M. Isambert, the administrator, has just been converted to Protestantism and occupies his few leisure hours studying exegesis and theology. Unfortunately, I was too tired to talk to him as I should have liked. For that matter, all conversation fatigues me more and more. I can only make a pretence at it. One just manages to agree upon what is most banal or 'matter of fact' – if even then. I find it difficult to finish my sentences, I am so much afraid that if I really express my thought, I shall find no response to it.

All the women who came to dance at the tamtam here were dressed in bright, becoming cottons, made up into skirts and bodices. They are all clean and look happy and smiling; none of them seem poverty-stricken. Should we conclude from this that all these black races need only a little money in order to wear clothes?[7]

10 October

I felt well enough this morning to embark on the long expedition to Rafai, which I was very much grieved to think I might have to give up. The sultanate of Rafai is the last in Ubangui-Shari to keep its sultan. The régime will finally come to an end with Hetman (who succeeded to the throne in 1909). He is inoffensive enough to be allowed to retain a semblance of royalty and power. He accepts the situation with a smile and makes no claims for any of his sons. The A E F government has invented a fine comic-opera uniform for him, which he seems to enjoy wearing. His three eldest sons all went for a year's study to the island of Gorée, opposite Dakar (where the sons of native chiefs and notables receive an education in French, to prepare them for an eventual position of responsibility under the French government); one of them is at Bangui, the second is serving in the army at Fort Lamy; the third, who is not yet twenty, has returned to Rafai and is staying with his father. He is a tall, shy boy, who came to shake hands with us and then retired. The sultan's residence is on a rising piece of ground opposite the station-house. We drove to it in our car two hours after arriving. (But the sultan was there before us and had been sitting for some minutes on our terrace.) The whole population were drawn up along one side of the road on a wide esplanade and cheered us as we passed. Then we went into a kind of *zaouia*, where the sultan's entourage sits.

7. But they must be able to find stuffs – and stuffs they like – in the factories in the interior.

The black races are described as being indolent, lazy, without needs, and without desires. But I am inclined to believe that the state of slavery and wretched poverty in which they are sunk, only too often explains their apathy. What desires can a person have who never sees anything desirable? Every time that a well-stocked factory offers the native blankets, stuffs, household utensils, tools, etc., people are ingenuously surprised to see his desires aroused – if, that is to say, a fair remuneration of his work gives him the means of satisfying them.

11 October

The sultan, surrounded by his household and his usual escort, came to bid us goodbye. This decayed court made rather a lamentable spectacle. A few flute players, the last remnants of its splendour, might have come out of a masquerade. The flutes were vertical and tied round with two streamers of long hairs, which opened out into corollas when the instrument was blown into.

The station-house of Rafai, which has been abandoned for six months for want of sufficient staff, is in a dilapidated condition; the rooms look sordid; they are spacious and pleasantly disposed, but full of unspeakable rubbish: deteriorated instruments, broken, worm-eaten furniture, etc.; and everything is covered with thick dust. We should have slept in the veranda, but for the panthers, which, we are told, have no scruples about entering the village; a native was recently devoured in his hut, fifty yards from the station-house.

Yet we shall be sorry to leave Rafai. The terrace on which the station garden lies overlooks the majestic stream of the Chinko and is very fine. I think I even prefer it to the one at Ouango.

12 October

We left Rafai[8] yesterday and stayed the night at Bangassou, which we left this morning. We slept again at Foroumbala; the cars

8. The motor road comes to an end at Rafai (or a few kilometres farther east). After this begins the ex-sultanate of Zemio, the frontier subdivision of our colony, bordered on the east by the Anglo-Egyptian Sudan and on the south by the Belgian Congo, from which we are separated by the M'Bomou (the upper reach of the Ubangui).

It was through Zemio and the forest of the Belgian Congo that we had meant to return on our way back from Fort Archambault, and thence gain the region of the Great Lakes and the east coast. This, no doubt, would have been our itinerary if we had not been tempted northwards as far as the borders of Lake Chad by my friend Marcel de Coppet, who was appointed acting Governor of the Chad and obliged hastily to leave Fort Archambault, where we were staying with him, and hurry off to Fort Lamy.

The rapid motor-car excursion which, thanks to Governor Lamblin's kindness, we made in an easterly direction was meant merely as a kind of parenthesis, just to give us a first brief glimpse of the country. Being no longer of an age when I can entertain many more hopes or form plans for many more journeys, I find it very difficult to console myself (notwithstanding all my *amor fati*) for having been obliged to choose the dreary march across the Cameroon rather than the dark, mysterious forests of the Belgian Congo and the enigmas of Zemio.

had to be cleaned. The station is agreeable, but the people really too mangy. My foot hurts and I cannot put a shoe on. As I am obliged to sit still, I am going on with *The Master of Ballantrae*.

We have seen the little orphan leper, who has been cast off by everyone. The woman to whom Marc gave money for a week's manioc for him has not kept her word . . . Never in my life have I set eyes on a more miserable creature.

Bambari, 13 October

The recollection of the little leper – the thin and as though distant sound of his voice kept haunting me all the way from Foroumbala to Alindao, where we lunched; and from there to Bambari, where we arrived only at nightfall (ten hours in a Ford). There were a good many minor accidents on the road; the motor broke down several times; a bridge gave way as we were crossing it and I don't know how we escaped upsetting into the river.

Bambari, 14 October

This morning, as soon as we were up, there was a dance, given by the Dakpas.[9] There were twenty-eight little boy dancers from eight to thirteen years old, who were completely painted white from head to foot; on their heads was a kind of helmet stuck all over with forty or so red and black spikes; on their foreheads a fringe of little metal rings. Each of them held in his hand a whip made of rushes and plaited string. Some of them had black and red checks painted round their eyes. A short skirt made of raffia completed this fantastic get-up. They danced gravely, in Indian file, to the sound of twenty-three earthen or wooden trumpets of unequal lengths (about one to four feet long) which can each make only a single note. Another band of older Dakpas (these were all black) performed their evolutions in the opposite direction to the first. Then a dozen or so

9. This is the dance which is so admirably represented in the Citroën mission's film. But did the members of the mission really believe they were assisting at a very rare and mysterious ceremony? 'Circumcision dance' the screen calls it. It is possible that the dance may have had a ritual signification in primitive times; but at the present moment the Dakpas, who have been subjected ever since 1909, have no objection to offering it as a spectacle to passing travellers who are curious to see it. When requested, they come down from their village or, more accurately, from the rock caves where they live, north of Bambari, and exhibit themselves for payment.

women mingled in the dance. Every dancer advanced with little jerky steps which made his anklets tinkle. The trumpet-players were formed up in a circle, and in the middle an old woman beat time with a feather brush made of black horse-hair. At her feet a great black demon writhed in the dust in feigned convulsions, but without ceasing to blow his trumpet. The din was deafening, for, with the single exception of the little white dancers, they never stopped singing and yelling at the top of their voices a strange tune (I noted it down) which was heard even above the bellowing of the trumpets.

We left for the Maroubas at two o'clock. The weather was fine. The people here are very handsome, with clean, wholesome skins (at last!). The village is a fine one. The round huts are all alike, except for the paintings with which they are decorated on the outside – a kind of rough frescos in three colours, black, red, and white – schematic representations of men, animals, and motor-cars, which are at times not without elegance. The decorations are protected by a thatched roof, which has a wide projection all round the hut, covering a sort of circular passage.

There were admirable grasses on both sides of the road looking like oats made in old silver-gilt.

We were thrilled by meeting Governor Lamblin in the middle of the bush.

An hour later, twenty kilometres from the Maroubas, where we are to pass the night, we came upon Mme de Trévise and Dr Bossert, very busy making a census of the natives they have vaccinated.

15 October

Slept at the Maroubas.

Yesterday Lamblin advised us to push on to Fort Crampel – instead of going straight to Fort Sibut.

The country is changing in appearance: the forest is sparser; the trees not taller than ours; in their shade grow tall grasses and a new kind of fern. We lunched at the M'Brés. The scenery was very picturesque, all surrounded with rocks. One might have been in the neighbourhood of Fontainebleau. With the first shot I brought down a great vulture which was perching on the top of a dead tree. As I have never shot before, I was amazed at my success.[10]

We met a herd of dog-faced baboons (cynocephali) between the M'Brés and Fort Crampel; they let us get quite close up to them; some of them were enormous.

The villages are rather fine-looking, but very poor. In one of them there were about sixty women grinding rubber rhizomes and singing; it is an interminable job and miserably paid.

At Fort Crampel there was a sudden and terrific tornado at nightfall, which laid low a number of fragile cearas, whose boughs we saw flying all round the station, and particularly between our hut and the dwelling of M. Griveau, the administrator, with whom we were dining. The tornado caught us just as we were going across. It was so violent that we were almost carried away by the wind and blinded by the lightning and the downpour, so that Marc and I got separated (as in a Griffith film) and only found each other again, drenched to the skin, at the station-house.

Adoum and Outhman have met some friends here from Abécher, and when we got in, asked leave for the night to go and carouse in the Arab village on the other side of the Nana. We did not hear them come in, but at dawn they were at work again, cooking the bread, ironing our clothes, etc.

Fort Sibut, 16 October

We met with a violent tornado half-way here. Changes in the landscape (I mean in the appearance of the country) are very gradual – unless it be at the approach of the smallest stream, *marigot*, or depression of the soil, when very big trees with spreading trunks and aerial roots, tangled creepers, and all the dank mystery of the

---

10. I should have been less proud if I had known that it is not customary in AEF [Afrique Équatoriale Française] to shoot eagles, vultures, or carrion crows, which are considered (the latter especially) useful assistants in the public health service. They clean up the carcasses of the biggest game in a few hours; as well as clearing the villages of their garbage, they are responsible, no doubt, for the disappearance of a few chickens, but as long as enough are left to satisfy the appetite of the white traveller, all is well . . .

underwoods suddenly reappear. During long stretches, between two 'forest galleries', the low woods and copses are covered with creeping plants to such a degree that it looks like nothing but a kind of continuous wadding. These green bulgings only disappear to make room for fields of maize or rice, which allow the trunks of the trees, a number of which still remain standing among the crops, to be plainly visible; a quantity of these trees are dead, from some cause which does not always seem to be fire. Large groups of dead trees, even in the *marigots*, puzzle me. They are sometimes completely stripped of their bark, and then the tree looks like a perch for vultures. I am inclined to think that this continual deforestation, whether it be systematic and deliberate or accidental, may bring about a complete modification of the rain system.

We are always enthusiastically greeted by the women and children as we pass through the villages. Everyone hurries up; the children stop dead on the edge of the ditch by the roadside and make a kind of military salute; the biggest of them salute by bending their body forwards and a little sideways, with the left leg thrown backwards (as they do in music-halls), with a wide grin that shows all their teeth. When I raise my hand in reply to them, they begin by being frightened and running away; but as soon as they understand my gesture (and I amplify it as much as I can, and add all the smiles I am capable of), they break out into shouts and yells and caperings – the women especially – a delirious astonishment and rapture that the white traveller should consent to notice their advances and acknowledge them with cordiality.

17 October

Rose as early as four o'clock. But we had to wait for the first glimmer of dawn before leaving. How I like these early starts! But in this country they have not the stern nobility – the kind of farouche and desperate joy that were mine in the desert.

We got back to Bangui at about eleven o'clock.

✦✦

CHAPTER FOUR

THE GREAT FOREST BETWEEN BANGUI AND NOLA

18 October

A misty morning; it is not raining, but the sky is cloudy and everything is grey. Marc says, 'Not more melancholy than in France.' But in France weather like this makes one turn to meditation, to books, to study. Here it is to memory.

My imaginary idea of this country was so lively (I mean that I had imagined it so vividly) that I wonder whether, in the future, this false image will not be stronger than my memory of the reality and whether I shall see Bangui, for instance, in my mind's eye as it is really, or as I first of all imagined it would be.

However much the mind tries, it cannot recapture that emotion of surprise which adds a strange enchantment to the object. The beauty of the exterior world remains the same, but the eye's virginity is lost.

We are to leave Bangui finally in five days' time. And then our real travels will begin. It would be easy to reach Fort Archambault, where Marcel de Coppet is expecting us, by a much shorter route and a much easier one – the one that is taken by the parcel post and by travellers who are in a hurry: two days' motor drive to Batangafo and four or five days' boat. At Batangafo one leaves the basin of the Ubangui and follows the stream that flows into Lake Chad; one has only to let oneself be carried. But that does not tempt us and we are not in a hurry. What we want is precisely to leave the beaten track, to see what one does not see ordinarily, to enter profoundly, intimately, into the heart of the country. My reason sometimes tells me that I am perhaps rather too old to plunge into the bush and into a life of adventure – but I do not believe my reason.

20 October

Yesterday at sundown I went by myself along a road that climbs a hill immediately outside Bangui and leads into the depths of the forest. I never weary of admiring the immense columns of the trees; the height to which they soar is so dizzy and the spreading of their foliage so sudden. The sun's last rays were still lighting their tops. At first there was a great silence; then, as the shade grew deeper, the forest filled with strange, uncanny noises – cries and songs of birds, calls of animals, rustling of leaves. No doubt a troop of monkeys were stirring the branches not far from me, but I could not succeed in seeing them. I reached the top of the hill. The air was warm; I was dripping.

Today I returned to the same spot an hour earlier. I was able to get close up to a troop of monkeys and watch their prodigious leaps for a long time. I caught a few admirable butterflies.

21 October

We drove in the car as far as M'Baiki, through beautiful forest scenery. The car goes too quickly. This road, which we shall gladly do again in a few days' time, would be worth doing on foot.[1] In the forest round M'Baiki the trees reach prodigious heights. Some of them, the silk-cotton trees, have a gigantic spread at the base of their trunks.[2] It reminds one of the folds of a dress. The tree looks as if it were walking.

---

1. Alas! The most monotonous and dreary stretches, where one would be glad of a car, were the very ones we were afterwards obliged to traverse the most slowly.

2. This extraordinary spread is called *empattement* in French. It often begins to be noticeable at about 30 ft from the ground. It counterbalances the inadequacy of the roots and gives some stability to a column that sometimes rises to a height of more than 160 feet. Other trees, the umbrella tree in particular, replace the *empattement* by aerial roots, like flying buttresses. The thickness of the growth, the neighbourhood of other trees, the cable creepers that bind them together, are further protections against the assaults of the tornadoes. The forests here are associations.

The umbrella trees, as I learnt from Auguste Chevalier, in his excellent account of his travels in central Africa, only grow in the 'secondary' forest; that is, in the one that rises in the place of the great primeval forest when once it has been devastated by some more or less ancient fire. It was this primeval forest which I wanted to see, which we thought we should find farther on, which I sought for everywhere in vain.

On raising a piece of the half-rotten bark of a fallen silk-cotton tree I discovered a quantity of big beetle grubs. Dried and smoked, they are used, it seems, as food by the natives.

At M'Baiki we visited M.B., the representative of the Compagnie Forestière. We found two missionary fathers seated on a bench, drinking aperitifs.

How agreeable these agents of the Great Companies manage to make themselves! The government official who does not beware of their excessive friendliness finds it difficult later on to take sides against them. It is almost impossible for him not to lend a hand – or at any rate not to shut his eyes – to the little irregularities they commit – and then to the formidable exactions.

The native huts in the villages round M'Baiki are very different from those we saw in the region of the sultanates; much less fine, less clean, and often, indeed, actually sordid. We recognize by this that we are no longer in Ubangui-Shari, where Governor Lamblin insists on the native huts' being built according to almost a single type adopted by the administration. Some people protest against this interference and think the natives ought to be allowed to build their huts as they please; but the ones we see here seem to show that Lamblin is right. They are joined together in a single long file, no doubt to economize labour; straight mud walls, sustained by horizontal bamboos, and very low roofs. But perhaps these hideous hovels have also been built by order. (Nowhere else in our travels did we see uglier or less exotic villages.)

Bangui, 26 October

Great preparations for leaving. We are sending thirty-four packing-cases straight to Archambault. The luggage that we are taking with us was put into two small lorries. Adoum got into the Ford with us. We left Bangui at three o'clock. Night overtook us when we were well into the forest. Notwithstanding the moonlight, we could scarcely see our way . . .

27 October

We lunched at Boda with that gruesome man Pacha (see later) and M. Blaud, the administrator of Carnot, who is on his way home. Pacha never smiles. He is certainly ill.

We left Boda about three o'clock. There were nothing but old men, women, and children in the villages we passed through.

The road rises slowly. Then the ground suddenly slopes away and one finds oneself overlooking an immense stretch of forest. The night had fallen when we reached N'Goto.

N'Goto is on a height formed by a slight fold in the ground, but overlooking a fairly vast tract of country. The Forestière has a station here – an uninhabited house, where the representatives of the company had told me we might possibly stay. We were a little disappointed in the appearance of the country. And besides we did not wish to owe any obligation to the Forestière. Our one idea was to go on. But the motors need oil and petrol. We had relied on the assurance M. Bergos gave us that we should find supplies on the road. There were none, however, at Boda and none at N'Goto. We shall be obliged to leave our two cars here. Mobaye, Lamblin's chauffeur, the same man who took us to Rafai, is to drive us in the lorry to where the road ends, with Zézé, the cook, and our sleeping-bags; and then return by himself to M'Baiki to fetch oil and petrol for the two other cars. Our boys are to start in advance before six o'clock with the sixty porters who have been put at our disposal. We shall find some of them at the 'Grand Marigot', the terminus of the motor road, and some at Bambio, where they will arrive about midday, after having walked all night. This is the point where our real travels will begin.

Invited to dinner by M. Garron, a great hunter,[3] who has been settled for the last four months at N'Goto, which he is now longing to leave, as the hunting is not good and he is bored to extinction.

We went to bed early and were both fast asleep under our mosquito-nets in the post hut when, at about two o'clock in the morning, a noise of steps and voices woke us up. Someone wanted to come in. We called out in Sango: '*Zo niè?* (Who is there?)' It was a native chief of some importance, who had called before that same evening while we were at dinner, but, being afraid of disturbing us,

3. In this country 'hunter' means elephant-hunter, just as in certain milieus 'to smoke' means to smoke opium.

he had put off the interview he wished to have until the next morning; in the meantime a messenger, sent after him by Pacha, the administrator of Boda, had just arrived with orders that he should return at once to his village. He was obliged to obey. But in despair at seeing his last chance of speaking to us vanish, he had made so bold as to wake us up at this impossible hour. He talked with extreme volubility in a language of which we understood not a single word. We begged him to let us sleep. He could come back later when we should have an interpreter. We promised to take the responsibility of the delay on ourselves and to shield him from the terrible Pacha. Why should this latter be so anxious to prevent the chief Samba N'Goto from giving us his message? We easily understood the reason when next morning, with Mobaye acting as interpreter, we learnt the following circumstances from Samba N'Goto.

On 21 October last (six days ago, that is) Sergeant Yemba was sent by the administrator of Boda to Bodembéré in order to execute reprisals on the inhabitants of this village (between Boda and N'Goto), who had refused to obey the order to move their settlement on to the Carnot road. They pleaded that they were anxious not to abandon their plantations and urged besides that the people established on the Carnot road are Bayas, while they are Bofis.

Sergeant Yemba therefore left Boda with three guards (whose names we carefully noted). This small detachment was accompanied by the *capita* Baoué, and two men under his command. On the road, Sergeant Yemba requisitioned two or three men from each of the villages they passed through, and after having put them in chains, took them along with the party. When they arrived at Bodempéré, the reprisals began; twelve men were seized and tied up to trees, while the chief of the village, a man called Cobelé, took flight. Sergeant Yemba and the guard Bonjo then shot and killed the twelve men who had been tied up. Then followed a great massacre of women, whom Yemba struck down with a matchet; after which he seized five young children, shut them up in a hut, and set fire to it. In all, said Samba N'Goto, there were thirty-two victims.

We must add to this number the *capita* of M'Biri, who had fled from his village (Boubakara, near N'Goto) and whom Yemba came upon at Bossué, the first village north of N'Goto.

We also learnt that Samba N'Goto was returning to Boda, where he lives, and had nearly reached it when on the road he met Governor Lamblin's car, which was taking us to N'Goto. At this he turned back, thinking that it contained the Governor himself and anxious to appeal to him in person. He must have walked very quickly, as he arrived at N'Goto a very short time after us. He was determined not to let this unhoped-for chance of appealing to the white chief escape him.[4]

28 October

Samba N'Goto's deposition lasted more than two hours. It was raining. This was no passing tornado shower. The sky was thickly covered; the rain had set in for long. We started nevertheless at ten o'clock. I sat beside Mobaye; Marc and Zézé settled themselves inside the lorry as comfortably as they could on the sleeping-bags, though they found it very stifling under the tarpaulin. The road was sodden and the car's progress was despairingly slow. At the slightest hill and also in the parts where the road was too sandy, we had to get out in the rain and push, to prevent the lorry from sticking in the mud.

We were so much upset by Samba N'Goto's deposition and by Garron's tales that when, in the forest, we came across a group of women who were mending the road, we had no heart even to smile at them. These poor creatures, more like cattle than human beings, were in the streaming rain, a number of them with babies at the breast. Every twenty yards or so there were huge pits by the side of the road, generally about ten feet deep; it was out of these that the poor wretches had dug the sandy earth with which to bank the road, and this *without proper tools*. It has happened more than once that

4. Needless to say, Samba N'Goto was flung into prison as soon as he returned to Boda. A letter to Pacha which I had given him in order to excuse his delay and protect him if possible was of no avail. He was flung into prison with several members of his family whom Pacha was easily able to lay his hands on. In the meantime, Pacha absented himself on tour, accompanied by that very Yemba whose exploits had by no means brought him into disgrace. I hasten to add that this impunity did not last long, nor the incarceration of Samba N'Goto either. On the receipt of my letter the Governor ordered an official inquiry. It was entrusted to M. Marchessou, inspector of Ubangui-Shari, who confirmed everything stated above. This led to the prosecution of Pacha.

the loose earth has given way and buried the women and children who were working at the bottom of the pit. We were told this by several persons.[5] As they usually work too far from their village to return at night, the poor women have built themselves temporary huts in the forest, wretched shelters of branches and reeds, useless against the rain. We heard that the native soldier who is their overseer had made them work all night in order to repair the damage done by a recent storm and to enable us to pass.

We have arrived at the 'Grand Marigot', the terminus of the motor road. The greater part of our porters are awaiting us here. Our boys have gone on ahead with the rest of the party, which we shall find again at Bambio. It is two o'clock. The rain has stopped. We hastily devour a cold chicken and start off again. It is only ten kilometres to Bambio. We shall do them easily. As a general rule we use our *tipoyes*[6] very little, as much because we like walking as to spare our wretched bearers.

The 'Grand Marigot' is an admirable spot. So far, I have seen nothing here to compare with its strangeness and beauty. It is a kind of large swamp, crossed by narrow footbridges of creepers and branches, and makes a clearing in the forest, whose trees here are not very tall; its surface is covered with water plants, mostly unknown; there are huge arums, with thorny, fluted stems, lifting up

5. It is to be noted that this murderous road, which was particularly difficult to lay, owing to the nature of the soil, serves exclusively for the car which once a month takes the Forestière's representative, Mr M., accompanied by the administrator Pacha, to the market at Bambio.

6. The *tipoye* is a chair swung between two poles, which are not made of bamboo, as one might expect, but of the branches of the gigantic ban-palm tree. The bearers are placed between these shafts, two in front and two behind. Two straps, which are fastened to the shafts, one for each pair of bearers, pass over their shoulders and distribute the weight of the whole. I did not measure the length of these shafts; but one can calculate it by imagining four bearers, one behind the other, and the length for a chair added. They are about as thick as a greased pole. I looked in vain in the forest for a palm tree capable of providing poles of this size. Above the chair there is an arrangement of mats laid over an arched framework of stalks; this forms a roof and is called the *shimbeck*. It is a protection against the rays of the sun, but prevents one from seeing, weighs the whole concern down on one side if it is not properly balanced, and sometimes comes down on one in the most uncomfortable manner.

There are no horses in this part of Africa, on account of the tsetses and sleeping-sickness.

their half-open cups and revealing a hidden whiteness, striped with sombre crimson. Five hundred yards farther on, one comes to the river. A mysterious silence reigns, traversed by the songs of invisible birds. Numbers of low palm trees hang over the river and dip their branches in the running water. We crossed to the farther shore of the M'Baéré in canoes. The forest closes in here and becomes still more enchanting; there is water everywhere and the road, which is laid on piles, is constantly crossed by little wooden bridges. Here at last there were some flowers – mauve balsams and other flowers that reminded me of our Normandy willowherbs. I cannot describe my rapture and excitement as I walked on (not suspecting, alas, that we should never see anything so beautiful again). Oh! if one could only have stopped! If one could only come back without an escort of porters, who put every wild creature to flight! At times this constant company irks me, exasperates me. Wanting to get a taste of solitude and feel more intimately the closeness of the forest, I quickened my step and began to run, in an attempt to escape, to outdistance the porters. In vain! They all immediately started off at a trot to catch up with me. Thoroughly annoyed, I stopped and made them stop, drew a line on the ground, and told them not to pass it until they should hear my whistle from a long way ahead. But a quarter of an hour later I had to go back and fetch them; they had not understood, and the whole convoy was being held up.

A little before one gets to Bambio, the forest comes to an end, or, at any rate, wide clearings begin. The sound of cries and singing warned us that a village was at hand. Crowds of women and children came hurrying to meet us. We shook hands with some chiefs who were lined up and standing at attention; and even, by mistake – such was our enthusiasm – with some common guards. We played the part of great white chiefs with much dignity, saluting with our hands and smiling like ministers on tour. One huge fellow, ridiculously dressed up in skins, was beating on a gigantic xylophone, which he carried slung round his neck; he was the conductor of the women's dance; these, singing and uttering savage yells, swept the ground before us, waved great stalks of manioc or broke them under our feet by beating them noisily on the ground; it was a scene of delirium. The children, too, leapt and danced. Our passage through the village was glorious. Our procession led us to the travellers' hut, where we found our boys and the first convoy of porters awaiting us.

29 October

This morning I went to see one of the native chiefs who came to meet us yesterday. This evening he returned my visit. We had a long conversation. Adoum, sitting on the ground between the chief and me, acted as interpreter.

The information of the Bambio chief confirms everything that I heard from Samba N'Goto. In particular, he gave me an account of 'the ball' last market day at Boda. I here transcribe the story as I copied it from Garron's private diary.

'At Bambio, on 8 September, ten rubber-gatherers (twenty, according to later information[7]) belonging to the Goundi gang, who work for the Compagnie Forestière – because they had not brought in any rubber the month before (but this month they brought in double, from 40 to 50 kg) – were condemned to go round and round the factory under a fierce sun, carrying very heavy wooden beams. If they fell down, they were forced up by guards flogging them with whips.

'The "ball" began at eight o'clock and lasted the whole day, with Messrs Pacha and Maudurier, the company's agent, looking on. At about eleven o'clock a man from Bagouma, called Malongué, fell to get up no more. When M. Pacha was informed of this, he merely replied: "*Je m'en f –*" and ordered the "ball" to go on. All this took place in the presence of the assembled inhabitants of Bambio and of all the chiefs who had come from the neighbouring villages to attend the market.'

The chief spoke to us also of the conditions reigning in the Boda prison; of the wretched plight of the natives and of how they are fleeing to some less accursed country. My indignation against Pacha is naturally great, but the Compagnie Forestière plays a part in all this, which seems to be very much graver, though more secret. For,

---

7. They were all fined a sum equal to the price of their work. Consequently they worked for two months for nothing. One of them, who tried 'to argue', was besides condemned to a month's imprisonment.

after all, it – its representatives, I mean – knew everything that was going on. It (or its agents) profited by this state of things. Its agents approved Pacha, encouraged him, were his partners. It was at their request that Pacha arbitrarily threw into prison the natives who did not furnish enough stuff; etc . . .

As I am anxious to make a good job of my letter to the Governor, I have decided to put off leaving here till the day after tomorrow. The short time I have passed in French Equatorial Africa has already put me on my guard against 'authentic accounts', exaggerations and deformations of the smallest facts. I am terribly afraid, however, that this scene of the 'ball' was nothing exceptional, if the stories of several eyewitnesses, whom I questioned one after the other, are to be believed. The terror Pacha inspires makes them implore me not to name them. No doubt they will withdraw everything later on and deny that they ever saw anything. When a Governor goes on tour, his subordinates usually present reports containing the facts they think most likely to please him. Those that I have to place before him are of a kind, I fear, that may never come to his notice, and the voices that might inform him of them will be carefully stifled. A simple tourist like myself may, I feel sure, often hear and see things which never reach a person in his high position.

When I accepted this mission, I failed to grasp at first what it was I was undertaking, what part I could play, how I could be useful. I understand it now and I am beginning to think that my coming will not have been in vain.

During my stay in the colony I have come to realize how terribly the problems which I have to solve are interwoven one with the other. Far be it from me to raise my voice on points which are not within my competence and which necessitate a prolonged study. But this is a matter of certain definite facts, completely independent of questions of a general order. Perhaps the *chef de circonscription* has been already informed of them. From what the natives tell me, he seems to be ignorant of them. The circumscription is too vast; a single man who is without the means of rapid transport is unable to keep his eye on the whole of it. One is here, as everywhere else in French Equatorial Africa, brought up against those two terrible impediments: want of sufficient staff; want of sufficient money.

*

We held a grand review of our porters this evening by moonlight on the vast open space behind the shelter house. Marc counted them off, arranged them in groups of ten, showed them how to count themselves. The ones who could understand shouted with laughter at those who could not. We distributed a spoonful of salt to each man, which caused an outburst of lyrical gratitude and enthusiastic protestations of devotion.

30 October

Impossible to sleep. The Bambio 'ball' haunted my night. I cannot content myself with saying, as so many do, that the natives were still more wretched before the French occupation. We have shouldered responsibilities regarding them which we have no right to evade. The immense pity of what I have seen has taken possession of me; I know things to which I cannot reconcile myself. What demon drove me to Africa? What did I come out to find in this country? I was at peace. I know now. I must speak.

But how can I get people to listen? Hitherto I have always spoken without the least care whether I was heard or not; always written for tomorrow, with the single desire of lasting. Now I envy the journalist, whose voice carries at once, even if it perishes immediately after. Have I been walking hitherto between high walls of falsehood? I must get behind them, out on to the other side, and learn what it is they are put to hide, even if the truth is horrible. The horrible truth that I suspect is what I must see.

Spent the whole day composing my letter.

31 October

Up before five o'clock. A rapid cup of tea, while our luggage was being packed. Our porters were drawn up in the open space behind the hut (sixty men, besides a native soldier, a native guide, our two boys, and the cook; and also three women who are accompanying the soldier and the guide). The chief came to say goodbye to us. A misty moon was shining. We started in the uncertain light that precedes the dawn, and kept ahead of the main body, with our boys, our *tipoyeurs*, the guide, the soldier, and the men who were carrying our sleeping-bags.

Even our inexhaustible patience was severely tried by the interminable forest. I was not able to finish my letter to the Governor yesterday. Unfortunately it is impossible to write, or even take notes or read in a *tipoye*. I only resigned myself to getting into mine after five hours' rather tiring march, for the ground, which was sandy at first, became sticky and slippery with clay during the last kilometres. After a short rest in my *tipoye*, I walked for another five kilometres. There was no intermediary halting-place, and however long the stage, it had to be done, for it was impossible to spend the night in the forest, without food or shelter for the porters. The forest is extremely monotonous and hardly at all exotic-looking. It would be like an Italian forest – the one at Albano or the one at Nemi – except that there sometimes appears a gigantic tree (twice as tall as any of our European trees), whose top spreads out wide above the other trees, making them look in comparison mere brushwood. The trunks of these small trees are half covered with moss and are like evergreen oaks or laurels. The little green plants that edge the sides of the road remind one of our whortleberries; and others of enchanter's nightshade; just as in the *marigot* yesterday the waterplants reminded me of our northern willow herbs and balsams. Our chestnuts are not less curious nor less beautiful than the seeds, whose hairy shells were all we saw left of them on the ground. There were no flowers. Why were we told that this part of the forest was particularly fine and interesting?

At the end of our day's march the ground, which until then had been perfectly flat, sloped gently down to a little shallow, shady river, whose transparent water flowed over a bed of white sand. Our porters bathed.

Bathing, we are told, is dangerous in this country. I cannot bring myself to believe so, when there is no fear of crocodiles or sunstroke. That is not the point, say the doctors (and Marc repeats it after them), but risk of congestion of the liver, fever, filariasis, etc. . . . Yesterday, all the same, I bathed. And what was the result? A delicious feeling of comfort. I did not resist the appeal of the water today either and plunged rapturously into its cool transparence. I never had a more delightful bathe.

Some chiefs came out to meet us with two tamtams, carried by children. There are two considerable 'Bakongo' villages here.

('Bakongo' is the name given indiscriminately to all natives who work for the Forestière.) And near by is a tiny little village called N'Délé, which is at present inhabited by only five sound men (and they are away collecting rubber in the forest), and five invalids, who look after the plantations. Needless to say, these men in the forest, who are under no supervision, work as little as possible at a task that is so little paid. Hence the punishments with which the representatives of the Forestière try to recall them to a sense of their *duty*.

Long conversation with the two chiefs of the Bakongo village. But the one who was at first talking to us alone, stopped as soon as the other came up. He would not say another word; and nothing could be more harrowing than his silence and his fear of compromising himself when we questioned him about the Boda prison, where he has himself been confined. When he was again alone with us later on, he told us that he had seen ten men die in it in a single day, as a result of ill treatment. He himself bears the marks of flogging and showed us his scars. He confirmed what we had already heard,[8] that the prisoners receive as sole food, once a day, a ball of manioc as big as – he showed us his fist.

He spoke of the fines that the Compagnie Forestière are in the habit of inflicting on the natives who fail to bring in sufficient quantities of rubber – fines of forty francs – that is to say, the whole of one month's pay. He added that when the wretched man has not enough to pay the fine, he can only escape being thrown into prison by borrowing from someone better off than himself, if he can find such a person – and then he is sometimes thrown into prison 'into the bargain'. Terror reigns and the surrounding villages are deserted. We talked to other chiefs. When they are asked, 'How many men in your village?' they count them by putting down a finger for each one. There are rarely more than ten. Adoum acts as interpreter.

Adoum is intelligent, but he does not know French very well. When we halt in the forest, he says it is because we have found a 'palace' (for a '*place*'). He says '*un nomme*' (instead of '*un homme*'), and when we tell him to ask a chief, 'How many men have run away from your village, or have been put in prison?' Adoum answers,

8. Confirmed in turn by the official inquiry.

'Here ten *nommes*; there six *nommes*; and eight *nommes* farther on.'

A great many natives come to see us. So-and-so asks for a paper to certify that he is sorcerer-in-chief to a great many villages; so-and-so wants a paper to authorize him to go away and 'make a little village all by himself'. When I inquire how many prisoners there are in the Boda jail, the only answer I get, whoever it may be who gives it, is: 'Many; many; me can't count.' There seem to be numbers of women and children as well among the prisoners.

1 November

Too much preoccupied to be able to sleep. Started before five o'clock. Did a stage of from 25 to 28 km, without using our *tipoyes* for a single moment. One can only calculate the length of a road without milestones by the time it takes to cover it. We must have done on an average five to six kilometres an hour. The last kilometres, on a sandy track and in the full blaze of the sun, were particularly trying. The forest was again monotonous, with nothing peculiarly striking in it for the first half of the day's march; then we suddenly came upon a wide, deep river of admirably clear water; at a depth of, I should think, more than fifteen feet we could see an abundant growth of water-plants stirring in the stream, underneath a shaky, sinuous bridge, looking extremely fragile, and made of round stalks, held together by insecurely fastened creepers; it was almost on a level with the water and supported by big piles. It reminded one of those little bridges which are laid across boggy places to enable one to get across dryshod; it was impossible not to feel giddy as one looked at the alarming depths below. For a mile or two after the passage of the river (the Bodangué?) the forest again becomes extraordinarily strange and beautiful. I often use these two epithets together in this notebook, for when the scenery ceases to be *strange*, it at once recalls some European landscape, and the recollection is almost always to its disadvantage. Perhaps if I had seen Java or Brazil, I should feel the same about this undergrowth of wood overgrown with epiphyte ferns and great arum lilies; but as it reminds me of nothing, I am able to think it marvellous.

Before reaching Dokundja-Bita, where we are camping, we passed through three miserable little villages. No one but women was in them. The men, as usual, were out rubber-collecting. The chiefs came to meet us from a considerable distance, with three tamtams, beaten by a decrepit old man and some children. Then, a little outside Dokundja, the women and children gave us a reception – piercing vociferations and frantic caperings. The oldest women are always the most excited, and the grotesque jigging of these elderly ladies is rather a painful sight. They all hold palm leaves in their hands and large branches, with which they fanned us or swept the ground before us. Very like an 'entry into Jerusalem'. The women here wear nothing but a leaf (or a rag), whose stalk passes between their buttocks and joins the string that goes round their waist. And some of them have a large pad behind, made of leaves, dried or green – not much more ridiculous, after all, than the bustle that was in fashion in 1880. But in the last village in which we stopped they were all adorned with creepers as well.

A courier from Bambio arrived here two days ago to announce our arrival. At the entrance and exit to the villages (and occasionally in the middle of the forest or the bush) there are sometimes several hundred yards where the ground, for some reason or other, has been weeded and cleared of vegetation and had sand spread over the road. In places, and right on the surface of the sand, there are the most beautiful mauve flowers, something like our cattleyas. (I had already seen them in the forest near Eala.) Is it these flowers that produce the big coral-coloured fruit like a garlic pod in shape, which is also found on the ground, and of which the natives eat the inside – a white pulp tasting of aniseed? The leaf is seen near by, like a small palm leaf, about four or five feet long. Do these flowers come out after the road has been cleared, or are they not rather left deliberately? I like to think so and I admire this sandy track, from which everything has been cleared away except the flowers.

Every time we halt in a village, we speak to the chief and persuade him not to let the rubber go, unless the Compagnie Forestière agrees to pay two francs a kilo for it, as is right. For we are told that it often pays only one franc fifty, and only consents to pay two francs after the twentieth kilo. And, moreover, we try to persuade the natives to learn to weigh the rubber for themselves; for they only use measures of volume (they count by basket-loads), which enables the representative of the Forestière to cheat them over the weight, if he happens to be dishonest, and if the administrator is not there to protest.

Whenever we stop, a number of men hurry round to appeal to us, to submit their quarrels to us, to consult us as to their ailments. One of them, with a brother and sister on each side of him, asked us to make a neighbour of his pay him for having lain with his wife, who was three months gone with child, which, according to him, had resulted in the woman's having a miscarriage. He asked fifty francs for the loss of the child.

2 November

It was past noon when we arrived at Katakouo; after having left Dokundja-Bita at five o'clock, we walked without stopping for seven hours, of which only half an hour in our *tipoyes*. There was only one river-crossing; the bridge was of stalks tied together by creepers; a small creeper, covered with ants, served as handrail. The rest of the time the landscape was monotonous – a steppe covered with tall grasses and sown with small trees like cork trees, sometimes fringing the edge of a forest and following, no doubt, the hidden course of a river.

There were thickets formed by enormous fields of *unreaped* manioc; and farther on, castor-oil fields, also unreaped, all the men being out gathering rubber, or in prison, or dead, or fled. After we had left the last village of this abominable subdivision of Boda, an enormous fellow, who had been accompanying us since the preceding village, and who was walking along hand in hand with me (I thought he was a chief), suddenly declared that he would not return to his village or go on working at rubber any more. He announced his intention of coming with us. But his brother (of the same father and mother, he kept repeating, for in this country a simple friend is very often called 'brother'), who is a *capita*, tried to oppose his leaving. There followed a long palaver. It would all fall upon *him*. *He* was the one who would be thrown into prison, etc. . . . A *matabiche* calmed him down and he was persuaded to return by himself.

Katakouo (Katapo on some maps). One can tell that one has left the subdivision of Boda by the fact that there are men to be seen once more. The village chief hurried up to show us his book, in which was

65

written: 'Incompetent chief; without energy; cannot be replaced; the other natives in the village are no better.'

Katakouo is an enormous village, nearly a kilometre long. There is a single street, if one can give this name to the interminable oblong, on the sides of which all the huts are lined up.

Towards evening I came upon a small shady river and bathed, slipping off the big trunk of a tree into a transparent pool with a bed of white sand. A little squirrel came and looked at me, like the squirrels at home, but with a much darker fur.

3 November

Left Katakouo long before dawn; for a long time as we walked, the forest was so dark that without the guide in front of us we should not have been able to follow the windings of the path. The day dawned very slowly – a grey, dull day, unspeakably melancholy. The monotony of the forest was intense; sometimes there were fine groves of trees (but a great many dead trunks) in the middle of fields of manioc – also unreaped – though we are no longer in Boda. I tried to question the chief of a village where we halted, a stupid man (like the chief of the last village and of the next), who held out his book, on which was written as before: 'Incompetent chief; has no authority over his people.' It was obvious. Impossible to get an answer to my question: 'Why was the manioc not reaped at the proper time?' As a rule the natives cannot understand the word 'why?' and I even doubt whether any equivalent word exists in most of their idioms. I noticed before, in the course of the trial at Brazzaville, that when asked: 'Why did these people desert their villages?' they invariably answered *how, in what manner*. It seems as though their brains were incapable of establishing a connection between cause and effect (and I noticed this constantly during the whole of our journey).

The women dance at the entrance to every village. This shameless jigging of elderly matrons is extremely painful to look at. The most aged are always the most frenzied. Some of them are like lunatics.

One of our porters is ill. A Dover's powder did him a great deal of good, but he cannot walk and has to be carried in a hammock; Marc dressed another one's foot. We did not once use our *tipoyes* all day; Outhman, who has cut his foot severely, occupied one of them for a long time. Nothing to note except the descent towards the river at the end of the day (we arrived at Kongourou about noon). I have missed several shots, which has greatly damped my conceit. The success of my first shots went to my head. I stopped aiming.

4 November

We arrived at Nola about three o'clock this afternoon, after having skipped the stage at Niémélé and done more than forty kilometres, of which a good thirty on foot. The moon, when we started, was still almost at her zenith – 'at midday', as Adoum says. (It was not later than four o'clock.) Nothing could be more melancholy, more dreary, than the abstract greyness of the light that replaced it. The morning was very misty; but the wooded steppe through which we marched for hours had a temporary grace lent it by the abundance of great feathery grasses, which the mist had loaded with dew. They are so tall that they hang over the road and drench one's head and bare arms as one passes by. One is soon soaked as if by a shower. There were a great many traces of animals on the sandy track (deer, boars, buffaloes), but I saw no game. The noise and, no doubt, the scent of our escort put everything to flight. We missed several birds which were too far off. When we were crossing one of the rivers, a horde of cicadas were making a deafening noise. The native soldier seized a big assegai belonging to a little boy who has been accompanying us for the last two days (with his master, a messenger of Yamorou's, the Bambio chief), and pinned one of these enormous insects to the trunk of a tree. Its wings were striped and shot with emerald, and the underwings reddish. Yesterday evening, night had closed in by the time we reached the village where we were to camp, three kilometres from Kongourou, which is the station shelter; but a commercial traveller had just arrived before us and made a clean sweep of all the manioc that had been reserved for our porters. This is what we were told when, in despair at not receiving the promised rations, we went back to Kongourou the same evening, to interview the chief – an extra six kilometres. This chief had come to pay his respects, when he first passed through; he was dressed Arab-fashion and was extremely taking; he explained that he was obliged to serve the first comers first, which we readily admitted; but our porters had to be fed. By dint of hurrying round from hut to hut, armed with torches, we succeeded, with the chief's help, in collecting enough manioc, and went back exhausted.

A few kilometres before one gets to Nola, the path emerges from the dense forest and debouches suddenly on the Ekela (which becomes the Sanga later on). We left our *tipoyes* for a moment and sat down on the trunk of a Palmyra palm, in the shade of one of the huts of a little fishing village, built on the river bank. We watched six poor women dancing; out of politeness, for they were old and hideous. After another three kilomètres through the steppe and among plantations of bananas and cocoa-palms, we arrived opposite this strange Nola. We saw its roofs from the other side of the river, which we crossed in boats. We have reached our goal. It was high time. We are worn out with fatigue, all of us. But, on the whole, there has been no serious drawback during these five days' march. (Yesterday, for prudence' sake, we recruited five extra *tipoye*-bearers, for ours are in a pitiable state.)

The *capita* lent us by Yamorou to show us the way was commissioned to take back one of his wives with him from Nola. She had eloped with a native soldier. On arriving at Nola, we learnt that the soldier and the woman left yesterday for Carnot.

❖❖❖❖❖❖❖❖❖❖❖❖❖❖❖❖❖❖❖❖❖❖❖❖❖❖❖❖

CHAPTER FIVE

FROM NOLA TO BOSOUM

Nola, 5 November

A difficulty has arisen with our porters. They all want to leave; at any rate the sixty recruited by the administration. Yesterday they were brought a large quantity of bananas, but very little manioc, which caused great discontent. The administration pays 1 fr. 25 a day per head when the man is loaded, and 75 centimes when unloaded; but often the whole amount is handed over to the chief, so that the men themselves get nothing. This, our porters declare, is what is going to happen. We are in a very embarrassing situation, for, in the absence of any representative of the French authorities, it is extremely difficult to get men to replace them; on the other hand, it seems inhuman of us to take these people much farther away from their villages. We had thought at first that we should be able to go up the river in canoes as far as Bania, but the Ekela is swollen by the rains and so full that it is unnavigable except downstream; the rapids are dangerous. We shall be obliged to retrace our steps as far as Kongourou and reach Bania by the left bank, for the other road, we are told, has been abandoned. As soon as a road is not kept up, it is overgrown by vegetation and becomes impracticable.

Our porters use a very long bamboo switch, forked at the end, with which they are extremely skilful at getting hold of the nests of the 'mason flies' that hang from the rafters of our veranda roof. The nests consist of little colonies of a score or so of cells; the larvae or chrysalises, when they are still milk-white, make very good eating, say our people. We have seen them pounce, too, on the winged white ants, that are attracted in swarms by our lamp, and gobble them up straight away, without even pulling off their enormous wings.

Great difficulty in finding manioc for our men. Some was brought in at last, but it was not ground and the porters are out of temper. We have decided not to leave till the day after tomorrow, so as to enable a fresh lot to be recruited. All the same, we are afraid to dismiss our old ones yet, though they are getting demoralized and rebellious.

Towards evening we crossed the Ekela in a canoe and visited the Forestière's establishment, which is managed by two very young agents. They seem honest.[1]

1. Let them have no illusions; their honesty will do them harm. The company will necessarily prefer agents who bring to their coffers more than can be brought in *honestly*. Nothing can be more illuminating as regards this subject than the remarks of an agent of this very company, which I heard long after and in quite another region. It is easy to understand my reasons for not mentioning the names of persons or places. This agent came out on the same boat with us; he was amused to come across us again and began to talk freely, and without at first suspecting the disgust we tried to hide, for fear of interrupting him.

He told us first that he served for a long time on the Gold Coast; and when we asked him whether he preferred the French colony: 'Don't I!' cried he. 'There's nothing whatever to be done over there. Just think! Nearly all the Negroes know how to read and write.'

He employs the natives to work at rubber for a wage of twenty-five francs a month, plus one franc's worth of rations every Saturday; otherwise they are neither fed nor lodged, and of course the rubber they bring in is not paid for. They are what is called 'volunteer labourers', who prefer even this lamentable situation to being requisitioned by the administration. This terrifies them to such an extent that they desert their villages and hide in inaccessible places in the bush. They have another dodge for escaping from forced labour (this was said laughing), and that is to get blennorrhoea. 'The rascals know the administration doesn't take such cases; and it's easy to find women who will give it to them.'

He earns, he said, 4,000 francs a month, 'in addition to *bonuses*'. This year the company gave him a bonus (or share in the profits) of 12,000 francs.

He does not conceal his fury against the English traders, who are so stupid as to pay the native direct the price the stuff fetches on the market – 'which spoils trade'. He confesses cynically that when one doesn't get enough profit out of the stuff, 'one makes up for it by tampering with the weights'.

As I proposed giving 100 francs *matabiche* (gratuity) to any native chief who should bring me another *dindiki* (a little animal of which I speak later on), he shrugged his shoulders.

'Don't give anything.'

'It's only fair . . .'

'Nothing at all.'

'Why?'

'When one gives these fellows a *matabiche*, they at once think they are being

We made various purchases in their 'shops', and then went on to a large village on the river bank at the place where the Kadei falls into the Ekela, and the two together become the Sanga. Opposite the village is a mountain whose steep slopes are covered with a dense forest. It is said to be frequented by monkeys of every kind; and in particular by quantities of enormous gorillas, which the natives hunt with nets. The village people showed us these tough wide-meshed nets hanging on the doors of their huts. At the entrance to the village there was a snare for panthers.

The porter difficulty has been suddenly solved We are told that it is quite possible to go up the Ekela in whale-boats as far as Bania, and that it will not take more than four days.

7 November

Two natives have just killed a serpent about four feet long and very big in proportion to its length. Unfortunately the blows of the stick with which they killed it have damaged its skin. It is a very fine one; the back is marked, not with lozenges, but with very regular light-grey rectangles, encircled by a black ring and then an outer and paler ring; it is a variety of python I have never seen anywhere else.

We lunched with Dr B. and a representative of the Compagnie Wial, which trades in skins.[2] They have both just come back from Bania. The doctor spoke at length of the Compagnie Forestière, which manages, he says, to evade the wise regulations of the medical service, eludes the visits of sanitary inspectors, and treats with

---

robbed. For instance, the chief I was telling you about brought me a chimpanzee one day which I immediately re-sold at Douala for 1,500 francs . . .'

'And didn't you give him anything?'

'I? On the contrary, I pitched into him. Well! a few days later he brought me another chimpanzee. So you see!'

He complained of the administration because 'it kills trade'; but he was referring to the higher administration; on the other hand, he sings the praises of the chief of the subdivision where he operates: 'A Negro may come and complain as much as he likes; he gets jolly well put in his place.'

He would have said more, only he detected on our faces something that was not altogether sympathetic.

2. In the good season (the dry-weather season), he says, he exports as many as fifteen thousand skins of little antelopes a month. Needless to say, I do not guarantee these figures. I repeat them as they were given me.

contempt the system of health certificates for the natives, whom it recruits from village to village and groups in 'Bakongo' settlements; hence the propagation of sleeping-sickness, which in this way escapes all control.[3] He considers that the Compagnie Forestière is ruining and devastating the country. He has sent confidential reports on the subject addressed to the Governor, but is convinced they are held up at Carnot (to which circumscription Nola is temporarily attached for want of sufficient staff), so that the Governor continues to be ignorant of the situation.

Last night a tornado that ought to have burst was nipped in the bud. It was stifling; one longed in vain for a shower to cool the atmosphere a little. The sky was lowering. There was a great deal of lightning, but so high and so far off that no thunder could be heard. It illuminated the clouds from above and suddenly revealed the most complicated structure of banks piled upon banks. I got up about midnight and sat for a long time outside my hut contemplating the wonderful spectacle.

Two nights running, a great monkey (?) has come to dance on the roof of our hut, and his bounds and leaps were such that we thought he would break it through.

It is impossible to imagine anything more dreary, more colourless, more melancholy, than the grey-skied mornings of the tropics. Not a ray, not a smile from the sky before midday.

Dined yesterday at Dr B.'s with the representative of the Compagnie Wial. About half-way through dinner the alarm sounded. Was it a fire? They are frequent in this country, where the native sets fire to the bush without paying much attention to the huts that may be within reach. A great noise of voices drew near, and suddenly there burst onto the veranda where we were sitting the Portuguese owner of a neighbouring factory, which we had visited that morning to buy tobacco for our porters. He had nothing but his trousers on. In a tremendous state of excitement and almost beside

3. 'It should be noted that this region [of Bilolo] was up till now considered exempt from sleeping-sickness. In this region the Compagnie Forestière recruits numbers of labourers, whom it *refuses* to engage regularly, thus removing them from medical supervision and encouraging the spread of this illness in a country which had hitherto been preserved from it.' (Extract from report.)

himself he explained that the native soldiers want to 'bash his head in', because his cook had run away with the wife of a guard, etc., etc. The doctor talked to him very firmly and, I must say, very sensibly, and dismissed him. It turns out on inquiry that the woman in question is the very one that the guard stole from Yamorou, and that the *capita* Boboli, who accompanied us here for that purpose, was commissioned to bring back to him. Boboli went back yesterday without the woman, when he was told that she had gone to Carnot with the guard.

This morning we called the delinquents up before us. There appeared the seducer guard, another guard (the one who was in our escort), who acted as interpreter (in spite of being afflicted with the most uncontrollable stammer), the Portuguese gentleman's cook, and, finally, the woman, his four days' mistress. Her only garment was a little packet of leaves held in place by a bead girdle. She was very Eve-like, very 'eternal feminine' – handsome, if one excepts the sagging breasts; the curve of her hips and legs is of great purity. She stood before us with her arms raised and resting on the bamboo supports of the roof of the veranda. All the natives gabbled together in incomprehensible French with astonishing volubility. We finally made out that the gist of the whole affair is merely a matter of money. Yamorou does not so much claim the woman as the 150 francs he paid her parents to get her. Besides which there was a tax of 10 francs, which the guard paid and which the cook re-imbursed . . . An inextricable muddle. We decided that the woman was to go back to Yamorou, since neither the guard nor the cook agrees to give Yamorou the 150 francs she cost. The woman listened with an air of unspeakable resignation, as her two last husbands told her she was too much of a whore for them to keep. Nevertheless, we insisted that the loincloth she had when she left Yamorou should be given back to her, plus five francs, given half by the guard and half by the cook, to provide her with food during the journey. The whole affair took an endless time.

Afterwards we spent a long time examining some anteaters' funnels and dropping little ants down the sides.

Yesterday I managed to read a few pages of *The Master of Ballantrae* with great delight.

8 November

We have decided to give up the journey by whale-boat, but at the same time we have had to give up Bania; we shall go to Carnot via Berberati. We have disbanded our sixty-five porters; we have been promised forty fresh ones, who, we are told, should be enough. Nearly the whole time is taken up by seeing to divers practical matters and by revising and typing my letter to the Governor. Yesterday evening a courier brought me a letter from Marcel de Coppet, which had been waiting for me at Mongoumba for more than two months. The courier told one of the guards last night that Samba N'Goto had been imprisoned, as I expected; but when I questioned the man this morning, he denied everything, and even that he had ever mentioned the subject. He took some sand up from the ground, put it to his forehead, and swore that Samba N'Goto was at liberty. One can see that he is terrified of reprisals.

We leave tomorrow.

9 November

Gama, on the Ekela. Mokélo is opposite, on the other side of the river – a stream far larger than the Seine. It consists of a few huts on a sloping piece of ground, including the vast one which we are occupying. We are greatly bothered by swarms of very small flies, '*fourous*', no doubt. The inside of the hut, the bamboos, and the thatch of the roof are shiny and, so to speak, lacquered all over by smoke; which gives an appearance of polished cleanliness to this otherwise sordid hut. It began to rain as soon as we arrived, and night fell almost immediately after. The stage was much longer than we had been told, and though we left at eight o'clock, we did not reach Gama till the evening. Some of our porters were exhausted. One old fellow in particular showed me the glands in his groin, the size of a hen's egg. We were only able to get forty porters, so that some of them had to carry double loads. The question of porterage and even of *tipoye*-bearers spoils my pleasure. I cannot help thinking of it the whole time.

The forest we went through today was much more interesting than the one before Nola, because of the frequent small streams that intersect it. The path slopes down to them abruptly. The forest itself is stranger; a large plant, whose name I do not know, with very broad, fine leaves, gives the woods an exotic look. There are some magnificent trees, with spreading trunks. The temperature is over-powering; not that it is very hot; but the air is so heavy, so steamy, that one is bathed in perspiration. I took off my waistcoat, which was sopping; I took off my shirt as well – it was wringing wet. I hung them on to the *tipoyes*, but they were still wet at the end of the day. The sky is low and uniformly grey; everything looks dull and dismal; one feels as if one were in a kind of oppressive dream – a nightmare. When one goes on ahead of the rest of the party and stays alone, as I did, lost in the immensity, the strange, uncanny songs of the birds make one's heart beat.

I should like to preserve here some record of yesterday evening's fantastic party. We were dining at Dr B.'s with A., the young agent of the Société Wial (only twenty-two years old), and L., the river steamship captain, who has just arrived from Brazzaville. We very soon noticed that the doctor was not in a perfectly normal state; it was not only his excited remarks, but I saw that when he offered me wine, I had the greatest difficulty in keeping my glass under the bottle – he kept trying to pour it out *on the other side*. And on several occasions he put the piece of meat on his fork down on the table-cloth, instead of putting it into his mouth. He got more and more excited, without, however, drinking too much; but perhaps he had already drunk a good deal, in honour of the steamer's arrival. But it was not so much drink that I suspected as . . . The day before, I had shown him my letter to Governor Alfassa, containing the serious charges against Pacha; he had seemed indignant; then, that evening, when I imprudently spoke of sending my letter to the minister, seized with fear no doubt, or from a sort of feeling of solidarity, he burst out into protests that there were numbers of officials and administrators who were honest, devoted, con-scientious, excellent workers. I, in my turn, protested that I had never doubted it, and that I knew a great many such; but that it was all the more important that a few unfortunate exceptions (and I added that of the quantities of officials of all ranks I had seen, I had never met but one) should not bring discredit upon the others.

'But,' he cried, 'you won't be able to prevent attention's being called especially to that exception, and public opinion will be formed on it. It is deplorable.'

There was a good deal of truth in what he said, and I was aware of it. He seemed to be afraid that he had gone too far in approving my letter the day before, and to be making a protest against that very approbation. For immediately afterwards he started approving a policy of brutality towards the blacks, affirming that one could get nothing out of them except by blows and by making examples, even bloody ones. He went so far as to say that he himself had one day killed a Negro; then he added hastily that it was in defence, not of himself, but of a friend, who would otherwise have certainly been done in. Then he said that the only way to be respected by the Negroes was to make oneself feared, and he spoke of a confrère, Dr X., the doctor who had preceded him at Nola, who, as he was peacefully going through the village of Katakouo (or Katapo), which we had gone through the day before, was seized, bound, stripped, daubed with paint from head to foot, and forced to dance to the sound of the tamtam for two days on end. He was only delivered by a squadron that was sent from Nola . . . All this was said more and more queerly, more and more incoherently and excitedly. We were all silent; no one else spoke a word. And if we had not finally broken up the party, because we had our packing to attend to for the next morning's start, he would certainly have said more. He almost went so far as to approve Pacha; at any rate, everything he said was with the unavowed object of excusing him and of repudiating me. He said besides (and, if true, this is very important) that the recognized chiefs of the villages are more often than not men who are held in no consideration among the natives they are supposed to rule; that they are former slaves, mere figureheads, chosen to shoulder responsibilities and suffer any punishments that may be inflicted; and that all the inhabitants of the villages were delighted when they were flung into jail. The real chief is a secret chief, whom the French government hardly ever get to know of.

I can only repeat his remarks more or less roughly; I cannot give any idea of the fantastic, uncanny atmosphere of the scene. One could only manage this with a great deal of art and I am writing as it comes. It should be noted that the doctor began the subject abruptly, by a direct attack, evidently premeditated; the soup had not been

cleared away before he suddenly asked me whether I had been to see
the Nola cemetery. And when I said no: 'Well! there are sixteen
white men's graves there,' etc.

10 November

Panthers abound in this region and have no objection, we are told,
to raiding people's houses. But our hut was so stifling that rather
than have no air, we pushed back the huge bark curtain and put our
deckchairs in the doorway.

In the absence of a watch, my eagerness was so over-zealous that
it got me up much too early – but it only got *me* up. The night was
still too dark; there was nothing for it but to wait – to go back to
bed . . .

We started at dawn, still stupid with sleep; this stage, which we
were told was very short, seemed the most interminable of all. We
did not reach the M'Bengué shelter till about four o'clock, after a
short halt at noon. I did fifteen kilometres on foot with extreme
effort; but I am taking more and more of a dislike to being carried in
a *tipoye*. It shakes one uncomfortably and I can never for a moment
get rid of the sensation of the porters' labour. Every day we sink
further and deeper into strangeness. All today I was in a state of
torpor and semiconsciousness, 'as though of hemlock I had drunk',
losing all notion of time, of place, and of my own self.

The sky grew a little clearer towards evening, and as I write this,
the night is drawing on in an admirable sky. At last we have escaped
from the oppression of the forest. At times it was very beautiful,
with more and more of the gigantic trees, whose trunks seem
suffering from elephantiasis. But the absence of any ray of sunlight
gives it a look of being sunk in sleep – in hopeless sadness. All the
leaves are shiny and firm, like those of the laurel and evergreen oak;
there are none like those of the hazel, for instance, which have a soft
felt-like consistency that is porous to the light and gives a golden-
green tint to the rays of the sun that pass through them and make
the Normandy copses abodes of mystery. The moisture was so great
till the middle of the day that it streamed from the branches and
made the clay path slippery, and walking very difficult. My
tipoyeurs fell flat three times. Occasionally at the crossing of a river
one would have liked to linger. M'Bengué, like Gama, is situated on

a vast open space, reclaimed from the forest which envelopes it on all sides – a sudden savanna of immensely tall grasses, among which, after a step or two, one is lost to view. I missed three shots at some odd birds, which I should have liked to see closer.

The obligingness and attentiveness and zeal of our boys is beyond words; as for our cook, his cooking is the best we have tasted in this country. I continue to think, and think more and more, that most of the faults people complain of in the servants here come more than anything from the way in which they are treated and spoken to. We can only be congratulated on ours – to whom we have never spoken an unkind word, to whom we trust all our possessions, and who, so far, have shown themselves scrupulously honest. More than that: we leave all our small objects lying about in view of our porters, and in view of the inhabitants of the villages we pass through – objects that are exceedingly tempting to them and the theft of which it would be exceedingly difficult to discover – a thing we should never dare do in France – and so far nothing has disappeared. A mutual confidence and cordiality have sprung up between our servants and us, and all, without a single exception, are as nice to us as we make a point of being to them.[4]

4. This judgement, which might seem premature, was only more and more confirmed as time went on. And I confess I cannot understand why all Europeans, almost without exception, officials as well as traders, women as well as men, think it necessary to treat their servants roughly – in speech, at any rate – even when they show them real kindness. I know a lady, who is otherwise charming and gentle, who never calls her boy anything but *'tête de brute'* ('blockhead' is a mild translation of this), though she never raises her hand against him. Such is the custom. 'You will end by it too. Wait and see.' We waited ten months without changing our servants and we did not end by it. Were we particularly lucky? Perhaps . . . But I am inclined to think that every master has the servants he deserves, and what I say does not apply only to the Congo. What servant in our country would care to remain honest if he heard his master deny him the possession of a single virtue? If I had been Mr X.'s boy, I should have robbed him the very same night I heard him declare that all Negroes were cheats, liars, and thieves.

'Doesn't your boy understand French?' I asked with some uneasiness.

'He speaks it admirably . . . Why?'

'Aren't you afraid that what you have just said . . . ?'

'It'll teach him that I'm not taken in by him.'

At the same dinner I heard a guest declare that all women (and he wasn't talking of Negresses this time) care for nothing but pleasure as long as they are worthy of our attentions, and that no woman is ever really pious before the age of forty.

78

I am going on with Adoum's reading lessons. His application is touching; he is getting on steadily, and every day I am becoming more attached to him. When the white man gets angry with the blacks' stupidity, he is usually showing up his own foolishness! Not that I think them capable of any but the slightest mental development; their brains as a rule are dull and stagnant – but how often the white man seems to make it his business to thrust them back into their darkness.

11 November

At last a short stage! We started about six in the morning and arrived two and a half hours later, after crossing a rather fine forest at Sapoua. The creeper-palm has made its reappearance.

We did the journey on foot. Sapoua is a triple or quadruple village, more than a kilometre long; it is situated in a wide stretch of savanna, sown with Palmyra palms and encircled in the distance by the forest. There were quantities of children, some of them so charming that we kept them with us; one man was playing on an extraordinary instrument – a calabash, held between the legs, in the middle of a bamboo, which was strung like a bow with six (?) strings. He sang with great subtlety and delicacy what our interpreter translated as meaning: 'I have so many hookworms in my foot that I cannot walk.'

Towards evening I crossed the savanna, accompanied by four children, and reached the outskirts of the forest. We came to a transparent stream with tea-coloured water and a bed of white sand, and everyone bathed. Some other children brought me a quantity of

---

These gentlemen have the same knowledge of Negroes that they have of women. Experience rarely teaches us anything. A man uses everything he comes across to strengthen him in his own opinion and sweeps everything into his net to prove his convictions . . . No prejudice so absurd but finds its confirmation in experience.

Negroes, who are prodigiously malleable, oftener than not become what people think, or want, or fear them to be. I would not swear that our boys too might not have been turned into rascals. One has only to set about it in the right way; and colonials are extraordinarily ingenious in this matter. One teaches his parrot to say: 'Get out, dirty nigger!' Another is angry because his boy brings vermouth and bitters after dinner instead of liqueurs. 'Double-dyed idiot! Don't you know yet what an aperitif is? . . .' Another time a poor boy who, thinking he was doing right, had warmed a porcelain teapot with boiling water is railed at before the whole company and again called a fool. Hadn't he been taught that hot water broke glasses?

pretty little cockchafers. I am astonished to see how much these creatures differ among themselves, though of the same species and sex. I had already been shown several examples of this diversity at the museum. It seems to be restricted to the male sex. Is it peculiar to tropical regions?

The heat is stifling.

Arrival of the manioc for our porters; twenty-four little baskets carried by twenty-four little girls. On every loaf of manioc is a handful of fried caterpillars; and there are besides a few sugar-canes. 'Five francs' worth,' said the corporal; I gave double – for I learnt yesterday that the white man is always asked a price that is very much below the real value. For instance, a chicken for which the white gives one franc costs the native three. One of our porters yesterday asked us to buy a chicken for him, as he would have had to pay three times more for it.

We were brought some crayfish from the river; they were very big, with extremely long claws and little pincers at the end of them. When cooked, their flesh is soft and gluey.

12 November

Tonight an indifferent tamtam, which we had ordered. I left it early, but Marc stayed late. I had a very poor night. The goats kept up an incessant bleating round our hut. I got up at half past five; the dawn was clear, the sky washed, and in it, almost at its zenith, a quarter moon was floating. Quantities of enormous Palmyra palms (they have thickened trunks, fan-shaped leaves, and bunches of enormous orange-coloured apples) give the steppe an appearance of strangeness and dignity. Not a breath stirred the tall grasses; the road that we had to take was a white sanded path. Our start was rather difficult, because last night we dismissed four men, who had been lent us at M'Bengué on the understanding that they could be replaced at Sapoua. The four men we were expecting, however, did not turn up at the rollcall. We left the native guard behind. It was only at our first stage (the first village we went through, ten kilometres from Sapoua) that we discovered that our four new porters were women; all the able-bodied men, said our guard, having made off into the bush at the last moment, in order to escape being requisitioned. What added to our indignation was that the loads that our porters leave to the women are much the heaviest. Often the most strapping fellows seize on the lightest loads and start off ahead as quickly as possible, to avoid being noticed. We gave each of the women a five-franc note, hoping that our generosity would make the men regret not having come – a vain hope, for no sooner back in their village than the women will give the men the money.

This morning's march was like a triumphal progress; when we got to the first village, we had an enthusiastic reception, accompanied by singing and shouting, in a wonderful rhythm; the people here look clean and vigorous; we got out of our *tipoyes*; mine was ahead. And then it was no longer a march, but a sort of race, escorted by tamtams and a troop of laughing children; several offered their services as boys. From this village onwards as far as Pakori, where we arrived at about eleven o'clock and camped, we were escorted; the singing (in alternating choruses) of our *tipoyeurs* and the village people never ceased. Before reaching Pakori we passed through four or five villages, each more strange than the other, filled with more and more excited people. I am afraid my memory of it is confused. It was too strange. At last we are out of the nightmare of the forest. The savanna is beginning to look like a thinly planted wood; the trees are not very big, like cork-oaks, and are often covered with a beautiful creeper, like a wild vine. There are a great many guinea-fowl, we are told; but the yelling of all this delirious crowd sets everything to flight. The inhabitants of this country, as I have already remarked, look happy and healthy; the men are almost all oddly tattooed, with a line in high relief[5] that starts from the top middle of the forehead and goes to the base of the nose.

Our escort (it consisted of forty porters, plus eight wives of porters, three of whom have babies on their hips) is grown out of all knowledge. Even the chiefs insist on following us – at any rate as far as the next village, where we all stop and shake hands at parting.

At Pakori, where we halted, and which is the finest village we have yet seen, the number of children was incredible. I tried to count

5. This is done by introducing into the cut some kind of powder that raises the skin.

them; but at a hundred and eighty my head began to swim and I had to stop; there were too many. And the whole population crowds round one, pressing eagerly up to have the joy of shaking the hand one holds out – all shouting and laughing in a kind of lyrical demonstration of affection – almost cannibalism!

Pakori at night. This large village is marvellous. It has a style about it, a kind of grandeur; and its population seems happy. There is an open space with a ground of white sand, that forms an enormous half-street, half-*place* (like a longer Piazza Navona). The huts, unlike the sordid, insalubrious, uniformly ugly ones of the country round M'Baiki, are vast, fine-looking, and different one from the other; some of them (of which we occupy one) are larger, they are approached by six steps, and built on a kind of hillocks, whose formation I cannot account for, something like those which are supposed to be termitaries on the plain between Mobaye and Bambari. We had a long conversation with a sergeant in the Fort Archambault medical service, who is on six months' leave. We learn here that in all the neighbouring country (and, I think, in the whole Carnot subdivision) the native is allowed to work at his own plantations, after he has paid his taxes[6] – that is to say, after he has gathered enough rubber in the forest to pay it – which takes him about one month. In this region they cultivate only manioc, sesame, yams, and a little castor oil.

It is true, said the sergeant, that the white man pays much less than the native for kids and chickens – than the native *would* pay, that is, for he rarely buys kids or chickens and hardly ever eats them. (He never eats eggs either. Sometimes he gives the bad ones to the children; the others, except those that are reserved for hatching out, are kept for the white travellers.) Kids and chickens are used as objects of exchange. Money, until quite recently, consisted, and even still consists, in assegai iron, which he forges himself and which is valued at five francs the piece. A kid is worth from four to five assegais. A woman is bought indifferently either with kids or assegais (ten to fifty assegais – that is, from fifty to two

6. The country here has not been conceded to the Grandes Compagnies, which accounts for this liberty.

hundred and fifty francs). The white man is not supposed to buy the kid which the chief offers him. It is a gift; then the white man, who, in theory, owes nothing, gives a *matabiche*, patently inferior to the value of the kid, but which the chief must always accept with gratitude. Nevertheless a certain tariff gets established – one franc for a chicken; four to five francs for a kid. It is understood that the native never knows the real value of anything. In this whole countryside there is no such thing as a market or an offer or a demand. From one end of the village to the other no native possesses anything but his women, his flock, and perhaps a few bracelets or assegais. No object, no stuff, no piece of furniture – and even if he had the money, nothing offers itself which could by any possibility awake in him the desire to buy.

13 November

We arrived at Berberati at about 11 o'clock. The country here is utterly different; even the sky, even the quality of the air are changed. At last we can breathe. We crossed a fine stretch of open country – a savanna covered with grasses ten or twelve feet high, and occasionally interrupted by a recrudescence of the forest. The country is undulating, with hills of a considerable size; the views are extensive. The station itself – the administrator's house in which we are lodging (it has been abandoned for want of sufficient staff) – is very well situated on the side of a plateau which commands a vast prospect; but, as usual, in this immeasurably vast country, there is no focus; the lines run incoherently in all directions; there is no limit to anything. The villages alone sometimes have some kind of form. They are no longer arranged in a line on each side of the road, but open out into perspectives; and the huts are grouped together in little clumps which are sometimes charming.

The chief of Zaoro Yanga, the first village after Pakori, made us a present of an odd little animal in a sort of little basket, made of plaited palm leaves of the kind that is used in these parts as a hen-coop. I think it is a sloth.[7] Its front paws have only four fingers,

7. I learnt later that the real name of this charming little animal is *Perodicticus potto*.

the forefinger being atrophied. Its hind paws are very prehensile, with the thumb placed opposite the other fingers. The neck processes of its backbone protrude sharply under its skin. It is the size of a cat and has a very short tail; its ears look as if they had been cut off. It moves very slowly; though it walks clumsily and awkwardly when on the ground, it is very clever at climbing and hangs head downwards from any kind of support. It eats anything we offer it with pleasure – jam, bread, honey – and particularly relishes condensed milk.

Someone has brought me an enormous Goliath beetle, which I had the greatest difficulty in getting into my poison-bottle, though it has a very large opening.

We have paid a visit to the mission house, where we were very kindly received by the fathers, and treated to some excellent milk.

When we got back to the station, we spent a long time watching a mason fly at its extraordinary work (this one had a canary-yellow, not a black, waist, like the more ordinary kind). In the space of a few minutes it completely walled up a spider in a mud cell, into which it began by forcing it. I cut the cell open with my knife and brought to view several small spiders as well as the large one; a few moments later the damage was repaired. In the evening I took possession of the whole construction, after having detached it with difficulty from a bamboo lath on to which it was solidly cemented. It was as big as a pigeon's egg and made of four oblong cells, in earth as hard as brick or nearly. Each cell, when I cut it open, contained four or five spiders; they were small, but plump; quite fresh, and looking more as if they were asleep than dead; there was only one maggot with them, something like a weevil in size and appearance. This arrangement is no doubt the grub's larder, and I think that the mason fly (is it a sphex?) had laid an egg, out of which this maggot had come, either beside the spiders or in one of their abdomens. Unfortunately my eyesight is not so good as it was, and I find it difficult to focus things that are so minute.

Marc has just delivered a masterly 'rowing' to one of the station guards, who took the liberty of boxing our cook's ears.

In response to the kind invitation of the father of the mission we have decided to spend another day at Berberati. During the night our *sloth* managed to untie the string that was fastened to his paw and to escape. After some searching we found him perched on the roof of the veranda. Two horses were sent us by the mission, to take us to lunch there.

This morning we had to dismiss our forty porters. Some of them were such excellent fellows that the tears came to my eyes as I took leave of them. They have been with us since Nola. One, in particular, was sorry to part with us; he wanted to come on with us to Carnot; he looked something like a Mohican, with the feather of a falcon we had killed stuck in a hole in his ear – a tall, loose-limbed clown of a fellow, full of jokes and absurdities. When he saw the footprints of game on the ground, he used to say: 'It's a small meat . . .'

Very interesting conversation with the father of the mission. Before lunch he took us to a place two kilometres off, where he keeps his large herd of zebu cows, which he has had brought from N'Gaoundéré. We did not leave the mission till evening.

I was unable to take any notes yesterday; we were too tired when we arrived at the station of Bafio towards evening – a stage of thirty-five kilometres, though we did it almost entirely in our *tipoyes*. Nothing is more fatiguing than this form of locomotion, when the *tipoyeurs* are not thoroughly trained. It shakes one like the trot of a bad horse. Impossible to read. The appearance of the country has changed. The valleys are deeper and there are large plateaux. After Berberati, there are no more tsetses and no more sleeping-sickness; hence the mission herds and the horses of the village chiefs. The villages are no longer set in long, straight rows by the sides of the roads; the huts are no longer square, but round, with mud walls and pointed roofs of thatch and reeds. One feels the beginnings of Arab influence; the chiefs at last have proper clothes and are no longer ridiculously rigged up in odds and ends of European dress. They wear the *boubou* of the Bornouan or Haussa tribes – blue or white, and ornamented with embroideries. A thing that is rather disconcerting is that when we pass through the villages, a tamtam is organized – on our account, indeed, but it is round the chief that the dancers are grouped; it is not to us that the inhabitants do the honours, but to *themselves*. Most of them are on horseback. They gallop and caracole; it is almost the Arab fantasia; they have an air about them, a certain nobility and, no doubt, an incommensurable vanity. One of them, to whom I gave a five-franc note, in addition to the price of the manioc which had been brought for our porters, and the eggs and chickens for us, took the note haughtily and passed it on disdainfully to an attendant who was accompanying him. Another, who had no horse, was carried, as though in triumph, on his subjects' shoulders; everybody greeted him with acclamations. Bafio's[8] two sons, very handsome, clean (in appearance), and dignified young men, came to meet us on horseback. When we reached here, they were thirsty and asked for drink. Could I have been mistaken? One of them *crossed* himself, before putting the calabash to his lips. Very much astonished, I made inquiries. Could he be a *convert?* . . . No, he has not abjured Islam. If he crosses himself, it is merely as an extra. They are both of them still quite young and their courtesy was charming. The father keeps his chin wrapped up in a *lehfa*, which he wears as a turban; we are told that it is to hide his beard, after the manner of the Haussas (?).

There are very beautiful butterflies every time we come to a river-crossing. They fly in *shoals*; and yesterday I saw for the first time a shoal of tailed ones; one, that I had never seen before, was black with broad markings of green *lamé*; the under part of the wing had a curved line of *gold* spots on it; this is the first time I have seen *gold* on a butterfly's wings; not yellow, but *gold*. These butterflies settle on the ground in swarms, probably on a trace of excrement; they are so close together that their wings, though shut, are touching; they remain motionless and so busy or so stupefied that one can catch hold of them with one's finger and thumb – not by their wings, which would risk spoiling them, but by their corslet. In this manner I caught a dozen of them – admirable ones in a state of perfect freshness.

8. According to the custom of the country, the name of the chief and that of his village are the same.

But what was most amazing was that there were numbers of bees walking busily about on the edges of their closed wings; at first I thought that the bees were nibbling and cutting at them; but no; they were merely sucking them . . . that is, I think so; the butterflies were quiescent, and the whole thing is incomprehensible.[9]

Marc is unwell, with a touch of the sun, no doubt. The atmosphere is stifling; not very hot, but the air seems charged with electricity or with something that makes it difficult to breathe. We have settled to rest here for the day.

I spent a considerable time this morning training my 'sloth'; he is very fond of being petted, and once he has snuggled into my bosom, it is exceedingly hard to get him out again.

Yesterday, at about ten kilometres out of Bafio, an express messenger sent from Carnot appeared with the most unexpected of mails from France.

Carnot, 19 November

Carnot is not in the least like what I imagined. The town lies spread out on the shoulder of a hill, overlooking the country that lies on the other side of the Mambéré; but the landscape is still formless; it undulates in immense waves of ground covered with forest. But the general slope and lie of the land seem undecided, as though the watercourses had a difficulty in choosing which way to flow.

The great event of the 17th (the day before yesterday) was our meeting with an administrator called Blaud, who has been suddenly recalled (we knew of this) by the demand for an official inquiry consequent on an action brought against him by the management of the Compagnie Forestière. Blaud is a big stout fellow, with a florid complexion and a jovial countenance. He is forty-two years old, but does not look it. I have already said that we met him at Boda, when we were passing through. His time here was up and he was on the eve of returning home to France, where his wife and little girl of six were expecting him. During the lunch which we took together at the table of the wretch Pacha, Blaud told us he was bringing an action

9. I think the butterflies had just come out of their chrysalises and that their wings were still imbued with a sweet juice, which the bees were feasting on.

against the Forestière for grave breaches of the regulations and of the terms of their agreement. As soon as they heard of this accusation, the Forestière forestalled it and, after an exchange of telegrams with the Paris management, decided to discredit Blaud. Their method is extremely simple – to accuse him loudly of having an understanding with private traders and of being bribed by them. How otherwise could he possibly have anything to say against the Forestière? We were therefore on the lookout for Blaud, as we knew he had been recalled to Carnot (where the administrator mayor of Bangui is to hold an inquiry on his official conduct) and that from Carnot he would be returning to Nola. We had arranged so as to meet him half-way at lunch-time, hoping we might take our meal together. But as we were leaving Bafio, there was a fuss and a confusion over our porters, some of whom failed to turn up, so that we were nearly an hour late in starting. It was about eleven o'clock when, at a turning of the road, our *tipoyeurs* and his came face to face. We were in the middle of the savanna; the few stunted trees with which it is dotted gave no shelter worth speaking of . . . Blaud, who was even more anxious for a talk than we were, offered to turn back and go along with us as far as a river-crossing, which is the usual place for eating. So it was arranged. The site is a marvellous one; with big trees shading it, beneath which the water flows in a swift, full stream, so transparent that it was all I could do to resist the temptation to bathe. I feel that in this way I communicate more closely with nature . . . On this occasion, however, I contented myself with bathing my feet. Blaud's large table was set up, and places laid for three; and while the meal was being prepared, Blaud brought out the whole set of papers containing his accusations. I know nothing of the actions with which the Forestière charges him, but it was impossible for me – after all I have seen and heard during the course of my journey – to doubt the truth of those with which Blaud charges the agents of the company; I therefore sincerely hoped he had not laid himself open to their counterattack; on this point, however, I was obliged to withhold my opinion. Blaud seemed extremely perturbed; and there was really good reason to be, for the powers and influence of these great companies are formidable. Blaud told us, incidentally, of the change of ministry and that Antonetti was prolonging his stay in Paris.

We have seen Lamblin's chauffeur (the man who drove us to Bambio and who brought M. Marchessou here); he tells us they heard as they were passing through Boda that Samba N'Goto and his son had been imprisoned. Pacha, in the mean while, is on tour and *Sergeant Yemba is accompanying him*.

M. Marchessou has, however, now left Carnot; he is holding his inquiry at Nola, to which place Blaud has been summoned.

Long conversation with M. Labarbe, who is doing the work of the absent administrator. Labarbe is a voluminous person, with a well-developed chest and a hearty ringing voice; he is still young, intelligent, and very conscious of the effect he wishes to produce and succeeds in producing. Sometimes he puts the forefinger of his left hand up to his eye in a knowing way, as much as to say: 'There is no green in it.' As though to bear out his name, a thick black beard covers the lower part of his face. His only assistant is gentle M. Chambeaux, who is suffering from anaemia and has asked to be sent home, where his wife and child, a little girl of two, whom he has never seen, are expecting him. Labarbe himself declares he has had enough of it – too much of it . . . It is no good his asking for help. M. Staup, his predecessor, who has been sent somewhere else, dismissed 'the writer' of the circumscription, who ought to serve as the administrator's secretary, on the pretext that his own wife was a typist; and now it is impossible to get hold of him; he – Labarbe – is obliged to do everything himself. And Antonetti, who during his visit talked of 'axing'! There was not a soul as it was, and he wanted to dismiss people! But after all, it was a very simple matter; if he was given no one to help him, he – Labarbe – had made up his mind just to let his papers accumulate on his table; we should see what we should see. He had left all his things at Baboua, because he had been suddenly ordered to replace Blaud at Carnot; he was going back tomorrow to fetch them. Another station left to go to the dogs! Everything was going to rack and ruin in this country! No doctors! No officials! The few people who were still there were in a state of exasperation and their one idea was to go home again. Yes! everybody was making off – everything was in a mess. In this wretched Upper Sanga, a country no one would come to, there was nothing to be found – neither food nor anything else; the strict application of the customs tariff made the smallest article of commerce cost a prohibitive price.[10] And what annoyances and pin-prickings! . . . He had had his field-glasses confiscated by the customs people the last time he had come back – glasses he had had from time immemorial and that everybody knew . . . because he had lost the receipt of the duty he had already paid on them, and had not been able to show the bill of what they had cost. What the devil! One couldn't always keep all one's papers! . . . Besides, let them keep his glasses; he wouldn't so much as take the trouble to claim them when he went back . . . etc.

Yesterday, after a violent tornado (thunder, lightning, and the whole bag of tricks), which we heard vaguely through our afternoon nap, we went in our *tipoyes* to Saragouna, half an hour from Carnot. The crossing of the very fine river was amusing and rather dangerous (over a swaying, half-ruinous bridge). At first we rather doubted Psichari's veracity, as he places this 'oasis of greenery' at three days' distance from Carnot; but we have since learnt that the village, like so many others, has changed its quarters; the inhabitants suddenly abandoned their huts and rebuilt them a few days' journey farther on. Why? Because a few deaths had made them think that the place was cursed or haunted or what not . . . People who have no possessions and nothing to leave never have much difficulty in going away.

Noted the way in which all the women of the village suddenly fell to weeding as we appeared.

We left Carnot this morning much later than we had intended, as we had to wait more than an hour for the new porters. It was past eight when we took the ferry outside the town. There were three boat-loads; we were in the last and not very easy in our minds, for the current is extremely rapid. After an hour's march through a monotonous steppe (a kind of thin forest of trees that are hardly taller than the very tall fine grasses in which they are enveloped and hidden and which make a thick incessant curtain in front of one's

---

10. Labarbe's recriminations, such as I report them, are, I fear, only too well justified.

eyes) we met a great quantity of porters; after them came a file of fifteen women and two men, tied round their necks by one and the same cord and escorted by guards carrying five-thonged whips. One of the women had a baby at her breast. They were the 'hostages' who had been taken from the village of Dangolo, where the guards had been to requisition forty porters by order of the administration. All the men had made off into the bush when they saw them coming . . .[11] Marc took a photograph of this painful procession. The stage was much longer than Labarbe had told us. We were obliged to stop at the place at which we had planned to arrive for our midday rest and which we did not reach till past four o'clock – Bakissa-Bougandui. It is a kind of village, but very different from those of the Bambio region and from those we passed through before reaching Carnot. The huts are round, with very low mud walls and pointed thatched roofs; they are scattered and grouped with a charming carelessness, according to no plan at all – set neither in streets nor in lines, nor arranged round any open space. We are here on the highest part of a bare plateau. All round, or at any rate east, west, and north, there is a vast view over a dreary expanse of ground, heaving in immense undulations and covered with forests of a dark uniform green, beneath a sky that is discouragingly grey.

Not to be unfair, I must say that the weather became very fine about midday. But the mornings are, every day without exception, grey, dull, clouded, unspeakably, incomparably melancholy. This morning, at any rate when we started, there was a thickish fog which gave an agreeable softness to the monotonous green and prevented one from seeing too far; for as a rule, at daybreak, one's eyes travel over a joyless stretch of green dullness, under a sky with no promise in it, over a landscape uninhabited by god, or dryad, or faun – an implacable landscape, with neither mystery in it nor poetry.

As I cannot read in my *tipoye*, I amuse myself by repeating to

11. According to Labarbe, whom we came across again a few days later, and to whom we expressed our astonishment, he ordered the women to be set free when they reached Carnot and condemned the soldiers who had taken them to fifteen days' imprisonment (?).

myself all the poems I know out of *Les Fleurs du mal*, and by learning some new ones.

This evening a tamtam is being organized in the village, not far off; but I have stopped behind and am still sitting at the little table that has been set up by the dim light of the storm-lantern, reading the *Wahlverwandtschaften*, as I have finished *The Master of Ballantrae*. The moon in its first quarter is almost straight above my table. I feel surrounded on all sides by the strange immensity of the night.

A little later, however, I went to rejoin the dance. There was a meagre fire of sticks in the middle of a big circle; two drums and three resonant calabashes, filled with hard seeds and mounted on a short handle, so that they can be shaken rhythmically, enlivened the dance. The rhythms are learnedly unequal; there are groups of ten beats (five and five), succeeded in the same space of time by a group of four beats – with the accompaniment of a double bell or a metal castanet.[12] The instrument-players are in the middle. Near them is a group of four dancers, *vis-à-vis*, two by two. The rest go round in a circle, arranged in order of height, the tallest first, then the boys and children, down to tiny ones of four or five years old; the women come after. They all jig their shoulders, with their arms dangling loosely, as they go round and round very slowly, looking at once gloomy and violent. One of the children, when I put my hand on his shoulder, left the circle and came and pressed up against me. When some men, who were watching the dance, saw this, they called another child, who came to my other side. When the dance stopped, the children followed me. They sat on the ground near my chair, during our meal. They would like to become our boys. Some more children joined them. In the darkness that swallowed them, all that could be distinguished was their eyes, which were fixed on us, and, when they smiled, the whiteness of their teeth. If I let my hand hang down, they seized it, pressed it to their breasts or their faces, and

12. The chanting on this occasion was exceedingly odd (the chorus was composed mostly of children); quarter-tones were employed – all the more noticeably because the voices were in perfect tune – which produced an excruciating effect that was almost intolerable. As a rule, all the singing is in the notes of our scale.

covered it with kisses. On my chair, the little *sloth* was sleeping beside me; I felt its warmth against my back. I call it now by the name the natives give it: *Dindiki*.

It is to be noted that when we arrived, the people of this village (and the last one) were exceedingly disagreeable, not to say hostile; but their hostility soon melted away before our advances and was succeeded by an excess of sympathy and warm, effusive demonstrations. The chief himself, who had begun by declaring he could not find eggs for us or manioc for our men, afterwards showed himself extremely attentive and offered us more than we had at first asked for.

22 November

Left Bakissa-Bougandui (what a name!) before six o'clock; the children all came running to escort us out of the village. We plunged into a thick fog. The landscape is growing vaster, the undulations of the ground greater. For a long time we followed the ridge line and then went down into a deep valley. We walked the whole morning (with an hour's halt), almost till noon, without the least fatigue; we must have done nearly twenty-five kilometres. It was only the rain that began to fall heavily that forced us into our *tipoyes*, before we reached the stopping-place. So far we have avoided tornadoes; they have always burst during the night or while we were at meals. But this time it was not a storm; the sky was uniformly grey and one felt the shower was going to be a long one. The rain was heavier than ever as we arrived at the first village – which did not prevent the usual tamtams, and shouting and singing. But in this district there is no chorus of Bacchantes; and, in particular, the crazy old woman, who always seems to be the same in every village, was absent.

After an hour's rather dreary wait the rain stopped and we set off again. I took Dindiki into my *tipoye*, which made me get into it for a little. An hour and a half farther on we came to Cessana, a large village (arranged like Bakissa-Bougandui and like all the villages in this region) where we stopped for lunch. Then, immediately after, another very long stage, but this time in our *tipoyes*. We arrived at Abo-Boyafé about four o'clock, exhausted. And this was the village where the administrator assured us we should be able to sleep after one day's march. The directions given us by Europeans are nearly always wrong. [13]

23 November

For fear of exaggeration I underestimated the length of our march yesterday. We did a ten hours' day – including a two hours' halt and an hour and a half of *tipoye* – that is, six hours and a half on foot at about six kilometres an hour; for we walk very quickly. I was so tired that I hardly slept. The weather is at one and the same time almost cold and absolutely stifling. We were told that the next day's stage was a very short one; but I must acknowledge that this information, though given by natives, was not any more accurate than the other. We did not reach Abba, where we were supposed to arrive at noon, till four o'clock in the afternoon, though we started before six and walked well. It must be admitted that this immense tract of country was most disappointing. The savanna unrolled before us for hours and hours and miles and miles, and always identically the same. The giant grasses became reeds. Above them the same stunted, ill-grown trees, worn out, I suppose, by periodical forest fires, formed a sort of thinly sown coppice. The single interesting moment of the whole day was the crossing of a bridge of creepers (our first), flung over a wide, deep, rapid river – the Goman – in the place of a wooden bridge which has collapsed. Nothing could be more elegant than this arachnean web, which looks so fragile that one trembles as one sets foot on it. Near by, a gigantic pandanus, dipping its branches in the river, added to the exotic impression of the scene. And during the whole day's march that was taking us so terrifyingly far away, I thought desperately of France and home – of M. with incessant and sickening anxiety. Oh, if I could only know that she is well, that she is bearing my absence well! . . . And I fancied myself at the Tertre with Martin du Gard, at Carcassonne with Alibert . . .

13. The explanation of this is that it is never a question of distances, but merely of the time taken to cover them. Now, most Europeans never leave their *tipoyes*. Double (sometimes triple) shifts enable the porters to relay each other and allow the white man to discount their fatigue and insist on an acceleration of pace, thanks to which the stage is covered with much greater rapidity. As for the rest of the caravan, it starts first and goes on ahead – or follows and catches up as best it can.

When we arrived at Niko, the village chief was exceedingly disobliging. We had sent a runner on in front, so that we might find our men's manioc ready prepared and be able to start again as soon as possible. But no manioc appeared. There was nothing for it but to search the huts. Nevertheless we paid the man, stupid and pigheaded as he was, giving him to understand that he would have had twice as much if he had brought us, of his own accord and with a good grace, the food that our porters required, and which he can easily and promptly make good out of the fields. This is the first time we have been obliged to use our authority.

As soon as the sun got the better of the mist, the heat became overpowering. We used our *tipoyes* a great deal, for after a little walking I sweated monstrously. Towards the evening the light became very beautiful. As we approached Abba, a messenger, who had been sent out to meet us, two kilometres from the village, began ringing a bell to announce our arrival. He went on ahead and our *tipoyeurs* began to run. Then the chief appeared on horseback. As he dismounted, we got down also. The population were collected on a piece of rising ground. It was highly imposing and we stalked forward majestically. The huts of the village are spacious and handsome, similar to those of the preceding villages, except that on the top of the pointed roof is placed a large, round jar, made of black earthenware, with its mouth uppermost; the huts are arranged without any order, but they fall into harmonious groups because of the lie of the ground. The view overlooks an immense tract of country. The sunset was glorious and then at once a curtain of very thin blue haze, made partly of the village smoke, spread horizontally over the landscape and gave distance to the neighbouring belt of forest. Not a cloud was left in the sky. In the zenith the moon was in her second quarter, and a long way off her shone two extraordinarily bright stars. The lights of the village began to come out. An immense silence, and then the air filled with the strident concert of the crickets.

Our belated porters come dropping in one by one; a good many of them are limping and they look thoroughly done up. We have given some of them a dose of quinine. The manioc has been distributed, and they are now sitting grouped round a large fire. The sky is full of stars.

I have not put my Dindiki back in his cage. He has spent the whole day (yesterday too) in my *tipoye*, either clinging to one of the bamboo poles that support the mats of the *shimbeck*, or else cuddled up against me. It is impossible to imagine a more confiding creature. He takes without hesitation any food he is offered and eats indifferently bread, manioc, custard, jam, or fruit. There is only one thing he cannot endure – being hurried or being made to leave his perch. This puts him in the most terrible rage; and he screams and bites as hard as he can. Impossible to make him let go; he would rather have his joints dislocated. Then as soon as you get him in your arms, he calms down and begins licking you. He is more caressing than any dog or any cat. When I walk in the village, he comes with me, clinging to my belt, my shirt collar, my ear, my neck.

Read a few pages of *The Affinities* with rapture. I give Adoum a reading lesson every evening.

25 November

We spent the day at Abba yesterday, resting. Marc visited the inside of the huts; in some of them there is a kind of thick half-wall, half-screen made of mud, which he took me to look at; it is slightly concave and makes a high back to a low bench that is placed opposite the entrance. Behind its shelter is the *créquois*, or sleeping-mat.[14] This large screen is soberly decorated with a very broad geometrical pattern in shiny black, on a ground which is left the red colour of the earth. The effect is very fine. On the sides, against the circular walls of the hut, are masses of enormous, varnished earthenware jars, which are decorated in relief, as if they were tattooed and which the natives use for keeping their water and manioc in; these, with the *créquois* or mat, are the only articles of furniture in the hut. A troop of children escort us, as usual, wherever we go; most of them are unwashed. We shamed them into going into their huts, out of which they emerged soon after, all shining from their ablutions.

Marc organized races for the children in the village square, while the parents looked on amused and delighted. There were about sixty competitors. The village chief was an excellent fellow, who we felt

14. A kind of low bed made of bamboo laths.

was conquered by our manners and whom we paid handsomely. The porters organized a tamtam; a solo dancer aroused the enthusiasm of the spectators (especially of the children, who thronged to see him) by imitating in an extraordinarily *stylized* dance a hen, a mare in heat, and other animals.

Several of our porters came to have their feet dressed; we were obliged to dismiss four. A fifth, who dragged himself along with difficulty, seemed to us to be shamming. And in fact he came with us the next morning and made no further complaints when he understood that he would not be paid if he refused his load.

Started this morning before six o'clock.

Halted at noon in a very fine village (Barbaza). The huts are of the same style as in the last and disposed likewise without apparent order, but according to the lie of the ground. And gradually a kind of paths, almost streets, are formed, bordered sometimes with wicker palisades, which separate the groups of houses. The same big black varnished pots are to be seen on the tops of all the roofs.

Another stage much longer than the ones between Bambio and Nola (with the exception of the first from Bambio to N'Délé). We left Abba before six and did not reach Abo-Bougrima till four in the afternoon, with only an hour's stop for lunch. The view is becoming more and more extensive, the valleys wider and deeper, the accentuation of the ground more marked.

In the first village we stopped at after Abba – a very large, very important one (I think it was Barbaza, which I have just described) – we were attracted by the sound of singing. It was a funeral. We made our way into one of the enclosures – a minute assemblage of from four to six huts, forming a subdivision of the big village. An old woman had died. Her children, her relations and friends were present. They were all giving vent to their grief in a rhythmical song – a sort of psalmody. We were introduced to the son, a tall man, who was himself old; his face was streaming with tears; while we were saluting him, he did not cease from singing as he wept, or weeping as he sang, punctuating his chant with frequent sobs. For that matter, all their faces were bathed in tears. We drew near the hut which seemed to be the focus of the cries. We did not dare go in, but as we were leaning forward towards the opening of the hut, which is like the opening of a pigeon-house or a beehive, the singing stopped.

There was a stir inside the hut, and some people came out. It was in order to make room for us and allow us to see the body. It was lying on the ground, not specially dressed, on its side, in the attitude of a person who has gone to sleep. In the semi-obscurity we saw a crowd of people, who went on with their funeral observances. Some of them went up to the old woman's body, bent over her, seemed to be trying to wake her up precipitately, and stroked and raised her limbs. All the faces we could see in the dark were gleaming with tears. In the enclosure, not far from the hut, two natives were digging a very deep, narrow hole, which suggested that the dead are buried in an upright position. Continuing our tour through the village, we saw dotted here and there near the huts a number of very small rectangles strewn with white gravel and surrounded by a low trellis-work of branches. These, we were told, were graves; we had supposed so. And yet how often have we heard it repeated that the natives of Central Africa have no care for their dead and bury them no matter where! At any rate, the people here are an exception.

Reached Abo-Bougrima somewhat exhausted and, after a tub and tea, I wanted nothing better than to plunge again into the *Wahlver-wandtschaften*, which, in spite of my having no dictionary (alas!), I understand better than I had dared hope. But when evening came on (Marc in the meanwhile had gone with Outhman to try to shoot a few guinea-fowl), I began to follow, quite vaguely, a tiny little path which I found behind our hut, and which was half concealed by tall grasses. It led us almost immediately to a quarter of Bougrima which has been allowed to fall into ruin. There was a large piece of sloping ground on which one could see the trace of a village square, formed by the spaces between the deserted and roofless huts. The walls of the huts, which were standing rather far apart, were broken in and showed the kind of inner partition, forming a curved niche and back for a low bench, such as I have already described. I was able to admire at my ease the fine decorations on these screens, which, though night was coming on, were still fully visible. I satisfied myself that there were three colours employed – and not black alone, as I had thought at first, but brick-red and ochre as well. And the whole thing is so varnished and so polished that the weather has hardly injured or even dimmed the tones. On one side (and always on the right, it seemed to me) there were very curious beginnings of pillars, which serve as stands for large jars, placed one on the top of the other. In consequence of the roofs' having disappeared (either destroyed by fire or removed to use again), the ruins have a clean and tidy appearance, without any litter of straw or wood.

The vegetation of the bush has closed in on these remnants, and at times a creeping plant, with its large beautiful leaves, framed or festooned the strange, ruined partitions, showing up the richness and sonority of their paintings. It was like a kind of Negro Pompeii, and I regretted Marc was not there and that it was too late to take some photographs. Solitude and silence and falling night! Hardly anything I have seen in this country has moved me so much.

26 November

At last a glorious day. The first clear morning for a long time; it seems to me as if we had never had any but grey misty mornings ever since we have been out here. True, the sky was not absolutely pure, but the light was warm and more abundant than ever. Is that the reason that the scenery seemed to me finer? I think not. At moments enormous boulders of granite jutting up out of the soil gave a more pronounced line to the landscape. The trees, some of them no bigger than our own, made a kind of thin, continuous forest in the savanna. The sky was a deep soft blue. The air was dry and light. I breathed it with rapture, and my whole being thrilled with excitement at the prospect of the long march across the immense country that stretched far into the distance before us.

Nothing particular to note, however, except our meal on the banks of a river, and, later on, the passage of the Mambéré under a burning sun, when our *tipoyeurs* took the opportunity of bathing. Marc restrained me from doing the same and I grumblingly submitted.

At a considerable distance from Baboua the new chiefs came out to meet us. They are the two brothers of the chief recognized by the French administration, who has lately fled into the Cameroon, taking with him the seven hundred francs that the administrator had given him to pay for the mats made by the men of his village.[15] These two chiefs were on horseback and appeared towering above

15. At fifty centimes apiece.

us, with their tall lances pointed towards our *tipoyes* and uttering such fierce cries that at first I thought they wanted to prevent us from advancing. One of their horses began to kick, burst a tamtam, and knocked up against Marc's *tipoye*. I got down and advanced smiling. Explanations and a great hubbub followed; then our vanguard started off again preceded by five men on horseback, amongst them the two chiefs, very handsome in their Arab garments, which fluttered about them in the breeze they made as they rode. We were so far ahead of our porters that as I write these notes, after having shaved, washed, and partaken of mandarins and bananas, they have not yet arrived.

Baboua, 27 November

Adoum came in limping last night, and long after the others; he is suffering from a swollen gland, which makes a large lump on his groin. I was afraid it might be a phlegmon, which I did not know how to treat except by wet compresses. I gave him besides some quinine and *rhoféine* and he lay down in the dark and went to sleep. The heat was very trying.

The house of the 'commandant' (the administrator) and the travellers' hut, where we are staying, are a few hundred yards outside the village, which we went to visit before sunset, accompanied by the interpreter and the two new chiefs. We were astonished to find the village completely deserted. The flight of the real chief entailed at the same time the desertion of a great many of the village people, who thought to show their devotion in this way. Thirty men (and their families), we are told, accompanied him into the next subdivision in the Cameroon territory. About two hundred more went off in different directions into the bush, where they have been living for some months past. We went into the chief's deserted house. It is reached through a labyrinth of mud walls and reed partitions, constructed with a view to ambush and defence. Behind the house are the women's huts, arranged in a semicircle and opening on to a sort of courtyard. Everything was empty and desolate.

The night was splendid. In the evening we heard the sounds of a tamtam, first in the distance and then drawing nearer. After a good slice of *The Affinities* and Adoum's reading lesson we went to see. In spite of the emptiness of the village, there managed to assemble about sixty people of both sexes and all ages. It would be impossible to imagine anything more dismal and more stupid than this dance, unrelieved as it was by any breath of spirituality. To the sound of a drum and a single musical phrase, taken up by the chorus and repeated untiringly, they all go round and round in an enormous circle, one behind the other, with extreme slowness and jigging their bodies almost as if they had no bones, bending forward, with their arms dangling and their heads shaking backwards and forwards like fowls. This is how they express their emotion – manifest their joy! By the light of the moon this obscure ceremony seemed the celebration of some infernal mystery; I stayed gazing at it for a long time, fascinated by it as by an abyss – like St Anthony by the stupidity of the catoblepas: '*Sa stupidité m'attire.*'

This morning the sky was the purest, the brightest, I have perhaps ever seen in my whole life. The air was light; the sky filled from end to end with dazzling radiance. I believe Baboua is about 3,500 feet high. Last night it was almost cold. Labarbe arrived about midday, so overwhelmed with business that he was unable to accept our invitation to lunch. He said he would not eat till he had settled up certain urgent affairs and given judgement – perhaps would not eat at all. We decided to go to him at about three o'clock and take Adoum, who is in great pain, for him to see. The poor boy has not been able to sleep or even to lie down, and spent almost the whole night doubled up on a *créquois*. Labarbe has studied medicine and I was impatient to have his opinion and perhaps his surgical assistance. He told us he would have to lance the boil and to dress it. Adoum dragged himself to the house, which is not far off, refusing all help from the porters. He appeared extremely reluctant when he was told to undress. I thought at first it was modesty. Alas! when he let down his breeches, his thighs were seen to be covered with large suppurating pustules. On observing his reluctance Labarbe began to chuckle, for he guessed how the land lay and overwhelmed Adoum with his sarcasm. It is not from inflamed glands that he is suffering, but from a venereal boil, that has to be treated differently. The boil, however, is on the point of bursting, and Labarbe began by simply applying hot-water compresses. He questioned Adoum jocularly. The poor boy got his trouble exacty forty days ago, on the occasion of that festive night out, which we had always thought rather mysterious. It was a sad sight to see his body – so handsome, so young still, and so pure of line, all marred, disfigured, dishonoured by such frightful sores. Labarbe, however, declares that the natives know certain herbs capable of curing syphilis radically – and that the disease never has the gravity it sometimes has with us. He thinks he has never known a native who was free from it – nor one who has died from it.

Baboua, 28 November

Still the same splendid azure of the sky. We took Adoum to see Labarbe again this morning. The boil had burst during the night, so that the patient was greatly relieved and at last able to sleep. He lay down on the mat and I held his hands while Labarbe pressed the swelling and squeezed out an incredible quantity of matter. He writhed with the pain and it was worse still when a dressing soaked with iodine was introduced deep down into the crater of the boil.

Spent the day resting and reading. My brain feels as fresh and limpid as the sky. About four o'clock the fugitive chief Semba came riding up on horseback, escorted by another horseman. He knows that imprisonment awaits him; but he knows too that four warrants are out against him and that there is no place he can escape to. He was wearing a kind of glittering coat of mail, made of quantities of fifty-centime pieces which had been drilled and sewn on to a kind of black doublet. He looked very handsome, very noble, and even a bit fierce, as he galloped up, with his lance pointing forwards; he dismounted at the approach of Labarbe, who, with great dignity and the most imposing and authoritative manner, dropped his raised hand on to Semba's breast and delivered him over to the guards to be led off to prison. But Semba, who has decided to submit, stalked on before them in the direction of the jail. He is accused and has been convicted of innumerable crimes – sale of slaves, murders, and cruelties, keeping arms, cartridges, etc., without permission, and so on. The populace watched him go off without a murmur of protest or even of surprise. Everything has taken place according to expectation. In the meantime the village, which I revisited in the evening (the heat in the daytime was overpowering), is more or less repeopled. It is an enormous village, and one is always discovering new quarters, new groups of twelve, fifteen, or twenty huts – either in a dip of the ground, or where they had lain concealed from the eye by the tall bush grasses. The sun went down, a globe of scarlet, behind a curtain of violet mists. And at the same moment, high up in the sky, the full moon began to shine.

29 November

Left Baboua at daybreak this morning with a new batch of porters, which led to delay and disputes as to the distributions of the loads. Besides which a hammock had to be prepared for Adoum, who is incapable of walking. I left the arrangements to Marc and went on ahead. I was feeling magnificently well and did almost the whole march on foot, at the head of the column. The weather was superb. The road had not been cleared; and even the long grasses on each side of it had not been beaten down, as they had been the whole of the previous way, in order to facilitate our progress. I had no idea what an obstacle they would prove; for the road is very wide (from two and a half to three metres), but the grasses are so tall that as they droop down, they cover the whole of it and are a great impediment; they were still all wet with dew and I was soon drenched as a result of forcing my way through them. Matters are much worse when one gets to a *marigot*; for then the road completely disappears in the mass of vegetation.

After about six hours' march we reached a stream, which crossed the road, not, as usual, beneath an arch of tall trees, but in open ground. The stream was neither particularly transparent, nor very deep, nor very full; but it broke and fell between such sharp, smooth rocks of granite, and a little farther on a bush made such a delightful shade, a tall tree gave out such a delicious perfume, that I yielded to the water's invitation.

Now that from time to time rocks make their appearance, the landscape is becoming more definite, more accentuated; the lie of the ground seems better marked. The country is very sparsely populated. About ten o'clock we reached the village of Gambougo, a wretched enough place; the chief was obliging, but we made no halt. It was past one o'clock when we reached Lokoti, where we lunched. This village is on the move. There are already visible the skeletons of the new huts, with their unfinished roofs, about a hundred yards away from the old village, which has had a spell cast upon it. It is impossible to cross the Nana by night, though we should have liked to continue our march by moonlight; we were compelled to halt at Dibba – a miserable village – with a still more miserable rest-house, which we had to make the best of; we had some of the openings stuffed up with straw and burnt a nest of ants whose hordes were menacing.

30 November

Three trees – one of them enormous – on the vague kind of place round which the huts are dotted – perfect moonlight – an immensity of soft warm night. In the early morning it was chilly and the dew as abundant as if there had been a shower. We started at the hour when the radiance of the full moon is beginning to fade in the coming of dawn – that rather eerie hour when witches come home from their sabbath. The road descends to the basin of the Nana; the sun made a crimson gash in the dove-coloured sky. As our ascent the day before had been quite imperceptible, we were surprised to find ourselves suddenly so high up, overlooking an immense tract of country, in which the belated mists formed great lakes and rivers in the distance.

On foot to Nana. Carrying the luggage across in a narrow canoe took a long time. On the other shore was a thicket of enormous trees; the steepness of the shore made them look still taller. The sky, which had been full of the rising mist, grew clear and there was a return of the radiant weather of the last few days. It was the sight of the canoe, as it left the opposite shore and emerged from the overarching shadow, impelled by the effort of the boatman bending double over his punting-pole – it was the man's slightness, his skiff's fragility – which gave the scale for measuring the hugeness of the surrounding trees.

Half an hour before getting to the Nana was a village where we might have spent the night if we had known. All these villages – Babouan *kagamas*[16] – are more or less deserted, on account of

16. A *kagama* is a village depending upon another, more important one, and in the charge of the same chief, who is represented by a *capita*, chosen by himself.

Semba's flight and for fear of the reprisals which may result from it, and also for the fear (only too comprehensible, alas!) that we white men, immediately followed, as we are, by the commandant, may be scouring the country in order to requisition men for the railway and seize them by any means in our power. However kindly and considerately one treats them, they are suspicious – and no wonder.

When we had crossed the Nana, however, the next village welcomed us with great demonstrations. They were all there, picturesquely grouped on a staircase whose natural steps were formed by the roots of some kind of gigantic tree – the chief, the tamtams, the chief's suite, among whom was his son, a clean, handsome boy of thirteen, his face oddly scored by black lines and his chest crossed slantwise by a strip of grey fur. Near him were three rather curiously handsome creatures, from fourteen to sixteen years old, covered with necklaces and belts made of blue and white beads, and with brass bracelets on their wrists, forearms, elbows, ankles and calves. I put one hand on the shoulder of one of them, the other on the shoulder of the chief's son, and drew them along with me at the head of the escort. Later on, these two boys accompanied me to the village, about half an hour off, carrying our bags for us of their own accord. They went with us into the travellers' hut, where we had our deckchairs put out, and sat down on the ground beside me; then the chief's son, while we were talking to his father, came and crouched between my knees, like a little tame animal.

The scenery is magnificent; this word is no doubt too strong, for there is nothing particularly enchanting about the site – which reminds one of a good many of our French landscapes – but my rapture at getting away at last from the recent formlessness, at once more seeing definite hills, decided slopes, and clumps of trees harmoniously disposed, was such that . . . Well! This morning, at last, the country is opening out before our eyes; for, since we left Bambio, with very few exceptions, we have been completely shut in, walking either through forests or through savannas, where we were enveloped by a vegetation so tall that we could see no more than fifty yards in front of us – and often not more than ten. What rapture it was when we had climbed the heights that lie in front of Déka, and that half encircle it, to see the tall grasses give way at last to a kind of close-shaven turf of a soft green colour, which allows the eye an uninterrupted view into the distance, so that the trees (they are not large) which are dotted here and there and which until now had seemed drowned and stifled by the tall grasses, were seen to full advantage! (Have I said that these grasses were so tall that a man on horseback could not see over them? One felt like a cat walking in a field of oats.) And then I felt in a state of physical well-being, which made me inclined to find joy, nobility, and even beauty in the least striking scenery. I had walked for an immense time; but when at last I decided to get into my *tipoye*, the cords on which it was slung snapped and dropped me brutally on to the ground; so I was obliged to go on walking. The sun was at its height and the ascent was steep. These hills, which are here called mountains because there is nothing higher in the whole country, cannot be much more than sixteen hundred feet high. But after a long bout of plateau, the country goes down in an extraordinarily deep dip, and again one has much more of a bird's-eye view than one has been led to expect from the amount of one's climb. A little later a ridiculous accident obliged me nevertheless to wait till my *tipoye* was mended. The interminable climb in the sun had put me in a violent perspiration (it was the hottest time of the day) and I was longing desperately for a river where I could bathe. We came to a *marigot*, but the water was thick with mud and no good at all; so I prepared to jump it, as there was no bridge; but the stream was wide, and when I put my foot on a log of wood to get a good take-off, my foot slipped and I came down at full length in the mud. I picked myself out of it covered with horrible filth and proceeded to change my clothes at once, seated on a burning rock. I found some linen in a bag, a pair of trousers in a box, but it was impossible to lay my hands on a pair of shoes. My extra pair had gone on ahead with the first set of porters. I had to content myself with slippers, which were totally unfit for walking. I still, however, managed to go on for a few more kilometres, carried along by a kind of ambulatory enthusiasm – an intoxication of health – which led me just now into calling the scenery magnificent.

I am writing this after dinner – the full moon is shedding its immensity of light over the village of Dahi, where we are spending the night; towards the east the heights of Bouar, which we are to climb tomorrow, are visible, through a faint blue haze. There is not a breath in the air, not a cloud in the sky, which is not in the least black, but azure like the sea, so intense is the moonlight. Not far from us are our boys' and porters' fires; and farther off again, the village's. The people here have not fled. There were a good hundred of them who hurried up to welcome us after nightfall, crowding round us with cannibal-like expressions of joy, and so close as almost to suffocate us.

Bouar, 2 December

It is now several days ago that the bush fires began. One can hear their crackling a long way off, and at night one can see their glimmer still farther; they pour out torrents of smoke into the sky. We arrived at Bouar yesterday about one o'clock. Notwithstanding the great heat, the air is sharp. We do not seem to have made much of an ascent, but the station of Bouar, which is some distance from the village, although less than thirty-five hundred feet high, looks over an immense expanse of country; towards the west lies the tract we have covered in the last two days, and edging the horizon are the heights where we slept the day before yesterday. Farther south, towards Carnot, one's eye follows the basin of the Nana to a greater distance still.

Yesterday the sun in setting filled the sky with crimson rays. This morning, as I am writing this, the heavens are ineffably pure; but the air, too heavily laden with moisture to be perfectly limpid, has spread a film of pearly azure over the dark greens of the forest and the glaucous greens of the savannas. In front of the hut there is a foreground of arid soil, broken here and there by great boulders of granite; then the last huts of the village, which stretches out towards the right behind the station; then a few trees, which in France would be chestnut trees – and then, immediately after, the farthest distance, in all its variegated immensity, for the fall of the ground is too abrupt to be visible. There is nothing between these trees, which are fifty yards off, and the plain – so amazingly distant.

Bouar, 3 December

Paid a visit to the old German station, one kilometre away; it has been half ruined by a tornado; but the view from it over the country is admirable. Saw the remains of some avenues of mango trees, and some of a curious kind of aloe, which harbours the younger generation on the top of its spike and sometimes all up its stalk, so that when one shakes the spike, there pours down from it, instead of seeds, a rain of little aloes, already formed, with quite large leaves and roots. A few tomato plants were growing against one of the station buildings; I came back loaded with their fruit.

Neither jasmine, nor lilies of the valley, nor lilac, nor roses have such a strong and delicious scent as the flowers of the shrub near which I bathed the day before yesterday – a corymb of little pinkish-white quadrilobed flowers round a slender tubing. The carriage, leaves, and flowers of the shrub are like the laurel's; its scent is concentrated honeysuckle.

4 December

We left Bouar this morning rather late, for we had to wait for fresh porters; and Labarbe, who arrived yesterday evening, was to start with us; but his destination was Carnot and ours Bosoum. We settled up with our porters yesterday so as to let them go; but we did not know that the administration had already paid them a franc in advance for their food. We ought therefore to have given them only three francs instead of four, and moreover we need not, said Labarbe, have paid for their manioc, for which I allowed about fifty centimes per day and per head. [17] Labarbe declares they do not spend more than twenty-five centimes a day for their food. It is a far cry from the time (not so long ago either) when, at Port-Gentil, I was near being indignant that the state's grant to prisoners was only thirty-five centimes a day. Porters are paid a franc a day by the administration (and not one franc twenty-five, as I thought), fifty centimes a day when not on the march, and twenty-five centimes a day for the return journey. In general the return journey is counted as taking half the time of the journey out.

Sometimes they wear a leather or cord belt, which exactly follows the fold of the groin, drawing a single simple line on the black skin; a

17. Needless to say, we continued to pay for our porters' food, as moreover every administrator does when he is on tour – that is, if he is at all anxious to gain their liking; it has been too often and falsely said that they are incapable of gratitude.

piece of brown or red bark, or a rag of cloth, covers the sex tightly, passes between the legs and rejoins the belt at the back above the sacrum. It makes a line of admirable purity. Sometimes the bark, which is of a beautiful rich tone, spreads out behind like a corolla.

Last night we had a small unofficial tamtam; it was very dark, for the moon had not yet risen. A dozen young boys met together for a little unimportant dance. The fires were lighted outside the huts in the guards' camp, and the evening's entertainment lasted late. While we were lingering near the fires, Zézé and Adoum played for money with the guards and were completely cleared out of their whole month's pay, which we had just given them. Adoum lost last month's pay as well, which he had been carefully keeping and which he sincerely hoped (I think) to take to his mother at Abécher, where he left her four years ago.

These guards had waited till the last evening to bring off their coup, thinking that we should be too busy this morning before starting to look into the affair. And as a fact we had already left Ouar far behind when I questioned Adoum, who was looking depressed, and he confessed. I tried to make him understand that he had been an idiot, that he had been taken in by dishonest players, and that the guards were cheats. He was very much amused by this word, which he did not know.

5 December

A thick fog this morning; we made our way along an overgrown track through tall grasses sopping with wet. It was not till ten o'clock that the sun succeeded in overcoming the clouds and re-established a sky of wonderful purity. The country is not very interesting. Yesterday at an hour's march from Bouar the villages succeeded each other about every two kilometres. This is an ill-subjected region and we expected to find a good deal of bad feeling. It is true that some of the villages were half deserted. A great many of the natives had scattered into the bush against our coming. But we had not the slightest difficulty in winning over those who were left behind, as soon as they understood we had no intention of harming them. And as news is quickly transmitted from one village to another, the inhabitants came thronging more and more and their welcome became warmer and warmer. We had the flattering impression that we were winning these people over to France.

It is to the spaced fruit trees in an orchard, to the apple trees of a Normandy farm, to the elms that prop the vines in Italy near Sienna, that I should have compared the dotted trees in the savanna we have been walking through for so many days past – trees whose trunks are submerged in tall grasses. And I admire the hardiness of these trees in resisting as they do the periodical burning. Today the greater spacing between the trees is the only modification in the desperate monotony of the landscape. The village in which we stopped last night – the second stage on the road to Bosoum – is without any beauty but that with which the light floods it. When the procession forms up to welcome our entrance into a village, my custom is to choose out a favourite on whom to lean, or who holds my hand as he walks beside me. It very often happens to be the chief's son – which produces an excellent effect. This one here was particularly handsome, slender, and elegant, and reminded me of Baudelaire's Sisina. In the evening he and two of his companions told me they all wanted to accompany us as far as Bosoum.

What a delicious bathe I had at noon and how limpid the river was! How clear the night is this evening! I do not know even the name of the village where we are spending the night. The road we are following is very little frequented (by the whites, I mean). An unknown immensity encompasses us.

While I am re-reading *Romeo and Juliet* with delight and rapture, Marc is dressing wounds, distributing medicines, and 'rendering justice' – which takes an enormous time.

6 December

Halt at Batara. On the outskirts of this considerable village, which we reached about eleven o'clock, we recognized by the young cearas plantations that we were back again in Lamblin's territory – in the subdivision of Bosoum.

After such a long time spent in wandering through regions where everything was savage, formless, embryonic, inexistent, it is the greatest joy to find oneself again in a village that is tidy, clean, and prosperous-looking; a decent chief, dressed in European clothes that are not ridiculous, in a freshly whitened helmet, speaking correct French – a flag run up in our honour – all of this moves me absurdly – almost to sobs.

We were tormented by the idea that we had not been sufficiently generous to the village chief at our last stage, so we have sent him two five-franc notes in an envelope, by messenger from Batara. His air of consternation this morning when he received his six francs *matabiche* has been weighing on my heart. The absence of any priced goods, the impossibility of knowing whether one is paying for the services one receives well, or too well, or not well enough, is one of the greatest discomforts in travelling in this country, where nothing has an established value, where the language has no word for thank you, where, etc. . . .

8 December

We arrived last evening at Bosoum, where the road again begins to be accessible to motor traffic. Here we are at an end of a long chapter of our travels. Lamblin's car is to pick us up here in order to take us to Archambault. Three weeks ago we wrote to the Governor, at his request, from Carnot to let him know the date of our arrival at Bosoum. We are one day in advance. We should have done the last part of the journey in two stages; but, having started from Batara at four o'clock in the morning, we arrived at Kuigoré as early as one, and decided to leave at three, as we still had time to cover the twenty kilometres that lay between us and our goal, before nightfall. We got out of our *tipoyes* and did part of the distance almost at a trot, so impatient were we. All the morning the landscape was *intensely monotonous*. Noticed by the way clematis gone to seed, ranunculus, or adonides (not yet in flower), and peonies in bud (as near Andrinopolis). After Kuigoré, there were very fine granite rocks, which sometimes looked like the big upheavals in the forest of Fontainebleau. Whenever the landscape becomes more formed, when it sets itself limits and attempts to be a little better planned, it evokes in my mind some corner of France; but the French landscape is always better constructed, better drawn, and of a more individual elegance. And so, at the crossing of a river a little before we came to Kuigoré, the flow of the water under the great trees, the rocks that broke the current, the road that followed the bank for a moment, all of this made us laugh with rapture and exclaim: 'One might be in France!'

The approach to Bosoum is very fine. Yves Morel, the head of the subdivision, was expecting us. As he never listens to what one says, he keeps on repeating the same things half a dozen times – but he is by no means stupid; his judgement, it seems to me, is often correct, and he says – though too slowly – things that are extremely interesting . . .

CHAPTER SIX

FROM BOSOUM TO
FORT ARCHAMBAULT

Bosoum, 9 December

The absence of individuality, of individualization – the impossibility of differentiating – which depressed me so much at the beginning of my journey, is what I suffer from too in the landscape. (I experienced this sensation as early as Matadi on seeing the population of children all alike, all equally agreeable, etc. . . . and again on seeing the huts of the first villages, all alike, all containing droves of human cattle with the same looks, tastes, customs, possibilities, etc. . . .) Bosoum is a place that looks over a wide stretch of country, and as I stand here on a kind of terrace, made of red-ochre-coloured laterite, gazing at the marvellous quality of the light and admiring the vast undulations of the ground, I ask myself what there is to attract me to any one point rather than to any other. Everything is uniform; there can be no possible predilection for any particular site. I stayed the whole day yesterday without the least desire to stir. From one end of the horizon to the other, wherever my eye settles, there is not a single point to which I wish to go. But how pure the air is! How beautiful the light! What a delicious feeling of warmth envelops one and fills one with pleasure! How easy to breathe! How good to live!

This notion of differentiation, which I have acquired here, and from which proceeds the sense both of the exquisite and of the rare, is so important that it seems to me the principal thing I shall bring away from this country.

Yves Morel spreads himself, unbuttons himself. He is still quite young, but already very like old Karamazov. Every now and then a twinge of rheumatism makes him wriggle and give little squeaks. For the rest, an excellent fellow. We talk politics, morals, economics, etc., etc. His remarks about the natives seem to me especially just, as they confirm the result of my own observations. He thinks, as I do, that as a rule people greatly exaggerate the lasciviousness and sexual precocity of the blacks, and the obscene signification of their dances.

He speaks of the hypersensibility of the black race as regards everything that has to do with superstition, their fear of mystery, etc. – which are all the more remarkable because he thinks, on the other hand, that their nervous system is much less sensitive than ours – whence their resistance to pain, etc. . . . In the subdivision of the Middle Congo, where he was at first stationed, custom demanded that a sick man on his recovery should change his name, to make it quite clear that he was cured and that the person who had been ill was dead. And when Morel, who was unaware of this, came back to a village after rather a long absence, to make a census of the population, a woman's terror and shock at hearing her old name would often be so great that she would fall down as if she were dead, in a semi-cataleptic fit, which it would sometimes take hours to get her out of.

I picked up a minute chameleon on the road, which I brought back with me to the hut and spent nearly an hour observing. It is certainly one of the most astonishing animals in creation. There is a charming little macaco sitting near me as I write this. It was brought me this morning; but the appearance of my white face terrifies it. It leaps for shelter into the arms of any native who passes by within reach.

There is an almost Neronic pleasure in lighting a bush fire. A single match and in a few moments the fire assumes outrageous proportions. The blacks immediately come rushing up to seize the huge locusts that are driven out by the heat of the flames. I picked up a very small mantis which looked as if it was made of dead leaves and was even more peculiar than the long insects like bits of straw that are so frequent. Yves Morel is ill – the after-effects of his yesterday's rheumatism; he never ceased vomiting all night, and about noon, when we arrived at his house for lunch, he was still vomiting, stretched on his bed in the dark, while we took our meal in the next room. We made him take a dose of magnesia and bicarbonate, which relieved him a little. There is absolutely no other medicine but quinine in the station.

Nothing can describe the beauty of the evenings and nights here at Bosoum.

10 December

Morel's vomiting continues. At one moment we wondered whether drink was not partly the cause of it; the bottle of bitters which had been uncorked the day before, and which we had hardly touched, was half empty this morning, and a whisky bottle too; we thought he smelt of spirits . . . well, I ended by asking him point-blank; his denial was so evidently sincere that we came to the conclusion that his boys have taken advantage of their master's illness and our presence, hoping that their excesses would be put down to our account.

The car Lamblin promised to send us has not appeared.[1]

11 December

The bush fires at nightfall are wonderful – in the plain, close at hand, far away, at every point of the horizon; and there are some too that are invisible and yet make a strange redness below the horizon, like the coming of dawn. The fire runs over the tall grasses, which are often still full of sap, without consuming them; and then the flame can be seen through the network of their blackened stalks.

Bosoum, 12 December

The sky is ineffably pure. I think there can never have been a *finer* day anywhere. The morning is very cool; the light silvery; one might be in Scotland. A slight mist lies over the lowest parts of the plain. The air is soft and gently stirring; its touch is a caress. I let Marc go to cinematograph a bush fire and stayed behind quietly sitting with Goethe as a companion.

13 December

Still no car and no news of Lamblin. What are we to do? Wait. The weather is splendid; the sky could not be purer, deeper – the

---

1. As we supposed, Governor Lamblin was in no way responsible for this delay.

light more beautiful – the air softer at once and fresher . . . I have finished the first part of *The Affinities* and run through quantities of the *Revue de Paris*. Morel is better. The vomiting has at last yielded to an injection of morphia which we gave him last night.

14 December

Finished reading through La Fontaine's fables from end to end. Has any literature produced anything more exquisite, wiser, more perfect?

16 December

Still held up at Bosoum. This is no longer a rest, but an irritation. As I am not taking any exercise, I am sleeping much less well. Morel has persuaded us that it is imprudent to leave our doors and windows open at night, because of panthers. So we keep everything shut and suffocate. It is high time to go – even if we have to go on foot.

In the collection of newspapers Morel has lent us and which the post has just brought him, there is a delightful article by Clément Vautel, in which I am taken to task, in company with 'Rimbaud, Proust, Appollinaire, Suarès, Valéry, and Cocteau', as an example of those 'abstruse' writers whom France has no wish for 'at any price'. – I read in Goethe: *'Durch nichts bezeichnen die Menschen mehr ihren Charakter als durch das, was sie lächerlich finden.'*

A radio message of 19 November has just been communicated to us: Valéry has been elected to the Academy.

N'Ganamo, 17 December

We finally had to make up our minds to leave Bosoum without waiting any longer for the government cars. We are sorry we waited so long; we reckon the time we have lost and calculate we might have been at Fort Archambault by now . . . A fresh batch of forty-eight porters (of whom sixteen are *tipoyeurs*) has been requisitioned. That makes the seventh. Nothing could be more thankless than this road; we sat, letting its perfect monotony sink into us in the overpowering heat, without getting out of our *tipoyes*. The shaking is too great to allow one to read. But as soon as we arrived at the end of our stage, I plunged into *The Affinities*. The evening was splendid, as all the last evenings have been. The sun, when it is still a good height above the horizon, 'turns into a mandarin orange', as Morel says. It loses both heat and radiance, and becomes an orange-red mass which the eye can contemplate without being dazzled. This is the delicious hour when a helmet is no longer needed. Exactly above that point of the horizon that is still coloured by the dying sun, a very fine crescent moon makes its appearance. I went down to a river which flows near by and which a little path in the forest glade enabled me to follow for a time. How tranquil it all was! The birds were calling; then, as soon as the sun had set, the concert of locusts began. In the twilight, almost directly over our hut, I saw the most amazing bird. It was a little larger than a blackbird; two feathers of prodigious length made a kind of balancing-pole on either side of it, which it seemed to use for performing the acrobatics of an aviator.

A little later, when night had closed in, I went with Marc to a little village from which he had just returned; its huts were extremely miserable; a group of them, behind a pile of huge granite blocks, took on an almost prehistoric appearance by the light of the evening fires.

Bossa, 18 December

Today we did a stage of twenty-five kilometres (the same as yesterday), but, though we started at 5.30, we only arrived at one o'clock, in consequence of a long halt on the road. The *tipoye-*bearers who have come from Bosoum do not sing like the others. The trees of the savanna are spaced farther apart; and at times they make way altogether for great open spaces. They are no longer the size of our small fruit trees, but fine trees, as tall as the tallest of our European kinds, though they do not reach the height of the giants of the forest. I should like to see these spacious meadows in the spring, when the grass is still short and a delicate green colour; but I am afraid that the frightful tangle of stalks that have been blackened by bush fires without being burnt may last on and cover up the young grass. The immense burnt tracts we have been passing through show a worse desolation than that of any winter. The trees have not lost their leaves, but they have become a monotonous bronze colour, which, in the burning sun, makes a gloomy, implacable harmony with the blackness of the soil. It seems as though no life could ever again spring from this calcined soil, and the bright green of the grass that is already shooting up between the blackened stalks three days after the fire, seems almost a false note – like an indiscreet confidante, who spoils the effect of the drama by prematurely giving away a secret likely to reassure the alarmed spectator.

What delayed us was our meeting, an hour after sunrise, with a troop of prisoners who were being led off by the *capita* of a neighbouring village. There were eleven of them, with a rope round their necks – to tell the truth, it was nothing but a string – that tied them together. They looked so miserable that our hearts ached with pity at the sight of them. They were all carrying a load of manioc on their heads – a heavy one, no doubt, but not excessive for a man in good health; but these men seemed hardly capable of carrying themselves. Only one among them had no load; a little boy of about eleven or twelve, frightfully thin, and exhausted with misery, hunger, and fatigue; at moments he trembled all over and his stomach quivered spasmodically. The top of his head looked as if it had been scraped and as if his scalp had been replaced in parts by the kind of skin that forms over scalds. He seemed incapable of ever smiling again. And all his companions in misery were so lamentable that there was hardly a gleam of intelligence to be discovered in their eyes. While we were questioning the *capita*, we emptied the contents of our provision bag into the boy's hand, but, as ill luck would have it, they contained only three bits of very stale bread. As we had been certain of arriving early at our stage, we had let our porters go on ahead without providing ourselves with food for the journey. The boy devoured the crusts like an animal, without a word, without even a look of gratitude. His companions, though not so weak as he, seemed no less famished. As a result of our questions, it appeared that they had eaten nothing for five days. According to the *capita*, they were fugitives, who had been living in the bush for the last three months – like hunted beasts, I imagine. But the accounts were contradictory, and later on, when we questioned, first Koté, the chief of the neighbouring village, who gave the order to capture them, and then, in the evening, the people of the village they come from, where we camped for the night, we could not make out whether they had gone into the bush for the sake of their goats, which were falling ill, or in order to escape the evil spell that had caused the death of several of their children, or in order to collect sacks of groundnuts, which had been ordered by the chief for the administration, or just simply from insubordination and in order not to work in the plantations. (It must be noted that these plantations are more important than any we have seen for a long time.) Some people say they had been settled in the bush for a year and had made a village there. According to their own deposition, they had been violently ill-treated by Koté and by the people of his village, who had tied them to stakes and covered them with filth. How difficult it is to learn anything, to understand anything! And even, it must be admitted, these men's thinness, their apparent misery, did not seem very different from those of the inhabitants of the other villages we have been passing through. Nothing can be more wretched than the huts where they live crowded up together pell-mell (in one hut we saw, there were eleven of them; in another, twelve). Not a smile or a sign when one passes! Oh, how far we are from our triumphal entries in the region of Nola! I ought to have prepared the mention of this meeting of ours with the prisoners by speaking of the combined 'operation' which Morel told us about and which began the day before we left Bosoum. Morel sent out five native soldiers (they had twenty-five cartridges apiece and orders not to shoot unless necessary), and these were to meet at a given spot other native soldiers under the orders of three other administrators. The four columns on their converging march could not fail to rake in a certain number of irreconcilables, who have been living on the borders of four conterminous subdivisions and passing from one to the other every time that one of the four administrators has tried to catch them; this has been going on for a long time, until now Governor Lamblin has made up his mind to put a stop to this resistance. Was this morning's convoy an indirect result of his orders?

19 December

As usual we started this morning at daybreak. Yesterday evening we saw a considerable number of sick people – frightfully thin – in the villages we passed through. Sleeping-sickness perhaps? Then perhaps the gad-flies that have been covering our *tipoyes* for the last two days, and only waiting for a moment of inattention to bite us, are tsetses?

The appearance of the country is changing. There are now vast prairies, bigger trees and farther apart. One of our porters signalled a herd of antelopes; about two hundred yards from the road we could make out a score or so of light-coloured patches in among the grass . . . Outhman and one of the porters seized the carbine and the Moser rifle, while I watched from the top of a bank. At the first shot the herd took flight – all the antelopes we had seen and a quantity of others that had been hidden by the tall grass. Their bounds were prodigious. Then they suddenly all stopped as though they were obeying a word of command. But they were too far off by then. There was no time to follow them.

It was very hot, but the air is so dry that we walked without perspiring.

Then at last we came to the Ouham. The country is very much the same; what had happened to it or to me that I should have thought it so beautiful? An imperceptible slope led me down to the river, which is bordered by a great prairie. The other shore is a little higher; and on the left, not far off, is a range of hills which, in so flat a country, one is tempted to call mountains. The Ouham is about as wide as the Marne – or as the Seine . . . One's sense of scale is altered and it is as difficult to judge the width of the river as the height of the trees. I went down to the river shore with the idea of fishing; but the grasses were too tall and my rod too short; it was all I could do to reach the water with my metal bait. Lower down the stream, there were some fine rocks that broke the current. The sun went down over the marshy prairie, which had been lately set fire to; there were traces of game everywhere. Above the rapids, the Ouham spreads into a great calm sheet of water . . . It is decidedly as wide as the Seine – at least. Its waters are muddy, like all the rivers we have seen since Bouar.

20 December

Got up this morning a great deal too early and read by the insufficient light of the camp lantern, while waiting for the dawn. It was cold and the air biting. The porters had lighted themselves great camp-fires, which they were unwilling to leave; and when we started, each man carried away with him a burning piece of wood, which he held in front of him, as close as possible. As we crossed the Ouham, there was a river of mist flowing over the stream of water, only more slowly; it unrolled and drifted away in shreds, faintly coloured by the dawning day.

We passed quantities of insignificant little villages – if one can give this name to the groups of wretched huts, whose inhabitants sit squatting beside a miserable fire, or on the threshold of their doors, and make no sign of greeting – hardly turn their heads to see us pass. These huts remind one of the rough sheds our charcoal-burners make in the woods. A trifle less and they would be like animals' dens. And this absence of welcome when we arrive, of smiles and greetings as we pass through, does not seem to mark hostility so much as profound apathy, the benumbed dullness of stupidity. When one goes up to them, they stir hardly more than the animals of the Galapagos; when one holds out a new sou to a child, he is terrified and cannot understand what is expected of him. The idea that he might be given anything is incomprehensible to him, and if an elder, or one of our porters, tries to explain the kindness of our intentions, he looks astonished and then holds out his two hands like a cup.

The village where we are camping is no whit inferior to the others we have been passing through, in wretchedness, dirt, poverty, and sordidness. Inside the huts the stench is unspeakable. I doubt whether the children have ever been washed. Water is used no doubt for cooking, but after that there is none left for cleanliness. It comes from a meagre stream that flows out of a marsh more than two hundred yards from the village and then loses itself in a hollow.

And yet on the road this morning, we passed cultivated tracts of considerable importance: millet (which is tending to replace manioc), sesame, and, above all, cearas – real orchards of cearas – though still too young for commercial purposes, and some fields of cotton.

The millet and sesame crops are kept in great oblong baskets which are hung to the branches of trees round the village.

21 December

We left at six-thirty and arrived at Bosangoa at about eleven o'clock. We passed a great many gangs of workmen on the road, which they were just completing and over which our cars should have been the first to go. The land was well cultivated (especially with millet), but the villages and populations were even more miserable than the day before. Sometimes, standing a little back from the road, there are a few rudimentary huts, built without any care; leafy branches take the place of the door. Not a greeting, not a smile, hardly a look as we passed.

At Bosangoa, M. Martin, who is temporarily replacing the administrator, M. Marcilhasy, away on tour, received us. The station is an important one; we noted avenues of aloes, also quantities of birds, including flocks of the beautiful white wader, called *pique-bœuf*; also a few tame phacocheres (a kind of large boar).

After the afternoon siesta the heat was overpowering.

Bosangoa, 23 December

The night was very cool – even cold towards morning. After starting with a single sheet, I was glad to end up with two blankets, two sweaters, two pyjamas, and a cloak. I went to bed directly after dinner, feeling very unwell with a heavy cold.

In the meanwhile Marc went exploring round the camp, according to his excellent custom of trying to find out things that are hidden from the light of day. He came in late and very much upset by what he had just discovered: not far from our hut, in the middle of the guards' camping-ground, a large band of children of both sexes, from nine to thirteen years old, are herded out in the open in the bitter cold night, with only a few inadequate weed fires. Marc, who wanted to question the children, sent for Adoum – but Adoum cannot understand Baya. A native offered himself as interpreter and translated into Sango what Adoum retranslated into French. The children seem to have been taken away from their villages with halters round their necks; they have been made to work for six days without pay and without anything to eat. Their village is not far off; their parents, brothers, friends were expected to bring them food. No one did. Very unlucky, but it can't be helped!

The double transmission of questions and answers involved some confusion; but the fact remained clear . . . So clear that the well-meaning interpreter, as soon as Marc's back was turned, was arrested by a guard and thrown into prison . . . So Adoum informed us at our early breakfast.

And this morning, when Marc and I tried to see the children, we were told they had gone back to their villages. As for the interpreter, after having spent the night in prison, he was taken away at daybreak by two guards to work at a distance; no one can or will tell us on what road.

Decidedly there is something here that someone is afraid of our finding out. Is this to be a game of hide-and-seek? We are determined to play it out to the end. And first of all we must get the interpreter set at liberty; it is inadmissible that he should be punished like Samba N'Goto for having spoken to us. We began by asking his name; but everyone had some excuse for not knowing it. The utmost information we were able to extract was that at one or two kilometres from the station there was a group of huts where a native was living who might know the man in question. Under a baking sun we made our way to this little village and managed to find out – not the name of the man – but of the two soldiers who took him away this morning. And while we were questioning, up came the first guard – the one who had arrested the interpreter the evening before. He seemed uneasy and suspicious and held a sheet of paper in his hand – the list of our porters – which he asked us to sign; as we could have done this perfectly well later, it was an obvious excuse for joining us. He wanted to know who was speaking to us and what was being said. But we cut our inquiry short, for fear of compromising more people; and as the spy seemed determined not to leave us, we went with him to M. Martin's and told him the whole story. Sad to say, he too avoided the issue and seemed to attach no importance to our tale. On our insisting, however, he at last undertook to hold an inquiry – a mere semblance – for when we saw him a little later, he assured us that there was no cause for our uneasiness. It was not for the reason that we suspected, but for a theft of kids, that the interpreter – an old hand at stealing – who in no way deserved our interest – had been put into prison. He affirmed, on the other hand, that the children were all very well fed and in no need of our pity. They had been sent back to their homes simply because they had finished their work – a very light job of weeding. It was merely an accidental coincidence – nothing suspicious about it. Are you satisfied? – Not yet.

Will our perseverance get the better of this imbroglio? We began
to take a more authoritative tone with the 'first-class' guard, who
grew confused, contradicted himself under cross-examination, gave
himself away, and finally admitted that the kid-stealer he had
spoken of to Martin was not the interpreter and that he had only said
so with intent to deceive. The interpreter was imprisoned immediately after his conversation with Marc; two soldiers took him
away this morning to the Bosoum road (the one we have just come
by and which we are certain not to take again) and placed him in the
charge of the guard Dono, with orders 'to make him work'.
Adoum's story, therefore, was correct.

This encouraged me, and the firmness of my attitude is beginning
to impress the natives. Some of them have made up their minds to
speak. We sent for Dono and questioned him separately, notwithstanding the protests of the 'first-class'. It has been confirmed that
this morning all the children went back to their village, together
with a certain number of women who had been brought away with
them; the children did not actually take flight of their own accord –
they were made to take it hastily, for the 'first-class' was making
them work in the teeth of all regulations. And he gave them nothing
to eat. An intelligent Sudanese woman (whom we visited later), the
wife of the sergeant who is accompanying Marcilhasy on his tour,
took a few of them under her special protection, out of pity, had
them in to her compound, and warmed and fed them. The 'first-
class' has also been keeping on starvation diet certain indented
labourers whom he was supposed to feed, as also the porters
employed in carrying the supplies of millet for the feeding of the
railway gangs at Pointe Noire. These porters have had nothing to
live on for the last six days but the grass or roots they could manage
to pick up, or what they may have been able to steal.[2]

2. 'If you begin to worry about what your boys have to eat,' said B. to me at the
beginning of our journey, 'you are done for. And the same with your porters . . .
Never fear. They're a lot that won't let themselves die of hunger. They'll always get
along all right. You needn't bother about them.'
Another colonial gave us 'a good tip' – always to throw away what was left over
from our meals – 'otherwise the cook gets into the habit of making the dishes too big,
expressly with an eye to the remains. It's a serious economy,' he said. And so forth.
Three quarters of the natives' illnesses (with the exception of epidemics) are the
result of malnutrition.

These inquiries lasted till evening. We were supposed to start at daybreak the next morning and had already taken leave of Martin. But we could not leave him in ignorance of all these things which it was his business to know and which we had discovered. On pretext of leaving a letter for Marcilhasy, we went to the station-house. It was nine o'clock and all lights out. There was no help for it. Martin had gone to bed, but he got up.

'Someone here is trying to hoodwink either you or me,' I said to him. 'The information given you by the guard does not tally with what we have just learnt. And as I dislike leaving behind me an affair that has not been properly cleared up, I have decided to delay our start tomorrow for a few hours – the time necessary to get to the bottom of things.'

So this morning we called up the two soldiers who had taken the interpreter away, who were not to be found last night. But I had *insisted* that the 'first-class' should produce them. For that matter, he had taken fright at my firmness and had himself sent for the interpreter to come back. The whole thing is now perfectly clear. In the absence of the sergeant, who left ten days ago to accompany the administrator, the 'first-class' guard had abused his powers, practised forcible recruiting, contrary to rules, and kept for himself the food that he should have distributed among the labourers and carriers. What is more, the sergeant has just now come back; he is an Islamized Sudanese, who speaks French very fairly well and has impressed us most favourably. We informed him of what had taken place and handed over to his care the unfortunate interpreter, with instructions to protect him from the resentment of the guard, who had already ill-treated him for having spoken to us. We gave a full account of everything to Martin and put it in such a way that it will be hardly possible for him not to intervene. It is inadmissible that he should protect and encourage such abuses, if only by shutting his eyes to them. If nothing reprehensible had been going on, the guard would not have taken such precautions to conceal it.

Before leaving Bosangoa we went back to the camp. Perfect order was reigning; there were only adults there and they were sitting round fires made not only of weeds, but of branches. But they looked timid and terrorized and pretended not to understand Sango, so as not to be obliged to answer us (a little later we found out that they spoke it perfectly). They did not dare take the cigarettes I offered them, or at any rate not before an hour's coaxing and encouraging. It is impossible to imagine more wretched objects than these human cattle.

We left Bosangoa about two o'clock, after a visit to the school of agriculture recently founded by Lamblin and very intelligently managed, we thought, by young M.

We crossed the Ouham about a quarter of a mile from the station; the people here seem less lethargic; some of them saluted us, some almost smiled; the huts of the numerous villages we passed through were once more built with walls; the inhabitants were cleaner. There were a few handsome women and a few men with admirable figures. When we stopped, it was five o'clock. The sun, though it had ceased to be actually burning, seemed none the less ferocious. Then, suddenly, its fires glowed and went out. There was a fine large village before we came to the station. The station village too, Yandakara, was very fine. We stopped there for dinner in front of an immense esplanade. Near the post-house we saw, just emerging from the soil, a number of great flat stones of grey granite.

24 December

The moon was shining brightly when we left Yandakara after supper. It was too cold sit for long in one's *tipoye*, though I managed to have a doze in mine. At eleven o'clock we reached a village, whose name I don't know, and left again at dawn in the bitter cold. It can't have been much above 40° Fahrenheit. The road was monotonous, with a few plantations.

A sudden miracle! The motor-car we had given up hoping for! It had not gone to Bosoum, but was coming straight to meet us; for Lamblin very sensibly imagined that, seeing the delay, we should already have started. Chambaud, instead of sending the letter in which we notified the date of our arrival at Bosoum direct to Bangui, had, for some unknown reason, forwarded it via Mongoumba, where it had to wait for the *Largeau* to pick it up. Hence a fortnight's delay. In case of illness or an appeal for help this blunder might have been fatal.

A lorry filled with three packing-cases of salt for Bosangoa was following the car. These cases were too enormous to be entrusted to porters. We have decided, therefore, to keep ours until the next stage, where the empty lorry will meet us on its way back from Bosangoa.

The post-house is at the farther end of a small village, whose name I don't know; not far from here flows a river, the Bobo, across which our road lay. Near the bridge the stream makes a bend and forms a deep, clear pool, where some children were bathing; then its abundant waters disappear from sight under the great overhanging trees.

Thanks to the motor-car, our last stage was not tiring. We gave up our siestas and went back to the Bobo immediately after lunch. A narrow path, hardly visible among the tall grasses, enabled us to follow its course up stream. The trees do not stop short at the river bank. They bend forward and stretch over and into the water, fling great hanging props towards the other side of the river, as if they wished to cross it, thrust them down into the stream, and spread over its surface a wide network of aerial roots – making by anastomosis a thousand little bridges along the water's level. Then a fairly vast space of ground stretches under the great, spreading, powerful branches; a religious shade reigns beneath them; the black soil is heaved into a number of little mounds, regularly spaced – like tombs. Can it be a cemetery? No. Merely an abortive coffee-plantation – a failure, like so many others in this region.

The motor enabled us to reach Bouca the same evening. We paid off our porters and started off again at about two o'clock. One of our boys got into the car with us. Zézé, our other boy, and a small cook's boy, who has followed us ever since Carnot, crowded uncomfortably into the lorry on the top of the pile of luggage. Two other small cook's boys, who have been following us since Bouar, do not want to be left behind; they stick to us like Dindiki to his perch. No room in the motors. Never mind! They will go on foot; and, in fact, we found them next morning at Bouca, which they reached after walking all night – and they had already walked nearly all day. They want to go with us to Archambault (or at any rate to join us there). Such fidelity touches me, though in reality it is chiefly a matter of poverty and the need, which all parasites have, of hanging on to anything that seems in the slightest degree substantial. These two cook's boys are, for that matter, frightful, know not a word of French; and I have not addressed two words to them since we left Bouar. But merely not to be brutal is a great thing. I had given them each a five-franc note; but in the morning at Bouca, in face of their determination to go to Archambault on foot, I gave them each a few extra fifty-centime pieces, as I know how possible it is to die of starvation with fifty francs in one's pocket, for want of a little small coin – for there is no change to be had in any of the villages one goes through. This is one of the principal difficulties of this journey; we were warned of it beforehand, and brought with us from Brazzaville bags of sous, fifty-centime pieces, and francs.

25 December

We arrived at Batangafo for lunch. The road seemed, paradoxically, longer by motor. The strain is overwhelming; one feels the monotony more because it lies less in the details than in the ensemble; and the rapidity of one's motion confuses one's sensations, turns them grey.

We shall try to reach Archambault this evening, so as to keep our promise to Coppet to spend Christmas with him.

A wild flight through the dark; the landscape becomes gradually barer, *nobler*; Palmyra palms reappear. A great antelope in a clearing quite close to us stood still, like a picture of St Hubert, and did not take flight when our motor stopped. Great wading birds. Enormous Sara villages dimly seen through the dark. Trellis-work walls bordering the road.

The lorry cannot keep up with us. We are obliged to wait for it.

We waited round a fire by the road-side. The Saras, who were warming themselves at it, fled at our approach; then came back one by one and accepted our cigarettes.

We arrived at Archambault a little after midnight. We woke up Coppet, who prepared a midnight meal for us, and stayed talking with him till morning.

FORT ARCHAMBAULT, FORT LAMY

End of December

Even in the early morning the splendour – the intensity – of the light is dazzling. We are on the other side of hell. At Fort Archambault, on the marches of Islam, barbarism is behind one, and one enters into contact with another civilization, another culture. A still rudimentary culture, no doubt, but yet one that brings with it a fineness, a comprehension of nobility and hierarchy, a disinterested spirituality, and a feeling for what is immaterial.

In the regions we have just been through, there are nothing but downtrodden races, not so much vile in themselves perhaps as made vile by others, enslaved, without an aspiration but for the grossest material well-being. Here at last are to be found real homes; at last, individual possessions; at last, specializations.[1]

Fort Archambault

The native town consists of rectangular enclosures, fenced round with palisades made of rushes (*seccos*). Behind these are the Saras' huts, where they live in families. The rush mats are just high enough to allow a medium-sized man on horseback to see over them. As one rides by, one can look down upon the strangest privacies. This is the quintessence of the exotic. The beauty of the

---

1. On re-reading these notes they seem to me greatly exaggerated; but when I wrote them, we had hardly shaken ourselves dry after a long soaking in the realms of limbo. And yet this impression of the non-differentiation of the individual from the herd receives confirmation and explanation in the following words taken from a recent circular issued in Ubangui-Shari, forbidding the native to exploit any kind of plantation whatever for his own personal profit:

'Each native *group* is the sole owner of the plantations and cultures created by the *collective* labour of its members.'

huts with their trellised roofs, edged by a sort of mosaic made with straw, is very great – like the work of insects. In these enclosures the few trees preserved from the annual burnings become very fine. The ground is of level white sand. There are quantities of little hanging granaries, so placed as to be out of reach of the goats, which make these minute settlements look like a Lilliputian village, built on piles. The climbing plants (kinds of hipomaea or flexible, broad-leaved Cucurbitaceae) enhance one's sensation of long-drawn-out hours, of slowness, of idleness, of sinking into a delicious dream. The atmosphere is one of peace, forgetfulness, happiness; the people here are all smiling; yes, even the suffering, even the sick. (I remember an epileptic child in the first village of Bosoum; he had fallen into the fire and one whole side of his handsome face was frightfully burnt; the other side of his face smiled – an angelic smile.)

I have left off putting down dates. Days here go by all alike. We get up at dawn, and I hurry down to the Shari to see the sun rise. The air is cool. There are quantities of birds on the river shore – tame enough, for they have never been hunted or shot at; fishing eagles, carrion crows, hawks, sparkling emerald-green bee-eaters, little purple-headed swallows, and quantities of small black and white birds like those we saw on the banks of the Congo; on the farther shore flocks of big wading birds. Then I come in for breakfast – porridge, tea, cheese or cold meat or eggs; read; pay visits; lunch with Marcel de Coppet; siesta; work; take tea with Coppet and look over his translation of Bennett's *Old Wives' Tale*; go out riding.

The way in which these people, who are so sensitive to rhythm, caricature and distort our bugle calls is very curious. They keep the notes, but change the rhythm to such an extent that they are unrecognizable.

. . . The sou here is worth eight blue beads. When a child buys a handful of groundnuts, he gets four beads as change.

The two cook's boys we left at Bouca rejoined us here on the evening of 1 January.

The contact of Islam elevates and spiritualizes these peoples. The Christian religion, of which they only too often absorb nothing but the superstitions and the fear of hell, only too often turns them cowardly and sly . . .[2]

Fort Archambault

Paid a visit to the two principal chiefs – Bézo and Belangar, Sara-Madjingayes by race. They have both sent their eldest sons to the school at Fort Lamy. The boys are just returning to Fort Archambault. The curious thing is that an exchange has been effected; and when we said to Bézo: 'And now you will have both your sons back again?' 'No,' he answered, 'I shall take his and he will take mine.'

'Why?'

He then explained to us that each of the two fathers is afraid of being weak and over-indulgent with his own son.[3]

The Banks of the Shari, going downstream, are admirable. Took a long walk by myself (very imprudent, says Coppet). Islands; long sandy stretches; varieties of strange birds.

I am reading *Cinna* again with rapture, and learning the beginning of it by heart – re-learning it.

What a headlong and stupendous flight of our literature towards the abysses of artificiality!

It would be impossible to push abstraction, preciosity, inflation, anti-realism (not to say factitiousness) further than in Emilie's opening soliloquy. And I know no more admirable lines.

> *Impatients désirs d'une illustre vengeance*
> *Dont la mort de mon père a formé la naissance,*
> *Enfants impétueux de mon ressentiment,*
> *Que ma douleur séduite embrasse aveuglément . . .*

2. I take care not to generalize, and what I say is, in any case, only true of certain races.

3. But perhaps, as an eminent anthropologist has pointed out to me, this is merely an example of the 'maternal family'. In certain tribes – the Sérèces, for instance (the region of Thies in Senegal) – fortune and situation are transmitted, not from father to son, but from uncle to nephew; the chief transmits his power to his sister's son.

This is the triumph of art over nature. Mallarmé's abstrusest sonnet is not more difficult of comprehension than the tangles of this sublime rigmarole would be, if the spectator were not prepared beforehand and prepossessed in its favour.

I re-read *Iphigénie* immediately after. What an extraordinary writer Corneille must have been to have made it possible to talk of Racine's 'realism'!

Archambault, 10 January

Marcel de Coppet has been appointed acting Governor of Chad and must be at Fort Lamy within five days. We have settled to go with him. The weather has been very hot for the last three days – too hot. I have a little fever towards evening and rather bad nights. I am disturbed by the bats that come into my room, in spite of the mats I put in front of my window, and the newspapers I put over the doors.

As soon as I had finished reading *Iphigénie*, I began it over again. Today I have finished it, with an ever-increasing wonder and admiration. I now think that this play is as perfect as any of the others and in nothing inferior to its sisters; but probably not one of them is as difficult to act. Not one of the parts can be left in the background or afford to be sacrificed. One might almost say there is no principal part, and that, turn and turn about, Iphigénie, Agamemnon, Clytemnestre, Achille, and Eriphile demand the actor's finest interpretation.

Agamemnon's character is admirably drawn by Racine. His shameful answer when Arcas says he is afraid that Achille may object to Agamemnon's using his name in a way that in fact amounts to forgery:

> . . . *Achille était absent.*

And, even in the smallest details, his irresolution, his self-contradictions:

> *VA, dis-je, sauve-la de ma propre faiblesse.*
> *Mais surtout NE VA POINT . . . etc.*

And this vileness:

> . . . *D'une mère en fureur épargne-moi les cris.*

17 January

Descent (I was going to say ascent) of the Shari, that strange river that turns its back upon the sea. A whole people assembled on the bank when we left Archambault.

The *d'Uzès* is flanked by four whale-boats. Marc and I occupy the starboard ones. We embarked at about three o'clock in roasting heat.

5 o'clock

Great strips of golden sand, of a burning purity, are pieced together at long intervals by stretches of prairie – the pastures of the hippopotamus and the buffalo.

18 January

The *d'Uzès* stopped not far from an extraordinary upheaval of great granite boulders. This is the place where Bretonnet's mission succumbed. Although the sun was on the point of setting, I could not resist the desire to see these strange rocks (I thought at first they were made of sandstone) close to. I led my companions at a breakneck pace, first through sand and then through bog. I climbed one of the heights – but I was being waited for and the night was already falling.

19 January

This is a landscape 'for lines', with little doum palm trees and burnt brushwood – wonderful in its ferocity.

An antelope shoot. Coppet killed three enormous ones.

The zebra-like markings of the crocodiles are very fine.

I have neither time nor inclination to note anything. Entirely absorbed by contemplation.

20 January

The landscape, without being exactly changed in appearance, is broadening out. It is tending towards a desert-like perfection and gradually becoming more and more denuded. There are still a great many trees, however, which are not palm trees; sometimes when the height of the ground protects them from the periodical floods, they grow quite close to the river banks. They are trees with which I am unacquainted – like large mimosas or terebinth trees.

Then little doum palm trees, which have the bearing of dracaenas, began to show themselves, and for some kilometres there was nothing else.

But it is in the fauna rather than in the flora of the country that its perpetual interest lies. There are moments when the sand-banks are all abloom with wading birds and snipe and ducks – quantities of birds so charming and so various that one cannot turn one's eyes away from the shores; and sometimes a great cayman half rouses himself at our passage and lets himself drop into the blue.

Then the distance between the shores widens; there is an invasion of azure. The landscape becomes spiritual. The waters of the river broaden like a plated sheet.

I shall have to throw away the box of beetles I was collecting for the museum. I had thought it would be a good plan to dry them in the sun; they have become so brittle that not a single one has kept its legs or antennae complete.

We frequently stick in the mud; the crew then get down, and, with the water up to their waists, they push the boat along as if it were a motor-car. This process sometimes lasts an hour before we are dislodged. But the landscape itself is so vast, so slow, that one has no wish to go quickly.

An enormous crocodile came quite close up to us – two balls and a convulsive leaping in the river! We stopped the boat and went back to the place in a whale-boat. There was nothing to be found. Animals that are killed in this way sink immediately and come to the surface only a few hours later.

At twilight, when it was already nearly dark, we again saw the strange bird which I have already mentioned (before Bouca). It was flying over the sandy shore and a shot from Coppet brought it down. It fell into the river and Adoum fished it out. Two enormous *pennae*, consisting merely of a bare central rib, start from under the wing almost perpendicularly to the other feathers. They are about twice as long as the whole length of the bird, and at their extremities, at a paradoxical distance, are two biggish disks, which it seems the bird is able to move and raise independently of the action of its wings. Coppet, who gave me the bird for the museum, calls it the aeroplane bird and declares that some naturalists offer six thousand francs for it; not that it is extremely rare, but it comes out only at nightfall and its fantastic flight protects it.

Boingar

A small village. Numbers of weaving-looms being worked, chiefly by children. Marc took a cinematograph of one of the children, who was still quite young and prodigiously skilful. The strip he was weaving was only a few centimetres wide and looked like a strip of bandage. These strips are joined together by their side edges to make a piece of stuff. (It takes as many as forty-eight to make a pair of trousers that reach up to the waist.) The loom is as simple as possible: two pedals cross the threads of the web; a comb, which is hung across the strip, drops on to the chain every time the shuttle has passed. The threads of the web are kept tight by a little flat basket which is placed on the ground a little way off and which is kept steady by being filled with pebbles. The child, as he works and as his strip of *gabak* grows longer, winds it up between his legs and pulls the basket towards him. He sings as he works and the throw of the shuttle accentuates the rhythm of his song.

Farther on, in a *secco* enclosure, there were seven looms placed side by side. No doubt the administration exacts a certain amount of *gabak* from the village. This work, we are told, is often made over to captives – the work that is considered honourable being the culture of crops and the raising of animals.

These woven stuffs, of which the materials are native and which are entirely unadulterated, are particularly beautiful. One can follow the process of fabrication from the beginning; there is no outside intervention whatever. There is some talk of reforming it. What for? If it were taken up a little by fashionable people, this 'homespun' might be at a premium in the market.

A fishing eagle in the middle of the river – the captive of its too enormous prey – struggled anxiously towards the shore, using its wings as oars.

*

Fort Lamy. How ugly! How ill-favoured!

Except for its quays, which are fairly well laid out, and for its situation at the apex of the triangle made by the juncture of the Shari and the Logone, how poor it is, in comparison with Archambault! At the point where the river flows out of the town are two extraordinary towers – huge brick buildings of the same height, which one can see must have been terribly expensive to make, and of which no one knows the use.

The native town adjoins the French town and lies parallel to the river, widening out at each extremity, so that in reality it forms two towns, each equally sordid and dusty, with just enough of the Sahara about them to recall some of the south Algerian oases – but how infinitely less lovely! The houses are built of a rough clay and are ash-coloured; the clay is always mixed with sand and straw. The inhabitants all look timid and skulking.

We are told that this dismal town is becoming rapidly depopulated, owing to recurrent fever and emigration. The natives, who are not allowed to assemble for a tamtam, or even to go about their own villages after nightfall, quit out of sheer boredom. The whites are kept here by their functions, but are equally bored and long to escape.

I took Adoum to the Fort Lamy hospital and asked Dr X. to be kind enough to make a microscopic examination of his blood, as I am anxious to know whether the lad really has syphilis, as Labarbe declared.

The examination has given a negative result. But then what about the boils at Bouar? They were simply craw-craw, which Marc and I suffered from as well – in his case complicated by adenitis. There is nothing the matter with Adoum. He did not seem in the least surprised to hear it.

'I knew I hadn't got syphilis. Where should I have caught it?'

'No doubt at Fort Crampel that night you went out on the loose.' (Labarbe had calculated that the exact time had elapsed to allow for the breaking out of the boils.)

'I didn't go out on the loose at all. I told you so to begin with.'

'But afterwards you told us yourself that you had been with a woman that night.'

'I told you so because you seemed to expect it. People kept on telling me I had been on the loose. It was no good saying no. I shouldn't have been believed.'

This little story will convince no one and will only serve to strengthen my conviction that one makes foolish mistakes quite as often through excessive suspicion as through excessive credulity.

28 January

We have decided to leave Marcel de Coppet to his new functions and to go down the Shari as far as Lake Chad. By starting tomorrow on the *d'Uzès*, we shall be back at Fort Lamy in a fortnight.

30 January

The landscape is without nobility. I expected to find sandy shores and the desolation of the desert. But no! Quantities of medium-sized trees with their rounded clumps make a very indifferent trimming to the river banks.

After being astonished at seeing so few crocodiles, I am now amazed by suddenly seeing incredible numbers of them. I have just counted a group of thirty-seven on a little sandbank fifty yards long. They are of all sizes; some hardly longer than a walking-stick; others enormous, monstrous. Some are striped, others of a uniform grey colour. Most of them at the boat's approach drop heavily into the water, if they happen to be on a sloping sand beach. If they are a little farther from the river, they get on to their legs and run. The way in which they slide into the water has something voluptuous about it. Sometimes they are too sleepy or too lazy to move. During the last hour we have certainly seen more than a hundred.

We got to Goulfeï (Cameroon) too late; but perhaps by broad daylight our visit to the sultan would have left us with less extraordinary recollections. The night had fallen when we passed through the gate of the town, which is entirely girdled by ramparts. In front of us was a long, straight wall, with a single black hole in it; through this, preceded by a few of the sultan's chiefs, we passed, and found ourselves in the most mysterious gloom. Then we followed a street between two fairly high mud walls; it was like a narrow, winding passage, with continual breaks in it. Every now and then we caught a glimpse of a shadow effacing itself in the embrasure of a door; it would raise its hand to its head and murmur a salutation. After a little the street widens for a moment, and we saw a sort of porch, roofed with woven branches, where people were sitting. How delightful it must be here during the hot hours of the day! Still farther on, the walls of the street open out into a *place*. The palace entrance is shaded by a big tree.

The presentations had taken place rather sketchily in the narrow street. We had intended to pay our visit on our return and had made our apologies for arriving so late. (I have the greatest difficulty in not being too courteous and even a little obsequious to a Mussulman chief; the nobility of his bearing and of his slightest gestures makes more impression on me than the highest-sounding titles.) But the sultan insisted, and, urged on by curiosity, we followed him through a series of little rooms and passages; the whole time in the dark. At last a servant brought a lantern. We were able to see that several of the little rooms we went through had smooth walls, as if they had been plastered with stucco, and that they were covered with paintings and ornaments, rudimentary, but rather fine-looking. We arrived at last in a room hardly bigger than the others, where there were some chairs. The sultan invited us to sit down and sat down himself. On my left, near the entrance, a superb boy of about fifteen or sixteen crouched down on the floor beside me; he was the sultan's son. The captain of the *d'Uzès* acted as our interpreter. We exchanged vague compliments Arab-fashion and then took leave of our host, with the intention of returning to the village when the moon rose.

What shall I say of this nocturnal walk? Nothing can be stranger or more mysterious than this town. Here and there, at the corner of a street, in a public place, are admirable trees, venerated no doubt – at any rate, preserved. The town walls on the inside are circled by a walk, and then slope down rapidly, but not inaccessibly. There is a large open place with a half-ruined fort. The whole thing was fantastic by moonlight. Above the walls of the houses one could see the cupolas of the roofs. We spoke to four lads on the threshold of a door; they were other sons of the sultan. They came with us for a time. We must have gone round in a circle without being aware of it, for after a quarter of an hour's walk, we found ourselves outside their dwelling again, where we left them.

31 January

The wind is very cold. This morning some large tortoises raised their heads out of the river in the track of our boat and followed us for some moments. The banks are much greener and are covered with little thorny bushes.

I omitted to say that yesterday, during a four hours' stop (we had to 'make wood', as we had none ready), we went shooting in the bush. There were incredible numbers of guinea-fowl. We brought back seven and lost three, which we wounded, but could not find. The bush is not thickly wooded; there are great spaces of bare earth, sown with cassia mimosas. Herds of big antelopes.

The fishing boats are very odd-looking – large canoes made of quantities of pieces of wood joined together with string or creepers, for there is no tree in this country big enough for a boat to be carved out of it. The stern of these boats is raised high enough to serve as leverage for a large net, stretched between two long antennae; a system of weights enables the net to be dipped into the river and pulled out again without an effort.

1 or 2 February

We stopped yesterday as early as two o'clock near a village on the right bank of the river. A tribe of children on the shore ran away as soon as they saw us. Rather a wretched village. A great many indigo-dyers (as in the preceding villages).

The women use a stick to beat the fruit of the doum palm tree so as to soften its woody pulp, which the natives chew like betel. The millet harvest has been very poor; it is feared there may be a severe famine.

The heat and especially the light are overpowering. I waited till evening to explore the country. As Marc had gone photographing with Outhman, and Adoum had gone shooting with a guard, I went by myself, in spite of recommendations. A marvellous orange light shone down slantingly on the vast natural orchard through which I walked on in a state of rapture. There is a network of paths on the ground made by the herds of oxen that form the chief wealth of the country. Quantities of birds were singing in the intoxication of evening. I imagined what these bushes, which are now for the most part dry, would be like in the spring, when they turn green, blossom, fill with nests, with bees on the wing, when the ground clothes itself with young grass, when butterflies . . .

We started again in the night, about two or three in the morning, as the captain wished to take advantage of the moonlight. We were fast asleep at the time we entered the lake; and even if I had got up, the light would have been too dim for me to see, as I should have wished, the change of vegetation. But the wind got up and obliged us to stop, so that we soon lost the time so uselessly gained by our early start, the only result of which was to cheat me of the sight I particularly wished to see. The wind whipped up the water into little precipitate waves which, as they were throttled between the whale-boats and the boat, spouted up like geysers and flooded the deck. In a moment the whole place was soaking. We hastily picked up everything that was lying about and folded up our beds. The little boat was tossing to such a degree that a table turned topsy-turvy, with its legs in the air; it was like the turmoil of a big shipwreck. And that with a depth beneath us of four feet! The dancing of the whale-boats beside us and the violence of their bumping against the hull of the *d'Uzés* were almost terrifying. We hurriedly found a temporary shelter between two vast clumps of papyrus and a kind of enormous carex.[4]

It is in this precarious haven that I am writing. In front of me, under a sky that is uniformly blue, stretches a limitless expanse of water as grey as a northern sea. Beside me is a tuft of great papyri – like water palm trees – rising out of the water, and exceedingly handsome, though the greater part of them are faded; and behind me the strangest mixture of grass and water that it is possible to imagine. Again I see the enormousness, the formlessness, the indecision, the absence of direction, of design, of organization, which so excessively disturbed me during the first part of our journey, and which is indeed the chief characteristic of this country.

4. A kind of grass.

But here this perplexity of nature, this wedding and welding of the elements, this *blending* of grey and blue, of grass and water, are so strange and recall so little anything in our countries (unless perhaps certain pools in the Camargue or in the neighbourhood of Aiguesmortes) that I cannot stop gazing at it.

We had to wait from sunrise till near noon in the shelter of the papyrus islands for the wind to go down a little. The wind, for that matter, is not very violent – compared to the sirocco or the mistral, it would seem the merest breeze. The papyrus tufts are of an admirable reddish-green colour; the water of the Chad a greenish grey, turning to a pale golden. The two whale-boats have been removed from our sides and fastened to our tow-line . . .

After a crossing of about three hours the islands of the opposite shore are beginning to make their appearance. The papyri now alternate with bushes, hardly taller than they, which have yellow flowers (Papilionaceae, as far as I can see) and among which climb occasional trails of great mauve convolvuluses – and with gigantic reeds, like those we call 'pampas-grass', whose tall hempen-grey plumes are of the greatest beauty. I admire the effort which so many plants of the equatorial regions make, to attain a symmetry of form which is almost crystal-like and of which we have no idea in our northern lands, where Baudelaire talks of the *'végétal irrégulier'*.

Papyrus, palms, cactus, euphorbia candelabra are all arranged round an axis according to a definite rhythm.

We cast anchor off an uninhabited island, as the channel through which the captain had intended to get to Bol was impassable. The evening was closing in. We landed, but did not go far from our mooring-place, for in one moment our legs were covered with an exceedingly prickly little seed, which it is impossible to remove without the risk of its barb breaking off in one's fingers and causing abscesses.[5] For that matter, the scenery had nothing to show of any

5. This horrid little grass, the *cram-cram*, abounds in the plains of Fort Archambault and in the whole Chad region; but when its grain is ground in a wooden mortar and freed of its envelope, which bristles with minute hooklets, it furnishes a kind of semolina of the finest quality, called 'krebs'.

interest, except perhaps a strange plant growing in the vast dried-up lawn which we crossed – a plant that is almost a bush, with very broad, thick, furry leaves of a delicate greenish-grey colour. The flower is rather a fine purple, but very small.

The night was not very cold, but the crew made up big fires and slept beside them, because of the mosquitoes. We stopped in an island peopled with white goats. It is impossible to understand what they can find to eat, for the ground is nothing but a stretch of arid sand, sparsely sprinkled with the strange plant which I have just described, the grey-green foliage of which makes an exquisite harmony with the whiteness of the goats. Numbers of the goats are hobbled by one leg to a stake stuck in the sand. I think they are the ones reserved for milking and kept apart from their kids. Not far off were a few huts, which seemed more like temporary shelters, and some miserable, cross-looking natives. The captain of the boat had great difficulty in getting one of them to come and pilot us among the islands. They brought us, however, four eggs and a jug of milk. The captain took a kid; one might almost say he took it by force; however, he left five francs in exchange; but the owner held out for two francs more, which the captain resigned himself to giving. This is the first time I have seen a native stick out for a price, or even name a price. We had been told, indeed, that the inhabitants of the Bol region were difficult. In other places, however little one gives them, they accept it without a murmur. The day before yesterday one of our soldiers (the sergeant) gave fifty centimes for a chicken, in the little island where we stopped. I told him it was a pre-war price and that for the future he must pay one franc for a chicken. He let himself be persuaded and went back with me to make the extra payment. As he had been pleasant about it, I offered to make it up to him; but he refused the fifty centimes I held out to him and, as I insisted, he made a present of it to a passing child.

It is natural enough that the natives, who are paid only fifty centimes for a chicken, should dread the arrival of the whites and do nothing to increase such an unlucrative business.

We came upon the *Léon Blot* lying up near a small island. We saw the old pilot on board, who had once upon a time guided Gentil across the lake. Marc took his photograph, and in our enthusiasm

142

we gave him a big *matabiche*, which brought a smile to his lips and tears to his eyes.

The old fellow whom we took by force to be our pilot evidently expected to get nothing, for when I slipped a *matabiche* into his hand, his face, which had before been lowering, lighted up. I chaffed him about his gloomy looks; he began to laugh, took one of my hands in both of his, and pressed it over and over again with touching warmth. What excellent people they are! And what diabolical art, what persistent want of understanding, what a policy of hatred and unfairness were necessary to obtain anything that could justify brutality, exactions, and ill usage.[6]

As soon as the wind gets up, the deck is deluged with great packets of water. One doesn't know where to take refuge.

I have given up the idea of translating *Mark Rutherford*. My interest in it is a little too special.

I have plunged into the *Second Faust* with the keenest pleasure. I must own that I had never read it all through in the text.

The islands are becoming larger and rising more decidedly out of the water. The sandy slopes of low sand-dunes are now visible. Besides the papyrus, reeds, and bastard senna trees of the shores, mimosas and doum palm trees are reappearing. But, on one island in particular, why are a quantity of these trees dead? By a natural death? And if so, from what cause? Perhaps the natives set fire to them round the base because of the accumulation of old leaves, which prevents people from getting at the fruit?

The quantity of dead or dying trees one sees has been a matter of astonishment to me ever since I came out here.

Arrived at Bol towards the middle of the day.

The little walls surrounding the station are very strange-looking – crenelated, with worn, blunted angles – the whole thing no higher than a man, so that from the outside one could almost put one's head through the battlements. The colour is like baked Indian corn. On

---

6. Conrad in *Heart of Darkness* speaks admirably of 'the extraordinary effort of imagination that was necessary to make us take these people for enemies'.

the extreme right there is the arched roof of a small fort; on the left, nothing.

The village is a little way off on the right – a few miserable huts with very few inhabitants. They nearly all, both men and women, wear clothes. There is nothing to be seen but sand with, for sole enlivenment, the strange grey-green plant,[7] whose fruit I am at last able to see; it is like a huge bivalve fritter or shell-fish, with a packet of seed hanging from its centre and embedded in a kind of filigreed felt-like material. The seeds form a coating round the feathery down with which they are crowned and by means of which they are enabled to fly away. Nothing could be more ingenious or odder. The grains are at first so closely fitted together – like the tiles of a roof – that one has no suspicion that they are protecting this down; at first one can see nothing but a horny outer shell something like a litchi's. When one presses this shell, it bursts; the grains separate and disclose a silken treasure, beside which even a dandelion's plumes would look dull – a marvellous silvery wonder, which puffs out, increases, multiplies, and shakes itself free in readiness for the first breath to carry it away.

It is sometimes exceedingly difficulty to make a census of the livestock, as the natives often believe that counting a herd and pointing out individuals brings them bad luck.

'How many goats have you?'

'If I count them they will all die.'

These enormous fields of papyrus are mobile, floating. If the wind blows, they move away, and one sees tuft after tuft of them detach itself and float off to form the broken prairie up afresh in another place. This is the reason that the channels in the lake become sometimes impracticable in the course of an hour.

Yakoua

Since Touggourt I have never seen so many flies.

There is no wood for making canoes. The people here construct a kind of floating rafts out of a very thick papyrus matting. They are

7. *Calatropis procera* (asclepiad).

very long and the prow is bent upwards like the beak of a gondola. Nothing can be stranger. They are punted through the water with long poles, which are often imported from a long way off.

The bush with yellow flowers of which I have spoken grows by the water's edge. Its wood is porous and so light that it would float on a cloud. One is astonished to see a child carrying on his shoulder an enormous beam. He uses it to cross the water with. He puts himself astride across it, lies flat on his stomach, and paddles with his hands and feet, and, if the wind serves him, gets across a good-sized *bahr* in a very short time.

There are quantities of crocodiles in this part of the lake, we are told;[8] but, strange to say, they never attack men[9] – perhaps because they are overfed with the fish that abound in the lake. They destroy the nets of the natives, who, moreover, find the floating papyrus such an impediment that they have almost entirely given up fishing.

Along the shore towards the east, the water lies out of sight and out of reach behind a thick screen of papyrus and reeds. They conceal tracts of bog, into which it is possible for people to sink up to their knees or up to their waists, or indeed to disappear altogether. At intervals there are breaks in this curtain of reeds which allow the approach of canoes, of ferry-boats, of cattle that come to drink. I have never seen more magnificent cattle. The first I saw was an ox standing beside a group of women; it was the colour of a camel and very different from any that I had hitherto seen – like some Egyptian bas-relief. Its enormous horns had only a slight inward curve, they continued the line of the frontal bone and formed a kind of diadem like the pschent. It is impossible to describe a line, but the grandeur of the curve made me think of the bull Apis.

A little farther on I met with a herd of quite a different race; cows and bull were a very delicate grey colour, almost white; their enormous, monstrous horns were bigger, not only than any I had ever seen, but than any I had imagined possible; they were

---

8. I myself, however, never saw one, either in the lake or on the banks.

9. This, at any rate, is what the natives declare. But Lévy-Bruhl puts me on my guard (*La Mentalité primitive*, chap. i, 4). The accidental does not exist for a native; he has not the slightest notion of the fortuitous; the crocodile is 'naturally inoffensive', and if he happens to eat a man up, it is because he has been *delivered over* to him by a magician.

extraordinarily curved – unlike those I had just seen – and the head that carried them looked so formidable that, not knowing what the animal's temper might be (it was a bull), I thought it prudent to retire. It was not till later, when I went that way again with Marc and Outhman, that I noticed that the terrible monster was hobbled.

Quantities of marvellous birds. There was one of a lustrous blue, so charming that I could not make up my mind to kill it. Curiosity to see it close to, however, carried the day. Its head is brown. The feathers of its back are of a soft pastel-blue, all the under part of its body is light blue; the wings go from this very soft shade of blue to a blue that is very dark. Its tail is dark blue and very long and ends in a sharp point. A little farther on I saw as many as seven black and yellow birds, as big as starlings, on the back of an ass.

I walk in the midst of a cloud, like a divinity – a cloud of flies. There are great quantities of mistletoe on the mimosa trees; the tree is rather like ours, very thick and strong, with a great many ramifications, long, greyish leaves, and dull red long berries.

We followed the curve of the shore till we reached the opposite side of the island; and we walked back across it. I was amused to find growing in the sand the same orobanche which I had admired in the dunes south of Biskra; but there it was a very delicate pale mauve; here it is nothing but a dry twist of weed, almost black.

The natives, who are continually crossing from one island to another, ferry themselves over the *bahrs*, which are sometimes half a mile wide, on logs of that extraordinarily light wood I have mentioned, called *ambash*; the swimmer lies down on the log so that his head and shoulders, though dripping wet, are kept out of the water – very like Arion on the dolphin.

– February

We went this morning in a whale-boat to the village of Yakoua, which is on a neighbouring island. We put in to another island on the way. Marc photographed a beautiful herd of oxen. They were being made to swim across a *bahr*. Their heads are borne up by their enormous hollow horns, which float like buoys.

The natives here were extremely pleasant – dignified too; they seem to become more refined and spiritualized as one gets farther north. A very old chief came to meet us riding on a horse; he got down and offered us his mount; but he needed it more than we did; for that matter the village was not far off, but the walk to it through the sand was extremely trying. There was a brief reception by the chief, who had dismounted, and an exchange of greetings in a kind of shed. The old chief had a very noble and beautiful expression of countenance. His hands were like a skeleton's and there were white spots on them. His two young sons (or grandsons) went with us through the village in his stead, for he was too exhausted. Marc tried to film some 'documentary' scenes, but was not very successful. He wanted to get some groups of swimmers, and principally of women swimmers. In spite, however, of their being carefully chosen out, these particular ones were not very good-looking. It was impossible to get any concerted action from them. We were given to understand that it is improper for men and women to swim together. The men must start ten minutes before the women. But, as the women remained standing on the shore, the men were suddenly seized with shyness and slipped on their trousers and belts. Marc explained to me that they would no doubt undress as they got into the water; he thought it would be rather effective to see them carrying their clothes on their heads to keep them from getting wet. But their modesty was too strong; they preferred wetting their clothes – which, after all, would soon dry in the sun; and when they were pressed to undress, they gave up altogether and went off to sulk under a doum palm tree. Marc began to lose his temper, and no wonder. The women then also refused to go into the water without their clothes on – which didn't, however, prevent them from insisting that all the men and all the onlookers, except us, should go away. All these absurdities gave very poor results. It was now twelve o'clock. The sun was baking. We got into our whale-boat again, but the wind was against us, and we had no oars, merely poles to punt with; but in this part of the lake, for a miracle, the water was deep and the poles barely reached the bottom. We made no progress. At last we decided to skirt along the shore and in this way managed to reach Bol, at about two o'clock, where our luncheon was waiting for us on board the *d'Uzés*.

The other whale-boat has gone 'to make wood' in another island and is not back yet. We shall not be able to go on before tomorrow.

Yesterday I went out again with my gun, but killed nothing. The birds let one get so close up to them that it seems a shame to fire. The end of the day was gorgeous. In spite of the lowness of the dunes, one gets a view from them over a wide stretch of lake, where the splendour of the golden sunset is reflected – serene, majestic, indifferent, hard.

We weighed anchor at five o'clock in the morning. The sky was Sahara-like in its purity. It was very cold again last night, but owing to the absence of wind the cold was bearable.

We stopped at about seven o'clock off a fairly large village, which has been completely deserted. Some of the huts are carefully shut and barricaded, which seems to indicate that their inhabitants have the intention of returning. We ended by discovering at the back of one of the huts a one-eyed old woman, crouching on the ground and dressed in rags that were caked in mud. She explained in a flood of words that she had not followed the general exodus because she was too weak and half paralysed. Just then we saw near by, and outside another hut, another old woman, who, the first told us, had stayed behind to look after her. We questioned each of them in turn, but their accounts were contradictory and Adoum transmitted our questions and their answers badly. If one asked how long it was since the other inhabitants had left, the answer would be the name of the chief of the village or the number of creeks between here and the island where they have gone. The loquacity of these two deserted old women was nightmarish. They kept up an unceasing drivel. The reason that they didn't go with the others was also that they didn't know how to swim (or were unable to). The others left twenty-one days ago. The most decrepit of the old women gave the number by making twenty-one lines in the sand with her forefinger. Whenever one asked her anything, she went through a kind of crazy calculation, making lines with her finger and immediately after wiping them out with the flat of her hand. The men had left in order to get something to pay the tax with, or in order to avoid paying it – one can't tell which.[10] These people would no doubt have

10. The island herdsmen of Chad, when the pastures of one island are exhausted, take their herds for some weeks to another island.

no difficulty in paying the tax, which is in no way excessive, if the census were kept up to date and if each of them had not sometimes to pay for three or four people who have disappeared, but who are marked on a census that is four years old.

We stopped at noon off a large island, rather difficult to put in to, choked as it was with papyrus, reeds, and bushes of ambash. I noticed in the water several water-beetles and an exquisite little floating plant, which gave the water a reddish appearance. Like our water-lilies, it has a single leaf – a triangular one, divided like a fern-leaf. We put the whale-boats end to end, but there remained a boggy space between us and dry land, which we crossed pick-a-back. An hour's walk in the interior of the island (the vegetation is as monotonous as ever – mimosas and especially the white-juiced senna tree) brought us within sight of a village; we drew near; all the huts were deserted. We made out a group of people, however, in front of a hut. At the sight of us, three men ran away into the bush. With the help of two interpreters – Adoum and one of the crew (a fellow with Herculean muscles and a fine-cut face, whose name is Idrissa, and whom we call Sindbad) – we spoke to the persons who were left behind – five women and three boys. Marc took some photographs and we distributed fifty-centime pieces, the value of which had to be explained to them. The eldest of the boys spoke to us and what a distinguished, gentle, noble face he had! Marc asked whether he was not the son of a chief; but no; his father was a plain worker in the fields, who had left with the other inhabitants of the village. The three boys, who at first seemed exceedingly shy, gradually grew accustomed to us. They told us that some of their relatives were taxed at thirty and even thirty-five francs a head; they themselves are taxed at seven francs, though the two younger ones were certainly not more than thirteen years old. They offered us some curdled milk in bottles made of plaited reeds and were extremely surprised, almost to tears, when I gave them each a *pata* (five francs). They told us that four days ago they had been ill-treated by some people belonging to the chief of the canton, Kayala Korami, who had seized their goats and tied up a man and flogged him . . .

*

More islands; they are all alike. I cannot understand how the captain manages to distinguish between them. Now that the boat has unloaded its packing-cases (wireless sets, wine, flour, and various goods for Fada and Faya), we are in no particular hurry, so we asked to be taken to some of the populated islands. At five o'clock we stopped – again among papyrus and bushes. We landed and walked inland. There were quantities of goats' and oxen's droppings, the oxen's not very recent. After a quarter of an hour's walk we came upon a village that was fairly large, but completely deserted. Not even a poor old woman, as in this morning's. But in the distance we saw the white patches of a herd of goats and we walked in that direction. The vegetation had suddenly changed. It was on the edge of a fairly thick wood that we found the goats. They made light moving splotches in among the tangle of branches, through which fell the slanting rays of the setting sun. The herd was scattered over a large piece of ground and half hidden in the woods. There were perhaps four or five hundred animals. They were all going in the same direction and we followed, allowing them to guide us. Soon we came upon two huts lost in the thick of the bush. At the sound of my gun, with which I had just killed a guinea-fowl, there appeared an old native; he came towards us with raised hands. With him were a tall lad, decently dressed in a blue *boubou*, a woman, and two very young children. The boy in the *boubou* agreed to guide us across the *bahrs* to the island where the natives of the outlying villages have assembled for the time being, in order to pay their taxes to the chief of the canton (to be accurate, his son), who has come on purpose to collect them. It was late already. The sun was setting; not a breath of air over the smooth expanse of water. The night had closed in long before we weighed anchor. We found our way to the village, which was not far off, accompanied by Adoum and Idrissa/Sindbad, and preceded by our pilot, carrying a storm-lantern. The chief of the canton (his son-in-law, that is – the person who is accused of cruelties and exactions) presented himself. He had a horrid face, a hooked nose (particularly unpleasant in a black face), a shifty eye, and tightly screwed lips. He was more than polite – almost obsequious. We left shortly, promising to return the next day. The only object of this nocturnal reconnaissance was to coax the people out of their shyness, and especially the children, among whom we distributed a number of small coins. The children here, in the neighbourhood of Chad, have not the enormous stomachs one sees in Ubangui; but their hands and feet are often hideously deformed; the palms of their hands become, as it were, spongy and the backs scaly.

We had got back on board and were preparing to turn in for the night, when Adoum came to tell us that five natives had appeared with 'complaints' and that the captain had told them to return next morning. Remembering Samba N'Goto, and afraid that these nocturnal confidences might be lost for ever, we hurriedly sent Sindbad to pursue the 'complainants' and to persuade them to come back. Then, to beguile the time of waiting, we began to read by the wretched light of the photophore (*Mark Rutherford* and the *Second Faust*). A long time went by and I was getting more and more unhappy, imagining that Sindbad had had to go as far as to the village and would only be able to find the five men by giving away the step they had taken, with the result of compromising – ruining – them. After about half an hour Adoum came to announce the arrival of another 'complainant'. This one came from a neighbouring island; he had jumped into a canoe as soon as he saw our steamboat go by, in the hopes of meeting a white man to whom he could speak. He bent down and showed us a large and very visible scar of a recent wound on the back of his neck; and, opening his *boubou*, he showed us another wound between his shoulders. They were the stripes given him by a 'partisan' of the chief's. The 'partisan' had begun by seizing three of the four milk goats that the man kept in front of his hut for his wife's and children's subsistence; and as the 'partisan' seemed to be going to take the fourth goat too, the other had remonstrated; upon which Kayala Korami's agent had struck him.

A little later (the interview with this first complainant had only just finished), four other natives appeared. One complained that Kayala Korami had appropriated a herd of eight cows which should have come to him after the death of his father's brother. The second told how he had given Kayala Korami 250 francs to be appointed chief of his village. Kayala Korami had then asked for double the sum, and as the other declared he was not rich enough to give it, Korami had threatened to kill him and had kept the first 250 francs. The last two 'complainants', terrified by Kayala Korami, have been forced to take to the bush, and only come out at night and go to the outskirts of the village in order to get food, which is brought them by their friends and relations.

What I cannot describe is the beautiful expression of these people's eyes, the touching intonation of their voices, the dignity and reserve of their bearing, the noble elegance of their gestures. Beside these blacks, how many white men would look like vulgar cads! And what a sad and smiling gravity there is in their thanks and farewells, what a despairing gratitude to the person who has at last consented to listen to their grievances.

This morning at daybreak there was a fresh batch of 'complainants' awaiting our pleasure. Among them was a chief, who was the first we received. Everything I have just said about the men of yesterday evening was still more conspicuous about him. He was accompanied by one of his people, who, when we invited him to sit down, crouched on the floor at his chief's feet, snuggling, like a dog, into the folds of his dress, and from time to time laying his head on or against his knee in sign of respect – of devotion almost, but also, I think, of tenderness.

The chief showed us scars and traces of wounds and blows on this man's back. He described Korami's exactions, and said that the people of his village were terrorized and deserting to a neighbouring circumscription. Before the new rules laid down by the French administration, when the village chiefs were not subordinate to the chiefs of the cantons, everything was all right . . . No, no, he made no complaint against the French authorities. Oh, if there were only more whites in the country, or if only the whites were better informed! If only they knew the quarter of Korami's misdeeds, they would certainly put things to rights. But Korami is the very person who gives them their information – he or people who have been intimidated, terrorized by him. Unfortunately Korami's family is a large one; if he were to die, he would be succeeded by his son or one of his brothers and everything would go from bad to worse. We asked him if he knew any native outside Korami's family who would be capable of replacing this odious chief; then, very modestly and simply and naturally, he pointed to himself. Marc noted down his name, as he had noted down the names of the other 'complainants'.

As for that, he had nothing to complain of personally; it was in the name of the inhabitants of his village that he was speaking.

Then, as he was speaking, up came Korami himself, surrounded by his partisans, his guards, and his whole suite. He had come to pay us his respects, but at the same time to see if anyone had come to denounce his misdeeds. We asked our chief if he did not fear that Korami would bear him a grudge for having come to speak to us. He raised his head, gave a kind of shrug of his shoulders, and told us through the interpreter that he was not afraid.

We were exceedingly embarrassed to know how to manage so that the other complainers should not be compromised. We thought in vain of some means of intimidating Korami and of preventing him from ill-treating them after our departure. We decided to begin by receiving him; and as soon as we saw him, we said we were in a hurry to go and take photographs in his village. We breakfasted in a few moments and set off, escorted by the whole crowd. In the meantime we sent a message to the complainers behind Korami's back, that they were to come back at noon.

The village is built in the sand. The huts are made of reeds and all at some distance apart from one another. There were goats everywhere, mostly white, in huge herds. Those with sucking kids were hobbled to branches, stripped of their bark and stuck in the sand.

On leaving the village we said goodbye to Korami, as we did not wish him to come to the boat, where we were expecting the complainers. But soon his curiosity was too much for him and he followed us. Again we said goodbye and he went away, but left three of his guards behind him. These remained obstinately fixed on the shore, waiting for our boat to leave, and with obvious instructions to tell Korami the names of all the persons who should come and speak to us. (They were the very guards who had beaten the natives.) We sent for them, asked them if they had anything to say to us and if not, why they were waiting. They replied that it was the custom, in order to do honour to a distinguished white man. I showed them that I had noted their names, asked them if they knew there was a new governor, and told them that I had come on purpose, because I knew there were things occurring here that were 'not right', but that all misdeeds would be punished, and that they might tell their chief so. They then very cleverly protested that their chief and they were merely acting according to the orders and directions of the white chiefs.

(Evidently if the sergeant at Bol were more powerful and less overworked, it would be his business to see to everything and prevent ill usage.)

After that, came quantities of children, also possible spies, whom we had to send away too. There must have been about sixty people on the shore to begin with. But they gradually left. We went on board with four of yesterday's and this morning's complainers. They implored me to give them a paper in my handwriting to protect them from Korami's anger. He will never forgive them for having spoken to me! A paper from me, they think, may save them from being beaten. I finally left them a letter in an envelope addressed to Coppet, which they can send to Fort Lamy, if they are molested. They were obviously grateful for the little I could do for them. One of them, the eldest, took my hands and pressed them long and hard. His eyes were full of tears, and his lips trembled. This emotion, which he was unable to express in words, quite upset me. He certainly saw how greatly moved I was myself and his looks were full of gratitude and love. There was a world of sadness, of nobility, in this poor creature, and I longed to take him in my arms! . . . Then we started.

The turning-point is past. We have reached the farthest limit of our journey. From now onwards we are on our way home. It was not without regret that I bade a farewell that is no doubt final to all that lies on the other side of the Chad. (This is perhaps an opportunity for saying what it is that attracts me in the desert.)[11] I have never felt fitter.

> *Sicherlich, es muss das Beste*
> *Irgendwo zu finden sein.*

We spent the night close up against an island in amongst papyrus tufts – which didn't prevent our boat from tossing all night in a clatter of clanking chains and bumping whale-boats and slamming doors, which utterly prevented me from sleeping.

We weighed anchor very early in the morning – but merely to go

---

11. Perhaps, but a missed opportunity.

aground again time after time. The water swept the stern deck, so that we did not know where to go or how to keep our things dry. I think our excellent captain must have lost his way – unless he began by trying an arm of the Shari which turned out impracticable . . . in any case, we had again to head north.

At last we found ourselves in running water again. At first there was nothing to be seen but tufts of great reeds and huge termitaries. Then the ground grew gradually higher.

We coasted along the left shore (Cameroon), which suddenly became covered with a forest that was not very tall, but extraordinarily thick. The great spread of the enormous trees formed a vaulted roof, lined with creepers. It was like nothing we had previously seen. I would have given anything to penetrate beneath those mysterious shades – and nothing would have been easier than to tell the captain to stop, since it was an understood thing that we might direct the boat as we chose. And at that very time, we were passing parts where there were no reeds and where landing would have been perfectly easy. What prevented me from giving the order? The fear of upsetting plans, the fear of I don't know what, but, more than anything, the extreme reluctance I have to impose my wishes, to exercise authority, to give orders. So I let the favourable moment slip by, and when at last I consulted the captain, the forest was getting thinner, and the mattress of reed that separates it from the river, thicker. The captain, who himself wanted to stop to make wood, said there was another forest farther on. We soon reached it and put in to shore. The clay bank was as steep as a cliff, but not too high for us to climb with the help of the snags in it. Marc took the Holland and Holland (an admirable weapon, kindly lent us by Abel Chevalley) and I the rifle and quantities of cartridges of every calibre. Adoum followed. Unfortunately the forest was much less thick and dark than the one before it. There were no creepers, or hardly any; the trees were not so old, the undergrowth not so mysterious. But what we did see made me regret still more what we had missed. There were quantities of strange trees, some of them enormous, none of them perceptibly taller than our European trees, but with extraordinarily powerful and wide-spreading ramifications. Some had a network of aerial roots through which we had to squeeze. There were innumerable creeping brambles with cruel spikes and fangs, and a curious brushwood, generally dry and leafless, for it is winter-time. What makes it possible to thread these labyrinths is the incredible number of game tracks. What game? We examined the prints, we stooped to scrutinize the droppings. Those, white like kaoline, were a hyena's; those, a jackal's; those, the harnessed antelope's; those, the wart-hog's . . . We advanced like trappers, with straining nerves and muscles. I led the way and thought myself back again in the days of my childhood, exploring the woods of La Roque; my companions followed close at my heels, for it was not very prudent to venture out in this way with only one rifle. At moments the smell was horribly like a menagerie. Adoum, who is an adept, showed us a bank of sand with the quite recent traces of a lion on it; one could see that the creature had lain down there; those semicircles had been swept by its tail. But, farther on, there were other traces which were certainly a panther's. We came upon an enormous excavation at the bottom of a tree-trunk; the opening that led into the hole was so large that Adoum crept into it up to his waist – with prudence, I need hardly say, for he began by telling us it was the panther's den; and indeed it had a violent smell of wild beast. Quantities of feathers were strewed all about, belonging to the different kinds of birds the panther had devoured. I was surprised, however, that a panther should have a den, when suddenly Adoum called out: 'No, it's not a panther!' It was an animal whose name he didn't know; he became extremely excited, looked carefully on the ground, and finally showed us in triumph a large porcupine's quill. Yet it could not have been a porcupine that ate all those birds . . . A little farther on I started a large red fawn, spotted with white; then a quantity of guinea-fowl, which I missed ignominiously. I should very much like to know what the birds were that I followed for some time under the branches. They were about the size of partridges and had the same kind of flight, but the undergrowth was too thick to allow of my shooting them. A great grey monkey came and swung himself impertinently a few yards above our heads; then he took fright. We heard and saw the higher branches stirring; a leap – a run – and there was his little grey face looking at us from a long way off. At moments there were spaces between the branches – clearings that will soon be filled with the enchantment of spring. Ah! how I should have liked to stop, to sit down, there on the slope of that monumental termitary, in the dark shadows of that enormous acacia, and watch the gambols of the monkeys, and muse, and wonder! . . . The idea of killing – the very point of the chase – damps my pleasure. Assuredly, I should not have had to stay motionless many minutes for the world of nature to close over me. Everything would have been as if I had not existed and I should myself have forgotten my own presence and turned all vision. Oh, what an ecstasy it would have been! There are few minutes of my life I would sooner live over again. And as I pressed on in the midst of this strange excitement, I forgot the shades that are already at my heels; this that you are doing you will doubtless never do again.

The wood grew thinner, the game tracks more and more frequent; and soon we found ourselves in a savanna like that we had recently passed through before getting to Chad.

We re-embarked after having killed only one guinea-hen.

In the clay bank beside the boat, there were quantities of bee-eaters' holes. The marks of the scratching of their two feet were plainly visible.

We stopped an hour before sunset in a very large village (on the French shore) – Mani – where we found the same children we had made friends with on our way out. The sultan – arrogant, unsmiling creature – no doubt considered us people of no importance, to judge by our familiarity with inferiors, and did not deign to appear. But his young son came and sat on my knee in the armchair I had ordered to be brought on shore – and his tenderness made up for his father's disdain.

I have lost count of dates. Let us say: the next day. We started at dawn. The sky was cloudless. It was cold. Every one of these mornings, I have got up at about half past five, and stayed till half past nine or ten wrapped up in two sweaters and three pairs of trousers, two of them pyjamas.

The guinea-hen we killed yesterday was delicious.

I am never tired of watching the enormous crocodiles on the sandbanks; they get up indolently at the passage of the boat and sometimes slide along the sand towards the water, and sometimes raise themselves on their four legs, looking antediluvian and as if they came out of a natural-history museum.

A small canoe, manned by two natives, hailed our boat. I did not see it come up, but we stopped for a moment and one of the natives came on board, looking very dignified in spite of his rather wretched *boubou*. He brought four chickens from yesterday's sultan and a great many apologies. He declared he had tried to find us last night as we were walking in the village. The sultan had sent the chickens last night, but so late that Adoum (very cleverly) had refused to disturb us – 'Governor sleeping,' he had said. All this was not very correct on the sultan's part, and I think that Adoum's refusal had very properly abashed him, so that he had sent us this messenger, himself an old village chief; this man had hurried overland, cutting across a bend of the river, so as to catch us up on the *d'Uzès* and make amends. We received him with dignity and magnanimity; and then I plunged back into the *Second Faust*.

The boat stopped at about ten o'clock 'to make wood', and we landed on the Cameroon shore. The country here is again very different. There is a curious alternation of trees – often very fine ones – and bare spaces covered with dried grass. Game is abundant and there are quantities of its winding tracks, which are easy to follow. The weather was splendid. We walked along the coast to begin with, and I succeeded in killing a guinea-hen. Then we plunged into the bush, as we had done the day before. We started a great wart-hog, which was resting in an impenetrable shelter of low branches that hung over what must have once been a marsh, but is now no more than a crust of baked clay. We pursued him for some time, but did not succeed in seeing him again. Our attention was then caught by a little herd of *am'rais*. So we came back empty-handed (except for the birds at the beginning), but enchanted. I shall remember the double tree-trunk I saw – a kind of acacia with low, extraordinarily wide-spreading branches, whose dark shadow sheltered a bare space edged round with other, smaller acacias – like a patriarch surrounded by his sons. It was in this huge tree – more *powerful* than any French oak – that a troop of monkeys were leaping, who fled at our approach. The whole tree was covered with that extraordinary fleshy creeper, which is like a cactus, and sends its arms in every direction; they are all exactly the same size, wind like serpents through the branches, spread out into a network over the tree-top, and then hang all round about it, like the fringe of a tablecloth.

Incredible numbers of crocodiles on the mudbanks. They lie flattened out close against the ground, mud- and bug-coloured, motionless, and looking as if they were the direct issue of the quagmire. A rifle-shot and they all disappear – swallowed up in the water of the stream, as if they had melted.

Goulfeï again. It was dark when we arrived, notwithstanding which the sultan came to greet us, but we told him we should put off our visit to him till next day. The first part of the night I had a strange feeling of discomfort. The night was not particularly hot – almost chilly and at the same time stifling. It was a kind of feeling which sleep is powerless to overcome without some kind of assistance. So for the first time I tried Soneryl ('talc and starch,' reads Marc on the prospectus) and soon began to feel its effects. But the whale-boat was rubbing against the tent-flap just behind my mosquito-net at the level of my ear – a little continual scratching sound which was perfectly unbearable. I got up three times and dragged my bed to a place where I thought I should escape from hearing it. Long before dawn a tumult of birds awoke me; I distinguished the guinea-fowls' cry and the ducks' chuckle. They were quite close. Finally I could bear it no longer and got up and dressed in the dark. Adoum, who had been wakened by the same din, came at that very moment to get the rifle and cartridges. We went out together on tiptoe. With three shots we killed four ducks. At the last shot, which was fired almost in the dark, I was surprised to see three little birds fall at the same time as the duck. The second duck fell into the river a little way off; a number of others flew right away – and I saw an extraordinary spectacle: one of the fugitives came back to its fallen companion and alighted on the water – at first a little way off it and timidly; then it swam nearer, regardless of my fresh shot, which, however, missed it. It was only at the third shot that it flew away, and even then unwillingly, for it came back again and hovered round its comrade; it was not till the canoe went to pick up the slaughtered bird that it flew finally away. Marc joined us and I handed him the gun; he made four more victims before sunrise.

We came in to dress and have breakfast; but before we had finished, the sultan and his court made their appearance. We let down the flaps of our tent to change our linen and make ourselves smart. A white man (with a considerable touch of colour – a Martiniquer) also arrived to see us – Sergeant Jean-Baptiste, belonging to the prophylactic sector of Logone. He does as many as six hundred inoculations a day, he said. The country is terribly ravaged by sleeping-sickness.

We revisited the town, which had seemed so strange when we had seen it by night on our journey out. By day it is no less strange and we were not disappointed in it. Goulfeï is absolutely amazing. The sultan conducted us to his abode – a series of very small, very low rooms in a building of sun-baked earth; one reaches it through a labyrinth of passages and corridors and courtyards; the whole thing is very small, but manages to have a grand air, like a highly primitive dwelling. The walls are extraordinarily thick. What it reminds one of most – the Etruscan tombs of Orvieto or Chiusi. And during our whole visit, at the turning of a passage or as we stepped into a courtyard, there was a rapid flight of women and children at the other end, running to hide in other still more secret retreats. There were staircases besides, leading on to the roof terraces. When our visit was finished, Marc went up to them to turn some films. Before this the sultan left us for a few moments in one of the numberless little rooms, where deckchairs had been unfolded for us and a fire lighted, and went to put on his state robes. He came back gorgeous; but very simple in spite of it, and smiling like a child. He had left us with his uncle (a brother of the late sultan's) and his son, a superb youth, as reserved and shy as a young girl. Both were admirably dressed. The son in particular was wearing a pair of vast trousers of grey silk, embroidered with dark blue (said to come from Tripoli). Both had on little *chechias* (fezzes) of plaited reed, embroidered with many-coloured wools. Their courtesy was charming.

We left again at noon.

Stopped about three o'clock at a new Cameroon village.

There was a great scattering at our approach. Little boys and girls fled and hid like wild game. The first we caught served to tame the others. Soon the whole village was conquered. Some of the children were charming and were hanging on to our arms and cajoling us with a sort of lyrical tenderness; but they bid us goodbye very quickly when we drew near our boat, for they are a little afraid of being carried off.

We expressed a wish to see the crocodiles closer up. A canoe, manned by two men from the village, was tied to the *d'Uzès's* tow-line. At about four o'clock we stopped off the French shore. We hastily took our places in the canoe, crossed the enormous Shari, and reached a vast sandbank on the other side. But it was too late for the crocodiles. So we went into the bush with Adoum and the two boatmen. We had not gone three hundred yards before Marc killed a big fawn, striped with white. And a hundred yards farther on we found ourselves in front of an enormous den. From the description the natives gave us of the animal that lives in it, we thought it must be an anteater. But the anteater had now made way for another big animal, whose muzzle could be seen at the back of the hole. From where I was I could not see it myself, but Marc saw it and took aim; his gun, however, missed fire. The wart-hog, for that is what it was, bounded out of the hole, followed by two others, also very big, and a litter of young ones. The whole lot rushed out and into us; I can't understand why no one was knocked down. A second gunshot brought down one of the three big ones. Adoum was doubled up with laughter, because one of our boatmen, in his fright, had backed, knocked up against a stump of wood, and rolled over on to the ground. Though one of the boars had run straight at me, to within two yards, I never for a moment thought of any danger. I mean, it seemed clear that the creature was trying to escape and not to attack. Nevertheless, I was expecting to be knocked down, for it was of a good size, bigger than the one Marc had just killed; but at the last moment it sprang to one side. We continued our hunt in a great state of excitement, but killed nothing further, except a guinea-hen. We very distinctly heard the roaring of a lion; the natives say there are a great many of them. This one must have been quite near us. The sun had set by now and it was beginning to be too dark to see. To our great regret, we were obliged to go back. The tracks and droppings that covered the ground were numerous beyond belief. Some – belonging to wart-hogs, antelopes of all sorts and sizes, monkeys, and many kinds of big game – seemed quite recent. In the meantime we did not want to abandon our victim, which we had left behind some way off, in the charge of a man, who had to keep off hyenas and jackals. The wart-hog was terribly heavy and the two boatmen had the greatest difficulty in carrying it as far as the canoe, slung on a long branch, with its legs tied together two by two. Adoum in the meantime loaded the deer on his shoulders; it was almost as heavy as himself. As for the wart-hog, it must have weighed at least as much as Béraud.

Our return journey across the river was made in the dark; sitting in the canoe on a level with the water – right against the water – and very unsteady equilibrium.

Got back to Lamy on the 13th. Our journey to Bol lasted eleven days.

Ever since they have been out in the bush with us, our boys have had meat every day. Outhman says: 'We happy when we eat. When we eat, we no think.' And when we ask: 'Think of what?' he evades the question and talks of his companion: 'Adoum, when he not eat, he think of Abécher, he think of his mother. Not think at all when eat.'

The French mail in, but no letters.

I note in the *Rire* this delightful legend to a poor caricature:

'Why, my good fellow, I've told you again and again that if you didn't drink, you might be a corporal.'

'Yes, sir, I know; but the fact is that when I drink, I think I'm a colonel.'

Dindiki rushes at the winged white ants, seizes as many as he can in his little hands, and gobbles them up in a kind of frenzy.

I must study Dindiki's ethics and aesthetics, his peculiar manner of moving, defending, protecting himself. Every animal has succeeded in finding out his own particular manner, outside of which there seems to be no salvation for him.

Fort Lamy, 16 February

Yesterday Adoum was quietly asleep in a native hut. Two whites came in – a sergeant and a corporal. They wanted a woman, who they thought was being hidden or kept away from them. Adoum, who kept quiet at first and pretended to be asleep, objected when he saw the two men light some straw and set fire to the hut.

'Why doesn't the dirty nigger mind his own business? If you say a word, you'll be locked up.' 'Yes,' said Adoum, '*you* set fire to the hut, and *I* get locked up.' Upon this the sergeant seized hold of him and gave him a violent blow with his cane – this morning he still bears the mark of it across his back. The breaking out of the fire brought people up to see, amongst whom were Zara, the procuress, and Alfa, Coppet's boy, who implored Adoum to say nothing about it.

This evening I hear the affair is being followed up. A long report has been made to Coppet, in which the administrator-mayor demands with great energy that the military authorities should punish the guilty parties.

A number of wireless sets, for which an order had been given in 1923 for use in 1924, had not been delivered, nor even announced at Fort Lamy at the time of our leaving . . . Such delays, we are told, are due to the administrative system of wheels within wheels. Official orders have first to be centralized at the Ministry for the Colonies by a special board, whose special agents communicate with the necessary firms. These agents, who have never set foot in the colonies, are free to modify the orders according to their fancy, and for the most part pay no attention whatever to the specified demands.

Long visit to Pécaut, the veterinary – a very interesting man. He told me that the red butterfly I let go several times in the forest of Carnot is particularly rare and sought after. I reproach myself bitterly. I think that the red butterflies I have seen (five or six times) were of two species or at any rate of two distinct varieties – not very big – of a beautiful scarlet – rather dark.

We leave in two days.
We have ordered eighty porters to be ready for us at Pouss, where

we shall go in whale-boats belonging to the Ouham and Nana Company.

In order better to divide the loads and overhaul the ammunition, Marc has opened all our packing-cases. We find that of the twelve tins of flour (ten kilos each) which we brought with us from Brazzaville, every single one has been perforated by the nails used for packing. The tins are carefully soldered, but worms have got into the holes and part of the flour has been spoilt by the damp.

20 February. Morning

We left Fort Lamy in three whale-boats. The homeward journey has begun. Every day now brings me nearer to Cuverville.

PART TWO

BACK FROM THE CHAD

CHAPTER ONE

◆◆

ON THE LOGONE

20 February

Left Fort Lamy in three whale-boats.[1] Homeward bound. We are ascending the Logone; it seems to me almost exactly the same width as the Seine. The waters are low and the natives prefer punting to rowing. There are four in front and four behind; they bend down on their poles and then raise themselves in cadence. We are thus deprived of their singing, which they keep for the more regular rhythm of the canoes; this almost silent progress, however, is less alarming to the game and enables us to get nearer the birds that people the shores.

In the narrow tunnel formed by the whale-boat's *shimbeck* the temperature is not too hot, and however slowly we go, a delicious draught blows through it. Lying in my deckchair, which by day takes the place of the camp-bed, that is folded away, I am re-reading the *Barbier de Séville*. More wit than depth. A sparkling brilliance – but its comedy is wanting in gravity.

21 February

Started before sunrise. A slight mist was silvering the shores of the Logone, which are more human in their proportions than the shores of the Shari. Its sandy banks have a smiling austerity; there is no softness about them. There are quantities of grey-green bushes like the willows and osiers of France. In the same way there

---

1. A whale-boat is a boat between thirty and forty feet long, made of plates of sheet-iron fastened together by rivets. It is generally sheltered in the centre by a roofing of mats, arranged archwise and forming a kind of tunnel; this is the *shimbeck*; at night one's camp-bed is set up beneath it; there is just enough room beside the bed for a narrow camp-stool on which to put one's clothes.

grow on these banks simile-watercress, false willowherbs, imitation forget-me-nots, ersatz-plantains – as though only the actors had changed, but not the parts nor the play. Who will play the part of the scrophularia? . . . Sometimes we find a plant of the same family, as happens in the case of the balsam. But this explains why one feels so little a stranger here, though sometimes the star actors of our countries are reduced in this to the rank of supers. For the landscape to take on a really exotic appearance the eye has to be caught by one of those plants which are *regularly disposed round an axis* – palms, cactus, euphorbia candelabra, etc. – of which we have no equivalent in our northern countries – with the single exception of certain conifers.

The drawback to a journey that has been too well planned is that it does not leave enough room for adventure. And yet we are approaching the place where our boy Outhman's first master (the administrator Noumira?) managed to get crushed to death by hippopotamuses. And we have in fact been warned that a band of thirty or so of these monsters is barring the Logone not far from here and that the natives dare not go upstream in their canoes. Well, well! we shall see.

Since leaving Fort Lamy we have been living on game – ducks or guinea-fowl. I am in the habit of inviting friends, or sometimes people I have never met, to share my pleasures with me in imagination, so this morning I went shooting with Pesquidoux, who assuredly has no suspicion that I was among the first to fall in love with his writings – among the first with Marcel de Coppet; at Fort Archambault we amused ourselves with recalling to each other his early articles, which at that time no one, or hardly anyone, had noticed. Yes! I invited Pesquidoux to partake of our duck '*à la rouennaise*' with us and to tell me if he had ever eaten a better.

The tall grasses on the shore hide the sudden falling away of the banks. Groves of a darker green, peopled with monkeys that fly at our approach – great trees overhanging the water, roots which the stream has washed bare and hollowed out into grottoes – a somnolent advance – enchanting idleness – cries of guinea-fowl – in the distance a herd of *katambours*[2] . . . We landed and followed the tracks at random; and soon, in the excitement of such novelty, forgot all about the chase.

Some of the trees attain amazing dimensions; but their tops are not lost to view, like those of the giants of the equatorial forest; theirs is a squat enormousness; and all round the trunk stretches a vast shady space over which the tree broods, over which it reigns, spreading its colossal branches as though to keep all other vegetation at bay. These branches curve and arch; their extremities droop till they touch the ground in the far distance. One can breathe for a moment in these beautiful covered clearings; but as soon as one gets out of them, one is inextricably caught in the confused tangle of branches; one stoops, one drops to one's knees, one crawls; after a quarter of an hour's creeping, one has completely lost one's bearings, and in the absence of landmarks we should never find our whale-boats again without the help of the natives, who never lose their whereabouts.

What a mistake to think that the birds and insects of tropical countries are always brightly coloured! Even the kingfishers here are black and white and it is only their form that reminds one of the Normandy kingfishers – shouts of blue, which in old days used sometimes to ring out from the little stream of La Roque, and to which my heart would shout a rapturous response.

The tsetses are very harassing. It is impossible either to kill them or to drive them away. It is with difficulty that one manages to see them. Their sting, though not very painful, becomes in time extremely wearing to the nerves.

About four o'clock the hippos appeared upon the scene. The surface of the water was suddenly ripped up by their enormous snouts. We counted seven of them, but no doubt there were more. They all breathed together almost at the same time. Our whale-boats stopped. Marc fired a few shots at them; then, wanting to get nearer, had himself landed on the other shore. I sat down on the trunk of a tree on the river bank almost opposite him. A great monkey came near me to drink.

*

2. Arab name for a species of antelope.

I took Outhman out with me into the country; the trees and undergrowth were covered with a prodigious number of locusts; if one goes near a low bush, they fly off with a great noise. Under one of the trees on which they were perching, too high to be afraid of me, there fell a continual rain of little long-shaped projectiles – their droppings.

High dry grasses, furrowed with tracks; traces of all sorts of animals, and especially of lions. But we saw nothing but monkeys or guinea-fowl. Yes; a herd of *katambours* – from a distance one would take them for small horses – came to drink in the river. There was an admirable sunset; the grass, the sky, the river, all turned golden. We were at the place where the Logone makes a great bend – opposite us was the sandbank where we are going to spend the night. Immediately after sunset the sky became dark – it was the horde of locusts starting eastwards. Their passage lasted not less than five minutes.

The landscape is less vast and less vague; it is growing more temperate and more organized.

22 February

The river banks (on the Chad side)[3] are fairly steep. We are interested by the *norias* – I do not know what other name to give this curious water-raising apparatus. It is a simple beam with a receptacle at one end and a counterbalancing weight at the other, by means of which water is taken from the river and easily raised to the level of the field that has to be irrigated. Nothing could be more primitive or ingenious than this elementary machine, which has a Virgilian elegance about it. A big calabash serves as receptacle.

One native raises the water; another distributes it; he uses a hoe, with which he opens and shuts by turns a number of little mud sluices. The water is first poured out of the calabash on to a wicker mat, so that the earth may not be washed away by the water and lose its slope. The whole field is on a gentle slope. They are cultivating egg-plants in this particular one; although not very big, there are six *norias* in it, about sixty feet apart from each other. I note this at

3. The Logone separates Equatorial Africa (Chad Colony) from the Cameroon.

length, for I have not seen these machines described in any book of travels to the Chad.

Stopped at Logone-Birni[4] (formerly Carnak). The sultan came to meet us in a canoe. He had on a blue *boubou* and blue spectacles and was holding in his hand an indigo-dyed cow's tail, to keep off the flies. We were welcomed by a concert of four instruments – two drums, a sort of clarinet, and an extremely long, thin trumpet, which is in separate joints; it gives out strange bellowings that are full of harmonics.

There is a hospital here with sixty patients. In the absence of the head doctor of the prophylactic department it is being managed by three natives. They claim that they are able to cure trypanoso-miasis, even in its third period. The impression they made on us was excellent; order, cleanliness, decorum; four microscopes; well-kept registers; an obvious desire to be up to the mark, and to the work – to give satisfaction.

Stopped at various places along the river. Looked in vain for hippopotamuses. Passed the night on a large sand island, out of reach of the lions, of which we are told there are great numbers in the neighbouring bush.

23 February

It is a strange thing that as one ascends the Logone, it becomes wider without apparently becoming less deep or less rapid. The shores are farther apart and lower and the country all round seems to be sinking down. How I wish I could see it in flood time, when it is transformed, we are told, into an immense lake, sown here and there with little islands of greenery, where all the animals come to take refuge. We stopped at midday at Logone-Gana (on the east shore). I left my whale-boat and visited it on foot – a large village built in terraces on the river bank and surrounded with battlemented walls. One goes in by a small postern gate. A number of marabous were standing like sentinels on the battlements; I counted seven on seven successive battlements – motionless – enormous – they might have been stuffed. In flood time, we are told, the water washes right up to

---

4. In the Cameroon. The most important settlement of the Kotoko tribe after Goulfeï.

the foot of the walls. Fairly high houses, sometimes round, sometimes like cubes, all crowded together in no particular order;
tortuous alleys; small irregular places; and suddenly an enormous
tree sheltering a little market. An intolerable stench of fish pervades
the whole village. Fish are the chief trade of the country; half-dried,
large and small, they are to be seen spread out on wicker hurdles at
every corner.

I bought a mark (worth three fifty-centime bits); there are still
some in circulation in the country, but the natives do not like them,
as they cannot be used for paying the tax.[5]

Forgot to note that we met a band of pelicans – the first. I counted
fifteen of them; they were quietly sailing like swans and when we
drew near, flew off to only about fifty yards' distance, when they
again alighted. They were not so fine as some I have seen in the
Jardin des Plantes, or as those La Fontaine describes so charmingly.[6]
These were grey or white (I think that the grey are the young
ones), but their wings were edged with black. I seem to remember
that the others were all white, with a tinge of saffron and flesh
colour.

But this afternoon, after my siesta, I saw a whole host of them on
a tiny island in the middle of the river – between 100 and 150. We
landed so as to cinematograph them from the shore. They are not at
all wild and come back after having been shot at. A quarter of an
hour earlier Marc had killed one of them. Not a thing to do – they
are too charming and too confiding. Our men will cut it up this
evening and make themselves caps with its feathered skin.

Stopped the night in another village. Douboul (marked 'Divel' on
the German map).

The village floats in a vast space girdled by a forest of Palmyra
palms. Very picturesque; washed by a backwater of the Logone.
Marshes; fever; mosquitoes.

---

5. A little later we saw a *chef de canton* insist on receiving the whole of the
capitation fee in marks, in a country where the mark fetches two francs.

6. '*Leur plumage est blanc, mais d'un blanc plus clair que celui des cygnes: même,
de près, il paraît carné, et tire sur la couleur de rose vers la racine. On ne peut rien
voir de plus beau*' (*Les Amours de Psyché*).

24 February

An almost sleepless night. I was kept awake by the splashing and the slapping of water. It was as if people were bathing just outside my whale-boat or as if fishing birds were pillaging the river. In the end my curiosity gained the upper hand. It was damp and cold. The camp-fires on the shore were nearly all out. At times one of the Saras coughed, sat up, blew on the dying embers, and then went to sleep again. A half-moon was in the middle of the sky. Have I said that our whale-boats had gone a good way up one of the Logone's backwaters, which ends a little farther on in a marsh under the walls of the village? The noise which had been keeping me awake was that of fish playing. There are so many of them that at times and in certain places the water looks as if it were boiling; I could see them in the light of the moon, half out of the water, pursuing each other, chasing insects, leaping and falling again with resounding splashes. Over the surface of the water a number of large odd-looking birds, which I could not recognize, were flying backwards and forwards silently and fantastically. Four great water-birds – royal cranes, marabous, or jabirus – flew across the sky with necks outstretched in front of them, and legs behind, uttering a long, hoarse cry. And then I suddenly understood that the others that were skimming the water were bats.

This morning the Logone is fairly like the picture I had made of it in my mind beforehand. The rays of the rising sun are gilding the sand and clay of the Cameroon shore, which rises in a low abrupt cliff, topped by a crest of reeds. Here and there are a few palm trees; the sky and water are a perfect blue. The east shore, which is lower, is covered with green grass that makes a silky swish when the whale-boat grazes it.

Out of a large flock of plovers (?) two gunshots killed and wounded eleven, which one of our crew pursued, picked up, and brought back; the others flew away in a dense crowd.

We stopped near a group of fishermen. Two boys in a canoe went to fetch some packets of bait which, when they first saw us coming, they had hidden in the fields, for fear we should take them away. And on the other side of the Logone we came upon another group of fishermen. They were extremely obliging, and most touched and grateful when I gave them a five-franc note in exchange for a big fish they offered us.

Passed an extremely wretched village (Cameroon), temporarily inhabited by people who have come from Moosgoum for the fishing season. All the women – even the youngest – have plates on both their lips – not made of wood, but of silver or some white metal – and also in their ears. Although the plates are not larger than bottle ends, the appearance is hideous.

Reached Kolem about three o'clock. Why is it marked so large on the map? It is not more important than last night's village. Extremely picturesque. There are ponds of stagnant water in four places in the town; one is covered with a thick green scum and pieces of floating wood. And half encircling the town, but on the other side of the ramparts, is a very large piece of water, which in the rainy season no doubt becomes part of the Logone. This large pond, which is parallel with the Logone, comes into the town, and the town begins again on the other side of it, as at Martigues; and still farther on, beyond the pond and the additional portion of the town, one has another view of the Logone and its other shore. The most astonishing thing we have seen since Goulfeï.

I made a point, however, of not sleeping at Kolem. The neighbourhood of all that stagnant water alarmed me. We started again at sunset and punted on by moonlight. We soon reached a sandbank where we shall be able to dine and camp, and where I am writing this before going to bed in the whale-boat.

Our boatmen are settling themselves on the sandbank and preparing for the night, which threatens to be cold. There are nearly forty degrees' difference between the day and the night. And I am speaking of the *shade* temperature; but they toil in the full sun and with no clothes on. I cannot understand how they bear up. (But some of them do not.) They have lighted fires round which to group themselves. Some lie at full length; others curl up with their stomachs to the blaze. One mat covers two of them, lying back to back, each with his face to a fire. They make a hollow in the sand in order to lie down in it, and put a mat over its edges so as to be better sheltered from the wind, which, thank God, is not very strong tonight. If it were to blow hard, they would catch their deaths. Nothing will ever make me believe that these people, who are supposed to have no wants, would not buy blankets if some 'shop' offered them the chance. I looked to see whether I had anything I could lend them and found the canvas sheeting of my camp-bed (which we had had replaced by leather at Fort Archambault). One of them accepted it eagerly. But there are twenty-seven of them, and I have been able to satisfy only one.

I must try in a few words[7] to make people feel the superhuman beauty of the night on this little golden sandbank, surrounded by water, sky, solitude, and strangeness. Sometimes there passes by a flock of big cranes, whistling in their flight like a night express – one can hear the noise of their wings.

25 or 26 February

Not a single tree for leagues and leagues; the shores hardly rise above the water's level. The landscape is becoming more and more marshy, more and more what I described in the second part of the *Voyage d'Urien*. On the sandbanks are companies of ducks – sometimes positive hosts of them. It was rather difficult to get up to them, and then a few shots fired into the mass brought down a dozen or so. Some that were only wounded fluttered back to the water and dived at the whale-boat's approach. There was one in particular at which we fired five times; it dived, swam under water, and re-appeared farther on. We wanted to put an end to it. Finally it was a mere wreck, but it went on diving and three Negroes who swam after it had the greatest difficulty in finding it among the reeds. At every shot that hits, our men rush up and leap out of the whale-boat, hustling each other in their anxiety to swim after the game. Excellent fellows! I wish I could understand what they say. Perhaps they are laughing at us and our bad shots; but their merriment is so charming, and their laughter so frank and so open! Their smiles are day by day becoming more confiding, more affectionate – I was almost going to say: more tender. And every day I am getting

7. I cannot rewrite these notes, but leave them just as they are without trying to polish up my recollections. (See *Journey to the Congo*.)

fonder of them. Marc followed a herd of *am'rais* for a long time yesterday over a stretch of burnt moor, but only succeeded in bringing down two. They are a little bigger than the harnessed antelope he killed the other day, but not so charming in form and markings. A single one would have sufficed for our whole crew; but they left not a morsel of either and also managed to dispose of the eighteen ducks we killed yesterday. These were not all of the same kind. Some of them were as big as geese and carried a black crest above their bills. They were all succulent, and indeed I doubt whether I have ever eaten anything better.

I also killed on the wing a curious bird with an elegant white crest, a long beak, large ruby eyes, and yellow legs, almost of the stilt species. It was as large as a rook.

Kaséré. A village that is perhaps not very poor, but unspeakably filthy. The soil is largely composed of refuse in the shape of dust. The inhabitants, nevertheless, look healthy and happy. No more *pian* here, no more scab; clean, wholesome skins at last.

A few very fine trees in the hut yards and in some of the village places – in particular some enormous Palmyra palms, with a great many branches, looking violently exotic. For the last few days there have been no more tsetses and in consequence no more trypanosomiasis (but then why no cattle?). Very little cultivated land. The inhabitants make their living by fish, which the people of Maroua come and buy, bringing millet in exchange. A great many mosquitoes on the bank where we camped. The stream is only an arm of the Logone. This morning we left the other more important arm and shall only get back to it again tomorrow evening. It is too deep for the men's punting poles. The higher up one goes, the more paradoxically full of water the Logone seems to be.

Mazéra. The last Kotoko village. This evening while Marc was filling his cameras, I went up to a group of children who were dancing to the sound of a drum. I had great difficulty in making friends with some of them. But as it was partly also a matter of money, the mothers forcibly dragged their offspring up to us, in the hopes of getting a fifty-centime bit. Most of the time the children yelled. They had to be coaxed round afterwards very slowly.

We got up at five-thirty. But about seven o'clock what a breakfast! Porridge, cold duck, *am'rai* kidneys, custard, cheese, washed down by an excellent cup of tea.

Adoum still continues to limp. The sore place above his foot has not healed; on the contrary, it seems to get worse. After having been told by the French doctor he had syphilis, when he hadn't, he has lost confidence and refuses to have recourse to any but native medicines. An old Negro (rather an attractive old fellow) took some powdered herbs out of a little bag and sold them to him for the price of two francs. Adoum spread this dirty dust on his open sore. The next day his foot was no better, and last night, after we had landed, we saw the poor boy sitting in the sand plastering his bad leg with a thick cake of mud and dung. This morning a native soldier who is in our party persuaded him to use a vegetable juice which is highly recommended – a viscous latex, a few drops of which the soldier brought on a stone. Adoum painted his sore foot with it, which made it smart horribly.

The country is becoming more and more desolate; the desolation of fire is added to the desolation of aridity. As far as the eye reaches, there is nothing to be seen but russet and black. There is a slight touch of green on one of the river banks, and on the other an edging of golden sand. The blue of the sky is almost tender, and the water – a mingled green, blue, and gold – is of an exquisitely lovely shade. Passed a little village in the making, with no name as yet on the map. As soon as they saw us, fifty or so natives, smiling and welcoming, got up a tamtam in the full heat of the midday sun. Some of the women would not be bad-looking except for the terrible plates which deform their lips. This is one of the most disconcerting of aberrations; nothing excuses or explains it; none of the theories that have been put forward (depreciation of the women to save them from raids, for instance) holds water for a moment. These unfortunate women, with their continually streaming lips, look stupid, but not at all unhappy; they laugh, jig, and sing, and seem to have no suspicion that they are not captivating. Every single one over the age of fourteen or fifteen is disfigured in this way.[8]

Towards evening we arrived at Gamsi and saw the first gun-shell-shaped huts. This is quite a small village, belonging to the Massa tribe and situated after the junction of the two arms of the Logone. The sun was on the point of disappearing; everything was pink and blue, vaporous, unreal. A sandbank in front of the village.

In the middle of the river was a curious, long island – a narrow strip of bushes. Here we watched a prodigious quantity of wading birds – white, black, and grey – coming up to perch. From moment to moment fresh arrivals flew up and seemed to hesitate: 'Full up!' 'Never mind! With a little squashing we shall manage.'

A little downstream was another large island, ending in an obtuse angle, on whose shores a population of ducks, snipe, and cranes came to roost for the night.

On the horizon a barrier of flames; it was the prairie that had been set on fire and was reddening one side of the night sky. An immense plain, with here and there, at long distances apart, a few sparse shrubs; in this barrenness the three great trees of the village looked magnificent. In the midst of a number of round huts the first shell-shaped ones looked even more beautiful than I had imagined. The perfection of their form makes one think of the work of certain insects or of a fruit – a fir-cone or a pineapple. In the inside sleep cattle, poultry, and people; but not pell-mell; everyone has his own place; everything is tidy; and everything is clean. The roof is sometimes supported by three or four big tree-trunks or branches, set slantwise, as if they had been flung into place by a whirlwind; almost at their feet is the hearth, which gives heat and also enough light to distinguish the herd of goats or cows, which are ranged against the circular wall and separated from the rest of the hut by a very low wall, like the wall of a well, so that the animals' manure does not dirty the floor of the hut, which is kept extremely tidy and clean. The hens live in a separate little corner of their

8. These plates, nevertheless, are not nearly so big as those of some other tribes – the Saras, in particular.

own. The whole thing is so exact, so well planned and proportioned, so neat, so cosy, that one's chief impression is perhaps one of comfort.

Moosgoum

I am astonished that the few rare travellers who have spoken of this country and of its villages and huts have only thought fit to mention their 'strangeness'. The Massas' hut, it is true, resembles no other; but it is not only strange; it is *beautiful*; and it is not its strangeness so much as its beauty that moves me. A beauty so perfect, so accomplished, that it seems natural. No ornament, no superfluity. The pure curve of its line, which is uninterrupted from base to summit, seems to have been arrived at mathematically, by an ineluctable necessity; one instinctively realizes how exactly the resistance of the materials must have been calculated. A little farther north or south and the clay would be too much mixed with sand to allow of this easy spring, terminating in the circular opening that alone gives light to the inside of the hut, in the manner of Agrippa's Pantheon. On the outside a number of regular flutings give life and accent to these geometrical forms and afford a foothold by which the summit of the hut (often twenty to twenty-five feet high) can be reached; they enabled it to be built without the aid of scaffolding; this hut is made by hand like a vase; it is the work, not of a mason, but of a potter. Its colour is the very colour of the earth – a pinkish-grey clay, like the clay of which the walls of old Biskra are made. Birds' droppings often whiten the top part of the flutings and unexpectedly show up their relief.

Inside the hut the coolness of the air seems delicious, when one comes in from the scorching outside. Above the door, like some huge keyhole, is a kind of columbarium shelf, where vases and household objects are arranged. The walls are smooth, polished, varnished. Opposite the entrance is a kind of high drum made of earth, very prettily decorated with geometrical patterns in relief, painted white, red, and black. These drums are the rice bins. Their earthen lids are luted with clay, and are so smooth that they resemble the skin of a drum. Fishing tackle, cords, and tools hang from pegs; sometimes too a sheaf of assegais or a shield of plaited rush. Here, in the dim twilight of an Etruscan tomb, the family spend the hottest hours of the day; at night the cattle come in to join them – oxen, goats, and hens; each animal has its own allotted corner, and everything is in its proper place; everything is clean, exact, ordered. There is no communication with the outside as soon as the door is shut. One's home is one's castle.

These huts give shelter to their own fauna as well as to human beings and cattle; swallows with black and white tails have built their nests in the top of the rounded roof; bats flutter round the single ray of light, in which their wings look transparent; little lizards run along the walls, on which the mason flies have built their nests like warts.

When a cow goes into one of these shell huts to pass the night, it has just room enough to get in by lowering its head. The door exactly fits the shape of the cow, which explains why it is wider at the height of the cow's body. The door-frame is in relief and very often decorated. At this place alone the wall is so thick that the embrasure forms what is almost a passage, like the opening of a conch. Certainly these curves, these angles, these splayings have been the same for centuries. Yes, these huts are really as beautiful as products of nature. If only some over-zealous administrator does not come in the name of hygiene, and order walls to be cut through and windows to be opened, and reduce the purity of these prime numbers to some sort of common divider!

These conic shells, which are of unequal height, are placed together in small groups. Their bases often touch, but do not impinge on each other; for their curve always starts from the ground, and the tangent circles which their plane would trace are perfect. The top of the passage which thus connects them forms a terrace half-way up their sides. Sometimes a round tower completes the ensemble and breaks the uniformity of its aspect. A very low wall goes from one hut to the other and throws, as it were, a circular girdle round all the buildings belonging to one community.

In front of some of these huts there is a floor of smooth beaten earth, where the Massas water their millet, which has got to sprout and ferment for the preparation of their *pipi* (a kind of beer). And this floor too, like everything else belonging to the Massas, is accurately laid out and perfectly shaped.

Besides the shells and round towers that serve as dwellings for the natives and their flocks, there are to be seen in the same enclosure other shells, considerably smaller; these have no flutings, but are sometimes decorated with vermicular markings and hatchings. These minor shells do not rest directly on the ground, but on a trellis-work of branches. They are granaries for storing millet, which has to be protected from rats, insects, and damp. A double belt of plaited grass enables the natives to reach the opening of the granary so as to draw upon its stores of grain.

Here and there near the dwellings we noted a sort of smooth, round, cup-shaped protuberance on the ground – a tomb.

On this first day the village was practically empty. The inhabitants were working in the fields. We decided to go on to Pouss, where the porters who have been requisitioned to accompany us to Maroua are waiting for us.

The station of Pouss on the other (the Cameroon) shore of the Logone, where we arrived at the end of the day, is very disappointing. Rather dirty too. So we went back to sleep at Mala.

As we are anxious to choose the best place to film, we wanted to compare Moosgoum with the most important village next it – namely, Mala, which we have now reached in our whale-boats. (I leave out of account quantities of minor groups of huts.) The *chef de canton* came to meet us on horseback. We put in to shore in order to greet him. An enormous fellow with a fat round belly – very amiable, smiling, deferential, and obviously anxious to prove the excellence of his intentions. He was wearing a white *boubou* with a black sash. With him was his vizier, or some such dignitary, wearing a dark purple kind of Tunisian waistcoat over his *boubou*. The four horses of the sultan and his suite began to get impatient. So we left after an exchange of compliments.

Mala seen from the river is very fine. There are a certain number of trees in the surrounding country, and a few in the immediate neighbourhood of the village and in the village itself – enormous trees. The one which is shading our mooring-place is particularly monstrous. It must be a ficus. The trunk, which is excessively odd and of a complication that looks as if it were intentional, is like a bundle of intertwined creepers.[9]

The race of the Massas is one of the finest in Central Africa. The natives of this country have none of the hideous skin-diseases which almost all the natives in the regions near the Congo suffer from. Not only are the people here robust, agile, and slender, but also clean, thanks to the proximity of the river, in which they bathe several times a day. The men as a rule simply wear a goatskin, which they let float behind them and which leaves them completely bare in front. Sometimes, however, they clothe themselves in stuffs which they buy from nomads, for they either do not know how to weave or else have no textiles. The women remain naked no matter what their age; for I cannot call the bead necklaces they adorn themselves with by the name of clothes. There is not one of them who has not her lips frightfully distended by metal disks. The old women have nearly all a pipe in their mouths, where the plates allow of it – that is to say, at the corner of their lips. I must add that the wearing of these plates causes a continual flow of saliva.

Mala

A shameless white-bearded old man, with a blanket on his shoulder and a stick in his hand, looking very like an ancient bard, told us about the first white man's arrival in this country – the explorer Gentil.

'When the white man arrived,' said he, 'all the village people cross the Logone and make off into the bush. The village chief is the only one who dares stay behind. He receives the necklaces the white man gives him. The village people come back in the night, but they are still terrified by the arrival of this supernatural being who comes in a

---

9. It *was* a ficus, as I afterwards ascertained, and learnt at the same time that this tree does not at first spring direct from the ground. It is sown by a seed contained in some bird's excreta falling upon another tree. The ficus begins by using this tree as a support, and from this perch drops down a quantity of aerial roots, which, as soon as they reach the ground, sink into it and grow strong. Then by a process of anastomosis these roots are welded into a complicated network, which gradually envelops and strangles the original tree, so that it ends by entirely disappearing. The strangest thing of all is that, according to certain naturalists, a cross-section of a ficus trunk a few years old presents an absolutely homogeneous appearance.

boat that moves by itself and who has already disappeared the next morning . . .'

We listened to this tale under the great tree I have described. In its shade, which stretches as far as the river, a hundred or more people were seated, and among them the forty-five men we have chosen among the men of the village to compose our troop of actors. They were all grouped in concentric circles. There were three old hags and three old men who had lost all sense of shame; they were as naked as the Saras, but the men did not, like the men of that tribe, make the modest and absurd attempt of hiding their sex between their legs. A certain number were young and charming; one, dressed in a goatskin, came and sat beside us, and leant on our chairs.

Yesterday evening, at our request, there was an immense tamtam. People came crowding up from moment to moment. To begin with there were nothing but children; then finally everyone took a part in the dance. It began as soon as we got back from Pouss, and from the way they carried on, it was clear they would not be able to hold out long. This dance has nothing common with the slow, gloomy circling in which certain colonials pretend to see an imitation of sexual acts, and which, according to them, always ends in an orgy. It is clear, precise, rhythmical, like their dwellings – like everything I know connected with the Massas; and varied too. It begins with a strongly accentuated march, the heel of first one foot and then the other smartly striking the ground so that the crotala which the women tie above the calves of their legs are violently shaken. There is no languor. The girls and boys form two separate circles, which revolve in opposite directions.

I said 'crotala' for the sake of simplicity; in reality they are little funnel-shaped bags of woven rush, fastened off at the point by a plaited thread. The base of the bag is attached to a thin, sonorous disk of wood, upon which, at every shake, a handful of small gravel (held in a little cage) is thrown. This bag is so proportioned as to fit exactly the calf of the leg against which it rests. It is charmingly made, as perfect as Japanese wicker-work.

The tune changed at last and the dance grew animated. In the moonlight it ceased to be lyrical, and became frenzied – demoniac. Some of the women looked possessed. One old woman executed a solo in a corner by herself. She went on like a lunatic, waving her arms and legs in time to the tamtam, joined the circle for a moment, and then, suddenly giving way to frenzy, went off again to a solitary place, fell down, and went on dancing on her knees. A very young girl almost at the same moment left the circle, like a stone shot from a sling, made three leaps backwards, and rolled in the dust like a sack. I expected spasms and hysterics; but no, she lay a lifeless mass, over which I bent, wondering whether her heart was still beating, for she gave not a sign of breath. A little circle formed round her; two old men bent down and made passes over her, shouting out I know not what strange appeals – to which she made no answer. But the tamtam seemed to wake her; she suddenly revived; her strength, however, had left her; she dragged herself along, forced herself to dance, and fell down again for the last time on her side, her arms stretched out, her legs half bent, in an exquisite pose – and nothing succeeded in stirring her from it. Since the scene of exorcism among the Jewesses in Biskra which I have described in my *'Feuilles de route'*,[10] I have never seen anything more strange or more terrifying.

28 February

I have seen some of the bags I spoke of yesterday being made. A man was joining the ends of the rushes and closing the point of the bag with plaited threads. He worked with a stiletto, which lightly raised the other threads so as to enable him to introduce the thread that was to bind them together. This was threaded to a long needle.

I had not imagined there were several ways of threading a needle. But this one had no eye. It was merely a very long, fine splinter of a very tough textile plant. The end opposite the point was pliant and divided into filaments which were plaited up with the thread and dragged it along after the needle.

All last night the flying and calling of birds made a tremendous noise. Our boatmen slept in the shell huts – warm at last. We, in our whale-boats at the foot of a little cliff ten feet high, on which the town is situated. At the place where we moored, the cliff is nothing but a gentle slope, on account of the immense heap of garbage which is cast out of the town in order to keep it clean.

10. See *Amyntas*.

A gunshot, fired in the middle of the river, a cry uttered as one's boat strikes up against the low cliffs, re-echo again and again from shore to shore, up and down the stream, far into the distance – a prolonged rumour that starts a whole host of birds.

Went duck-shooting in a canoe at sunset. After the overpowering heat and blinding light of the day, what rest, what serenity! The sun disappeared in crimson behind a veil of mist. The sky grew golden and the water reflected its splendour. The Logone, which is about eight hundred yards wide, can be crossed on foot without losing touch of the ground. Not a flaw, not a wrinkle – nothing but the gentle fold in the water made by the skiff in which I was seated with Outhman and a guard, and which two tall Negroes steered with their poles, one fore and one aft.

When we took the names of the members of our troop of performers this morning, we were astonished at the numbers of boys and girls called Zigla. This is also the name of a familiar bush demon, whom the women who want children invoke (and sacrifice goats to). If afterwards they become pregnant, they make a vow to give the child the demon's name.[11]

Considerable tobacco plantations. The tobacco plants have white flowers and fine large leaves. There are quantities of fields – very small, but all the better cultivated – enclosed by wicker hurdles or little earth walls. The Massas sell their crops to the Bornouans or to the Haussas of Nigeria, who go about the country as commercial travellers.

The musical bar is in twelve time; the first note counts as two; the others are equal:

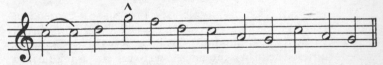

11. The names which the natives give their children often show their desire to save them from the evil spirits' notice or to appease their ill will. In M'Bochi: *Ilonguebé* (bad blood). In Ouolof: *Kenbougoul* (unwanted); *Amoul Yahar* (no confidence).

The first G is very much accentuated – almost shouted.

Another dance is accompanied by a melody which seems quite different owing simply to the fact that the A is replaced by B flat. The upper G is the only note that is pure.

Another:

and here again B flat replaces the A in the second part of the dance – and at that moment the C itself is replaced by an indistinct sound, intermediary between B flat and G, or composed of them both.

1 March

Yesterday evening another tamtam. Not so many people as the night before; the dances were as astonishing. It lasted two hours and then in a moment the place emptied itself and everyone went to bed. It was like a performance of rhythmic gymnastics.

In thinking it over last night, it seems to me that I transcribed yesterday's tune wrongly and that the intervals are greater than our tones, so that between C and the dominant below there is *only one note*. It may seem monstrous that I should not be certain of it. But imagine this tune yelled by a hundred persons, not one of whom sings the *exact note*. It is like trying to distinguish the main line among quantities of little strokes. The effect is prodigious and gives a polyphone impression of harmonic richness. The same need makes them put beads on the wires of their little 'pianos' – a horror of the clean sound – a need to confuse and drown its contours.

A short walk inland brought me unexpectedly to a very wide road of whose existence I was ignorant. When I got back to Moosgoum, I made inquiries. The road is intended to go to Laï. But as it is flooded every year by a sheet of water which reaches a depth of twelve feet in depressions and twenty inches in the raised parts, the probabilities unfortunately are that it will never be practicable. Every year, after the water has gone down, the natives have to work at banking and weeding it. All the able-bodied men are requisitioned for this work, which lasts at least a month. It is true that they are very poorly paid. The work has nothing excessive about it, and as it does not take them far from their village, they can go home to sleep every evening. They do not complain. But as for understanding the necessity of a precarious road like this that runs parallel with a river which does away with the need for porterage . . . !

I obtained the above information from a gigantic sultan in a dark-blue *boubou* and a white turban; an unimaginable number of amulets were hanging from a leather strap at his side (texts from the Koran in little red leather cases). He came from a neighbouring village with his suite and an interpreter to pay his respects. Charming, courteous, smiling, and well-mannered. He declared himself extremely satisfied and said he had never had any complaint to make against any Frenchman.

Sick of sleeping (at Mala) at the foot of a refuse-heap where the whole village empties its garbage, I decided to return to the very pleasant station of Mirebeddine. (I told Marc that we should catch something, and this morning, as a matter of fact, he got up with a bad sore throat and fever.) Two of our porters have got a kind of inflammation of the lungs. It is not surprising. What does surprise me is that any of them can hold out against the sudden variations of the temperature; this morning the air is a little warmer, but yesterday *after sunrise* the thermometer marked only 46° Fahrenheit. It must have gone as low as 40°. Then at ten o'clock the temperature leaps up from 58° to 76° or 85° and later goes up to 95° and even 98° (winter temperature). We are told that in the hot weather it reaches 122°.

We left directly after breakfast.

Our boatmen splash water on to the plate of burning metal on which they rest their bare feet. They are all coughing and spitting as hard as they can. Some of them went this morning to the market at Pouss; they have been replaced by lads from Mala.

We reached the station of Mirebeddine (a mile and a quarter from Moosgoum) at about two o'clock. Marc went to bed at once, his temperature is over 102°. After a siesta I made a little excursion to the neighbouring shell huts, which are particularly well made. In one of the principal enclosures (one goes in by a postern) a gigantic

vase-granary made me think of a stage setting for Rostand's
Chantecler.

I have arranged my whale-boat so as to be able to leave Dindiki in
it at night. All day long he lies like a compress, plastered against my
stomach, or clinging to my neck, and utters the most frightful
shrieks if I try to unfasten him. I have long ago given up tying him
by the leg; he turned and twisted to such an extent that in the
morning I used to find him half strangled by his string. I have tried
shutting him up in boxes, in hen-coops, in bags; but he was too
unhappy. If I left him free at night in my whale-boat – an island he
could not escape from – it was all up with my night's rest; for the top
of my mosquito-net was the spot he preferred for his gambols; he
thought it a delightfully elastic springboard, and leapt and bounded
and careered about on it, going on like a lunatic. At Fort Lamy he
could get from my room on to a terrace that had no outlet and where
there was plenty of room for him; but he always came to my bed; it
was my bed he besieged, trying to get under the mosquito-net,
teasing me with a thousand tricks, trying to force me to play with
him. When I was driven desperate, I used to get up and put him into
Marc's room, where he proceeded to torment him in the same way.
One night, when Marc left his door open, Dindiki took to his heels.
He made off downstairs, no doubt using the banisters. The boys in
the offices on the ground-floor found him next morning a long way
off in the branches of a small tree. During these last nights I had
relegated him to Zézé's whale-boat, which was kept apart from mine
by a pole; but Dindiki managed to use this pole as a bridge and found
me out three times running; finally I was so worn out that I popped
him into the dirty-linen bag. When I fetched him out in the
morning, what rapture! At last! He fastened on to my hand, my
arm, refused to let go even while I was dressing, even while I was in
my tub.

2 March

Last night Marc was 104°. I am horribly anxious. Haunted by the
spectre of recurrent fever which is raging in the neighbourhood. We
have made every arrangement to be able to get to the Logone-Birni
hospital in a hurry if things go wrong. I have moreover engaged a
double crew so as to avoid stopping at night. I had warned Marc of

the imprudence of sleeping at the foot of that mountain of filth, of going, as he did, into all the huts (but how much I like his curiosity!), of shaking every hand, of bestowing caresses right and left, and of stopping so long at night in the middle of the thick cloud of dust raised by the dances. His sore throat seems better. I have given him some aconite. He has not had a bad night (in spite of being disturbed by crowds of squeaking bats), and this morning his temperature has gone down to 101°. He is stopping in bed, but hopes to be able to get up and go on with his work tomorrow.

The boatmen in the big enclosure in front of the station hardly stopped coughing all last night. It was not very cold, but the wind got up. The feeling of their discomfort, for which I am indirectly responsible, kept me awake. How glad I am I bought an extra woollen blanket at Fort Lamy for each of our boys. But the thought that these poor fellows are passing the night beside me without any clothes on, their backs frozen by the north wind, whilst their fronts are roasted by the fire, and that they don't dare go to sleep for fear of waking up half cooked (one of them showed me the skin of his stomach this morning completely scorched and covered with blisters), and this after having toiled all day – is really too monstrous.

Bathed in the Logone a good way from the station, on a sandbank, in company with two egrets, a fishing eagle, and some small lapwings (?). It would have been perfect except that one is obliged to keep one's helmet on. Delicious feeling of comfort afterwards.

Des edlen Körpers holde Lebensflamme
Kühlt sich im schmiegsamen Krystall der Welle.

Marc's temperature has not fallen below 101°. If it goes up again this evening, we shall leave for Logone-Birni. He has a very severe headache again.

3 March

At about eleven o'clock yesterday morning I myself was seized with rather an odd sickness. While I was reading *Faust* in the veranda, I suddenly felt sleepy. I went to lie down on my bed and at once was seized with violent giddiness, cold perspiration, and sickness. Soon after came an attack of vomiting. I felt unwell till night-time. No fever.

Marc in the meantime again went up to 104°. Profuse perspiration and rather a bad headache.

At times I feel tottering on the verge of an abyss of horror. I think really that it was my violent anxiety for Marc that brought on my attack . . . unless bathing this morning? . . .

I am writing this lying down in the whale-boat, which I got back to with some difficulty, for the slightest movement makes me sick. I have again experienced that moments of respite between attacks of sickness are almost voluptuous. The body, even when it is on the verge of breaking down, may still find the mere sensation of *existing* almost delicious. Occasional oases of rapture between two attacks of misery.

We have sent a quicker boat on ahead to prepare the Logone hospital. Adoum's attentiveness and devotion are perfect.

CHAPTER TWO

❖❖❖❖❖❖❖❖❖❖❖❖❖❖❖❖❖❖❖❖❖❖❖❖❖❖❖❖❖❖❖❖❖❖

BACK AGAIN

I think I am better. I still have fits of giddiness, but I was able to sit at Marc's bedside and eat a little breakfast with him. Porridge and boiled rice, with some delicious stewed apricots (we have drawn upon our choicest stores), washed down with Vichy and Moët.

After this brief repast I went back to bed. And while I was trying to go to sleep, the boatmen in the stern – six Saras who have been with us since we left Fort Lamy (the other five in front are from Moosgoum) – began to chant the following words, which Adoum translated for me:

> The Governor[1] is ill.
> Row, row, that we may go quicker than the illness,
> And take him to the doctor at Logone

– the most extraordinary chant I have ever heard in this country. Oh, if only Stravinsky could hear it! It consists of a long phrase, beginning with a shout and ending almost *pianissimo*; but it is sung like a canon, so that the *fortissimo* of some of the singers coincides with the *pianissimo* of the others, which forms a kind of murmured bass. The notes are never *clean* (which makes it extremely difficult to take down the tune); just as in English there are no *pure* vowels. Our northern ears, which attach so much importance to *exactness*, find these sounds very difficult to understand. Here they never sing in tune. Moreover, when one of them sings 'do, re', the other sings 're, do'. Some of them sing variants. Out of six singers, each one of them sings something a little different, without its being exactly 'in

---

1. I have omitted to say that after Fort Lamy the boys, and with them the whole crew, promoted me. 'Commander' was no longer good enough. Or 'Governor' either. In their enthusiasm they called me 'Government'.

parts'. But the result is a kind of thickness in the harmony, which is extremely strange. The same phrase – nearly the same (sometimes with a little change after the manner of Péguy) – is repeated indefatigably for a quarter of an hour – for half an hour. Sometimes this song, shouted at the top of their voices, seems to go to their heads, and then they row madly, furiously. (This time we are going down the deep arm of the Logone.) How could I have said that the Saras do not sing? (Note, however, that they never sing when they are punting, but only as an accompaniment to the *regular* movement of the oars.)

Our popular songs, compared with these, seem coarse, poor, foolishly simple, rudimentary. This morning, in Marc's whale-boat, I listened to the Saras' chorus – very different from the one my boatmen were singing yesterday. It was like nothing I have ever heard. As profoundly moving as the songs of the Russian boatmen – perhaps more so. It began *pianissimo*, in a murmur, as though they were making a trial, and for some time they continued singing low – particularly the soloist. As always in this country, the chorus did not wait for the soloist's phrase to finish, but struck in on the last note and even sometimes on the last but one. The effect was astonishing. Little by little, as though gaining confidence, they became more and more animated. The soloist had an admirable voice, totally different in quality from what is required by the Conservatoire; a voice which sometimes sounded choked with tears – and sometimes seemed nearer a sob than a song – and sometimes had accents that are *hoarse and apparently out of tune*. Then there suddenly came a few very soft notes of a disconcerting suavity.

Adoum translated the chorus as follows:

> We are no longer taken away as captives,
> We are free to go where we please,
> To buy *boubous* and *fardas*.
> The white rule the country and they are kind.

The rest was improvised by the soloist as he went along.

Their rhythmical and melodic invention is prodigious (and apparently naïve) – but what shall I say of their harmonics? For that is what I find especially surprising. I thought that all the songs here would be monophonic. This is the reputation that has been made for them, for there are never any songs in thirds or sixths. But this polyphony, in its widening and narrowing of the sound, is so puzzling to our northern ears that I doubt whether it be possible to take it down with our means of notation.

The refrain is attacked on several notes at once. Some voices higher and some lower – like creepers winding round a central stalk, adapting themselves to its curve without following it exactly – like the trunk of a ficus.

4 March

Marc's fever has gone down; though he still felt very unwell last night, he is certainly much better. Ought we still to persist in going back?

We have at any rate decided to go on till we meet the head medical officer, who has been advised of our arrival and will be coming to meet us with medicaments. Marc will certainly not be fit to start travelling again or even working at the cinema for at least four or five days. We might as well spend them in this way; and if necessary go on to the infirmary and have our blood examined. We feel almost foolish to be getting better. We must really keep up our dignity in the eyes of the natives and not seem too much like weathercocks.

100° in the shade. If it were not for the draught in the *shimbeck*, we should perish. My whale-boat has lost its rudder, and my boatmen are extremely clumsy at keeping it straight, and especially at putting it straight. It heads into the rushes on the bank, swivels round on itself, and a great deal of time is lost. On this second day, however, we arrived at Logone-Gana about noon.

Nine or ten kilometres before reaching this village, we were delayed by a lugubrious sight. An Arab from the bush, who was going with one or two others to Fort Archambault to get work, was drowned almost before our eyes. The river is fordable in a great many places. At the very same place where his companions had just crossed, he lost his footing. A crocodile? They declare not. He simply 'didn't know how to swim'. Our people saw him raise his arms three times and call for help – and Adoum, who was watching from the whale-boat, thought he was fishing. 'Come quick and look at a fisher,' he called out to me. I looked for my spectacles for a moment, for I was reading. Then Adoum said: 'No, it's someone playing the fool.' It was someone who was drowning. When, a moment later, we wanted to go to his help, it was already too late. It may be imagined how impatient I was at the clumsiness of my boatmen, who let the whale-boat twirl round across stream and so lost the last hope of saving him – if there was still a hope. The Arabs, his companions, chattered volubly on the bank about the accident, but did not seem greatly affected by it.[2] For a moment I hesitated as

2. Here again I was extremely *naïf*. This is what I find in Lévy-Bruhl (*La Mentalité primitive*, p. 387 et seq.):

'What will be the feeling regarding those who have been quite close to "bad death", who have nearly succumbed . . . ? Will they be aided, will there be a helping hand held out, will the bystanders strive to accomplish the impossible to snatch them from a death which appears so imminent? . . . Primitives are nearly always driven by an irresistible instinct of fear and horror to do exactly the opposite . . . If anyone fell into the water accidentally, it was considered a great sin to help him out. Since he was destined to drown, it would have been wrong, in their opinion, to save him from his fate . . . If a man fell into the water in the presence of others, they would not allow him to get out again; on the contrary, they used force to make him drown, to make sure of his death.

'Can one imagine conduct more atrocious and inhuman? Nevertheless, just a moment before the poor wretch's life was in danger, his companions were ready to share everything with him, food, weapons, shelter, etc.; they would defend him if he needed defence, avenge him if a member of a hostile group did him a wrong – in short, they would fulfil, towards him as towards the rest, all the manifold obligations that the absolute solidarity of these communities demands. He falls into the water accidentally and is in danger of drowning, and immediately he becomes an object of dread and repulsion. Not only do they refrain from hastening to his aid, but if he appears to be saving himself, they prevent him; should he come to the surface, they drive him under the water again, if, in spite of all this, he does succeed in surviving his immersion, the social group refuses to admit that he has escaped death. They no longer know him; his membership is rescinded. The feelings he inspires and the treatment meted out to him recall the excommunications of the Middle Ages.

'All this is because cases of this kind are exactly like "bad death". It is not the death itself, nor the circumstances accompanying it, that terrifies the primitive mind; it is the revelation of the wrath of the unseen powers and of the sin for which these angry powers require expiation. Now when a man runs the risk of accidental death, the revelation is as clear and conclusive as if he were already dead. He has been "doomed", and it matters little that the sentence has not been carried out. To help him to escape would be to become a party to his wrongdoing, and draw down upon one's own head a like misfortune. The primitive dare not do it . . . The accident – which was no accident, since nothing happens by chance – is a kind of spontaneous ordeal. Just as the ordeal reveals to many of the African peoples the evil spirit imbuing such-and-such an individual, so does the accident betray the misdeed which has led to the culprit's being doomed by the unseen powers. In both cases, this terrible revelation brings about the same revulsion of feeling. In one moment the

to whether I should have the body looked for . . . But what would have been the good? They would nòt have buried it – and if it comes to a choice between caymans and hyenas . . .

A largish fish leapt out of the water between our boatmen's oars and fell into the boat.

Flocks of pelicans. Bruneau de Laborie says that certain of these flocks number more than a thousand individuals. I amused myself by counting the biggest and found 160 of them, which is not so bad. Bruneau de Laborie says there are two kinds – the grey and the white; but unless I am mistaken, the grey are young ones, as with swans.

What unforgettable hours! Captivity in a whale-boat! I am progressing in the *Second Faust* with rapture. I cannot re-read the dialogue with the Centaur without hearing Pierre Louys's voice reading it for the first time. (We were hardly out of *rhétorique*.[3]) I do not know whether he had discovered these admirable lines for himself; I think that probably his brother, George Louis, had shown them to him – but no matter.

Was Flaubert thinking of these lines when he wrote in the *Tentation*:

> 'Ici, Chimère; arrête-toi!'
> 'Non, jamais!'

With what religious *Schaudern* Pierre and I listened to Chiron's answer:

> . . . *Du stehst am Ufer hier,*
> *Ich bin bereit dich durch den Flusz zu tragen.*

And Pierre's lips and voice trembled with the fervour of his worship for Helen, as he uttered Faust's words:

---

man who was a companion, friend, and relative has become a stranger and an enemy, an object alike of horror and hatred.'

Authorized translation by Lilian A. Clare

This refers to the primitive natives of Kamchatka; but the same may no doubt be said of the peoples of central Africa.

3. About equivalent to the fifth form in an English public school.

Sie ist mein einziges Begehren . . .

words which were to dominate his life. This is how I like to think of him, now that distance has effaced many blemishes and imperfections; this is how I love him.

Long reading-lessons with Adoum. I am better. It has been terribly hot today.

Evening calm. This is the time Dindiki wakes up. Sense of pleasure in nocturnal animals.

> . . . Now is the pleasant time,
> The cool, the silent . . .

5 March

Camped yesterday at the same place we camped in on the third day of our journey out. A prodigious quantity of insects of all sorts (but no mosquitoes) assailed us at our evening meal. There was a thick coating of very tiny ones on the globe of our camp lantern. They get into one's eyes and ears, stick on to one's perspiring forehead, fall into one's buttered eggs and into one's glasses – most exasperating! There were some that were larger – earwigs, cochineals, a little mole-cricket, and an enormous mantis. I stuffed a number of them into my poison-bottle.

Marc's fever has almost gone, but it has left him very tottering and in a painful state of nervous irritation.

We started again at three o'clock in the morning. I was feeling rather curiously unwell. About eight o'clock the medical assistant came from Logone-Birni to meet us in a boat; he took specimens of our blood then and there. Half an hour later we arrived at the dispensary and we have taken up our quarters in the doctor's house, as he is absent.

Nothing whatever has been found in Marc's blood – or in mine either. A little abashed, both of us, at not being iller. Have written to Marcel de Coppet to reassure him and sent the letter by courier on horseback.

The weather is very trying; the sky leaden; the horizon lowering. The wind, which is fairly strong, is raising clouds of sand; the air seems full of it.

The chief came to visit us on our arrival. He is very amiable. Since we were at Birni last, he has lost his mother.

I was glad to see the three hospital assistants again; they are most attentive and obliging. Asked to see the boy with sleeping-sickness whom they hoped to cure, though he was in the third period; but he died the day after we left.

Adoum, after applying a plaster of cow dung to his sores, next put on the contents of the stomach of a newly-killed kid – a warm mash of grass. It was the first thing, he declared afterwards, that had done him good. I said I believed him. And this morning his sores really do look a little better. (He has one half-way up his leg and another on his ankle.) The contents of the kid's stomach formed a plaster which kept the places from unwholesome contacts. I proposed that he should go and have his leg dressed at the infirmary; but nothing would induce him to. He took out of his handkerchief a horrible powder (the dried remains of the stomach) which he is keeping in reserve; he powdered his sores with it after washing them with warm water, while our guard and an old Arab looked on and gave their advice.

Two of our boatmen have fallen ill.

Logone-Birni

This is a very large village, encircling the sanitary station on the river bank. A sordid place; quantities of houses that have fallen in; the enclosures round these ruined houses are filled with all sorts of refuse. The streets are filthy.

Like all the villages in this region, Logone-Birni is surrounded with walls (parts of them have fallen down, particularly on the side nearest the river); but the curious thing is the enormous stretch of waste ground that lies between the walls and the village. Its girdle fits it very loosely.[4] Enormous birds – carrion crows, marabous, eagles, perch on the ramparts; in parts of this waste ground there are marshes; in parts, trees.

---

4. This large piece of waste ground *intra muros* used to be reserved for cultivation in case of siege.

6 March

Nothing to note all yesterday. A day of waiting. Marc and I are depressed and weak. We learn that recurrent fever is again raging in the region of Maroua, through which we have to go. The medical assistant proposes that we shall take with us one of the hospital attendants who is going to make a round of inspection in those very parts, and who would be able in case of need to make the intravenous injections recommended against recurrent fever. I have written to the administrator of Kousséri to tell him and ask his authorization. I am anxious to get information as to the customs of the Massas and have been questioning Zigla, the very intelligent native who has been with us since Moosgoum. But one is never sure of understanding a native properly. In their endeavour either to say what they think you will understand, or on the contrary to avoid being pinned down, they arrange their remarks especially for your usage and adapt them to your questioning, however prudent and supple and cunning it may be.

The people of these primitive races, as I am more and more persuaded, have not our method of reasoning; and this is why they so often seem to us stupid. Their acts are not governed by the logic which from our earliest infancy has become essential to us – and from which, by the very structure of our language,[5] we cannot escape.

Yesterday a fresh visit from the sultan in his ceremonial get-up. A marvellous *boubou* of white *broché* silk with portraits of Edward VII scattered over it. On his shoulders he wore a big scarf of crimson and black *lamé* silk. Under his white *boubou* was a dress of canary-coloured silk. His head was covered with a sort of *bonnet grec*, slightly conical in shape and embroidered with different-coloured wools, like the wool-work caps of the days of Henri Monnier. While the medical assistant sent us a duck and a quarter of beef, the sultan on his part brought us an offering of young pigeons

5. During the early part of our stay at Brazzaville, I noted that the relation of cause and effect seemed not to exist for them. This is confirmed by Lévy-Bruhl, whose books on primitive mentality I made the foolish mistake of not reading till after my return. They would have spared me numberless errors and shed light in many dark places.

out of the nest, a kid, and food for all our porters. He seemed extremely desirous of pleasing us (and I think I produced the same effect on him). We each of us tried to say what would be most agreeable to the other and when Adoum, who acted as interpreter, transmitted some sentence which particularly touched him, he clapped his hands gently and silently to mark his heartfelt approval. Sometimes the guards who accompanied him imitated this gesture; for instance, after his photograph had been taken, when I told him that, not content with sending him a copy, I wished to keep one myself as a remembrance of his kind reception and of the extreme niceness of the people of Logone-Birni, I saw the three pairs of hands open and shut five or six times running, in time, up and down, down and up.

The town of Logone-Birni was for a long time the most important in the region; but it has been devasted by sleeping-sickness. And moreover in 1915, during the war with Germany, there was a great exodus of its inhabitants for Divel and Gofa. The quantity of deserted and ruined houses is explained besides by the fact that the Kotokos bury their dead in the enclosures round their huts and then abandon the house for fear of the evil eye. It is with the greatest difficulty that they are persuaded to use cemeteries.

One often hears talk of '*massâs*' – that is to say, 'corpse-eaters' – among these people. This is partly legend and partly fact; there are examples, it seems, of violation of graves that would be inexplicable otherwise.

All this information[6] was given me by young Lieutenant H., who arrived this morning on horseback, on his way to another subdivision.

7 March

Some difficulty in getting under way. Four more of our boatmen, besides the two others, have fallen ill (congestion of the lungs) – three of them too seriously for them to go with us. I gave them a line to Marcel de Coppet, which will ensure their being paid when they get back to Lamy. Thanks to the twelve extra Massas we recruited at

---

6. But here again Lévy-Bruhl makes me suspicious.

Moosgoum, we shall be able to get on, I hope, in spite of these defections.

Considerable numbers of tsetses. Outhman is prodigiously skilful at killing them, and ordinary flies too. He cuts off their legs with the blade of a knife which he slides up to them very quietly, as if he were shaving.

CHAPTER THREE

❖❖❖❖❖❖❖❖❖❖❖❖❖❖❖❖❖❖❖❖❖❖❖❖❖❖❖❖❖❖

SECOND ASCENT OF THE LOGONE

7 March

Left Logone-Birni this morning, taking with us the hospital assistant, Gabriel Loko, a German half-caste; he is an intelligent, attractive young fellow, who was going south on his service in any case. The air was once more pure and light; the light splendid. It was not too hot. But my whale-boat has again lost its rudder; the *capita* who is supposed to direct my ten boatmen is unfathomably stupid, and our progress despairingly slow, as we keep constantly heading from one side of the river to the other and the men do not even attempt to keep a straight course. I think we cannot be doing more than three kilometres an hour. The two other whale-boats are a considerable way ahead and will be impatient at having to wait for me. I submit without complaining, but at this rate it will take us a week to get back to Moosgoum.

I am reading Chekov's *Steppe*, in the translation sent me by Charles Du Bos, or rather the other stories that come after that very fine tale, which I had already read in English.

Our boatmen have been rearranged. The crews have been mixed; my incapable *capita* has been deposed, etc. . . . In short, there is a slight improvement.

After breakfast I was reading under my mosquito-net, when I was disturbed from *Samson Agonistes* by a strange noise like a waterfall. The whale-boat stopped. I came out from under my *shimbeck*. This noise of slapping water was being made by the wind in the fans of four big palm trees above our heads. Marc's whale-boat had stopped too. At that moment Adoum said there were hippos in view.

Marc, who had arrived a little before us, was posted on the lookout for them; our coming had disturbed the game for a moment, but they soon reappeared some way downstream. There were four of them quite close to us, and the river at this place is not at all wide. We climbed up the steep bank and peppered the poor beasts, who put up their snouts every five minutes to breathe. No apparent result, though some balls seemed to have hit. And then, suddenly, fifty yards away from us, up stream, appeared a fresh snout, more enormous than any of the others – and just beside it the snout of a young one, which Adoum declared was on its mother's back. What monsters hunters are! Marc fired, and this time there was a great eddy. Certainly the hippopotamus had been knocked over; it was one of its feet, not its snout, that came up again next and splashed the water about. Another ball; another somersault; all our boatmen on the bank and in the whale-boats were dancing with excitement. Then no more. We waited.

We waited till evening, on the assurance given us by our men that the monster was killed and that he would come up again with his belly uppermost; his not coming up to breathe was a proof he was dead. The strange thing was that the others, the four others, stayed obstinately in the same place, notwithstanding several further shots, as though they failed to realize their danger, or perhaps, like the *am'rais* and the ducks, so as not to abandon their wounded comrade.

I should like to know when it is that a hippopotamus can possibly sleep. It grazes all day. And in the night it lives in the water and is obliged to put its head up every five minutes to breathe.[1]

Night was coming on. We had to find some place where our boatmen could sleep. But as we were anxious not to give up, we determined to camp lower down the stream, in the hopes that the current would bring the hippopotamus's body down to us. So there we were going back again for the second time!

---

1. When I afterwards read Christy's excellent book *Big Game and Pygmies*, I was particularly amused to find that he had asked himself the same question about elephants. According to him, these great animals need very little sleep – hardly ever go to sleep.

We had not gone half a mile, coasting along the other (Chad) shore, when Gabriel rushed up to me in great excitement. 'A lion! A lion!' I sprang to the fore part of the boat, but saw nothing. 'There! Quite close to us. Lying in the grass. He's asleep.' And he pointed to something twenty yards off which I could not distinguish – much to his impatience. And if the beast was as near as he said, I was surprised it did not stir, for I had made a great noise by kicking over a canteen as I climbed on to the caisson. Marc's whale-boat was quite near. Armed with the Holland, he hoisted himself on to his *shimbeck*; at first, however, he could see nothing either; but suddenly, and really quite close to us, a good-sized lion rose to its feet. Three shots went off simultaneously. Not one of them took effect. But while I was watching the lion, which disappeared in a moment, something peculiar must have happened, for I suddenly saw four, five, ten men jump from the whale-boat into the river, diving in as quick as they could. Even Gabriel, with all his clothes on, jumped in. For a moment I was afraid it was an accident – someone drowning. It was only later that I understood what had happened. Marc, who was very unsteadily perched on the roof of the *shimbeck*, had lost his balance from the recoil of the Holland. He had only been able to catch on to the roof by letting go the gun, which had disappeared in the Logone; hence the men's precipitate dive.

After five minutes' search at the bottom of the water, the Holland was retrieved.

We are now camped on the Cameroon shore, exactly opposite the place we saw the lion, at the end of a very narrow island and almost in the water. I am afraid the night is going to be cold. All – nearly all – our boatmen are already coughing. Will the wood they have collected for their fires be enough? What is to be done? If there were a moon, we might go on again at once; but it is in its last quarter and only rises very late. Besides, they would be still colder in the whale-boats, even if they were rowing, and they prefer, they say, not to leave their meagre fires before morning. And not one of them complains – protests . . . On the contrary, even while they are coughing horribly – a loud, hoarse cough – they still smile. How well I understand that Coppet should have become attached to the Saras – excellent fellows that they are![2]

8 March

The thermometer is at 46° this morning. The Saras coughed, spat, wheezed, till late last night. In spite of the wax stopping I put in my ears, I could hear their breath whistling and rattling in their chests. Another two nights like last night and it would be all up with them. We must absolutely find a village where they can sleep in some shelter.

This morning, to make up for the bad night, there were great rejoicings – the dead hippopotamus was in sight. It looked like a heap of grass, a lump of earth, and formed a little island near the steep river bank. We sent one of the whale-boats to reconnoitre. Yes, there was no mistake! And our men leapt and yelled for joy.

We interrupted our breakfast and started on another whale-boat to go and look at the monster. It had drifted on to a shoal, from which it was dislodged with the greatest difficulty. The men pushed at it with their poles, all talking at once, but they could not succeed in coordinating their efforts and pushing together. These natives, who are so near nature and who, one would think, would be clever at such simple tasks, are incredibly clumsy and stupid whenever anything new has to be undertaken. Whilst they were all pushing on one side of the animal, one of them, who was on the whale-boat, stuck his pole right across in the opposite direction and considerably thwarted their efforts. Unfortunately those of us who would have been able to direct them did not know the language. Finally, however, the hippo, with a chain on its foot, got itself towed along by Zézé's whale-boat. We went into the other whale-boat and prepared the cinema. Unfortunately, the light was not good. At some distance from the shore, the hippopotamus foundered again. I saw its head for the first time, and for the first time understood the

2. I was glad to see the following passage in Bruneau de Laborie's account of his travels. Though he had at first been irritated by some of the African natives' defects – defects which are in vexatious contradiction to our own methods and customs – 'one afterwards discovers in these primitive beings,' he writes, 'unsuspected qualities of rude strength; one finds out that they are sensible to kindness, faithful in their attachments, grateful, and hospitable; their cupidity is capable of turning into unsuspected liberality and their selfishness into generous assistance.'

hugeness of its body. It took twenty men to roll it over, so that it showed in turn its back, its side, and then its pink belly, on which its short paws were daintily folded.

At last it got to the shore, and the work of cutting up began. Thirty-four men applied themselves to it with enthusiasm; they had three matchets and a few cutlasses – ridiculously small ones for such a task. Some of them held the limbs or pulled on the skin while the others cut. They all shouted, gesticulated, and danced about, but there was not the slightest dispute. Nothing but good humour and laughter. The cutting up, the slow, gradual dividing of the great bulk, lasted two good hours. The scouring of the entrails, the opening of the stomach, gave forth the most appalling smells. Luckily the wind was strong enough to carry them off. When the lungs were torn out, the blood issued from the *vena cava* like a long, purple serpent; I felt I was going to faint. Nothing was thrown away, nothing wasted. The vultures and eagles that hovered above us were disappointed. Every moment they became more daring; some of them, in a sudden, useless dart almost touched us with their wings . . . I went back to my whale-boat and took a glass of brandy to steady my inside. It was heaving with disgust.

Big as the animal was, Zigla tells me he has seen bigger. I should like to know its age. Perhaps one might calculate by examining its teeth, which I took away with me. I should like to see its brain; I would conquer my disgust in order to find out whether there were any of that hideous kind of worm which Ruyters told me he had seen in the cranium of the Abyssinian hippopotamus.

All the same, it was impossible to take it all away. We left behind us on the river bank the skull – which we gave up opening – one front foot and one back, and the pelvis. But the Kotokos came up in their canoes, only too delighted to wrest these titbits from the vultures.

At lunch we had hippopotamus steak – very good too, upon my word! Then we started off again in our whale-boats, which had been practically encased with raw meat. The smell is abominable, but it will be worse in a few days. In order to get to my bed, I have to scale a foot, and then climb a jaw and a big roll of skin thicker than any carpet. A heap of bleeding gobbets, of entrails, of unspeakably pestilential fragments, are spread out on the *shimbeck* to dry in the sun; and festoons of purplish strips are hung by long palm cords on the whale-boats' sides. Horror! it is raining blood through the roof of my *shimbeck*! And not only blood – worse! I gaze like King Canute at the red and yellowish drops, dripping on to the floor, the canteens, my bag, the top of my mosquito-net, under which I take refuge. But what is all this compared to the Saras' joy, their laughter, their gratitude!

Towards evening a kind of dry tornado; hardly any wind; the sun was overcast and the sky white and dull; the atmosphere became oppressive and the air seemed unbreathable.

Logone-Gana, 9 March

However agreeable a camping-place the sandbank on the shores of the Logone might have been for us, it was too dangerous for our boatmen, and we resigned ourselves to passing the night at Gana. We left the post hut to our men and slept in the charnel-houses that our whale-boats have been turned into. Adoum, however, has taken pains to clear mine of the most nauseous pieces. The floor is sticky with blood – or, more accurately, with the sanguineous liquid that flows, not from the pieces of flesh, but from the strips of skin that are carpeting the roof of the *shimbeck*. It needed almost courage to undress. A strong sickly stench pervaded the whole place, and when the wind is in the right quarter, there are sometimes mixed with it other unpleasant whiffs of a very obnoxious nature; for, as is often the case in these villages, we have been obliged to anchor near the post house, at the foot of a hillock composed of garbage and excrement. It is the village muck-heap and cesspool. On getting out of our boats we hardly knew where to step. When it is light, one can more or less choose; but tonight there was no moon, and the last globe belonging to our camp lantern has just broken.[3] The big lamps we brought with us were too complicated for the bush and have long since been out of repair, so that Zézé has to use the storm-lantern to do his cooking by. The consequence was that a little later, when I wanted to leave my whale-boat, I sank into a foul quagmire and was obliged to change my shoes, socks, and trousers – all the time groping in the dark.

3. A few days later we found another half-cracked one in a canteen.

It is astonishing that in spite of all this disgustingness we found a little appetite to do honour to the dinner that was waiting for us on shore, a little way off from the smells. Directly after dinner, with the help of the medical assistant, we gave the illest of our Saras a drastic treatment of cupping and blistering. The confiding way in which these poor fellows put themselves into our hands is touching. For lack of anything better, we were obliged to use our table tumblers for the cupping. When I left the station hut after looking to the patients, I failed to see where the terrace came to an end and tumbled right off it. Fortunately, refuse makes a soft bed. I didn't dare feel myself, but I sniffed . . . I was all right.

Extremely difficult to get a few calabashes of millet for our men's evening meal. 'There is none,' answered the chief, who looked a dull, stupid old fellow. He gave us the same answer when we spoke of sending a man on horseback to the next village to tell them to prepare cakes of millet for tomorrow night. 'In a canoe, then?' The chief declared the canoe would not get there before we did – which failed to convince me. But the guard who was with us explained, when the old fellow had departed, that he was a chief who had no authority over his men, that he was afraid of being disliked and didn't dare give them orders. However, as he was also afraid of displeasing us, he brought us three chickens and a few eggs – which of course we paid for; too much, if anything. The amount of millet that was brought was obviously insufficient, but it only meant that our men ate more meat. No doubt there will still be enough left to be pestilential.

I have omitted to say that we landed for a little before getting to the village. The country is monotonous: ex millet fields, sown with doum palms. Every fan of the palm has a vulture or a marabou sitting on it. Sometimes the palm tree is nothing but a skeleton on whose topmost withered branches are perched a few dislocated-looking marabous, which eye you up and down.

Immediately after leaving the whale-boat, I came upon the corpse of the poor man who was drowned the other day; it lay cast up on the bank, pale, swollen, and battered.

I shall not have drawn up an accurate balance of the day's

proceedings if I omit Browning and Milton. I re-read with delight, with rapture, some of the sonnets, the opening of *Samson*, and long passages of *Paradise Lost*; with less enthusiasm Browning's *In a Balcony*, of which I had kept a better recollection. It is often an advantage not to understand too perfectly. My imagination readily succumbed to mirage in those days and generously invested my uncertainties with the colours of enchantment. Now that I see more clearly, I am a little disappointed.

I lay down under my mosquito-net and read with a kind of frenzy (which ended by giving me a bad headache). I cannot remember having ever brought to bear on any text a keener, a more sensitive, a more perspicacious – or a hungrier – attention.

No doubt it was for Jules Romains[4] that Milton wrote:

> . . . Why was the sight
> To such a tender ball as th' eye confin'd?
> So obvious and so easy to be quenched,
> And not as feeling through all parts diffus'd,
> That she [the soul] might look at will through every pore?

Seized with a great desire for walking this morning. I can tell by that that I am better. The whale-boat dropped me with Adoum, the interpreter Zigla, and a guard, opposite the village of Divel. We were to meet again at Gofa, which there was every probability we should reach before the whale-boat. Our pace is as quick as the boat's and we should have the advantage of cutting across the bends of the river. Ten o'clock. It was already hot, but the air was light and almost sharp. I took my gun, and the guard had the Moser. On leaving the village I ignominiously missed some little brown ducks – the best kind.[5] That is, the one I wounded managed to get away, and the second shot was a misfire. These misfires are exasperating. A little while ago the Moser failed to fire six cartridges running. I must admit that when we bought the cartridges at Brazzaville, we were warned that they were the remains of the German stock and of bad quality. Next, it was against a herd of *am'rais* that we made proof of

4. Or for his friend Farigoule, the author of *La Vision extrarétinienne*.
5. No, I think now that the best are the bigger, black-crested ones, about the size of a goose, with green and brown-gold wings.

our incompetence. We had gone through an interminable field of tall grass along a narrow path, with our hands out in front to clear the way and with no view of anything but the next step, and came out on a vast space devastated by the yearly fire, where the young grass was already showing green again at the foot of the burnt stalks. As we raised our heads, we saw, two hundred yards ahead of us, the *am'rais*, who had already got scent of us and were looking up. At the first glance I could only make out two; but when, at the guard's approach, they fled – in single file, after the manner of the natives – I counted forty-eight or fifty of them. They ran for a few yards, then stopped and turned round; curiosity seemed to get the better of fear. A shot went off; they all bounded forward; the order of the troop was by then a little broken. Some of them leapt high above the burnt grass, no doubt to get a better view of the situation. But they did not go far and again turned round to look. They seemed to be waiting, to be inviting you to pursue them. We watched these manoeuvres from a distance; they would have continued, but we shouted to the guard to come back. The sun was beginning to be unpleasantly warm and we did not wish to risk missing the whale-boat.

A little farther on, two big black ducks. Ashamed of my first miss, I passed the gun to the interpreter; but his luck was no better than mine. The ducks flew away before they were within range.

A little later another herd of *am'rais*. This time it was Adoum's turn to miss them.

As we were walking, we picked up some little fruits of the colour and shape and size of dates. They were lying under small bush-like trees. The kernel, which is protected by a thin, fragile envelope, is covered with an extremely thin layer of pulp; this is dry, sweet and pleasant to the taste, and slightly subacid. One's teeth are set on edge, for the pulp adheres to the stone; agreeable enough when one is thirsty.

I waited patiently on the same bank on which Marc photographed the children who were fishing. The stench of the hippo meat is now so strong that one can almost smell the whale-boats before seeing them. I understood as I was waiting why I had been so anxious to do the road on foot.

*

Zigla, who had left me for a moment to go and negotiate with the chief of Gofa for some millet, came back without the cakes and with my gun broken. I am sorry I lent it to him. Adoum had forgotten to tell me that the fastening of the shoulder-strap had given way and been mended with a little piece of wood instead of the metal buckle. We ought to have carried it very carefully; it suddenly fell off Zigla's shoulder. I should never have thought that the butt of a gun would break with falling such a little way. 'We shall be able to patch it up with string,' said Zigla, who, I thought, might have been a little more apologetic. But natives who possess nothing . . .

Now it is the *capita* of my whale-boat — that is to say, the man who replaced the one who was so incompetent — who has fallen ill. I found him shivering at my bedside beside the little Sara whom we had cupped. They soon both went off to sleep; so did I, under my mosquito-net, after a little dose of Milton.

At four o'clock we stopped at the village of Karsé (Cameroon). I got on to Marc's whale-boat for tea. It was in this village that we first saw women with plates adorning their lips. They belong, it seems, to the Massas who have fled from their villages in order to avoid working at the Moosgoum road. They are preparing to come back, we hear.

The natives, according to Zigla (one of the most intelligent blacks we have yet met), have got more wives nowadays, because in cases of contention or repudiation they find it easy to get the white judge to support them in recovering the marriage money; moreover, they are no longer afraid of raids; and finally and especially because, when the tax has to be paid, if the village chief says to a native: 'You have several oxen, you must sell one to make up the capitation fee,' he cannot say the same of wives. So it is better to buy a wife than an ox. (We may add that the native makes the wife work and not the ox.)

The Kotokos complain that when last we went by, our boatmen carried off two of their poles. The latter admit it. We offered to give two francs per pole. The Kotokos shrugged their shoulders. They need the poles and ask that they should be returned. Nothing is more difficult to find in this country than tree-stems nearly sixteen feet long.

10 March

Kolem. Spent the night here out of devotion to our men. They were able to sleep under shelter. The night, for that matter, was not so cold. But it is impossible to imagine a more sordid village. Besides the unspeakable filth of the yards in the houses and streets, there are the stagnant ponds (I think I have mentioned them), the cesspools, and rubbish heaps, where the village empties all its garbage and manure, and which give Kolem its picturesqueness and its peculiar hideousness.

In order not to disturb our patients too early in the morning, we have agreed to put off our arrival at Moosgoum until tomorrow. We shall spend the night at Mazéra. One becomes resigned to this slowness. What does one day more or less matter? I have never read better nor more rapturously. The monotonous landscape soothes one's mind without distracting it. But sometimes the lookout signals a herd of *am'rais*; then we put in to shore; we climb the bank; the immense plain (ah, how I should like to see this country under water!) flickers and vibrates in the burning sun. I leave Marc to hunt the *am'rais*, and sit and gaze at the grey-green stream and its fringe of reeds.

I have learnt to beware of these reeds. In this country, grass cuts, trees scratch, creepers tear. A fortnight ago I tried to hoist myself up the bank by catching hold of the reeds, and ever since I have had two whitlows on my middle finger, which refuse to heal. They are caused by the almost invisible little velvety hairs which the reed leaves on your finger. These little barbs must be hastily extracted or one is punished by an abscess forming, which is small at first, but which grows, suppurates, turns into a boil or a whitlow, a foolish, horrid thing, which makes one clumsy with one's knife, one's fork, one's fountain-pen – and still more with one's gun.

Marc met me at Mazéra,[6] which I reached on foot. He had to wait on the shore a long time for his whale-boat. His long hunt after

6. The last Kotoko village.

am'rais in the burning sun had tired him, but at any rate he had killed a fine male. As for the ducks, they are, so to speak, invulnerable; their feathers wrap them round in a hard casing, and small shot slips off it.

Innumerable herds of *am'rais* on every side. I saw three quite close to my whale-boat, coming down to the river to drink. Gabriel, the hospital assistant, went after them.

Out of the thirteen occupants of my whale-boat, four are ill. They never stop coughing and spitting – a frightful hoarse cough.

It seems, from what the chief of this village (a very nice man) says, that the *chef de canton* (the very same who came to pay his respects in a boat, when we passed the first time) is expected to come tomorrow, in order to collect the tax (eleven francs per head), and that he insists on the whole of the payment being made in 'white money' (i.e., in marks).

I know that as the mark is no longer current, the administration is trying to call it in, and I understand that half the payment of the tax should be exacted in 'white money', and that amount the village chief says he is able and willing to find. But the whole amount, he says, is impossible. There is not enough of it – and even what he manages to get fetches here double the yellow token – that is to say, each mark has to be bought with two francs (tokens). The capitation tax is in this way doubled.

I have noted the name of this *chef de canton*, and I shall be curious to hear whether he is doing this with the knowledge and approval of the *chef de circonscription* – to whom I shall repeat the matter – or whether, as I fear, he puts the surplus into his own pocket.

We have decided to wait till tomorrow for the arrival of the *chef de canton* and to send him word, so that he may not delay too long. The village where he is staying is not more than an hour away, but our messenger cannot start before tomorrow at daybreak, for it is not safe to go out at night on account of lions.

11 March

The abominable stench makes night in the whale-boat a serious trial. The vexatious thing is that our men (not all of them at any rate) did not take the chance we gave them of sleeping in the village huts, a hundred yards away. In the middle of the night I got up and dressed to go and see why the men whose cough was keeping me awake preferred camping on the river bank; there were ten of them round three fires. One of the guards, Zézé, and the kitchen boy were warming themselves at the first. 'The village is too far,' said the guard. Round the second fire three Saras were dozing; round the third, Gabriel, Outhman, Adoum, and Zigla were fast asleep. But at any rate these latter have blankets. I think they have a horror of camping-places because of the lice, and a still greater horror of the Kotoko huts, where recurrent fever has lately been raging. This is what Gabriel ended by admitting. Recurrent fever is transmitted by lice;[7] he knows this, and that lice born of the contaminated lice can transmit the disease without themselves having been in contact with contaminated persons. None of this is very reassuring, and last night, feeling tormented by an odd kind of itching, I took some rhoféine to send me to sleep. Besides which, my bed is not steady and its thin mattress projects so as to touch the matting of the *shimbeck*; it is no longer an island and I no longer feel safe.

Imagine what life in a whale-boat is like! Among barrels, canteens, bags, toilet things, guns, stoves, provisions, etc.! And mine is occupied during the daytime by thirteen men (myself included), four of whom are ill. If an object chances to fall and slip between the laths of the movable flooring, one hardly dares fetch it up out of the nauseous liquid swimming at the bottom of the boat – which it is exceedingly difficult to clean, as there is no means of draining it.

Yes, however perfect a place for reading and meditation a whale-boat may be, I shall be glad to leave this one. It was all right till the hippopotamus came, but since the boatmen have hung us all round with these stinking festoons, one hardly dares breathe.

I got up before day-break, and in the cold early morning (46° under the *shimbeck* and 41° outside) I watched the arrival of the *chef*

7. Or, more correctly, by ticks.

de canton we were waiting for. He was accompanied by seven men; all on horseback; all fairly well dressed; he himself particularly decorative. The crossing of the river was very fine; the horses did not lose their footing, but the water was breast-high.

We hurried over the interview a little, as Marc wanted to go and shoot *am'rais*. But what was the need of much talk? The chief reassured us in a few words. It was certainly a misunderstanding. There was never any question of exacting the whole payment – or even the half – in marks. They pay what they can in marks, and the rest in francs.

As the chief of the village came up at that moment, I made the *chef de canton* repeat these reassuring statements before him, and we went out shooting, hoping the incident was at an end.

We came back empty-handed from our expedition and left Mazéra; after we had been going up the river for about two hours, the Mazéra chief (or, rather, one of the village notables sent by him) caught us up; we had no sooner gone than the *chef de canton* repeated his demands – he will accept no payments but in marks.

I immediately returned him the little bunch of egret feathers which he had given me (he had offered me a quantity; I had thought it disobliging to refuse them all, but had taken care to select the smallest; 'as a souvenir of our meeting,' I had said through the interpreter), I did 'not wish to keep the present of a liar'. Besides which, I immediately wrote to Thiébaut, chief of the circumscription of Kousséri (to which these villages belong) to inform him of the business.

I should be very curious to know what the end of this dispute will be – another chapter in the tale of deceptions.[8] It is one of the drawbacks of this journey that one has to leave behind one the answers to the questions that are raised.

And then I plunged back again into *The Flight of the Duchess*, which amuses and delights me much more than the first time I read it, when I did not understand it so well.

8. I learnt soon after that M. Thiébaut had done what was necessary to put an end to this abuse. Sad to say, I also learnt some months later that this excellent official had been carried off by an attack of bilious fever in one of the post houses of the long road we had just travelled over, when on his way home with his young wife.

The poor *capita* of my whale-boat is very ill. Pneumonia, says Gabriel. I had not thought it was so serious and had not seen him for some time. He is icy cold, in spite of being in the burning sun, and wet with perspiration. He breathes with difficulty and his pulse is very weak. Gabriel has just given him some ipecacuanha. It will be a relief to him to be sick, but fatiguing, and perhaps we shall have to give him an injection of caffeine. I have told Marc's whale-boat, which has the medicine chest on board, to keep close behind ours, well within hail.

With great difficulty we have cleared enough space to open a deckchair in the fore part of my whale-boat, where the sick man can be put. There have had to be moved: several canteens, two sacks of millet I have just bought from some passing traders, the hippo's jaws, some mats, some oars, two cases of films, the dirty-linen bag, the broken rudder, the half-burnt logs of wood, which the men are taking with them in view of the next camp-fires – for wood is rare. The patient's temperature is not more than 100°. As we hope to get to Moosgoum this evening, where we shall be able to have the whale-boat washed, I have told him to be sick where he is, for he is really too weak to lean over the side of the boat. What trust, what resignation these poor blacks show! But never a word or sign of thanks. I have often asked how one said 'thank you' in such or such native dialect. 'There is no such word,' is the answer.

Every day there are fresh cases of illness. The youngest of our boatmen has an abscess in his ear. I have put in a dressing soaked in carbolic glycerine (our medicine chest is of some use at any rate) which I was using myself a few days ago. And don't let anyone talk of malingering, for the little fellow goes on with his work all the same, and very courageously.

The water must have gone down considerably since we first passed (on our way back from Logone-Birni, we took the deep arm of the Logone). The whale-boat sticks in the sand two or three times an hour; all the boatmen jump into the river and haul and push for a long space of time. One hears the creaking of the metal on the wet sand. A curious mode of locomotion!

And quench its speed in the slushy sand.

Notwithstanding the efforts of our boatmen, we shall not be able to get farther than Ghamsi today. We have been greatly delayed by my having to write to Thiébaut, about the traffic in marks, and then by this constant sticking in the sand. Marc gave up hope of arriving at Moosgoum the same evening a little too soon perhaps. And then the man who was best able to steer the boat between the sand-banks is the very one who is ill. I have said that I told him he might be sick in my whale-boat, feeling certain that I should not have to sleep in it again. This forced halt is horrifying. But there is nothing to be done; our men, notwithstanding the best of wills (and the Massas of Mirebeddine were very anxious to get to their homes this evening), are really done up. We must spend the night here, exactly in the same place where we camped a fortnight ago, near the little island overgrown with bushes, where the egrets haunt (which I mentioned) at the foot of a hill made of oyster-shells – the enormous shapeless oysters which one finds on the banks of the river (and which I did not mention).

We went to the village to look for shelter for our men. We visited hut after hut and bribed a few old women to turn out. The *capita*, in a tottering condition, has been helped by one of his companions to the best of these huts; he has the vague, unseeing eyes of a dying man.

We took our evening meal on the river bank, by the light of the stars and a fire which was made up close by. Really this evening one feels rather distraught. I had found the heat very trying towards the end of the day and had a bad headache. But Zézé served us a duck, shot by Outhman, cooked to a turn, and capable of making one forget anything.

The appearance and smell of my whale-boat were such that I hesitated a moment whether I should not have my bed made up on shore (I must add one thing more to the rest of the horrors: being convinced that we were going to sleep at Mirebeddine, I had given Dindiki, who was constipated, a purge!). But the wind got up. We had to resign ourselves. At any rate I took a dose of Soneryl to give me a little saving oblivion.

*

The *capita* died last night. Gabriel came to tell us about three o'clock this morning. It was too late to try an injection; his heart had stopped beating. I was afraid yesterday that in the state of weakness he was in, the Sedobrol which we gave him (and yet it was a very small dose) ran the chance of sending him to sleep for ever; but at any rate it made his passing easier. From what his brother, who watched the night with him, says, he does not seem to have suffered much, or to have realized he was dying. An injection would only have been a temporary stimulus. He could not have been saved without the nursing and care we were unable to give him.

In the early morning we went to the hut where the poor fellow was resting at last. What a miserable existence his has been! He was lying there on a mat beside a small fire, completely wrapped up – shrouded – in a blue *boubou*, from which his bare feet projected a little. Four Boas (men from his village) were crouching round the fire near him. The sun was rising as we left the hut (the door was so low that we had to stoop). His brother has chosen a little site not far from the village for his grave. Kara was about forty years old. He was the eldest son of a large family. One wife survives him, but no children. He leaves life without a hope, and all his life he no doubt never had a hope of anything but of earning more than one franc fifty a day. It was he who accompanied Powel Cotton, the English big-game shooter, to the Chad. He showed us his chit.

The Saras and the Boas finished digging the grave. The earth was very hard and they had no tools but two small hoes made of a thin bit of metal, fastened at an acute angle to a forked branch.

The dead body was carried to the spot and put for the time being on the ground beside the hole. It was completely enveloped and tied round in a cloth. They then fetched branches, on which, it seems, the body has to rest so that it may be a little isolated from the immediate contact of the earth.

We left Ghamsi about eight o'clock. I read diligently during the whole journey.

When we reached Moosgoum, we landed to look at the village again, and we did the remaining two kilometres which separates it from Mirebeddine, on foot.

Amid the surrounding barrenness and after this second long

ascent of the Logone the station of Mircbeddine seems to us like a haven of grace. A fresh case of pneumonia has broken out among our boatmen. This time, at any rate, we are taking precautions. But the poor fellow, so young, and strong-looking, has a high fever and seems very seriously ill. We cupped and Gabriel blistered him, but not very successfully; then we made applications of iodine.

It appears from the sick man that the night before last at Mazéra, when it was so cold (I got up to see who the men were who insisted on sleeping in the open), the *capita* who has just died felt too weak and ill to go to the village (barely a hundred yards off) and had stayed shivering all night beside a fire. And the fresh patient had caught cold from staying with his friend and refusing to leave him. It would have been so easy to have had the *capita* carried to the village, if only we had known, if only he had spoken! But these poor people wait till the last extremity before complaining. Indifference, apathy, resignation, familiarity with wretchedness, and perhaps the fear of being rebuffed, of being considered discontented, molly-coddles, malingerers. The example of such self-sacrificing friendship, so simple, so modest, which the poor boy will perhaps pay for with his life . . .

An excellent nap has completely restored me. I had no sooner got up than the sultan of Mala made his appearance with a numerous suite. The sultan is an enormous lump of a man. One shuddered at the idea of offering him a seat. We have not a chair – neither deckchair nor English armchair – that would not break down under his weight. It was a great relief when we saw one of his servants step forward with a solid affair, specially designed for his use.

After the first compliments had passed, delivered by means of two interpreters, I inquired as to the value of marks in this country, and as to their greater or less abundance. We are here in the Chad territory. The mark, we were told, is current as well as the yellow French franc, and payments are made indifferently in white coins or in French yellow tokens. But in the country of the Fellatas (Cameroon) the mark is at a premium, and when people here trade with the other side of the river, the Fellatas demand ten centimes more than the yellow franc for a mark. What a trade the Fellatas must drive! The mark, which iş here worth one franc ten, is worth two francs at two days' march from here.

I was anxious to see whether I could bring a smile to the sultan's lips, and made Adoum relate the shooting of the hippopotamus, then its cutting up and the appalling smell of our whale-boats, which had been turned into tanneries. The story was highly successful. The whole suite (fifteen men) joined in the sultan's laugh.

'This shows,' he ordered the interpreter to say to me, 'that you are a great chief. A small chief would never have borne such a thing for the sake of his men.'

As I noticed that he was holding a whip in his hand, I asked whether he would like some hippopotamus hide. My offer seemed to delight him. More laughter and amused exclamations among the suite when I added that I was sure he would never use a whip to his men. So a huge piece of hide was taken out of the whale-boat's caisson (I didn't know it was there), and enough cut off to satisfy the sultan.

13 March

The natives' *indiscretion* can no doubt be explained by their *want of reserve*: one offers them a cigarette – they take the whole packet; a cake on a dish and they take the whole dish.

We set to work rather late to have our whale-boats cleaned out. The luggage was unloaded and arranged more or less tidily on the veranda – cases to left, tins to right, barrels in the middle. By the vacillating light of the camp lantern's candle (the globe is broken) the post house looks like the day after a shipwreck.

Our patient is better; his temperature went down in the night from 104° to 96°; but he is still far from cured.

I have sent a courier to Lamy with a letter to the Ouham and Nana Company to announce Kara's death and settle up his affairs. I have also written to Coppet in order to make sure that they will be settled up *properly*. After this we decided to go to Mala in one of the whale-boats. It was extremely difficult to get boatmen. Most of them tried to get out of it. I explain this sudden (and momentary) defection of men who are usually so obliging, as follows: the Ouham and Nana Company are in the habit of paying by the journey and not by the day. They get so much from Lamy to Moosgoum and from there to Bangor. What we asked for was an extra, which would not be counted to them. A few words of explanation would have avoided the delay caused by the men's disappearance this morning; but we only got to the bottom of it later. I am writing to Coppet about this too, so that the poor fellows may not be cheated; and a few *matabiches* will recompense them for their willingness.

CHAPTER FOUR

❖❖❖❖❖❖❖❖❖❖❖❖❖❖❖❖❖❖❖❖❖❖❖❖❖❖❖❖❖❖❖❖❖

SECOND STAY WITH THE MASSAS

It gives me the keenest pleasure to see Mala again. It is certainly one of the most astonishing things we have seen in our journey, and even one of the finest I ever saw. The inhabitants of Mala are charming; they seem sincerely pleased to see us again (it must be admitted that we rained a good many small coins on them).

The gravity of the forms, the subtlety of the colours, remind one of certain of Corot's Italian pictures. (I am thinking particularly of a view of the Forum.) This village would have charmed him. The relations of the tones and the masses, the soft blue of the sky, the grey pink of the walls of the houses, the dash of green given by a few enormous, admirably spreading trees in the open places, the greenish grey-blue expanse of the Logone, seen through a breach of the *carnak*,[1] all contribute to the enchantment.

The light and heat have been extremely trying lately in the afternoons. And for the last few mornings the sun has not come out of its limbo before ten or eleven o'clock.

In the evening and at night there is a barrier of fire in the distance along an immense stretch of the horizon. And here and there on the opposite horizon there are great red gashes which denote more fires still farther off.

14 March

We are stuck. The sun does not shine; the earth has no shadows; the light is soft and silvery – a Scotch light, and totally unsuitable for filming. Marc is in despair, and so am I, out of sympathy.

1. Town wall.

Our patients are decidedly better.

Some children (one boy in particular, a protégé of Marc's, about twelve years old, astonishingly robust and admirably proportioned, not so much a faun – in spite of the goat's skin round his loins – as an infant Hercules) brought me some coins to change. The franc is at a premium; at any rate they wanted to exchange their two-franc and their fifty-centime pieces for French one-franc tokens. Their cheeks were stuffed with coins, for their habit is to use their mouths as purses or money-boxes, out of which they extract their small economies, bathed in saliva.

At Mala we requisitioned ten film-performers, who arrived by canoe this morning, as had been arranged. But the light was so bad that nothing could be done but rehearse. The scene was laid in the compound of the Mirebeddine village chief (he is Zigla's father). Different episodes of everyday life were gone through, some of them exceedingly successful. The infant Hercules was admirable when he climbed up to the top of one of the gun-shell huts, step by step. The proceedings, however, were somewhat interfered with by the sixty or so village notables and other curious onlookers, who crowded into the enclosure, pressed round us, offered their help and advice, got in the way, and – worse than all – spat all over the place. Some of the actors proved incompetent; they had to be replaced, and Marc asked for volunteers among whom to choose. Thirty-two little boys and girls were brought up and a board of inspection was organized in the veranda behind the station hut. An almost intolerable odour of dried fish exuded from all these oiled and naked bodies.

It cannot be said that the custom of piercing the lips is disappearing. All the girls, as soon as they are barely nubile, begin to wear plates; the single exception is Zigla's sister. Zigla's father refuses to allow his daughter's lips to be pierced, but the girl herself is in despair, because she is convinced she will never find anyone to marry her with lips 'like a boy's' and she means to take advantage of her father's next absence to disobey the paternal commands.

The flocks of pelicans are most beautiful; every evening they fly through the purest of skies to the sandbank where they pass the night. They make a very long, gently undulating line, following each other one by one, at equal distances. Minute after minute a fresh flock deploys over the gold of the setting sun. I amuse myself by counting them. Once I counted eighty-six; another time more than a hundred.

15 March

The light was a little better this morning. The thick haze which overcast the sky turned into a nimbus of clouds.

Much grieved to hear that our principal patient is not so well; his temperature has gone up again. Yesterday we thought he was almost cured.

All the sick men this morning came to take refuge round the one and only fire in the kitchen; they kept spitting for all they were worth. Not very appetizing! But, on the other hand, they cannot be left without a fire. We proposed sending our boatmen, who have nothing to do, to 'make wood' in the bush; but we are told they would have to go more than ten kilometres before finding any. And yet there are a good many trees to be seen in the surrounding country – taboo, no doubt. The natives only burn cakes of dried dung and millet stalks.

I am trying to go on with *Faust*, after having abandoned it a week ago for Milton and Browning.

The sky has cleared. Marc was able to do some good work this evening. It is terribly hot. After one's siesta, when one goes out on to the veranda at about three o'clock, the light and temperature and peculiar quality of the atmosphere is such that one is overcome with dizziness – a kind of burning at the back of one's neck – a kind of heat-stroke. One looks at the thermometer – only 96°. One reflects with terror that it may go up to 113° (even to 120°, Coppet said). The air is so dry that the soft leather binding of the *Concise Oxford Dictionary*[2] has begun to curl up.

At sunset I went out to shoot partridge, of which Marc told me last night he had seen a flock in the neighbourhood. I brought back

2. When they heard that I was going to start on a long journey, the Clarendon Press were so exceedingly kind as to send me this book, by the good offices of Abel Chevalley; it proved of the utmost value to me.

two; but it was Outhman who shot them. I had to hand him over the gun, as it was too dark for me to see.

Zigla has mended the rifle butt that he broke, very prettily, by wrapping it round with a tight bracelet of kid-skin.

Some curious dragonflies kept in front of us; they had a black or dark-red spot on the tips of their transparent tulle wings (at least as far as I could see in the dusk). What surprised me was to see them coming out at this hour of the evening, for I did not think there was any kind of twilight dragonfly.

16 March

Yesterday there was a little insubordination among our men. Some of them refused to go and gather millet stalks, to make fires for our patients, in default of wood. The distance was too long. One of the *capitas* declares that he cannot touch the millet balls that are brought from the village – the women with plates in their lips who make them slobber over them, and it disgusts him. (I quite understand!)[3] He prefers grinding the millet himself and cooking it as best he can. Finally one of the boatmen demanded that we should insist on Zézé's paying him the remaining nineteen francs which he still owed him out of the thirty-four he won from him yesterday. The game is a kind of heads or tails, which is played with little shells. I do not know whether it is possible to cheat at it, but the boatman, it seems, won uninterruptedly. I have my suspicions. But Zézé had only to stop playing after he had lost the fifteen francs he had in his pocket (he had just asked us to pay him his month's wages in advance). The boatman, after having won these fifteen francs, lent them to him and then won them back again. Gambling, nevertheless, is forbidden. I told them so, and that at Fort Lamy their stakes would have been confiscated, and they themselves locked up in prison. They know it. I have forbidden the boatmen for the future to play with our boys. (Adoum, who has already burnt his fingers, refrains.) Zézé is to pay another five francs, which I shall stop out of his wages, and the other man, who has already won too much, is to hold his tongue. The incident dragged on for some time; the

3. I think now that I credited these people with sentiments of which they are incapable. No doubt it was not a matter of disgust, but of respect for the 'appurtenances', of which the saliva is one. See Lévy-Bruhl on this matter.

boatman went through a little farce of weeping, refusing to take the five francs, etc.

One of the principal traits in the native's character is his inability to lay by. The little he has he spends at once on drink, food, or play. When I spoke to Governor Lamblin about the possibility of introducing savings-banks into the colony, 'That is one of the most important – I should like it to be one of the first improvements to set about,' he answered, 'but I fear the natives are not yet ripe for it.' The best thing, no doubt, would be to enable them to make purchases that are not mere waste of money.

This morning the weather was splendid. Marc took a great deal of trouble to get a film of the natives rising in the morning and the cows and goats coming out of the huts; but they were all at sixes and sevens; and when things began to go a little better, the sun was too high, the shadows too short, the light too glaring; the atmosphere of early morning had disappeared.

On the whole, it seems to me that the best part of these photographs (and there will no doubt be a great deal that is excellent) will be things that have been taken by a happy accident – gestures, attitudes, which were just those one did not expect. The parts that were prepared beforehand will be, I am afraid, a little stiff, a little made-up. I feel as if I should have gone about it differently, and given up all idea of scenes and tableaux, but kept the camera in constant readiness to take the natives unawares, busy at their work or their play; for all the grace goes from anything when one tries to make them do it over again. More often than not it is after Marc has stopped turning – immediately after – that the naïve, delightful, uninventable, unrepeatable actions occur. A mother was told to give her child something to drink; she did so, more or less skilfully, and had to be instructed to incline the calabash a little more to the right or the left. Then, directly after, I saw her put the calabash down on the ground and take up a handful of water and let it stream over her thumb, which stuck out like a teat, into the baby's mouth – a charming action, quite unknown, I believe, to our French mothers, however rustic. But unfortunately Marc had stopped turning. We tried to get it repeated. But the child was no longer thirsty; it began to cry, to struggle . . . The woman's hand came in front of the child's face; the action was no longer comprehensible; nothing was the same. Ah! why couldn't he have caught the whole scene impromptu? Everything that is dictated becomes constrained.

I have just discovered that my little Dindiki is mentioned in Cuthbert Christy's excellent book, *Big Game and Pygmies*, p.240: 'The potto is very slow and deliberate in his movements. "Deliberate" is perfect. He is comparatively rare.'

Did I say that the messenger whom I sent to Carnot from Fort Archambault with orders to bring me back a pair came back without having succeeded?

I read in the same book, p. 281: 'In Africa the forest natives are full of little items of observation that delight the field naturalist.'

This encourages me to accept as true what the natives told me about Dindiki's habit of strangling monkeys, which are often much bigger than he; this is understandable, for the monkeys are asleep at the time Dindiki goes on the prowl. He has a powerful grip, and once he has taken hold, nothing can make him let go. The monkey is taken by surprise from behind, and when Dindiki creeps along the branch and seizes him by the neck, he is no doubt unable to defend himself . . . Curious to know whether Dindiki sucks their blood . . .

This afternoon, while Marc was working in the Mirebeddine chief's compound, a messenger arrived from Mala to inform us of the death of the father of one of the interpreters, after two days' illness. This sad news necessitates the departure of the interpreter and some other members of the troop. The result of our inquiries as to the nature of the illness leaves not the smallest doubt – it was recurrent fever. Why were we not told when we went through Mala? The hospital assistant would have given the sick man an injection which would very likely have saved his life.

We learn from elsewhere that recurrent fever is causing great ravages at Maroua. I do not think, however, that there is any possibility of changing our itinerary.

I sometimes feel that there is a gulf of flames separating me from M. – a Gehenna, which I despair of ever crossing.

Yesterday, at nightfall, we heard the sounds of a tamtam, some hundred yards from the station hut. I made my way to it, leaving Marc in an improvised dark-room, at work filling his camera. The moon was in its first quarter and gave very little light, but the trodden earth of a little path I followed glimmered faintly between the hummocks of a future millet field.

The curiosity that drew me was not very strong. If the camp lantern had given a better light, I should have stayed behind to read; but its glass is broken and the slightest breath makes the candle-flame flicker desperately. I pretended the professional duty of an observer and started off.

By now everyone in the village knows me, and the tamtam did not stop at my approach. A few children ran up to me; but it was so dark that I could recognize no one. It was all I could do to make out the group of black dancers. There were only about forty of them; they were singing rather badly and dancing rather vaguely to the sound of a single drum – it was just a little family tamtam. It seems hardly possible that such a trifling stimulus should have sufficed to provoke spasms and hysterics in five persons, during the brief time that I was a spectator. Ah! what a melancholy – what a hideous spectacle! The young frail body of a little girl (I recognized it as a little girl's by the glittering of her bead girdle) rolled in the dust, moaning like a wounded animal. She panted; her legs twitched convulsively; and then all was quiet. I bent over her; there was not the slightest rising of her breast to show that she was breathing. Her body seemed untenanted. The demon had left her. An old man knelt down beside her and began to exhort her. A long time went by; then the girl got up; she seemed waking out of a dream. But soon the dance, which had not stopped, drew her to it again; and twice more in the space of half an hour I saw her fall again on the ground. Decidedly the demon was a tenacious one and refused to relinquish his hold. Other demons subjected other women to their perturbing influence. An old woman leapt out of the circle with little backward jumps, to the great amusement of the onlookers, who urged her on with their shouts. Finally the old woman fell and lay writhing on the ground. Farther on there was another; and then another. And then a man. They seemed to take a kind of pleasure in it, as though this state of delirium was what they were longing for and trying to produce. The dance here (and also at Mala) in no way resembled the dances in other places. It seemed a kind of hygienic, anti-demoniac exercise. But, then, are all these people ill? Or do they become epileptic or hysterical by persuasion? Is the belief in the devil, like the belief in God, sufficient to determine his presence? This belief seems to play a great part in the Massas' existence. Here and there, sometimes in the country, sometimes on the outskirts of a village, or in the village itself, at the foot of a tree, no matter where, one sees with surprise a little mound, about as high as a beehive, generally made of earth and painted white, of an odd pointed shape, looking as if it might be a little mausoleum. When one inquires what it is, the answer is: 'It is the devil.' And I have never been able to find out whether they think that Eblis is really enclosed in it, whether it is a propitiatory altar, a trap for devils, a devil-repeller, or a devil-conductor . . . The fact remains that when one sees one of these little affairs, devil there is.

I have not made out that this belief in an evil power is counter-balanced in the minds of these poor people by the belief in any tutelary genius. The best they can hope for is the absence of enmity . . . But perhaps I am wrong. It is almost impossible for a person to penetrate very deeply into the psychology of a people whose language he does not speak and through whose country he is merely passing – in spite of all their friendliness and openness – their welcoming attitude, I mean. It seemed to me last night that they were not altogether pleased to have me assist at the celebration of these kinds of mysteries. I had no sooner left the dance than their cries became louder, as though my presence had caused some constraint and put a stopper on their frenzy. Moreover, while I was lingering among them, I was hit three times over by some projectile – merely a little lump of earth, which was thrown at me so gently that the first time I thought I had been accidentally hit on the stomach by the arm of some excited dancer; but the second hit enlightened me as to the first. The third, which struck me on the back, almost hurt me. I did not turn round at once, thinking it best to let it pass unnoticed, so I did not see where it came from. The affability of the last few days has been so great that when I told Marc about it, he declared I must be mistaken and that the lump of earth cannot have been thrown with any hostile intention; perhaps, on the contrary, it might have been a provocation, an invitation . . . As for me, I could only take it for an anonymous and discreet 'Go away!' without any intention in it of wounding, vexing, or hurting. Nevertheless, I did not go away at once, so that I witnessed the last three hysterical seizures. Giving way is a thing I dislike. I reflected afterwards that it was perhaps not very prudent of me to have come by myself, and to go away by myself, across open country and in the middle of the night. When once the devil takes a hand, no amount of affability counts. Anything may happen . . . I ought perhaps to have been afraid, but I could not manage to be. Two great strapping Negroes stepped out of the circle and followed me. The only plan was to be on terms of good fellowship. I held out a hand to each and walked along for some time holding their hands in mine. If you have dealings with the devil, the best way is to propitiate him. Massis knows I am marvellously good at it.

A long conversation with Adoum, who is the necessary go-between for talking to Zigla. Everything confirms what I have just said. The natives here believe in the devil, in many devils – and believe only in them. No other supernatural power helps man to defend himself against them. The most one can say is that certain objects, certain actions, have the property of frightening the devil and of thwarting his evil intentions; but this beneficent property does not issue from any supreme principle. Nor is there anything that can influence the conduct of man, whose whole wisdom consists in knowing what harms and what preserves him.

In the same way, after death there is nothing. 'After a man is dead –' repeated Adoum, who is a Mussulman himself and is quite certain of going to paradise –' among the people here, it's like after the wind has gone by.'

The dead are often not buried, but simply thrown into the river.

The morning has been extremely tiring on account of the excessive heat; the whole of it was spent taking photographs.

As we wanted to light up the inside of one of these curious huts, so as to be able to photograph it, we paid fifty francs for permission to pull it down. Three men who were set to work at it climbed up to the top of the gun-shell in twelve strides – with two matchets and a pestle. In a short time the outside wall was broken through and the building decapitated. A flood of light entered it and after the dust had gone down a little, Marc set his actors to rehearse.

Returned to the station hut about one o'clock, dead with heat – 100° in the darkest and airiest part of the veranda. The light was glorious, overwhelming, appalling.

About three o'clock, after our siesta, we went to Mala by whale-boat, with Adoum, Zigla, Gabriel and his assistant, and five members of our troop, not to mention twelve boatmen and a *capita*. The actors, who lay down at our feet in the whale-boat, gave out a perfume of dried fish-oil that almost made me regret the hippopotamus.

In the radiant light of evening I thought Mala more charming, more splendid than ever. But Gabriel, the hospital assistant, after making a tour of inspection in the village, came back in consternation at the amount of sickness: pneumonia, tuberculosis, recurrent fever. He advised us strongly not to sleep at Mala tomorrow night, as we had intended. And it would not be prudent even to spend much time in the village. It is the very place, however, where we wanted to work. Mala is incomparably finer than any other Massa village we have seen.

On our way back a lucky shot reconciled me with myself. I brought down four ducks with a single cartridge – those big ducks with gold-green wings and a black bill, that has a helmet-like protuberance on it. I say 'brought down', but when the boatmen went to pick up the birds, they found, as is nearly always the case, that they were not quite dead. They dive to the bottom and only come up again a long way off or not at all. Or else, wounded as they are, they fly off and find a hiding-place in the reeds or grass to die in. This time my boatmen were only able to bring back three.

A little farther on we came upon two dead bodies (one of them we had seen on our first journey). Drowned? Not at all. Dead men who had been thrown into the river with all their 'baggage', wrapped round in palm-leaves.

I went down to the river bank and did the rest of the way on foot, glad to walk a little and above all to get away from the horrible stench of the whale-boat.

Quinine and Rhoféine. A fairly good night. I was afraid of bad results from yesterday's excessive glare. This morning the air is cool, caressing, and delicious to breathe. We left Mirebeddine about eight o'clock.

Whether in the forest or in the bush country, my experience has been that the days are not long enough to study, or even to pay attention to, a quarter of the interesting things which pass cinematograph-like before one in the twenty-four hours. One has to keep to one's subjects and leave the rest, hoping for the next occasion, which unfortunately too often never occurs (Christy, p. 44.)

I note in Christy the passages that are *worth translating*: on the growth of the ficus (pp. 29 and 30); on the decrease of the primeval forest (pp. 30 and 31).

Very poor afternoon's work at Mala. Nothing that had been ordered was ready. People made off just as they were wanted; orders were misunderstood or carried out wrong. The sun was very fierce – 106° under the veranda, at two o'clock. But at four o'clock the light began to fade, the sun grew obscured with haze, and we were obliged to put off the rest of the seance till tomorrow.

Half-way back on our return journey we saw some men on horseback on the Cameroon shore, obviously waiting for us. Our boat drew near. They had been sent by the *chef de canton* and were watching for our return to Pouss to tell us that their master was expecting us at the station. And sure enough, we could see standing on the shore in the distance a stupendously big, fat man, surrounded by a numerous escort; he was underneath an immense canopy – a gigantic umbrella, like the awning spread over a merry-go-round, and striped alternately in red, green, and yellow. As we left our whale-boats, he rose and advanced towards us. Then, after an exchange of greetings in the oriental fashion, he signed to us to pass in front and precede him to the station hut; seats were brought into the veranda; fortunately he had his own chair like the sultan of the other shore. No armchair of ours could have borne him.

Sixty or so of his familiars or 'clients' and servants invaded our veranda with him and made a circle round us, either seating themselves on the ground or leaning against the railings. A fine sight, but rather stifling. 'Who are these people,' we asked, 'and what do they do?' 'Nothing,' was the answer. 'They are the sultan's clients; they live round him and sometimes come from long distances, if they are assured of finding food, shelter, and the rest, at his court.' It seems that every big chief in the country has numbers of such parasite partisans, who pay in incense for the privileges and favours he dispenses, and save him from too direct a contact with the common herd. This, I think, is true of all courts; it is shown here on a reduced scale, but in an exemplary and flagrant manner. A sovereign without an entourage is an undesirable – an impossible – thing. One can judge the courtier's worth by the sovereign's.

X. is very ill again. He complains of violent pains in the head; and his temperature is going up. This two days' respite has misled us. Gabriel speaks of sending him back to Logone-Birni. I am afraid he may not be in a state to bear the three days' journey in a canoe – with whom? How cared for? How fed? Sleeping where? But, on the other hand, what will become of him if he is left here without assistance and without nursing? . . . The practical impossibility in which I find myself of saving this poor man's life revolts, enrages, exasperates me. I sent for Gabriel, after I had seen the patient, and had a long talk with him. He assures me that the sultan here (the one whose visit we have just received) is very kind (he has been talked of for the 'medal'!) and will have no difficulty in finding an attendant to go in charge of the sick man as far as Logone-Birni.

Pouss, 19 March

We reached Mala early by whale-boat. But, as I foresaw yesterday, the light is dim and the sky hazy. Nevertheless, we did some very good work to begin with. Then, by degrees, everything went wrong. Some of the actors we had chosen turned out hopeless as soon as they had to leave their routine, and behaved like lunatics. I come back to what I said yesterday: everything one dictates and *tries* to get appears constrained. It would have been better to cull the things a happy chance brought in our way. But then we should have had to have more time and give up the idea of anything connected or continuous.

A baby crocodile which was brought to us this morning, and

which we should have liked to put in the film, pretended to be dead and looked more like a rag than a crocodile. The live fish, which we intended to film in the act of being caught, have died in the canoe reservoir where we were keeping them, in spite of the water's being constantly renewed. The heat is overpowering.

Matters too are greatly complicated by the double translation of every slightest order. And one is rarely sure that the original order has been properly understood by the first translator, Adoum, who repeats it in Arabic to Zigla, who repeats it again in Massa. The order reaches its destination completely mangled. Adoum always translates with great rapidity – but very often absolutely at random – for he sometimes entirely misunderstands what has been said, though he never hesitates for a moment. And sometimes one is petrified (contrariwise to the Bourgeois Gentilhomme) at hearing a brief order turn into a very long sentence – into a whole speech.

109° under the veranda; 104° in the rooms. It was quite 113° at Mala this afternoon when we were working. I thought I was going to faint. I am not sure the results will be worth it.

We have decided to leave tomorrow in the morning if possible, and not in the afternoon, as had been at first arranged. We have sent word to the *lamido*.[4] I have tried in vain to buy a blanket for our patient, whom we are sending to Logone-Birni by canoe. Fortunately the nights are warmer; he is better, and I have given the attendant who is to look after him on the journey the wherewithal to supply his needs.

How complicated these starts are! The station chief has to be paid for the millet balls; certificates have to be given to the guards, and *matabiches* to the boatmen. There were some of these I took leave of with real regret – Boïbossoum, in particular, the youngest of them. He would have liked to come on with us, and his smile was very sad as he said goodbye. Do not let it be imagined that I am blind; we had some bad lots among our men – and I even consider that our charming and very intelligent interpreter, Zigla, was a bit of a rogue. I didn't mind his having purloined the three big ducks that I had intended to give our boys, so much as his having denied it

4. Sultan.

immediately after. No matter; with a few exceptions, I say that one would look in vain for a body of forty men, in England, France, Germany, or Italy, who would be so easy to deal with – so smiling, so amiable, so trustful.

We are leaving the country without having managed to see a certain sorcerer whom we have heard of and whom we tried to get over from the neighbouring village where he was staying. Many people have seen this magician cut a chicken in half and then, after he had sprinkled a little water on the two halves, they have with their own eyes seen them come to life, join together again, and the resuscitated chicken run away, pecking up food as it went. But that is nothing. He has been seen on the public place to rub together a handful of leaves, tear them up, and throw the fragments on the ground, and then, in the presence of a crowd of spectators, turn these fragments into real, live little children, either boys or girls, at request. We promised a thumping sum to assist at this miracle. But no doubt the sorcerer is suspicious of us and afraid of divulging his tricks and losing his prestige. We were obliged to content ourselves with the secondhand account of his performances.

CHAPTER FIVE

THROUGH THE BUSH – MAROUA – ADOUM LEAVES

20 March

A short night. We did not finish our packing yesterday evening. It is incredibly hampering to have no lights. Got up with the first glimmer of dawn.

Eighty porters – four horses.

Crossed an immense and absolutely empty moor. Saw some royal cranes; they were flying either singly or in small groups or large companies (very like the people at Pontigny). Here and there during the first kilometres were a few Palmyra palms. It seems the sultan is to be decorated for having planted them. He might have planted a few more while he was about it. The species is not nearly so fine as the Bangassou kind. Some of their trunks are pierced with holes – palm rats, I suppose. A large spider had spun its web across the path. Incomprehensible! There was no support for it to be seen anywhere, though it was taut and vertical.

Halted after about fourteen kilometres. A few isolated trees on a baked soil (like terracotta pottery). It was about eleven o'clock and the sun was broiling. We rested in the shade of the biggest tree. The wind scorched one's skin as it passed; it was a curious plaited skein of mixed alternate winds; one, blowing no doubt from the river at a temperature of about 98°, seemed cool; the other blew from a furnace – a breath from hell. Every object one touched, unless it was wet, was hotter than one's hand.

I forgot yesterday to mention the whirlwind that passed over the village of Mala, when we got back from Pouss; it was perfect in form – a column of vapour or sand like a gigantic palm tree, absolutely even and vertical, without a bulge or dent in it from earth to sky. It dispersed very slowly, after having lasted perhaps ten minutes (certainly more than five).

The second part of the day was exceedingly trying – I really think the most fatiguing of our whole journey. The sky was thick – loaded with something – we didn't know what, except that it wasn't rain. The vast plain through which we rode was utterly without charm or grace – baked and parched; it was covered with short, dry grass of a dirty yellow colour, which made one almost regret the great stretches that have been burnt black by fires.

The station of Guirebedic was a terribly long way off; we thought we should never get there. We were so sick of riding, we dismounted, hoping to get a little rest by walking. We were dead beat.

This evening, after three hours' rest, shade, and night, I still feel as if I had not eliminated the excess of sunlight. I feel like a garden wall that remains saturated with heat long after the sun has disappeared. I was so completely parched when I arrived – with no saliva in my mouth but a kind of bitter froth – that during three hours I drank a quantity of liquid that would have been enough to drown a Brinvilliers. The strange thing is that one does not mind drinking water that is not cold – almost tepid. Fortunately the water we boiled before starting today has not got the horrible taste of crocodile which the river water has had for the last few days.

The sons of the sultan, who is away, are exceedingly obliging. We have not got into touch yet with our new porters. The few smiles we have bestowed upon them have met with no response. As they have not had any communication with our last batch, we cannot benefit by the reputation for pleasantness they would certainly have given us. We have got to begin all over again.

The shell huts that were so fine have disappeared; we asked why in the first village we came to – still Massa – there were nothing but ugly thatched huts. It is because the earth here is too much mixed with sand; a gun-shell hut would crumble away at the first rains.

Ginglëi, 21 March

Slept out of doors in the spacious *bordj* courtyard. Left again at five a.m. – too late, alas! A wide motor road, as wide as the royal road at Versailles. What for? We concocted a *tipoye* out of Coppet's long deckchair. Noticed a curious new kind of termitary, ending about eighteen inches above the ground in a series of pipe-like, trumpet-shaped openings, where the termites work *in the open*. Is there no danger of their being attacked by ants? Or have these termites, whose habits are so unlike the others', different modes of defence? How I wish I could study them seriously!

It was not too hot at first – not much more than 95°; but it is 110° now in the Gingleï rest-house, where I am writing this. It is killing. And the light is like a dagger in one's eyes.

We met a great many charming little deer, in groups of two, three, or four – hardly wilder than goats – *café-au-lait* colour, with cream-coloured bellies; across each side they have a wide stripe of chocolate colour.

Water is scarce. There are wells near the villages for domestic purposes, and watering-places where the cattle go to drink. A poor old woman defended one of these precarious reservoirs all by herself against our porters' thirst.

Yesterday we crossed two sham rivers – low banks put to prevent or turn aside flooding.

A very fine mimosa with white flowers.

Sausage trees; Bignoniaceae (?); large purplish flowers or sprays.

A flask in my saddle-bag – in the flask, lukewarm tea. There was only a mouthful, and I swallowed it the wrong way! . . .

It is my small Dindiki who bears the heat least well of us all, accustomed as he is to the constant moisture of the equatorial forest. He pants, refuses to eat, doesn't know what to do with himself. Purges and enemas have no effect. In the forest he no doubt knew what barks to nibble, what fruits to take a taste of, etc. . . . I arranged a damp cloth round his cage and put a dripping sponge on the top of it; but he grew impatient and bolted off to perch on the highest and consequently the hottest spot of the roof of the hut; where we were having lunch; and from there he rained down on us bits of wood and straw and a quantity of dusty rubble.

Gingleï, a large and hideous village – a fortuitous conglomeration of sordid, dilapidated cabins. Here and there in the surrounding country are a few fine trees – some of them non-deciduous –

emerging out of a monotonous but fairly thick undergrowth. A torrid winter.[1]

When we wanted to start again, Outhman climbed up the central beam of the hut to catch Dindiki, whom we had seen mounting higher and higher, through the tangle of rafters and thatch. It was a poor little crumpled-up, limp object that Outhman brought down with him. No doubt he thought that the higher he went, as in his native forest, the more air and coolness he would find (it must have been more than 122° in the place he had got to); or perhaps a scorpion or a spider had stung him? . . . I had grown attached to the little creature more than to any dog; he was my constant companion. His heart was still faintly beating. I took him on my knees and treated him as one does drowned persons – artificial respiration and friction – keeping his skin moist as I did so. At the end of an hour's time I had the joy of seeing him breathe again very faintly. Marc helped me. We sent Adoum hurrying after the porters, who had already started, to get canteen No. 4, where the medicine chest is kept. Gabriel injected three drops of caffeine. We did not start till Dindiki had revived a little. He was sick. I took hope again. I cleaned him and then put him to lie down in a helmet and took him with me in my *tipoye*.

A strange kind of *tipoye*, improvised by tying on to a long deckchair two long poles, which four enormous porters hoisted on to their heads. I was suspended in mid-air at more than two yards above the level of the ground. It was sunset before we reached the camping-place.

The sultan came to meet us with music and a dozen or so men on horseback. Their custom is to rush at one full tilt with their assegais and rifles pointed as though they were making an attack, and kicking up a terrific dust as they gallop. The old sultan – a delightful old fellow – had an ox killed for our porters, which was at once cut up and roasted in front of their big fires. We put up our beds in the open air, near a gigantic tree in the middle of the station compound. Dindiki drank a little tea. For the first time I called Zézé an idiot

1. Is it necessary to remind my readers that the seasons in equatorial regions are totally unlike ours? There is, properly speaking, neither winter nor summer, but a dry season and a rainy season.

because he twice running made a ridiculous failure of the prunes I ordered for Dindiki.

The station water looked like *café au lait*, but unfortunately did not taste like it! We slept for two or three hours and then gave the signal for starting.

The half-moon did not set for another hour; it must have been one or two in the morning. (At midnight the temperature was 82° – a delicious feeling of coolness.)

23 March

A prodigious night march! First through the village of Bogo, which looked immense; then across an indistinct plain; I could see nothing but the sky, pinned as I was in my deckchair, and so shaken that I confided Dindiki in his cage to the cook's boy. Marc, with all the others, went on ahead, galloping away on a spirited horse. I only joined him again at the first stage, a little before sunrise, at Balasa – the last halt before Maroua. We had given the *chef de circonscription*, Marc Chadourne, notice of our coming, and he was kind enough to send his English dogcart to meet us, filled with vegetables for our lunch – for he had not expected us so early. We got into the cart and gave the little horse its head. We were soon beneath the town walls. The *lamido* had to be given time to organize the traditional reception. (Until I saw Reï Bouba's later, I thought nothing could have been grander!) Thirty or so men on horseback; saddles and costumes of great beauty. But we were so delighted to have at last arrived that we hardly gave anything a glance. It was not nine o'clock. Chadourne had prepared a monster breakfast for us – *café au lait*, eggs, jam, papaw, bananas – followed by a profound siesta.

We have put Dindiki beside a wet cloth, on the top of a little three-cornered sideboard, underneath an enormous calabash, in the coolest spot in the house – only 98°.

Maroua

The heat has been terrible for the last few days. There is a curious, incomprehensible epidemic raging here. It is not recurrent fever, and the treatment recommended for the latter has no effect. People – women especially – are seized with sudden illness, fall down, and succumb almost immediately. The epidemic has been going on for about a month and now seems to be diminishing; but the number of deaths has been terrific. I do not dare give the figures.

24 March

We had gone up to the station without looking behind us. It was only a little later, when we went out on to the terrace, or rather the veranda, that we discovered the immense expanse of country before us. Chadourne has arranged the station hut with more than taste – with intelligence – a perfect comprehension of what is suitable to the country. The walls of the large centre room are burnt-sienna colour; the ceiling is of maize-coloured mats; these are divided up into compartments by dark-purple mats of the same kind, arranged in the places where the beams might come. On one of the walls is a large mat from Reï-Bouba, in a mosaic of reeds – black, ochre, and white. On the wall opposite is a bookcase, or, at any rate, a bookshelf; and on the top of it, native objects in basket- and wicker-work; then comes another, darker mat, also from Reï-Bouba. The proportions and colours of the whole arrangement – the big divans made of cane, and the few pieces of furniture – are perfect. Two big shuttered doors and four large windows face each other. They are all kept carefully shut, so as not to let in the flaming inferno from outside. But when the sun goes down, everything is opened. The circular gallery round the house (round three sides of it, at any rate) is bordered with beautiful, large, pointed arches – like a cloister; the walls and pillars are whitewashed. Chadourne has had the balustrade taken away, so that one can see the steep rocky descent, right down to the river. The river? The river-*bed*, rather. A wide river of golden sand which winds round the station rocks. The native huts, grouped between the river and the mountains, seem to have advanced as far as the station rocks, to have there been stopped and turned aside, to have crossed the golden river, and to have re-crossed it, in order to reappear again much farther on. The station itself is overlooked by a mountain, bare, bald, ashen-grey, and very beautiful. Here and there, at rare intervals in the immense plain, there are other impatient, sudden upheavals of the soil. One of the noblest landscapes that exist – one of the most eloquent, the most melancholy.

Yesterday I tried, very absurdly, to describe the landscape. Nothing gives any idea of its proportions. The mountains above the station are probably as high as the Esterel. The station hill is not at all high – not even up to the first story of the Eiffel Tower; but the expanse it overlooks is immense.

It is hot. One can think of nothing else . . . and of hurrying on.

In order to gain time we have given up an expedition into the mountains, which Chadourne suggested. All our remaining faculties and powers are centred on getting home.

Dindiki refuses to eat. I am astonished he is still alive.

We sleep out of doors on the terrace. After midnight the temperature goes down a little and becomes delicious. One feels that if it went below 86°, one would catch cold. The sheets one lies down on are as hot as if they had just been warmed by a warming-pan. Everything one touches – one's clothes, one's towels, the cushions one sits on – everything is hot. Chadourne, who is himself feeling the heat severely, has only managed to get on for some time past by taking injections of Cacodylate.

I am re-reading *Heart of Darkness* for the fourth time. It is only after having seen the country that I realize how good it is.

We have got to part with Adoum. It would be inhuman to take him farther with us. When we engaged him at Brazzaville, where some chance had stranded him, it was with the intention of taking him back to the neighbourhood of his own country – the Ouaddai. But at present, now that we are going southwards, every day is taking him farther away from it. He must go back to Fort Lamy, where Coppet will procure him facilities for returning to Abécher, to his old mother, from whom he parted more than two years ago. Gabriel Loko, the half-caste hospital assistant, who is with us and who has to regain his post, will go with him as far as Logone-Birni[2] –

2. It was only after I had got back to France that I had news of my boy and his travelling-companion. Gabriel Loko died the day after their start, at their first stopping-place; he was suddenly carried off by the terrible epidemic – a kind of cerebro-spinal meningitis – which was still ravaging the country. 'This decease was very little agreeable to us,' wrote the native hospital assistant of Logone-Birni, in the letter of touchingly bad French in which he informed me of this melancholy event.

an opportunity which will not present itself again and which must not be missed. Yes; for some time past I have been saying this to myself every day; I say it to him too and he knows it. But my heart fails me at the idea of parting from the poor boy, who would gladly go with us as far as N'Gaoundéré – as far as Douala – even as far as France, for henceforth he has nothing on earth – and I realize it perfectly – dearer to him than our confidence and friendship, the depth of which I can gauge by the sadness I feel at parting from him.

Such devotion, such humility of spirit, such a childlike desire to do well, combined with such nobility, so much capacity for love – all this, as a rule, meets with nothing but rebuffs . . . Adoum is assuredly not very different from his brothers; none of these traits belong especially to him. Through him, behind him, I have come to feel a whole race of suffering humanity – a poor oppressed people, whose beauty, whose worth, we have failed to understand . . . whom I wish it was in my power never to leave. And the death of a friend would not grieve me more, for I know I shall never see him again.

He had knelt down beside me, the better to mark his deference, with his head turned aside, so that I should not see him crying, just as I on my part hid my tears from him. He was icy cold, and I felt him trembling all over when I put my hand on his shoulder. He knew no words in which to express his grief or his gratitude, and simply murmured in a plaintive, lamentable voice: 'Thank you . . . thank you . . .' when I told him that I had written to the Governor to ask him to give me news of his arrival at Lamy and to help him to reach Abécher, where I had already sent his old mother some money on his behalf.

X. said to me: 'In a few days he will have forgotten all about you.' I hope to Heaven he may! Much good it would be if his life were darkened with regrets. And yet how often Marcel de Coppet and others have told me of cases of fidelity among Negroes – of a boy (Coppet's, for instance) going a twenty days' march to join a master whom he remembered affectionately!

I tried the following experiment: I gave him a bundle of eleven *patas* (five-franc notes) to do some commissions with, saying: 'Here are fifty francs.' I did this to convince a sceptic, for, personally, I did not doubt a moment that Adoum would tell me of the mistake as soon as he had counted the notes, which he did only the next day.

'I bought ten francs' worth of tobacco,' he said.

'Then you ought to have forty francs left.'

'No. Forty-five; because yesterday you gave me five francs too much.' And this was said in the most natural manner possible.

I see nothing in him that is not childlike, noble, pure, and honest. The whites who manage to turn creatures like him into rogues are worse rogues themselves, or else miserable blunderers. I have no doubt that Adoum would fling himself in front of any danger — even a mortal one — to protect me. I have never doubted him; and his gratitude comes above all from that.

But people are always talking of the Negroes' stupidity. As for his own want of comprehension, how should the white man be conscious of it? I do not want to make the black out more intelligent than he is; but his stupidity, if it exists, is only natural — like an animal's. Whereas the white man's as regards the black has something monstrous about it, by very reason of his superiority.

26 March

A sleepless night, in spite of Sedobrol and Soneryl. I am in great nervous anxiety and fear that I may not have the necessary endurance to get through the three weeks' furnace that lies between us and N'Gaoundéré. Yesterday I had an attack of giddiness while I was trying to pack my canteen. I was obliged to give it up and leave the job to Marc. Dindiki still refuses to eat.

One can think of nothing but the heat.

I have never seen anything more pathetic than poor Adoum's unhappiness. Perhaps he was surprised to see me so unhappy myself. His forehead — his whole face — was covered with perspiration, and icy cold. He was like someone who feels his muscles giving way and whose whole body is in a state of collapse. When I took him by the arm, it was the same as when I picked Dindiki up the other day from the top of the roof, in a faint.

I wish I could describe his qualities and show that in reality there was nothing particularly individual about them. I am sure that

243

Adoum is not an exceptional being. He seemed to me, on the contrary, a perfect representative of his race – and that is why I was so greatly overcome by his modesty and gratitude.

What an abominable crime to repulse, to prevent, love!

His deference was so great that when I gave him his daily reading-lesson, he never sat beside me on a chair or even a packing-case. He had the feeling, which I did not attempt to modify, that it 'would not be proper' – and always settled himself with his book on the ground, either sitting or kneeling.

He was continually going off by himself to be alone and study his lesson book or his exercise book, in which I used to write down short sentences for him to learn by heart – so great was his desire to educate himself and so draw nearer to us.

CHAPTER SIX

❖❖❖❖❖❖❖❖❖❖❖❖❖❖❖❖❖❖❖❖❖❖❖❖❖❖❖❖❖❖❖❖❖❖❖❖❖

LÉRÉ, BINDER, BIBÉMI

Mindif, 27 March

We are out of the furnace. At five o'clock this morning the air was *suave*. I could do with two sweaters on when I first got up. Not more than 75°. One feels hopeful again. Even Dindiki seems better.

Last night we drove the twenty-five kilometres that separate us from Maroua. We started a little before sunset and arrived in the dark. We were met at long intervals by the sultan's brother, then by his young son (a boy of twelve with a great many attendants), then by the sultan himself (the *lamido*). He had a considerable escort; a huge parasol, like the ones one sees on the beach at Deauville, was being held over him; it was mounted on an immensely long handle, for the sultan was on horseback, and the parasol-bearer followed on foot. The whole thing made a curious effect in the moonlight.

Mindif lies among three exceedingly curious upheavals of the soil. One of these, and by far the largest, resembles the great headland of Rio de Janeiro. It looks enormous – a sheer and apparently inaccessible block; this sudden geological formation seems to me inexplicable, either by volcanic upraising, or by earth folding, or by erosion. The ground all round is uniformly sandy. The two other upheaved masses are granitic – enormous monolith warts.

Crossed several *mayos* (rivers). The river-beds at this season are mere stretches of sand. If one scratches the soil, water at once comes to the surface.

Marc had an attack of bleeding at the nose. He gave his handkerchief to be washed. A carrion crow flew over the basin and carried off the bloodstained handkerchief.

*

I climbed up to the top of the enormous boulder which towers above the camping-place. I then perceived there were quantities of other such boulders of various sizes, scattered here and there over the country (about every three kilometres). The one that I climbed was one of the most remarkable. It was a single block – coarse-grained granite, of a rather ugly purple. At its base and on its sides lay large, sharp-splintered fragments of rock, among which creatures like marmots ran in and out.

In the fissures of the rock there were swarms of bees.

The *lamido* has sent us a present of milk, rice, dates, and honey. Marc's nose bleeds regularly, morning and evening.

28 March

We arrived exhausted, physically and nervously, at Lara about ten o'clock in the evening. The heat is appalling, terrifying. One longs to take shelter, but one doesn't know from what. The air is so dry that it shrivels up one's temples and eyelids. We dined by moonlight, but we could think of nothing but bed and sleep. Our beds were already set up close by, but before we were able to go off to sleep, such a violent wind got up that our mosquito-nets were in danger. We had to go in and suffocate in the camping-place.

Lara (there is no doubt a village of the name, but we were unable to see it) is sheltered by a circle of small hills – those sudden risings of which I have spoken, which reverberate down on us the heat they have accumulated during the day. The station is a group of huts – a sort of esplanade; and in front of the principal hut is one of those enormous trees I never tire of admiring. Soleiman, our new interpreter, begged us urgently not to go far afield, for fear of the great quantities of serpents that infest the country. 'Big serpents?' 'No; very small, but very poisonous.'

The wind has become ferocious. I rose twice, thinking it was a whirlwind. It seems to get up on the actual spot and go no farther. The roof of the hut will certainly be carried off. A blast from hell. Imagine a fierce wind that is hotter than one's body. The more violent it becomes, the deeper it burns; it cracks the earth; it withers everything.

The road was extremely tiring. We no doubt left Mindif too early (Chadourne accompanied us so far and went back to Maroua directly after breakfast); it seemed as though the sun would never set. I had the canvas awning of my *tipoye* watered; but in spite of this it was so suffocating that I thought my last moment had come. I did the end of the journey on foot and on horseback. Night came, but brought no coolness.

Left Lara at 4 a.m.

Arrived at Domourou before the hottest part of the day. From six in the morning onwards, one gasps. One wonders anxiously – almost desperately – if one will be able to hold out. Life in camp is like slow-motion film. This morning, thanks to a copious watering, which turned the bed coverings into rivers and lakes, where Dindiki came to drink, we brought the temperature down to 104°, but we were dripping. I went out into the furnace of the veranda to get dry. We reflect with terror that perhaps the heat has not reached its maximum. And it is no use saying that one will get accustomed to it. On the contrary; from day to day one gets weaker – from day to day less able to bear it.

I am, however, enjoying the third instalment of *Bella*, tasting it in slow, delightful sips. In the midst of a certain rather mechanical artificiality, at every turn one comes across charming things like this: *'Il venait chaque après-midi avec un pliant s'asseoir auprès du berceau et face à lui, comme auprès d'un fleuve.'*

Binder, 29 March

A stage that has not been at all tiring. We were almost astonished to arrive at our journey's end with so little difficulty. The road was rather monotonous, but nevertheless the country was hillier. A continuous thicket – not at all exotic in appearance – like a French coppice. Sometimes a tall tree or two. Some, very few, have kept their leaves. One species even is in flower – large, kind of canary-coloured sprays – analogous (in appearance) to laburnum – but yet not Papilionaceae.

Dined by moonlight. I have a sore throat. Slept in the courtyard of the *bordj*. At last the temperature is going down. It was almost cool this morning (61°). Unspeakably delicious rest.

The *lamido*, who is extremely amiable – and quite simple – organized a kind of carnival this morning. The horses of his men-at-arms (his knights, I was going to say) were clothed in their extraordinary caparisons (like counterpanes), which are quilted in black and white, or red and white, lozenges. They reminded me of the great Simone Martini of Sienna – which reminds me of Spenser's

A gentle knight was pricking on the plain.

But I have exhausted my power of attention.

I left my book, however, to go and look at the tamtam a moment, thinking to meet Marc there. Nothing could have been less characteristic – or more dreary.

Sudden and inexplicable modesty of the women. They are not content with wrapping themselves up in their *boubous*, which trail on the ground and cover them up feet and all. They turn their backs and hide like rabbits, with their heads stuck into holes and corners.

30 March

Arrived at nine or ten o'clock in the evening. Left at four o'clock in the morning to try to avoid the heat. One can think of nothing else. I have hardly strength to write these few shapeless notes.

Saw a stunted bush with a few large tubular flowers, white like a gardenia and very scented.

Léré, 31 March

The landscape is becoming more marked, with slight hollows and risings. We went uphill by an almost imperceptible slope, and the air became a little less stifling.

It was a fantastic moment when the porters cast a double shadow, the moon lighting them on the right, while the first glimmer of dawn fell on their left flank. Everything was grey and silver.

A few smiles, a few kind words, have got the better of the porters' remissness. Yesterday evening they refused to go any farther. And now, in their enthusiasm, they declare they are willing to go with us as far as Douala. One old man, who was carrying the heavy cinema packing-case, was seized with a fit of excitement. He began rushing wildly about in every direction, laughing and shouting; off into the bush and then back again; spinning round on his own axis; darting up to a tree he caught sight of and striking it three times with a javelin he had in his hand. Had he gone mad? Not at all; it was merely lyrical excitement. What we used to call 'savage ecstasy' when we were children. And at times the *tipoye*-bearers – to get a *matabiche*, no doubt – began thanking me, either separately or in chorus. They are no longer satisfied with calling me 'Governor'. They shout: 'Thank you, Government, thank you!'

Poor fellows! They really have no cause to thank the government. The Chad[1] administration pays them only 1 fr. 25 a day as porters, and nothing for the return journey. – 1 fr. 25 for thirty kilometres, with fifty pounds of luggage on their heads and without food. That is to say that out of this minute sum they have to pay for their own food. And mark well: the return journey is not counted. When they get back, it is easy to imagine how much they will have left.

The Cameroon is perceptibly more generous than the Chad. It gives 1 fr. 75 a day for porterage and 50 centimes a day for the return journey, unloaded. According to the regulations (specified in the station orders), the porter ought to pay for his own food out of this; I know that we were not the only persons to disregard this injunction. It is certain that the porters' alacrity greatly depends on the way they are fed – and, moreover, as they are foreigners in the countries they go through, and are very often no favourites, they have less facilities than the white man for getting the village people to supply them with millet balls and the little 'sauce' in which they dip them. If, when there is no game, they are given a few kids as an extra, they are enraptured – 'Thank you, Government, thank you!'

As we thought this remuneration derisory and considered that Cameroon people ought to benefit by the Cameroon tariffs – at any rate during the three days (out of five) they have passed in Cameroon territory, we suggested to M. Bénilou (head of the subdivision of Léré) that he should only pay them according to the Chad tariff the two days' porterage in the Chad – and that we should take upon ourselves the three other days; i.e.:

---

1. The subdivision of Léré, which we were then going through, belongs to our Chad colony and makes an *enclave* in the Cameroon.

2 days at 1.25	2.50
3 days at 1.75	5.25
Plus 3 days return	
at 0.50	1.50
	9.25

to which we added 75 centimes *matabiche* to make a round sum and to enable us to pay them with two five-franc notes. They were delighted with the *matabiche*, but extremely disappointed by the notes, which they did not know how they would be able to change, so I am not sure whether we should not have pleased them more if we had paid them at the famine rates of the Chad, but in small coin.

In the high parts before getting to Léré, the vegetation changed. We seemed to have changed seasons, almost abruptly. Torrid, desolate winter, bare trees, dry bushes, reddened, fire-blackened stubble disappeared. Suddenly, almost the whole of the plants were of evergreen species. More than that. Some of them, and those the biggest and the handsomest, were in flower – thick spikes, blazing in the crimson light of dawn. The gently undulating country was like an English park. How restful and refreshing the shade was to one's eyes! And the foliage was no longer dark green – almost black – like the green of the Congo forests, but an acid, joyous green, as thrilling as the fields of barley one suddenly comes across in Tunisia, at the dip of a dune, after leagues of tawny sand. Monster trees, of noble and majestic bearing, are mingled with doum palm trees, that are very much ramified, like dracaenas.

It did not last long. The country became once more baked and burning. Léré is not on the lake. Perhaps in the rainy season it is on the river, but the Mayo Kebbi, which joins the lake of Léré to the lake of Trêné, is partially dry.

The very considerable village is composed of a Bornouan quarter (I ought to describe the *seccos*, which are brand-new), a Goubléa (?) quarter, and a Moundang quarter.

An hour or two before we reached Léré, we saw the first Moundang village; it was about two hundred yards off the road; but we stopped to visit it. The architecture is exceedingly curious – but exceedingly ugly – chiefly on account of the material employed – a kind of very coarse clay, mixed with gravel. The walls, which are not at all high, are interrupted by kinds of little *donjons* or turrets – the whole forming a bracelet. One goes in by the clasp of the bracelet, and finds oneself in a minute inner courtyard, where the people live in a state of complete nudity. Some of the youths and men, however, wear loincloths; others a straw sheath. The women wear nothing but a string, or a row of beads, round their waists.

A good many of these *donjons* are millet granaries. They are shaped like a long thimble and are open at the top and at one side, which makes the whole thing look like the building of a mason-fly. The opening, which is just large enough to admit of a man's creeping inside, shows like a dark patch in the distance, except when it is shut with a mat of plaited straw, that fits it very exactly. The other small buildings – a kind of round towers – are used as huts. Walls, huts, everything except the granaries, are covered with roofs of thatched straw or reed and mud, extremely thick and inelegant. In the courtyard there were some curiously shaped ladders, made out of a tree-trunk in the shape of a Y, with notches cut in them for footholds; an accumulation of household objects, dust, disorder; a prodigious number of lizards of all sizes.[2] Some of the women have full, rounded forms, like Maillol's sculptures.

Last night there was a terribly dusty tamtam.

This morning, tired and incurious. Let Marc visit the village by himself.

To think that one has reached the point of thinking the air cool at 100°!

1 April

It is possible, we are told, for it to be 'much better'. A pity! We should have liked to experience the maximum. But how now? Am I, too, going to give way to the devil of record-breaking? – Impossible to do anything all day long. Spent the hottest hours of the day on a camp-bed in the dark, with only the thinnest ray of light thrown upon Christy's book, of which I only managed to read a page or two.

2. The largest, however, are not larger than a forearm. Some of them look as if they were painted – divided into four parts – red, blue, white, red. When at rest, they keep continually nodding their heads.

Left Léré towards the end of the day – much too late. But we never had a more difficult start. Marc had to do everything alone, and merely watching him exert himself made me sweat profusely. After a too abundant luncheon with Rousseau, the big-game hunter, a walk home in the sun, and a missed siesta I felt sick and unwell – incapable of making an effort or a decision.

We have dismissed our Maroua and Binder porters, except twelve who did not wish to leave us. The seventy-five new ones, who were requisitioned at Léré, seemed very ill pleased at having to start – and I can well understand it. The poor fellows have just paid their tax. The harvest has been good. They were expecting a rest . . . Nothing of the kind! 'You are to start on a journey – thirty kilometres a day, with forty or fifty pounds' load on your heads, in time of Ramadan' (they do not all keep the fast) 'and in sweltering heat; you will be taken twelve days' march away from your home – and all this for 1 fr. 25 a day, food at your own expense and nothing for the return journey!' This is slavery; *temporary*, I grant, but still slavery!

Are we to take the cook's boy on with us? The poor fellow, who has been with us ever since Carnot – a volunteer out of sheer enthusiasm – has been very unwell for the last two days. He was as thin as a rake to begin with, but had improved enormously in our service and had become as stout as the strong man in a travelling circus; of great endurance and invariable good humour – one would have thought him capable of standing anything. The excessive heat, however, has completely bowled him over. He complained of violent pains in the head and vomiting, and fell off his horse between Binder and Léré (for we had made him ride, as he seemed to be suffering from adenitis). His heart was beating fit to burst and his temperature was 102°. We gave him quinine and Stovarsol. And here is another case of a sick Negro giving himself up for lost. Not a word, not a smile. Yesterday, however, he was better. But we thought it more prudent to hand him over to the Léré hospital attendant, with fifty francs and instructions to send him off to Archambault as soon as he feels better. It is unlucky he speaks nothing but Sango, which nobody about here can understand.

Even Rousseau, who has been seven years in the country and is absolutely climate-proof, etc. (eighty kilometres a day shooting elephants, so he says), declares it is 'terribly hot'. The sky is completely overcast, not with mist, as at Mala, but with thick clouds. Bénilan, the head of the Léré subdivision, is ill and has written asking to be sent home.

Rousseau is like Claudel in personal appearance – low-browed and thick-necked. He comes from Tours and is an only son. During the war he did his military service out here and has never left the country since (he means, however, to embark, as we do, at Douala on 13 May, but with the intention of coming back in September). He thought of going by way of the Bénoué, and spoke of this itinerary in such a way as to make us feel extremely undecided. But when we saw him again, he told us that, according to the last accounts from Garoua, it may not be possible to get the big canoes there, which take one down the Bénoué (in twenty days) to Bénoué Bridge, where one finds the railway. Taking everything into consideration, there would not be much advantage in this route, even if one were certain of getting canoes.

The idea of getting home has become an obsession.

In spite of the unfavourable weather, Marc has been filming the whole morning – a dance of the Moundangs in the strangest ceremonial costumes – a large apron, embroidered in black and buff, and an immense skirt (which they make stick out from their bodies when they want to sit down, by twirling round). As usual, there were rather unpleasant jiggings right and left; but at times an imposing march forward with great strides; and then pirouettes and faintings and people lying flat on the ground.

I must also mention the enormous, fantastic figures that were completely covered up in black seaweed (one couldn't tell their backs from their fronts), with porcupine crests and Punch and Judy voices. The women and children fled in panic terror. I flung myself into the spirit of the thing and, to everyone's frenzied joy, rushed for protection into the chief's arms. Then there came up to me the smallest of these creatures, who is said to be the most terrible; he was holding a little wooden axe in his hand and brandishing and shaking it, making movements like an insect's. I ordered him to be given a *matabiche* of five francs to divide with the others; but he was fully conscious that he was playing Père Ubu, and declared he would keep the note 'for himself alone'. Ferocious and mysterious; he brought it off extremely well. Stravinsky or Cocteau would have been enchanted.

In the Léré station-house a mason fly of the largest species began to build its cells in the moulding of the door beside my bed (which was set up indoors in the afternoon, for at night one slept outside). The evening of our arrival I was much amused to see it bring a biggish grey-brown grub (I have broken my spectacles and could not see very well) and then proceed to wall it up in a cell. I determined to undo its work and take out the caterpillar (or worm), on which – in which – it had presumably laid its eggs. In the meantime I allowed it to go on with its work. It completely blocked up the cell, first chewing the earth it brought and mixing it with saliva, and then hermetically sealing the opening through which it had introduced its prey. Its work is as clean, as smooth, as perfect as a potter's – the size of an olive stone. To my great delight, I saw it begin another similar building beside the first. On the evening of the second day four or five cells had been added. The whole formed a single block; the partitions were no longer visible. The earth had hardened. My knife had some difficulty in breaking it, and when, as I was going to leave, I took down the nest to see the caterpillar that had been shut up in it, I was amazed to find *in its place* a very fat, very lively, greyish-white maggot, with no eyes, a tapering hind part, and a very large fore part – in the shape of an extinguisher. Could it really have had time to come out in less than two days, to devour the caterpillar, and to grow to such a size at the latter's expense? I must find out.

Very much grieved by Boylesve's death, which I saw in a number of *L'Illustration* lent me by Bénilan. I think that I stood in his eyes a little for 'the sins he had not dared commit himself' (in literature, of course), which was the cause of the special consideration and affection he always showed me. I think he made a mistake in urging me to stand for the Academy and that he was wrong in backing me. But he did it, in spite of my reluctance, with such charming insistence that in the end I was almost shaken in my determination.

One day after an attentive reading of *La Jeune Fille bien élevée*, which I had liked, I amused myself by piecing out the manner in which the book had been constructed. I wrote him a long letter, and after praising him most sincerely, 'No doubt,' I added, 'you composed it in the following way; am I not right in thinking that the character of the grandmother was added at the last moment, to the detriment of another character, who was at first more important and part of whose substance you used to build up the new personage?'

It turned out to be true. Boylesve was amused by my perspicacity, and our intercourse after this letter became closer, without, however, ever ceasing to be strictly literary. He was not so bourgeois as he seemed at first sight, but everything about him was modest and retiring – which made his sensibility appear all the more exquisite.

The Moundang women are generally completely naked. Some of them, however, wear a narrow piece of stuff, originally white, passed tightly between their legs and fastened to a row of beads in the form of a girdle. Others, and in particular the sultan's daughters, wear in front a little apron of embroidered beads, reaching half-way down the thighs. The patterns on these aprons are always geometrical (lozenges and triangles) and are sometimes very beautiful.

We did the next stage by night to avoid the heat. Ten or twelve kilometres, we were told, but there were probably more. I began the journey in my *tipoye*; but I was so intolerably shaken, and the *tipoye*-bearers, who had not been properly trained, went so slowly, that I chose to walk, after having tried a troublesome horse for some time. Marc succeeded me in the *tipoye* and arrived only half an hour after me at Kabi – an agreeable station, where we got some excellent milk. The night was very dark, for the sky was completely overcast. But there was no storm threatening, so we set up our beds out of doors, on a carpet of coarse river-sand.

There were a great many trees in the surrounding country, but none of them very fine. From the village and the station-house one catches glimpses of the rather dreary shores of Lake Léré, which we coasted along yesterday without being aware of it, and which we are now going to leave behind us.

We felt too tired to start off again before dawn, as we had at first intended. And this morning it is market day.

There were astonishing swarms of naked women. The men are dressed in breeches and *boubous* which reach to their feet. A great many of the young men wear numbers of necklaces under these *boubous*, which show, where the *boubou* is cut open on the chest. They wear bracelets on their feet and hands; some of them even have the backs of their hands covered with shells and beads, fastened to the bracelets round their wrists. The *boubou*, however, is not obligatory. Some of them wear only loincloths or sheaths; but however little dressed they may be, they are always more so than the women. Certain books of travel say that the Moundangs took the custom of clothes from the Foulbés, after having defeated these latter in war; till then they had gone completely naked and their women also, wearing at most a kid-skin floating behind them in the manner of the Saras, and a straw sheath.

The duty of carrying water is exclusively performed by the women, who use *bourmas*. Not to be able to wash *properly* is one of the worst trials of this journey. The state of dirt one is in is unspeakable, especially after having travelled through the burnt bush.

Arrived at Biparé before sunset. A short stage on horseback. The sky was more and more overcast. Continuous thunder was heard in the distance. We have the thrilling hope of soon reaching the region and season of storms.

The chief of the Bororos, a nomad race of grazers, of a strongly marked semitic type, accompanied us from Léré as far as Biparé. He came to the post-house and settled himself down; in vain we said goodbye to him, it did not make him budge.

The storm came nearer. It came over us. The temperature began to grow milder. Imagine what it means! The *first rain of the year!* We expected cataracts – alas! only a few parsimonious drops fell from an inky sky. A prolonged gust of wind swept up all the dust of the camp.

We went through a small village and pushed on as far as the Mayo Binder; the Mayo Kebbi is farther on, at the foot of the mountain we are approaching.

A great number of enormous flashes of lightning – and what I have never seen – *coloured* flashes – most of them *gold*, some *pink*, or, rather, *pale ruby*.

Left Biparé about four o'clock in the morning. The storm yesterday has completely changed the quality of the air. One breathes again. There is less electric tension. The Mayo Kebbi flows round the foot of a russet and black mountain, with deep valleys in it. It stands isolated in the landscape, though there are other hills in very small chains at several points of the horizon. The banks of the river are sandy. What joy to see running water again, though this, it is true, sometimes lost itself in the sand! Very fine white lotuses were growing in the still pools. We saw two big antelopes and some flocks of duck, which were difficult to get at. But I killed one (the large kind, with a black crest).

The sky was overcast. We reached the stage without much difficulty (on foot, on horseback, and in *tipoyes*) in six hours.

Golombé. A sufficiently good halting-place, close beside a big capoc tree (false silk-cotton), whose fruit our porters beat down – as big as very big bananas and the same shape, with a very hard, though fairly thin rind – and containing a silky down, with which each of the porters stuffed his carrying-pad.

We started again at about two o'clock, taking advantage of a very overcast sky. Nevertheless, the temperature was still at 100° in the shade, and we streamed with perspiration during our siestas, on account of yesterday's rain.

A transitional country – fairly hilly; a certain amount of rock. Sometimes the path, which was occasionally so ill traced that a guide was necessary, led through mimosa groves and wound uncertainly among upthrusting rocks. It must be beautiful in the spring. Then there were big sausage trees; then sudden dips of the ground, large spaces without any trees, where the grass was still green, and where there were sometimes big herds of oxen grazing. Everywhere else, tall tow-coloured grass – taller by a yard than a man on horseback. In the sun they turned a beautiful golden colour, under a sky that was violet – almost black.

Reached Déo at nightfall. Our horses' trot considerably outdistanced our porters. We ordered a large weed bonfire to be lighted on a piece of rising ground so as to encourage them on their way. At last they arrived. In spite of their double stage – six hours this morning and nearly six hours this evening – they were in excellent spirits, singing and laughing. The important thing for them is to be well fed. I gave them a sheep this morning and a sheep this evening (not much for eighty, but it was impossible to get more), and, in addition, abundance of balls of millet with sauce, fish, etc. I have promised them an ox at the next stage.

Some of them wear, hanging round their necks, a whistle made of a goat horn pierced with two holes. They blow into this indefatigably, like tiresome children upon their little penny whistles; it makes a thin shrill sound; an exasperating little tune of three notes, which in the long run would drive one mad. They have no other songs, no other music.

Since Adoum left us, Outhman has been promoted a step. He understands very little and speaks an almost incomprehensible jargon; but Madoua, Adoum's successor, understands less and speaks even worse. Moreover, I fear, he is slightly stupid. Each time we used to have recourse to Adoum, we now have recourse to Outhman. He puts all his sentences in the third person, whether he is talking of himself, us, or anyone else. One would think he was frightened of the word 'I'.

4 April

Camped last night in the village of Déo, on a little public place, in the middle of rubbish-heaps. An abominable smell emanated from one of them, to which our porters had set fire. It burnt slowly and without any flame, but with clouds of nauseating, acrid smoke, which the slight breeze obstinately blew back in our faces. However much we watered it, off it started again; and this morning we were waked up two hours sooner than we wanted to be by this same stifling smoke. We had not intended to leave Déo before dawn, but it was as early as four o'clock when we started. I felt so thoroughly done up that I was glad to use my *tipoye*, which Outhman had arranged so as to give my head a support – and very soon I lost consciousness. The night was beginning to fade when we reached the shores of a small lake, where the porters drank, watered the horses, and rested a few moments.

In about the middle of the lake, there appeared an eddy, and then came that noise of watery snuffling and puffing which used to make our hearts beat when we were going down the Shari or up the

Logone. The smooth surface was ripped across, and by the light of the moon we saw the snout of an enormous monster about thirty yards off. In those surroundings, which were on so small and homely a scale, the disproportionate size of the hippopotamus made the little lake look like an aquarium or pool at the Zoo. Unfortunately, at that very moment our porters were having a frightful shindy with Zézé, whom, for some reason or other, they were threatening to murder. Their clamours frightened away another monster which was wallowing in the reeds not far off and which immediately plunged into the water.

The country is hilly, with little hollows, which serve as jewel-cases for small Scotch lakes. We came again upon the Mayo Kebbi and recrossed it. This was followed by a large tract of savanna. Then there appeared on the horizon a little village which belongs to the dependency of Bibémi, where we decided to halt for our lunch and siesta. Doum palm trees, baobabs, and candelabra euphorbias. Not far from the village another lake. The sultan of Bibémi came to meet us – very fine and – as usual – very fat. The upper and *lower* part of his face was hidden by the black and varnished *lehfa* of his turban. He was escorted by a few captives, sumptuously clothed. He introduced us into his residence by the postern and we were brought chairs, milk, and two kinds of dates – one of them purplish (like carobs in colour) and without stones – groundnuts and corn. As I was admiring the boots of one of the men in his suite – they were in a kind of mosaic of plaited leather – the sultan sent for a pair of slippers in the same style and presented me with them, and Marc with a lion-skin. They had cut branches and requisitioned *seccos* so as to make a shady peristyle in front of the postern.

5 April

The *lamido* of Bibémi, who is in constant rivalry with his neighbour, the sultan of Reï-Bouba, is anxious to show us that he too knows how to receive guests. He preceded us into the capital of his sultanate, and then came back out of it to meet us, escorted by about a hundred variegated horsemen. He alone was in white, with a black turban. A dozen nobles, or captives, accompanied him and never ceased vociferating what one would take for insults from their tone of voice. They were translated to us as follows: 'How well he is!' (I think this must be a kind of optative like 'God save the King!' rather than indicative like '*fluctuat nec mergitur*'.) 'There is no one like him! No chief is as great as he. – He is good and generous; he benefits everyone with his riches' (and no doubt they speak from experience). When it is the sultan's heir who appears, as he did yesterday, preceding his father, to come and meet us – 'One has only to look at him to see that he is the son of a very great chief.'

The whole thing is very little varied, but there are several styles of saying it:

Firstly. Enthusiasm. It positively bursts out. 'I can't keep it to myself any longer.' In the style of 'Have you read Baruch?'

Secondly. Profound conviction; below one's breath, in a tone of fierce obstinacy. Style of '*e pur si muove*' – as if someone had been saying the contrary.

Thirdly. The matter-of-fact style – 'What else *could* I say?'

Lastly. The person who doesn't even attempt to enter into the game. Style of 'Here's your money's worth!'

These wafts of incense are flung out like stones from a sling or like the keening of paid wailers. Is it possible that the *lamido*'s ears are really gratified by them? But is it possible, either, that a God can take pleasure in prayers to order, or in the telling of beads and rosaries?

This morning we returned the visit the *lamido* paid us yesterday. On the other side of the postern there are a quantity of low huts which form a kind of interior city, with winding ways obviously arranged to make an intrusion difficult. In these huts, which are all more or less similar, the wives and children of the *lamido* hide away. I was presented with a superb pair of worked leather boots, some pyrograved and coloured calabashes, which, though not worth more than a few pence, are none the less charming, and some purses like the boots. In exchange for all this it was very difficult for us to know what to give him. We made Mahmadou, our interpreter (who has been with us since Binder), express our regret that we had nothing with us worthy of being presented to such a great chief, and say that we promised to send him some objects from Paris which we hoped might please him. He thanked us in anticipation. We promised too to send him the photographs Marc had taken of him, his son, and his court. I did not dare offer to pay for anything (except indirectly), even for the ox which was presented to our porters. We wanted all the people of the *lamido*'s suite to keep a pleasant recollection of our passage and I held out a hundred-franc note, which the *lamido* showed his escort, transmitting at the same time the chief of my good wishes. This was received with a concert of almost terrifying vociferations. Some of the courtiers had very striking and characteristic faces; one in particular with a hooked nose, whose photograph Marc took, might have been Acomat himself. The young chief of Biparé has been Bibémi's captive for a long time and he has always treated him, he says, as if he were his own son.

We started again at two o'clock and slept at Djembati.

6 April

Yesterday from Bibémi to Djembati the sky was white; a diffused and dreary dazzle. I forgot to mention the so-called *revolt* of our porters. I must say that at present our caravan is composed of seventy Moundangs whom we collected at Léré and ten Foulbés who have been with us since Maroua. Well, while we were visiting the sultan, someone came to inform us that the Moundangs had refused to go any farther; that they wanted to go back immediately to Léré; that a party of them had already left; that they must be brought back by force . . .

As soon as I got back, I sent for the *capita* and explained by means of the interpreter that I didn't want to make them do anything by force, that I had come to the country in order to defend the natives' interests, and that, if they desired it, I was ready to let them go. (This was saying a good deal, for if they had left me in the lurch, I should have been in great difficulties, as the sultan had expressly said that he had just sent to Garoua the entire number of valid men at the disposal of the village.) But, I went on, I was anxious as to the manner in which they would be paid; for if they were to leave me then, I should not be able to insist upon the Léré administration's giving them a different tariff from the Chad's, which is considerably lower, as they no doubt knew, than the Cameroon's, which I intended to apply if they came with me as far as Reï-Bouba. This speech in Livy's best style made a marvellous impression, and I should have imagined that I had brought my men round if I had not immediately discovered that they had never had any intention of leaving; that the man who had been suspected of running off had merely gone to fetch water from the river.

I tell this story just as an example of a misunderstanding that might have turned out badly if I had consented to use the high-handed methods that some people advise. Everything, as it was, ended happily with smiles and cheers.

The road – almost an invisible path, which we should not have been able to find without a guide – leads into hilly – almost mountainous – country, with great granite rocks that remind one of Fontainebleau.

Met with some enormous monkeys (cynocephali?) who went off quietly on all fours and barely hurried their pace when we rode towards them.

Not far from one of these miserable villages – or, rather, groups of huts, surrounded with *seccos* – we saw two enormous birds (every-thing is enormous here), a little bigger than pelicans and entirely black, except that their wings were edged with white, which showed when they opened them. They walked like geese, their heads and necks held very high, and seemed as if they had great difficulty in taking their flight, when we rode after them. They say that in the rainy season they lose their feathers, so that the inhabitants of the villages are easily able to catch them. I think that this and the jabiru are the biggest birds I have seen.

We urged on our horses a little and arrived at the end of the stage before sunset, having left our porters far behind. The stage was a long one, and we expected to see them come in exhausted. I had a bonfire lit to cheer them on their way. The night had long since closed in and we lay down on some reed mats to wait for them, as we ourselves were utterly done up. At last they arrived, invaded the enclosure, and, to our great amazement, as soon as they had put down their loads, began to dance round us a wild, extravagant dance, accompanied by shouts of 'Thank you, Government!' I pass it on.

Excellent fellows! how very unripe they are for laying claim to social rights!

*

Left N'Djembati a little before daybreak. After we had passed the granitic fold in the ground, we went through unspeakably monotonous country, without the slightest individuality. Small, sparsely growing woods – one might have been in the environs of Achères – and this for miles and miles. Sometimes there was a slight undrained hollow, where the crackled ground showed there had been a marsh in the rainy season. A few unhoped-for drops of water laid the dust a little and refreshed and moistened the air. One longed, after these months of drought, for some tremendous tornado, to drench the thirsty soil and bring the sleeping vegetation back to life. But no; there was barely enough to be surprised at; the drops scarcely seemed to fall; it was as if they were suspended in the air.

Crossed the dry bed of a little stream. On the other shore a horseman was waiting to welcome us; we were in Reï Bouba's country.

At the stage we found a party of four messengers, accompanied by fifteen carriers; the latter were loaded with ten baskets of rice, ten *bourmas* of honey, six of butter, five calabashes of honey cakes, besides an ox, which, however, had just escaped and which people were pursuing in the village.

Not knowing which road we were going to take, Reï Bouba, said these messengers, had sent similar presents on to the other road. He had not yet received the letter which the Bibémi scribe had written for us yesterday, but only Chadourne's, which had been forwarded from Garoua, where, it was thought, Reï Bouba had gone.

Crossed an interminable plain; every three kilometres a more or less fine tree. A few traces of game; but our porters, with their intolerable little whistles and shouts, frighten everything away.

Was it on account of this monotony that the approach to the Mayo Tchina seemed so beautiful? Water – and water that from a distance looked blue – a vast open space of sand. Our path followed the bed of the river for some time, then made up its mind to cross it just opposite the village where we were to camp. We had intended to arrive at Reï-Bouba tomorrow evening, but we are informed that the sultan wishes to put us off for a day, so as to be better able to prepare his reception.

REÏ-BOUBA

7 April

At what o'clock did we start this morning? Before four, no doubt. As early as three, perhaps . . . In order to cure our alarm-clock, which has a certain slowness of action (every now and then it takes it into its head to start going again), Marc has turned the regulator to *fast* – too far.

Another envoy from Bouba met me at dawn. He was the sultan's special interpreter. He talks French very decently. As far as I can judge from the pupils the Garoua school turns out (he is one of them), it is infinitely superior to the other schools I have seen in French Equatorial Africa. He was the bearer of a long and very interesting letter from Captain Coste, who commands the circumscription of Garoua. The interpreter also looked for us on the other road first. It is a much better one, they say (but considerably longer). More presents from the sultan.

At the stage, three led oxen were presented to us for our men (we accepted only one); some bowls of excellent milk, of which I managed to drink incredible quantities; some grilled, spurious pistachios – or, let us say, more simply, groundnuts.

I had started in my *tipoye* long before Marc; he came up with me at a gallop just at the place where the road strikes the Mayo Reï. Water! Clear, running water! I caught up a bath gown and hurried towards a fine granite rock on the river bank. Alas! the bottom was too muddy . . . There were a few enormous oysters, plastered like limpets on the rock.

The dreary aspect of the bush has been enlivened since yesterday by the appearance of flowers; they are not very noticeable, tubular in shape, fleshy, and of a creamy-white colour; not particularly beautiful, but with a sweet smell that recalls orange-blossom; today too we came across an exquisite plant, looking like a species of asparagus, except that it was a creeper, sometimes covering a whole shrub with a veil of white muslin; its flowers are very tiny, like spiraea. The stalks are furnished with a certain number of small thorns; it has bulbs – sometimes very large ones – with a very peculiar, rather strong, and not unpleasant smell.

A little before getting to Djoroum the road winds in between the *mayo* and a biggish lake, where we saw some hippopotamus snouts and the back of a crocodile breaking the surface of the water.

We reached Djoroum at eight o'clock.

A clean station hut; sand-strewn floor; well arranged; near an extremely poor and sordid village.

I went out with Outhman and killed two partridges (that is, he killed them). We are surrounded with a great deal of attention, very much honoured and watched over; neither Marc nor I can take a step without being escorted by the interpreter and two guards.

Now that we are visiting sultans, contact with the common people has become impossible.

During dinner an invasion of minute little flies, attracted by the light of the camp lantern. They stuck to one's bare arms, to one's perspiring forehead, got into the opening of one's shirt, and, without stinging, tickled most frightfully. We got frantic and rushed to the protection of our mosquito-nets.

The sultan Reï Bouba is the proprietor of all the goods of all his people.[1] The capital is a large centre, where an élite of notables and Kirdis of every race in the sultanate meet together. They are the old warriors of the preceding sultans who, after having defended their master, have settled round his dwelling. They work for their chief and are clothed and fed by him.

. . . The other *lamidos* of the circumscription, who were more or less under Yola, are considered by him as old 'captives'. He calls them his 'sons'

---

1. 'The Hilaga family conquered the country 250 years ago. Ardo Boudi died at the age of 100. Ardo Djoda died at the age of seventy-two. Boubandjiba died at the age of ninety-nine, after reigning sixty-nine years. His son Bouba reigned from the age of fifty-two to that of ninety-seven. Malou Hamadou was chosen sultan in preference to his fourteen brothers; these, after revolting, were all killed except the fourteenth, who escaped and became the father of Bouba, the reigning sultan.'

and shows his superiority by overwhelming them with his luxury and by constantly offering them presents, which they accept. He considers *giving* a mark of superiority.

Reï Bouba is able to see and judge things for himself. He does not believe that every white man is a superior; but he is capable of extreme devotion to anyone who gains his confidence.

(Extract from Captain Coste's letter)

8 April

We left Djoroum as early as half past four in the morning.

We had to reach Reï by nine o'clock, which was the time for which we were announced. It was a four hours' march to Reï and every hour a fresh messenger arrived to renew and enlarge upon the sultan's greetings and express the impatience with which he was expecting us.

At a certain spot, pointed out by the interpreter, we halted all our porters and dismounted, so as to wait for everything to be ready, and arrive neither too soon nor too late for this resolutely theatrical entry; also so as to lace up our boots and put on clean coats. We felt as if we were playing the children's game of '*Loup, y es-tu?*'

At last we were told that the moment had come.

And then we saw advancing towards us twenty-five horsemen, whose appearance, although bizarre, was sombre and sober; it was only when they had come close up to us that we saw they were dressed in dull steel coats of mail and had on their heads helmets topped by very strange crests. The horses were perspiring, prancing, kicking up the dust magnificently. Then they turned to the right-about and preceded us. Half a kilometre farther on, the curtain of horsemen divided and let through sixty admirable lancers, dressed and helmeted as for the crusades, on caparisoned horses, in the style of a Simone Martini. And almost immediately after, these parted in their turn, like the bursting of a dyke, under the pressure of a hundred and fifty horsemen in Arab dress, with turbans on their heads and each carrying a lance in his hand.

More floods of people then succeeded each other more and more rapidly, pushed forward by a thick wall of foot soldiers – archers in serried ranks and perfect order. Behind these could be seen something which seemed at first incomprehensible – this was a quantity of bucklers in hippopotamus hide; they were nearly black and held at arm's length by the performers in the rear. I myself was caught up into this extraordinary ballet, and everything seemed to melt into a glorious symphony; I lost count of details, and behind this last curtain of men as it parted, I beheld nothing but the sultan himself – surrounded by his bodyguard and standing before the town walls, a bowshot from the door through which we were to enter, at the foot of a little slope and in the shade of a clump of enormous trees. At our approach, he descended from a kind of palankeen drawn by stooping, naked men. There were two parasols over him – one, of crimson, shaded him directly; the other, much larger one was black, flecked with silver, and was held over the first. We dismounted from our horses and, extremely desirous of representing as best we could France, civilization, the white race, we advanced with dignity, slowly and majestically, towards the sultan's outstretched hand; we were flanked on either side by our two interpreters, the one who has come with us from Binder, and the sultan's, who came to meet us yesterday.

The sultan is very tall; less so, however, than I had expected from hearsay. I was struck by the beauty of his expression. He had certainly rather be loved than feared. He spoke in a low tone of voice, with his arm paternally, and as it were tenderly, laid on the interpreter's shoulder. After the first compliments had been exchanged, we mounted our horses again and went on in front of him into his town. Six trumpets sounded continuously (composed of a very long antelope horn, which is connected with an ivory mouthpiece by a sheath made of crocodile skin). The populace was picturesquely arranged in groups half-way up the slope.

We then rode to our camping-place, which is very neat and clean. Our followers' huts are of shiny golden straw and are quite new; the doors are bordered like the canvas cover of an English trunk. Our rest-house, according to the model followed nearly everywhere, is composed of two round, fair-sized huts, with doors that face each other; they are connected by a covered peristyle forty or fifty feet long, whose roof projects a considerable way over the little low wall . . . It is useless going on; descriptions like this convey no idea of the reality. Reï Bouba's presents were laid out in one of these huts.

An hour later we visited the sultan, after having announced our coming beforehand. At the foot of the big town wall (it is about twenty feet high and built of earth) were ranged about a hundred captives in ceremonial attire, their backs to the wall, and their javelins cast at their feet. The gateway is very wide and long. When they cross this threshold, the servants unclothe, as they are only permitted to enter the sultan's presence naked to the waist. The roof is supported by large pillars with false capitals, resembling the entablatures of the Susa palace. The wooden gates are extremely massive. Three men preceded us bent double. They advanced as though they were crawling, making their gestures on a level with the ground. We then found ourselves in an oblong enclosure, which was sanded with coarse river-sand, opposite a little piece of rising ground, on the top of which the sultan was sitting under a large tree. He rose at our approach, came down from the terrace, pressed our hands, and renewed his speeches of welcome. We followed him into a narrow, oblong room – a sort of passage. He made us sit down on a kind of divan-sofa, and himself lay down on a lower divan, not opposite, but beside us. The two interpreters remained crouching at the door; the sultan's private interpreter remained prostrate during the whole of our visit. An important subject of conversation was the Citroën which the sultan has ordered and which has no doubt been stopped at Lagos until the rainy season will enable it to be sent up the Bénoué. Marc is going to write the necessary letters to get it forwarded at once.

We have paid the seventy carriers whom we brought from Léré and who want to go back. Each of them gets twelve francs, according to the Cameroon tariff, which, as I have explained, is much more advantageous to them.

I sat outside the door of the hut, in the shade of the veranda, and had the men brought up one by one. To each of them I gave an A E F note, a French note, and four fifty-centime pieces. But the poor fellows have no more idea of what they are being given than of what they ought to receive. It seemed to me that they were all, without exception, amazed at getting so much; but also that they were more pleased with the four small coins than with the two notes; and I feel practically certain that if I had made them choose, they would have preferred the former. I made the experiment three times of giving a porter only one note and two coins; he went off with his six francs smiling and, to all appearance, nearly as satisfied as when I called him back and gave him double. This would be enough to prove that the poor creatures are at the mercy of exploiters and that if the administration does not protect them they are incapable of defending themselves in the least against traders who grind them down and who can always say: 'They are pleased with what they get. What more do you want?'

I inquired of the *capita* and the interpreter what they would do with their money, as I was afraid they might spend it all on their way home; but they assured me that, of the two notes, one would be kept to pay their tax.

'But they have just paid it.'

'Yes, this will be for next year.'

We have been round the village. Crooked streets between screens of *seccos*;[2] orchards of papaw trees; ceaseless activity; long processions of women fetching and carrying water. The streets emptied at our approach; the children hid; the women turned away; the people who did not run off stood up and kept their eyes lowered. Our two interpreters enveloped us with attentions and respect – circumvented us.

At Reï, as Marc was getting ready to film, the interpreter asked us whether it was true that in France there were people who came down from the sky with wings. (This is what they thought fit to show the natives of Garoua on the cinema.) I quote this as an example of stupidity, not, indeed, on the part of the natives, but of the people who chose a film likely to provoke such questions.

9 April

Fresh visit to the sultan, to whom we presented some trifling objects we thought might please him – a map of the country, a rubber hot-water bottle, a magnifying mirror, some Bengal lights, some rolls of cotton-wool. We promised to send him a watch and a new map from Paris. We also promised to do what was necessary at

2. A sort of long mats made of plaited grass.

Douala in order to retrieve a sewing-machine that is being held up there. So much amiability on our part no doubt encouraged him, and when I took leave of him, he held out his hand to me with a smile, but without rising. I should not have thought much of this if I had not been warned of the danger of letting him get too much puffed up. A similar adventure happened once before to Bruneau de Laborie; should I do as he did and return Reï Bouba his presents? No, not that; but when later on I came across the interpreter (Hamandjoda), I gave him to understand that I had noticed what had happened that day, and Marc, a little later, persuaded him that it would be proper for the sultan to return my visit.

Fresh visit from the sultan. Very simple, cordial, and interested by everything we showed him and said to him. No doubt his having remained seated, which had astonished me, had nothing intentional in it. At our request he gave orders for our departure. He never raises his voice, and even these orders were given in a whisper to the servant who stood beside him, and were then immediately transmitted by word of mouth from person to person.

We put up our beds in front of the rest-house, on the public place, in the shadow of a giant ficus. There were moments last night when the air seemed to thicken; the atmosphere became intolerably close and oppressive. My fatigue was intense. And in the deep silence of the night, after the turtle-doves in the ficus had grown quiet, we heard fits of coughing, as hoarse as the crowing of cocks, answering each other from hut to hut.

10 April

Although we were up before dawn, we did not leave Reï till rather late, for we had new porters to deal with, and the distribution of the loads is always very complicated.

On leaving the town the road crosses wide fields of millet, which at this time of year are empty. These fields are cultivated with spades. The sultan, it seems, judged it useless to introduce ploughs into a country where labour is so abundant and costs him nothing. For all the inhabitants and all the fields belong to him.

At last – or already – there are a few flowers on the roadsides, which are becoming more and more wooded: large blue panicum, big veronicas, some hypericum, and the promise of peonies.

Bouba has done his best for us; we have never had so spirited an escort. The porters, one and all, show a kind of ecstatic zeal; if a man is told that he has assumed a load that is too heavy for him, he protests the contrary, as if anxious to prove his valour. A boy of fourteen, Wilkao, seized hold of Marc's suitcase and made a point of honour of carrying it to the very end. Mala, a young bowman with a perfectly formed figure, dressed in a sort of blouse, which is tucked up on one side into a leather belt, and shows his bare thigh, looks like a Benozzo Gozzoli. He is not a porter, but a page – a companion *de luxe*, to whom we confided Dindiki's basket.

The forest grew thicker the nearer we got to the mountains, behind which the sun was setting; we skirted round them and discovered, situated at their foot, the village of Tcholèré, in Reï Bouba's dependency.

Majoresque cadunt altis de montibus umbræ.

We set up our beds outside the camp in the strange ambient of eight great ficus trees. They encircle and cover a platform of fine sand in front of the huts. Opposite the huts rises the mountain from which rolled the great boulders of granite on which our escort have seated themselves in little groups. Evening is drawing on. An ox – a gift of the sultan's – has just been killed for our men; they are eating and chattering, and at moments their laughter rings out so clearly that it is like the calling of birds. When I pass near them, they smile and raise their hands to their faces in a kind of military salute. 'Thank you, Governor!' What excellent people! This afternoon, as I was walking beside my *tipoye* in the sweltering heat, one of the *tipoye*-bearers made me a regular speech, which was translated by Mahmadou: 'It is too hot for you to walk on the road. The Governor will fall ill if he doesn't get into his *tipoye*.'
But under the baked awning of the *shimbeck* it was as hot as hell.

This evening I am lying on my deckchair, too tired to do anything but read a little Milton.

271

The night is wonderful. Is it a tree frog in the ficus trees which keeps dropping the same little pearly note so untiringly? No doubt. Outhman, when I question him, says it is not a bird.

11 April

We hoped to be able to wait here till night; but we are told that the stage is a long one. In fact, though we started at 7 o'clock in the morning, at 1 p.m. we had only done half of it and were thoroughly exhausted. How hot it is! The country is monotonous – an interminable forest, not in the least exotic-looking (the false karites look like Spanish chestnuts), but getting thicker and thicker and vaster and vaster. Big monkeys; an antelope. Zézé's boys are unlucky; the new one (who has replaced the old one we left behind at Léré) has been unwell for the last two days and seems very unfit to accompany us. I do not know what is the matter with him. Like all Negroes, the moment they are ill, he has become *limp*. He seems to be suffering from his heart. In that case it seems absurd that he should be obliged to make such an effort. I tried to persuade him (Marc wanted to force him) to remain behind. But the idea of being abandoned in this country, of which he doesn't know the language, terrifies him. He did not protest very loudly, but sweated great drops in his anguish. I think he was afraid of Bouba's keeping him as a captive and preferred expiring on the road with us. These unfortunate creatures stick to the caravan like limpets; they make one think of the soldiers who, when they are sick or wounded in an enemy's country, implore to be put an end to, rather than be left to linger abandoned.

I made the cook's boy get on to Mahmadou's horse and he took mine. And, as a matter of fact, I was glad to walk. But how long it was! We arrived exhausted at a place where we were able to rest for a few hours. It was on the summit of a hill that was burnt black with fire – a group of miserable mud huts with straw roofs – very ugly and very dilapidated. One of them had two entrances, which made an almost imperceptible and yet refreshing draught; we set up our table and beds to take an hour's rest and uncorked a half-bottle of Cliquot.

Started again at 4.30 p.m.

The road plunged into the mountains (very humble mountains). False acacias, false chestnuts, false Cévennes. The sun set as we reached the small and very picturesque camping-ground of Jet, which is perched on a buttress of rock and would be more picturesque still if one of the two big trees that sheltered it had not been laid low, either by lightning or by fire.[3] It has most unluckily fallen on the remaining one, making havoc of its finest branches. These bush fires will end by making another desert region of the whole of this country.

12 April

Set off very early in the hopes of getting as far as Tsatsa. I even began by getting up all by myself at 1 a.m., deceived by the porters' fires into thinking it was time to start. But there was no moon; the night was as dark as the inside of a coffin. I went back to bed again, drunk with fatigue and sleep, but slept badly and did not wait for the alarm to give the signal for starting.

The path was very bad, rocky, steep, and littered with rolling stones on which one was afraid to step in the dark. One could only creep on very slowly, with one's nerves strained, stumbling and slipping at every step. I was full of pity and admiration for our poor porters; each man helped himself with his assegai. At last, as the day was just breaking, we got to the bottom of the valley; a *mayo* flowed along it, whose abundant waters ran tumultuous and clear. Marc and I sat down on a granite rock that emerged from the stream to watch our troop cross over. In places the water was fairly deep, the current swift, the bottom uncertain. When they had all crossed, we mounted our horses to cross in our turn. All day long I was haunted by the desire and the regret for those clear waters.

An hour later we met Captain Coste's sister, who, with her escort of carriers, is going to join her brother at Garoua, where she is directing a technical school.

We gradually got farther into the heart of the mountains. They are still the Cévennes, but the high Cévennes. The ground became steeper and the path lost all pretence to being a straight line. We did nearly the whole way on foot and arrived fairly early at the little camping-place of Manne, where we were told that it would not be

---

3. See two pages later.

prudent to go on that day as far as Tsatsa, for we should not be able to reach it before nightfall; the road is bad and difficult; it would be impossible in the dark. Much use it had been getting up so early in the morning! At times one feels completely done up with fatigue – at the end of one's tether; one would like to give the whole thing up, like a child who calls out 'Pax!' in order to get out of the game he is playing. But perhaps the finest thing about this journey is the necessity of going on, the impossibility, as a rule, of taking into account the state of the weather, of one's own fatigue . . . I was told that a *mayo* was near at hand with plenty of water in it; I hurried off to get a bathe. Alas! I found nothing but a few puddles of brown water in among the rocks, on a bottom of mud and dead leaves. For we were in the middle of the forest. (One would have sworn the trees were oaks at that moment.) On all sides, on the flanks of all the hills, it stretched as far as one could see.

I followed the dry bed of the torrent for a few hundred yards downhill. The vegetation here was rather different; it seemed a small part of the great forest; there were big trees again, leaning over what was left of the pools, enormous creepers, and singing birds.

Then I went back to the camp, where Marc was awaiting the arrival of the main body of our troops; in the meantime he had organized a contest of assegais and arrows between our *tipoye*-bearers and pages. The sun had become overpowering. I sought some shade at the foot of an enormous boulder. Fire had shrivelled, blackened, dirtied, disenchanted everything. An uneven carpet of dead leaves, cinders, and charcoal lay on the burnt soil at the root of the trees. Not a blade of grass, not a trace of anything fresh, tender, or green was to be seen. But how was it that the dead leaves had not been burnt? They had not died, but had been suddenly withered by the fire. Will the trees that bore them be able to resist having been baked in this way and temporarily smothered? A great many of them will certainly never recover. The trunk will end by drying up and next year will fall an easy prey to the flames – it will become one of those trunks that can be seen in the surrounding desolation, that burn slowly, and gradually turn to ashes, continuing to smoke for days and weeks after the fire has gone by. As a rule, the fire attacks them at the base and performs the office of woodman, felling them to the ground. If the air is still, the form of each branch is traced on the ground by its ash. Sometimes the tree is hollow and, as it burns standing, turns into a chimney. At night it looks like a factory chimney, with showers of sparks and flames shooting up from its summit. Sometimes even, during the day's march, holes in the trunk form a draught and look like large red eyes – like incomprehensible signals. Often the burning continues below the surface of the soil; it follows the roots deep into the ground.

And here and there, in the midst of this desolation, grow those large mauve flowers, like cattleya flowers, that produce, I believe, the coral berry the natives are fond of eating.

On account of these perpetual fires, on account of the repeated displacement of races and villages, on account of the old forest's having been replaced by more recent vegetation, the constant and dominant impression – mine, at any rate – is of a new country, *without a past*, of immediate youth, of an inexhaustible spring of life, instead of the ancestral, prehistoric, prehuman feeling which travellers in this land prefer to talk of. The most gigantic trees of the equatorial forest do not perhaps appear so old as certain French oaks or Italian olives.

We gave the village people who brought our porters balls of millet a plateful of salt, which seemed to please them greatly – more even than notes. We are told that this is because the latter have to be paid in their entirety to Bouba, as likewise the smallest *matabiche*; all they will be able to keep for themselves is the salt, which can be consumed on the spot.

To take enough tinned provisions with one is not by any means everything. We have been too economical with ours, keeping them for worse days. Has the moment come to open the stewed pears? . . . Had an extra breakfast today with a delicious Olida ham.

13 April

Started at five o'clock this morning and arrived at the end of our stage at about one o'clock – after two brief halts of twenty minutes – in a state of physical and nervous exhaustion. I am filled with remorse as I think of our porters. Not only do Marc and I carry nothing, but we have our horses and our *tipoyes* to help us (it is true we hardly ever use them), and cold drinks of tea and mint water to refresh us *en route*. We know that at the end of the stage we shall find a deckchair to sink into, a bed to sleep on, a table ready served. They have got to do the march with a load of forty or fifty pounds on their heads. One expects to see them arrive completely exhausted – they are singing. Grumbling? – They say, 'Thank you, Governor.' Not a recrimination! Not a complaint! Always a pleasant smile in response to the word or two of friendly greeting we give them when we pass. They are admirable people.

The invisible village that lies hidden somewhere or other not far from the station was warned of our coming by advance runners. The caravan, on arrival, must find their 'balls' ready and a good sauce. The sauce today will be enormous white mushrooms, like *mousserons*, but their smell is too disagreeable to give us any desire to taste them.

The sky was overcast. The night brought no freshness. Going up one slope after another, we have gradually reached a good height. On looking round, indeed, nothing seems to be much higher – nothing *is* higher. The ground is still dry almost everywhere; but it must have rained lately, for there were some fresh stalks, some tender sprouts, some green grass . . . I tot up today's balance-sheet:

The botanical interest has been very great. Peat-mosses have formed in some of the depressions where the constant humidity permits of continual vegetation. Many of the flowers are unknown to me. Others are relations of flowers I know. There are balsams on the banks of the rivulets – with mauve, wide-open, almost flat flowers – not so beautiful as the little yellow-flowered balsam in the neighbourhood of Gérardmer. In the bed of a dried torrent there were some big amaryllis whose white flowers had veinings of a rather peculiar wine colour. Not far from them a charming orchis showed its tall spike of modest, greenish flowers, the lower petal spotted with dark crimson. A number of plants were still in seed – in particular some aconites (?) and another kind of Ranunculaceae, with innumerable tufts of fluffy seeds, like those of our clematis. A little dark-red aster. A new kind of eryngium. But the most astonishing was the beautiful big, pale mauve flower which I mentioned yesterday, growing flat on the ground, and often in the places that are the most burnt and the rockiest. The higher one gets, the more abundantly it grows. A strange thing is that some of these flowers have a sweet scent, though most of them do not smell at all. I have found another variety here, just a little less wide and of a dark crimson. The keels of both kinds are tinted with saffron. This flower has neither stalk (its stalk is in the ground and bears several flowers, all of which bloom on a level with the soil) nor leaves, and springs out of the ground like the colchicum, which it resembles in colour and delicacy; it is one of the most beautiful of this country. A few butterflies have made their reappearance.

There was one delicious moment whose recollection almost banishes that of my fatigue – the moment of bathing. Since . . . before Bosoum, we had not come across clear water. And here was a thickly flowing, cool, transparent stream! . . . I left the path, with Outhman to carry my bathing-gown, and found a pool deep enough to dive into, under a thick vaulted roof of foliage.

To my great surprise, on going up a little stream during one of the caravan's halts, I found some palm trees; and, still more surprising, some banana trees[4] (they are very rare – I have only seen four of them), or, rather, the skeletons or mummies of banana trees, without either leaves or fruit, showing merely some miserable remains of scorched stem. They were apparently wild – a very long way from all human habitation, on the high part of the plateau, before coming to Tsatsa.

We gave up the idea of reaching Haldou that evening, though we were told it was quite near – but we were all exhausted.

What an unspeakable relief – rain, an attempt at a storm! Although it was not much, all nature seemed immediately washed, refreshed, revarnished. After months of drought and waiting, the rapidity of the growth after a first shower must be amazing.

Outhman this evening came running to tell me that he had seen a 'balancing bird', like the one Coppet killed.[5]

---

4. My astonishment came from thinking that the banana had been imported from America.

5. See pages 134–5.

I have questioned the people of the country about the banana trees I saw on the road. They are really wild bananas. A certain number are to be found on the plateau near damp places. They dry up in the way I saw and then sprout again at the foot, after the rains. Their fruit is worthless.

14 April

Rain; a gentle, quiet, slow rain; not at all the appalling tornado I was expecting – longing for, almost. This rain, in fact, is as little exotic as it could well be. It relaxes one's nerves deliciously. The road makes an enormous circuit on the plateau – incomprehensible, because it leads to an exceedingly abrupt descent. There was very little variation in the vegetation. I saw no more bananas. In one damp hollow was a brilliantly coloured tree, with bracts of a rather orange-red – most striking; very small, insignificant flowers, tubular and yellow in colour, recalling those of the bougainvillea so much that I wondered whether it was not an allied species, though very different in its bearing.

Perpetually and everywhere, there are traces of more or less recent fires. Even in places where green grass is coming up again, this constant black grime is visible beneath it; there are great stretches of carbonized soil on which nothing remains to be seen but blades of grass stubble, which have come to look like the spikes of a porcupine.[6] Not a tree-trunk that does not fill one's hand with soot if one touches it. The whole countryside is spoilt – dirtied.

After this experience I think no country will ever seem monotonous again, nor any journey tedious. Yesterday, when after the interminable ascent (though it was interesting and there was water to be seen again) we thought we had nearly arrived, we were not even half-way.

Reached Haldou about eleven o'clock. Great nervous exhaustion. Exasperated with the carriers' chattering, which prevented us from

---

6. These burnt blades are marked with regular alternate stripes of black and white, exactly like the quills of the porcupine, which can move amongst them without being visible. The white part is due to the momentary protection of the leaf, which is itself consumed, but the base of which forms a sheath for the stalk and protects it in that place from being carbonized.

sleeping. It is not ill-will on their part, but the impossibility of understanding that such trifling noises can disturb us. As a rule, they obey the first signal with alacrity, and when once I cry: 'Silence!' there is no need to repeat it. But the camp here is arranged in such a way that we are all on top of one another. I got up three times – had a horse taken away, stopped the cleaning of some saucepans, interrupted some game or other . . . In the end my exasperation was so great that I gave up my siesta altogether.

About five o'clock, a little less strung up, if not really rested, I went out, and took Outhman to carry the gun; for this morning, while I was looking for a place to bathe along the banks of the little *mayo* that flows two hundred yards away from the camp (in vain; the banks were protected by a barricade of reeds), I started a partridge. We struck off sideways towards the left and reached a rather fine part of the river, where it flowed over great granite slabs. Then, after crossing it, we walked along the hill-side through some old millet fields. We recrossed the river a little farther on and reached a burnt village. With the sole exception of two huts which have been miraculously – and quite uselessly – preserved, everything was burnt: I mean, all the roofs, wood and thatch. Nothing was left but the mud walls of the deserted huts.[7]

A fairly large village; the huts were not all of them wretched. A number of them had a double entrance; they were nearly all arranged in the same manner, divided up into compartments by an ingenious system of low partitions.

Where have all these people gone to? In the deep silence of the evening, in this wild country, the appearance of this deserted village was unspeakably melancholy. The dismal sky might have been in Normandy.

Haldou, 15 April

So tired that I did not fall asleep till morning, in spite of *rhoféine*. And I was sleeping soundly when Marc came and shook my mosquito curtain. Rain. The beds which had been set up out of doors

---

7. The hut 'walls' in this country (and in particular the walls of the rest-houses) sometimes simply consist of a *secco*, set up like a round screen against twelve stakes, planted circlewise.

had to be hastily taken in. The next stage was a very long one. We had intended to make a start as early as five o'clock, but we had to put it off a little. The sky was black. But we could not go to sleep again. I was thoroughly exhausted. I think perhaps that it is by the dimness of my sight that I can best measure my fatigue . . . If people think that I complain a great deal, I reply that I see no reason why I shouldn't. Out of pride? I have very little, and place it elsewhere. The stoical silence which people admire in Vigny and which made him put one of the worst and most absurd lines in our language into the wolf's mouth:

Puis après, comme moi, souffre et meurs sans parler

(as if it were stoicism that prevented wolves from speaking any more than carps!) seems to me more ridiculous than admirable; and, as Molière would have said, 'pure affectation'. As for me, my habit is, when I suffer, to heave great romantic sighs, so profound that my suffering feels slight by comparison.

Nevertheless, I recovered a little freshness of mind, a little vigour, and even a little joy on the road. The uninterrupted forest became denser and finer. Even the soil changed. Great slabs of what I suppose was laterite began to cover the ground, which in places was bare of vegetation. When rock showed – in the beds of the streams, for instance – it was no longer granite, but a very hard stone, which was slightly vitreous where it flaked, and the colour of boot-leather.

One of our carriers brought us some of the wild bananas that grow in the bush; they were still green, but as big as market bananas and edible, we are now told, in contradiction to yesterday. That is the way in this country.

This morning Mahmadou and Outhman gathered some little fruits off the trees, of the colour, shape, and size of plums; they were slightly sweet, but almost intolerably harsh to the taste; as with almost all the fruits of this country, the flesh is undetachable from the stone, so that one can do nothing but suck them a little and then spit them out.

I used my *tipoye*, which I had not done for a long time past; this caused great enthusiasm among the *tipoye*-bearers, who for the last few days had continually lagged behind, but who at this immediately started off at a trot, singing, laughing, shouting, saying all kinds of things in which the words *'matabiche'* and 'Governor' recurred again and again. If I slipped my hand down at the back of my *tipoye* and let it hang, Ghidda would seize it rapturously. 'Thank you, Governor, thank you!'

With a few exceptions, there is very little shirking among these people. The youngest especially make it a point of honour to carry the heaviest loads.

We had gone on in front with our *tipoyes*, horses, and guards (the porters had been left far behind), when we came upon a herd of big antelopes. They were close to us – about ten of them, I should think, slowly crossing the path and apparently unaware of our presence. We stayed a long time watching them. I urged Marc to go after them, but we did not have the rifle with us. Mahmadou was dispatched back to the caravan to fetch it, and while Marc was waiting, I went on by myself on foot and got well ahead of the others. It was intoxicating to feel oneself all alone in the midst of this strangeness, far from everyone, all contact with the world lost, with no sound to be heard but the songs of birds, etc. – great empty spaces about one, where one hoped to surprise wild creatures – and here and there, in the monstrous forest, astonishing low palm trees with wide leaves.

Arrived at Mandakou at about one o'clock. This is the extreme limit of Reï Bouba's territory; a *mayo* forms the frontier. The river is in a deep cutting, in the manner of this country. As at Beaucaire and Tarascon, there are two rest-houses on the two opposite banks. We occupied the one on the Reï side, and, in order not to be disturbed by the noise of our porters, we sent them over to N'Gaoundéré, where they let themselves go.

This evening I saw another 'balancing bird'. But there must be several varieties of it; for this one did not seem exactly like the one I saw on the banks of the Shari; and that was not like the one I saw near the Ouham. Its flight is very rapid and erratic, and it must be very difficult to shoot.

Evening dragonflies. At noon, while bathing, I saw a *coral* one on the banks of the river. Night dragonflies.

*

I have been re-reading *Horace* – a play that particularly exasperates me. Its sentiments appear forced in the extreme, and forced all the more easily in that they remain abstract. And yet I am surprised; after an opening that drags, full of arguments and logic-chopping, Corneille soon rises to the highest flights; the character of Curiace is admirably drawn – admirably contrasted with that of Horace. The whole of this should be read over again with the utmost attention. All the second act is admirable – Corneille at his best, and so fine that I know nothing finer. In old Horace's farewell to Curiace the liveliest and most delicate emotion is reached.

16 April

As I go with my reading I am reinforced in my first impressions. The beginning of the third act, starting with Sabine's soliloquy, is a model of false, artificial psychology and of rhetoric without either warmth or beauty. And as to what follows! In particular scene iv, in which the two sisters-in-law discuss whether the loss of a husband or that of a lover is the more painful . . . etc., and with what arguments! None of this is human or sincere or true or natural. The whole of Act III is exceedingly mediocre when it is not exceedingly bad.

Equally absurd is Camille's soliloquy in Act IV, in which the imprecations of the later scene are prepared and worked up to. What actress could play this résumé of the situation, this recapitulation of its reversals and cross-purposes – what actress could carry it off?

But the fifth act is admirable in every respect. How greatly it pleases me that, after the action is over, the tragedy should be wound up and crowned by pleadings at the bar!

Woke up as early as four o'clock. My extreme fatigue yielded a little to the curiosity and interest aroused by the forest. It was denser here and taller. Never too dense, however, to prevent one from riding through it in every direction, regardless of paths. My horse has a very pleasant canter; I took advantage of it and we started, Marc and I, escorted by Outhman, Mahmadou, the interpreter, and the guards; we soon got far ahead of the porters, who had been in front at first. The ground was everywhere intersected by sudden dips and little *mayos*, mostly dry still. Nevertheless one had the feeling everywhere that it had rained. – A rather fine orchid on a tall stalk; its flowers, of a velvety purple, reminded me of the bee orchis. I left the path for a little and started an exquisite little fawn, almost under my horse's very feet. It was lying hidden in the grass. It bounded off with marvellous grace and lightness.

A little farther on, while Marc was behind, Outhman, who had come on with me, signalled a dog-faced baboon (*Cynocephalus*). '*K'bir, K'bir*.'[8] A moment later I saw it, and as it went off very slowly, I urged my horse after it through the undergrowth. The monkey was really enormous, almost as big as a man. Although my horse was bearing down on him, he did not quicken his pace; and even, after a little, he actually stopped, took up his stand on a rock, and when I came still nearer, turned round, stood up, showed his teeth, and began to utter a series of cries – a kind of yelps – more as if he were calling than as if he were angry. 'He is calling the ones that are bigger than he,' said Outhman, and advised me to go no farther. I have been so often told that all animals, without exception, fly from man that I could not believe that the monkey might attack me. No – but perhaps hold his ground . . . And, in fact, he took two steps towards us. We were not twenty yards away. I thought it more prudent to turn. But at that moment, seeing Marc in the distance on the road, I called him. At the approach of this reinforcement, the monkey fled.

A very fine ravine; big trees; big granite rocks. Running water; but it was not the hour for bathing.

The forest came to an end. And then began an immense space of bare plateau. Here and there on it, one or two kilometres from the road, were scattered little groups of five or six huts. We arrived about ten o'clock at a fairly large village (the first *Drou* village), where we thought the rest-house was. The cleanest, neatest village I have seen since I have been in Africa. All the *seccos* were new. Unfortunately this was not Gangassao, our goal. We had to go on again. We were told the rest-hut was 'quite near' – i.e., four kilometres in the blazing sun – more fatiguing than the whole of this

8. 'Big' in Arabic.

morning's road. We hoped to find some milk. But the herds belonged to the Foulbés, and this place is the Drous' – who are not on speaking terms with the former. (We succeeded, however – but with great difficulty, and after sending a deputation – in getting a bowlful.)

Gangassao. A half-deserted village. Quantities of burnt huts. The inhabitants fled about two years ago from a village chief they disliked, and settled down in the new, clean village, which we passed through just before. Impossible to get to the bottom of what really happened. As far as we could make out, the chief tried to curry favour with the powerful, and did not defend his people from the *lamido* of N'Gaoundéré's exactions. Impossible to get a definite answer from the natives – even to questions that need merely a yes or a no.

We started off again after a siesta which at last was quiet and restful, for Marc insisted on the porters' camping a long way off. They started before us, and as the stage was not very long, we only came up with them again at the little Foulbé village of M'Bang, though we did the eight or ten kilometres at a hand-gallop and without once stopping, hurried on by a threatening sky. This gallop over a great bare plain, under a cataclysmal sky, was so exciting that for a little while it got the better of my fatigue.

Rejoiced to find some excellent bananas again at the station. The village was a mass of greenery. The dry season is over. We dined outside the hut on the public place, which was extremely clean and well sanded. But as soon as we sat down to table, there was an invasion of *bobos* – a kind of ephemeral insect with very long wings,[9] which drop off almost at once. The table was soon covered with wings. As for understanding what became of the insects . . . !

18 April

N'Gaoundéré. The *lamido* came a long distance out of the town to meet us; as usual, he was the only one to be dressed in white. He waited to receive us on the top of the highest hill (the third before

9. Adult termites.

reaching N'Gaoundéré), surrounded by a considerable body of cavalry; so that the march to the town, at a foot's pace, as decorum requires, seemed almost interminable. There were about five hundred performers; a great number of French flags; cheers; yells. The whole thing was very fine, but without order and fearfully dusty.

Unable to note anything yesterday. Nothing exotic in the landscape, which, however, seemed too big for a France to contain it. Grey sky. No adventures on the way. Fresh, almost cool, air. We must be already nearly three thousand feet up.[10]

10. I leave these notes just as they are and apologize for their formlessness, which is due to my fatigue. I was afraid that if I endeavoured to rewrite them, they would lose that accent of sincerity which is doubtless their sole merit.

CHAPTER EIGHT

‹•••›

N'GAOUNDÉRÉ

All the amiability of the administrators, M.L. and M.N., has failed to get us comfortably lodged. The only hut which they would have liked to give us has just been burnt down. There was nothing to do but to fall back on a wretched two-roomed building, barely furnished, and still white with plaster, paint, and putty – for there are panes of glass in the windows; the floor is carpeted with a thick dust of brick, earth, and rubble, which the wind raised in eddies. Neither tables nor chairs. But the hospital is next door.

Considering the importance of N'Gaoundéré, one is likewise amazed at the ugliness and discomfort of the public offices. Their thin roofs of corrugated tin, laid upon barrack walls, are a blot on the hillside that faces the native village. It might be beautiful and it is hideous.

Yesterday evening Marc suddenly declared that he was utterly done up. And I at once felt ashamed of my fatigue and complaints. For the last ten days (and even for longer) I have fallen into the habit of allowing everything to rest on him. All the difficulties, arrangements, management of the porters, have lain on him. I have allowed myself to be easily persuaded that it is better that only one person should look after the commissariat department. But it is an exceedingly fatiguing task.

Yesterday evening an attack of fever obliged me to take to my bed, while Marc went to see the *lamido*. We decided nevertheless to leave on Monday the 19th (we arrived on the 17th), so as to try to catch the boat at Douala on 13 May. Unfortunately the telegrams we wanted to send – to order a car to meet us at Yoko, to engage our cabins in the *Asie*, and to let them know in Paris that my letters are not to be forwarded — have been held up, as the line has been temporarily interrupted in consequence of a tornado.

We have paid off our porters – both those from Maroua and those from Reï-Bouba. Six men of the last batch, however, are to come with us as far as Douala; we are to help them retrieve a certain sewing-machine which the sultan has ordered and which is being held up at the customs; these six men are then to take it back to him. It was with real sadness that we said goodbye to the others, and I think they too were sorry to leave us. A real feeling of reciprocal attachment very soon arose between us and these excellent fellows . . . People go on saying that nothing can be got out of the natives of this country except by force and constraint. If they would only try another method, we should soon see the result. The Negroes are perfectly able, no matter what anyone may say, to distinguish between kindness and weakness, and there is no need to terrorize them in order to make oneself feared. It is better to make oneself loved. This, I think, is the sultan Reï Bouba's system. It was ours. After a few days we saw a devotion arising in these simple creatures' hearts, which would very soon have turned into fanaticism.

I have already said that no subject of Reï Bouba's possesses anything of his own; he cannot even dispose freely of his own person. Everything he receives, whether as wages or tips, must be handed over to the sultan. We understood the reason for this custom, which at first sight appears abusive and contrary to the rights of individuals, when we learnt that all our free porters (those from Maroua) had let themselves be cleared out of the whole of their pay the very same evening that they received it, by gambling with some crafty and unscrupulous native soldiers; Reï Bouba's subjects, on the contrary, had refrained from risking pay that had to be handed over to their master.

Amane, 20 April

The commissariat service becomes particularly difficult with every fresh change of porters.

Left N'Gaoundéré yesterday very late. Sorry we were obliged to do a great part of the road by night; it looked to me, by the dim light of the half-moon, beautiful and somewhat novel. But perhaps it was not so much the forest that was changing as the season. We are getting into spring. The forest is traversed by quantities of steep ravines. In one of them, which we crossed long after sunset, we heard a strange croaking, which must have come from an enormous frog, to judge by the volume of sound. Curious fireflies, much larger than those of the Congo – *fulgores* probably. It was impossible to catch them – the ground was too rough.

Arrived at Anan about nine in the evening.

I have said nothing of N'Gaoundéré. I hardly saw it – too tired – and no curiosity. In the early morning, however, seen through the mist, from the hill opposite the station, the town looked very beautiful. Towards evening I decided to take a walk in the streets; they are wide and clean; everyone gets up as one approaches and bows very low. The women run away and hide. The marketplace was extraordinarily animated; but it was late; people were beginning to pack up. The streets have mud walls on either side of them; inside the walls are huts with pointed roofs, with quite a different thatch from the other huts we have seen (the kind they take a handful of to use as a rag); the straw of these is finer and more pliable; it makes a sort of dishevelled mat and falls in an uneven fringe along the edge of the roof (very Indo-Chinese-looking), covering it like an extinguisher.

Nakourou, 21 April

Another stage accomplished. The indications again say twenty-nine kilometres. Rather fine country. Still the same forest (false karites, for the most part), but more varied. New species of plants in the ravines.

Our troop has never been larger, though the loads are diminishing. We left two vast deckchairs, given us by Coppet, behind at N'Gaoundéré, as they will be of no further use to us – also various superfluous supplies. But we are taking on two *tipoyes*, which means sixteen bearers. We use them very little, however. They are more a precautionary measure. But in the state of fatigue I am in after two or three hours' march and another two or three hours on horseback, I was glad to get into mine. And, besides, at Tibati we shall be obliged to send our horses back to N'Gaoundéré, on account of tsetses and consequently of sleeping-sickness.

Keigama Tekel, 22 April

Here we are at Keigama Tekel, exactly half-way between N'Gaoundéré and Tibati. After a good night's rest we did this stage – the longest – without too much fatigue. Started a little before six o'clock, after having sent the porters on ahead. Did the first hour on foot; the rest on horseback. The ravines are more and more overgrown with vegetation that is getting more and more tropical; we have almost got the great forest again. The *vernonia* has reappeared. Again saw two banana trees right in the forest; the old stem was dried up, but the young one had sprung up close beside it, all burnished gold.

Some of the river-crossings were thrilling. The trellised bridges of dried branches are often eaten away by termites and are far from inspiring confidence, so that one prefers to attempt the acrobatic feat of sending one's horse down the steep slope beside the bridge. He goes down it gingerly and then, once the ford is passed, scrambles up the other side in one or two bounds.

Halted at one of these *marigots* to take a meal of hard-boiled eggs, Cheshire cheese, and cold tea, under an enormous tree and in the circling embrace of its roots, that made a vaulted roof over the water. Tasted some very pleasant, 'sleepy' little fruits; there were others exactly like our sloes, but with a milk-white sticky pulp round a mauve kernel; extremely astringent and tasting of turpentine.

Met two white men, accompanied by their convoy – Lamy, a 'special agent' who is being sent to Maroua, and T. Monod, who is employed in the ichthyological department of the Museum, and who has been commissioned to study the fish of the Chad.

I am almost astonished to be feeling better. Some of my ductless glands seem to have begun working again – the ones that supply one with energy and curiosity.

We were waked up from a deep siesta by the approach of a tornado. The sky looked really terrifying. It was the colour of ink and uniformly dark on the north side. A violent wind blew this menacing mass towards us, raising whirlwinds of dust, overturning the *tipoyes*, tearing off a great bit of the roof. We sat down on the edge of the plateau (the station hut is built on it and overlooks an immense expanse of wooded, very hilly country) to watch the approaching catastrophe. The colours were admirable; a sunny *ocellus*, of pale green, moved rapidly along, surrounded by the dark green of the neighbouring forests, while in the distance was a background of violet hills washed with rain, which appeared to be falling in abundance. At times there were monstrous flashes of lightning on the horizon. They flashed three or four times in succession over exactly the same place, each flash in the very track of the first, just as we had seen at Coquillatville. The whole affair travelled rapidly towards us. The first drops fell. We hurried indoors . . . But no! It was a false alarm. The storm appeared to respect the station. It rained all round it, but we came in for nothing but a very short, slight shower – hardly enough to freshen the soil and lay the dust.

Niafayel, 23 April

Marc was seized yesterday with violent toothache, which lasted all night and only yielded towards morning to a double dose of Soneryl and *rhoféine*. And this morning, during the march, the pain, which had been calmed for the time being, began again worse than ever.

Started rather late (7.30 a.m.), but the stage was not so long. The country is becoming more and more interesting. Flowers now cover the ground on the borders of the *marigots*; round about the first *marigot* we came to after leaving the station, there was in particular a crop of amaryllis as abundant as the pheasant-eyed narcissus in the fields round Uzès. Enormous flowers – and sometimes seven in bloom at once on the same stalk – but smelling a little of chloride of lime.

Found another amaryllis in the bed of another *marigot* – still larger – completely white.

In a meadow – a tiny kind of lawn on the margins of a *marigot* – there was a brilliant yellow flower; it was very strange and I cannot tell what family to ascribe it to. It grows on a level with the ground in a cup of round leaves.

There was a third species of amaryllis in the river, or on the sandbanks that were half covered with water; six petals (or three petals and three sepals), very long and very white.

But the most astonishing flower of all was found by Marc as we were going down the hill, a little before getting to the station. It had no leaves and had sprung from a bulb, which was very near the surface of the soil; it was like an enormous coral-red dandelion seed (a crinum?).

The descent from the plateau was very fine. The road was extremely steep, skirting along thickly wooded ravines. The trees taller than ever.

While Marc was resting, I went on foot through the savanna to the bed of a river (still dry) that follows the bottom of the valley. Much interested by the termitaries. I disturbed a score or so of them and discovered six or seven varieties; they are sometimes frequented by ants; sometimes they are inhabited by little black termites and ants living all together (?). Others are occupied by adult termites with very long wings; one wonders how they will ever be able to get out from underground, for all the issues seem to be stopped up. These are the same winged insects that fell upon our table the other evening in such masses, the same that Dindiki fed upon, and *that lose their wings*; the table was strewn with them in a few minutes; but we couldn't see what happened to the insects after they had lost their wings. When I held Dindiki over a termitary that had been disturbed, he dashed at it and attacked it repeatedly with his tongue, so that he filled his mouth with termites and earth.

Ganlaka, 24 April

Every day there are new flowers. A tiny saffron crocus. A large flower the colour and shape of purple cistus. Again, in considerable numbers, the canary-coloured flower we saw the day before yesterday, in a cup of thick leaves. These leaves are as fleshy as those of the sedum or the echeveria; they are shaped like those of the latter and delicately edged with carmine. They grow on an extremely fragile rhizome, which I could not succeed in getting out of the rocky ground without breaking.

*

Slept well, thanks to Sedobrol. This stage, though one of the longest, according to official information, did not tire me. Started at five o'clock and arrived at Ganlaka at 11.30 a.m. If we had to go on again this evening, I should be ready. We knew that the road passed near a lake (in an old crater, people say, but I doubt whether this is correct). At first a mass of dense mist lying in a dip of the ground that was bare of trees might have been taken for a lake. Yes, really; through the branches it looked like water. But farther on, it really *was* water we saw as the mist parted: it was like a Scotch loch, partially surrounded with low woods, and then with tall reeds and black rocks; there was an open space between the road and the lake, which looked like peat-moss, but it was in reality quite dry and we rode our horses over it. Shreds of mist were still floating over the water; the sun had only been up an hour. As we came to the waterside, three big does ran off along the shore. There were quantities of fish, some fairly big, and striped like perch; also other smaller ones, which Outhman and Zézé tried in vain to catch, wading into the water after them. I should have liked to bring some back for the Museum, as I heard yesterday that Monod, in spite of his being an ichthyologist, had not stopped here. I consoled myself by capturing two cicindelas (tiger beetles). As I didn't have the poison-bottle with me, I put them for the time being into the same box, without thinking of their pugnacious habits. When, a little time after, I opened their temporary prison, I found nothing but a few remains.

A swarm of dragonflies (two kinds – some with dark red or black spots, some with entirely transparent wings) followed me, skimming along the ground and hovering round each of my footsteps.

One or two kilometres from the lake, in a thickly wooded place, looking rather damp and shut in, there were quantities of wild bananas growing. Nothing can describe the beauty of these great leaves in the shade and freshness of the morning – light green in colour, still intact and *cabbage*-like in form. On one of them I found a little tree frog – yellow all over, with pink suckers at the end of its feet.

25 April

The last stage before Tibati. Said to be the longest. We left by 4.30 a.m. and the porters by 4. Arrived at 11 o'clock, only slightly tired. We started on foot, ahead of the horses, which we had put to spend the night in the village. At dawn we had to cross a *marigot*, and I sat down by myself to wait for Marc by the waterside; after a little I heard the most singular noise among the dead leaves at my feet. It was like the crackling of a shower, not of rain or sleet, but of hail. The sound was not continuous; it went over the ground like a wave, swelled, died down, and swelled up again at regular intervals. I came to the conclusion, after careful observation, that it was produced by an army of insects, evidently under the leaves. It was too dark among the undergrowth for me to be able to see anything. Outhman, who came up just then, at once recognized the noise, which was as rhythmical as a chorus of boatmen; it was termites at work. He struck a match and raised a layer of dead leaves – the devouring host was there.

Crossed two large wadis; halted in the shade on the banks of the first, after fording it on horseback; the water came up to the horse's belly. Parallel to the wadi, and not far from it, was a German trench. Crossed the second wadi by canoe. We were very near Tibati by that time. Two sets of messengers came to meet us (without counting those who were waiting for us at the stage yesterday, and who presented us with some horribly rancid butter). Soon after, the *lamido* himself, with an escort of people dressed in a sort of red uniform, made his appearance. Salutations passed and then everyone mounted and rode the last three kilometres at a foot-pace.

This is a large village. Groups of Sara dwellings, as usual enclosed round with *seccos*. There is a permanent market in the public place: large butchers' stalls; two kinds of salt – grey and white; manioc flour in calabashes, which the bees rifle; antimony (?); beads; a few mangoes; various spices; cloves; cigarettes.

But on my side there is a growing *lack of curiosity*. The station is agreeable. A Swedish missionary is settled not far off.

Two days ago hookworms made their odious appearance again; this morning the extractions were highly unpleasant, followed by sousing the places with iodine to cauterize them.

Yesterday forty-two of our porters asked to return at once to N'Gaoundéré. It had been agreed that they should come with us as far as Yoko – or even, to be more accurate, as far as Matsa, the next stage, which is accessible by the car that is to come and take us to Yaoundé. Query: are these men really wanted for their work on the land, as they say themselves? In that case they should be allowed to go, as the *lamido* here undertakes to provide us with other carriers. It is indeed inadmissible that for the sake of a white man's convenience a whole village should risk being starved. We should be taking these people twelve days away from their homes – an absence in all of twenty-two or twenty-four days. The lack of administrative stations on this Cameroon road, which would allow of relays between Yoko and N'Gaoundéré, necessitates this. We discussed this case of conscience with the interpreter; he declared that work on the land had not really begun yet, that the men should have said what they are saying now before they started; that they had not been taken by surprise. I pointed out to them that there was no administrative station at Tibati, so that they would have to go back to Yoko before being paid; that moreover their pay was good – considerably better than in the Congo – and that besides I would give them a good *matabiche* if I was satisfied with them. In short, I tested the force of their objections, which at last gave way before my arguments, and soon there was no trace of them left. But I must add that we have never had a batch of porters to whom I have said goodbye with less regret. For the first time there has been no cordiality – or hardly any – between them and us, during these six days. They are professional porters, who have already taken on certain professional habits of mind and body. They submit to this hard imposition on the part of the administration (or of their sultans), but with a bad grace, and because they cannot help themselves.

The natives of Tibati are more evasive – more unapproachable than ever. As soon as they see you, the children run away and the women hide. I no longer have the patience – nor the curiosity – it would need to gain them over slowly and cunningly. These town people, moreover, are spoilt – less simple, I mean, and consequently less interesting than those of the bush.

26 April

Yesterday evening we were invited to take tea with the Swedish missionary. I have not enough imagination to take this simple and *naïf* creature for a spy. The tea-party dragged a little; it was followed by an open-air sermon, as on every Sunday. The good man learnt the Haussa tongue in *Denmark*! He admits that so far he has not made a single convert and that no one listens to him. These lectures of his must be curiously painful. 'They go on talking to each other, but they listen all the same,' he said, 'and Christ's truth sinks slowly in.' Marc wanted to film the scene, but a violent storm dispelled these projects. The first tornado. Diluvial rain and terrific claps of thunder.

Towards evening Marc was seized again with violent toothache. The perspiration poured from him and he was writhing with pain. The pain soon became so severe that we decided to make an injection. But what a business! The morphia and the syringe were stowed away in canteen No. 1 among the most complicated medley of small objects. I managed to get it out, however, while Marc was bathing his aching tooth in mouthfuls of brandy and *eau de Botot*. I woke up Zézé, who re-lighted the fire. First of all, the syringe had to be boiled, for it had been put away unwashed after having been used for Dindiki's injection of caffeine; and then the glass piston stuck. In my vain efforts to free it I only succeeded in breaking the instrument and making my fingers bleed. Fortunately a double dose of Soneryl took effect, and the night ended in slumber.

We left Tibati this morning rather late. Yesterday's rain had cooled the atmosphere. I started by myself on foot, after the porters, but before Marc and the horses,[1] who only came up with me an hour later. I was feeling well. I had been able to sleep without a soporific. I took pleasure in walking, breathing, being alive. Extremely interested by the spurt the vegetation has taken. The traces of fire are disappearing, either because they did not exist in this region or

1. For though we were begged not to take the N'Gaoundéré horses farther than Tibati, the *lamido* of Tibati offered to lend us fresh ones for the two or three first stages towards Yoko, as the tsetses do not begin till farther on.

because they have been covered by the outbreak of spring. But the insects here interest me even more than the plants. The better part of the morning was occupied by hunting cicindelas. I have found seven species of these in the last few days. Some of them are very difficult to catch, not merely on account of their agility, of the promptitude and rapidity of their flight, but also because of their cunning, and the singular habit they have of not flying *before* the enemy, but of immediately going behind him, so as to escape from being seen. One faces round as quickly as possible, but it is extremely difficult to make out where they settle. Several of us together set about chasing them on all fours along the path. Outhman, as usual, was particularly clever at it, and it is always he I call to my help when I see a new species (often when I am on horseback) which I am afraid of missing, for my sight has failed a great deal in the last few months. The smallest species of all, which I was unacquainted with, is no bigger than a fly and of a perfectly dull appearance; in spite of their being particularly quick to take alarm, we succeeded in catching a few of them, and I rolled them up in toilet-paper till I could lay my hands on the spirits of wine.

There was a big violet orchid in the bush, on a spike, like an artistic foxglove.

It was no doubt yesterday's tornado which broke the telegraph-wire that follows the road from N'Gaoundéré – an accident of frequent occurrence. We retraced our steps, with the vain intention of repairing it. Impossible without tools. I was astonished that the wire was not fixed to the insulators, but merely laid on them, so that it remains loose and much more liable, I should have thought, to yield to the first onslaught of the storm.[2]

Near the station of Niandjida, which we reached after midday, a few pineapple plants made their reappearance (but only their leaves). We have also seen several times within the last few days a

2. The line was repaired that very evening by a workman, who was at once sent from Tibati and who joined us in the evening at the station. It had been broken in two places. The service seems admirably organized.

large solanum with dark-violet flowers and a fruit like a shiny white egg.

No sooner do we arrive than we all set to work to examine our feet. The Congo hookworms were nothing to these. There are superabundant quantities of them here. They have a little respect for our white feet, and for our porters', which are, I suppose, particularly horny; but our poor boys, although they wear boots, are covered with them. And up till now I had only seen them when they were embedded; but Zézé called us to point out four, five, six, running over his foot, on the search for a crevice or a tender spot.

After my siesta I took a little path which led to the neighbouring *marigot*. The farther south one goes, the more tropical is the vegetation which surrounds each of these streams. I followed the belt of forest till it took me deep into a marsh. Delighted to see once more the big climbing palm (*Eremospatha cuspidata*) which we had left behind on the other side of the line. But no! This was not it, though it looked very like it from a little way off. I went up to it; the stem from which the palms spring is bristling with thorns; on the other hand, the palm leaf itself has not got the kind of harpoons that make the other such a formidable creeper.

Voudjiri, 27 April

These latter stages are by far the most interesting. It is as though the country were trying to make us regret it. I question it anxiously; not that I expect any 'lesson' from it, but I want to speak to it alone, from heart to heart, as to a friend one must soon leave. As the night was drawing to an end, I went on in front, ahead of our troop. The day was dawning as I reached the margin of a deep, full *marigot*. I heard a sound coming from the other shore, which I recognized as the yelpings of baboons; in the dimness of early morning twilight and the forest gloom I did not manage to see them, but only a band of very small monkeys performing acrobatic feats in the branches of the tallest trees and announcing their presence by shrill squeaks.

I left the path to observe closer at hand the vegetable drama of an enormous tree being stifled to death by a ficus. The tree-trunk was growing slantwise. The ficus, which had dropped down perpendicularly from one of the branches, which was ten times bigger than itself, had wound tightly round its middle; its rootlets, which in their turn had become trunks, were squeezing it like the arms of an octopus. The tree is doomed.

When I got back to the path, five natives were standing on it. One of them was carrying a load of banana slips ready to graft. All five went off almost at once into the forest depths, along a very narrow and almost indistinguishable track; I looked after them for a moment and saw them cross the river on the trunk of a fallen tree.

A new orchis has cropped up, which in the distance I took for a gladiolus. The flowers are citron colour and delicately streaked with carmine.

Another *marigot* hidden under vegetation still more exotic. Among the great trees of the forest, and almost as tall as the tallest, was a prodigious and extraordinarily ramified pandanus. But why were there such a quantity of dead trees in one of the dells near this *marigot*? Their death did not seem due to fire,[3] for the soil is very swampy and does not lend itself to any sort of cultivation.

I lingered some time on the road where I was looking for cicindelas, in order to watch a mason fly which was dragging a large spider after it backwards. Where was it being taken? No doubt to an earth-hole like the one we saw yesterday evening, into which a mason fly of the same species was burrowing. After every backward dive, it brought back a scoop of earth with it, which it proceeded to smooth down all round the hole and to some distance from it, so that there should be no fear of falling into it again.

I have again come across the astonishing aroid I admired so much at the falls of the Djoué; it is composed of a single leaf – the same plant, I think, that Costantin mentions in his book on tropical vegetation.[4]

A porter brought us one of the most curious flowers I have ever seen. A score of little wide-mouthed pentagonal bells are arranged round a central point (like the garlic flower), on limp and rather drooping peduncles. The strange – the prodigious thing about it is the colour and texture of the flower. It looks as if it were cut out of

3. The natives as a rule employ this method for clearing the land with a view to cultivation.
4. *Dracontium gigas* (?).

velvet, and its colour is *grey* – an unknown colour in flowers – as grey as half-mourning suède kid gloves (and very much the same material). A little later I saw the plant itself in the bush; it is about eighteen or twenty inches high, like the alstroemeria in bearing, with a similar seed, as far as I remember (must verify this), which is pentagonal like the flowers. I had it dug up by the roots, and brought up a fairly large-sized bulb, as flat as a pancake, which I intend to take home, though without much hope of being able to grow it.

Met M. Pascalet, who is going up to Garoua to study the growing of cotton. When he heard my name, he said: 'I am reading a book of yours.' But, as usual, this was a mistake. It was my uncle's *Traité d'économie politique* he had with him in his *tipoye*.

The road followed a saddleback between two deep and thickly wooded ravines. It was the finest and most interesting part since we left Pouss.

Saw a large purple arum with a short, very wide-mouthed flower.

On the edge of the forest were a quantity of flowering bushes; some with white bracts, others with sumptuous scarlet bracts. Then in the bush there were other isolated shrubs with flowers like perfectly round balls; they were as big as chestnuts and made in milk-white corded velvet with an orange ground. Many of the shrubs were covered with fruit. Since the recent rains the grasses have already grown to a height of nearly three feet. It is true that we are farther south, where everything is more forward.

The descent, after leaving the saddleback, was exceedingly fine. Caught sight of a little village hidden away in the fold of a deep-lying, shut-in *marigot*; the huts were round, with pointed straw roofs. But the road passed it by on the right and went on up the opposite slope.

Beautiful as the road was, the distance to the stage was too long. We arrived at Voudjiri after midday, dead-beat.

The village has been deserted – removed farther off. After our siesta we visited the *marigot*, which is a very large one (quantities of crocodiles, we were told). The water is muddy and flows sluggishly under the drooping branches of the great trees. A little path that is barely visible follows the stream downhill as far as the rapids.

Luxuriant vegetation. Enormous ruby-red and emerald-green bugs, edged with a yellow and black check; in spirits of wine, alas! they turn black.

Hardly able to sleep last night. Again extremely tired. A sort of internal stiffness; a stitch in my side; I couldn't turn in my bed; obliged to give up riding. I started on foot in the dark, before the porters and without having breakfasted, and reached a village which was still fast asleep. We woke up the chief – an enormous, laughing black, who was amused at having been caught in his sleep. He ordered some bananas to be brought for me. Then up came my *tipoye*; I was exhausted.

Dindiki has made a meal of cicindelas, flinging himself upon them furiously. Two new species – nine in all:

1. Black, with four pairs of light yellow spots arranged like those of our French cicindelas, and ivory-white mandibles.[5]
2. Black, edged with pink.
3. Bigger, with a slower flight (perhaps the wing-cases are fixed – can it be a carabid?). Its hind legs too seem shorter and not adapted for jumping. Black, with a yellowish-white spot in the middle of the wing-case and on the side.
4. Great numbers of the small, round kind; emerald-green, which turns blue or purple in spirits of wine.
5. Black, with brown transversal stripes.
6. Very small; black, resembling a fly.
7. The size of our French cicindelas; brown, with a wide black velvet stripe down the middle.
8. Large; dull green; considerably bigger than the others.
9. Black, with a little blood-red spot on the side.

I was so much distressed to see them turn a uniform dull black in the spirits of wine that I tried to keep some of the last species I captured in the cyanide bottle, and then in a matchbox.

Cicindelas, with their powerful and murderous mandibles, are

---

5. The same one, but perceptibly larger (the female, perhaps?), has black mandibles, edged with white.

incapable of making holes in the paper in which I wrap them up, while certain small, apricot-coloured coleoptera (chrysomelids), with apparently inoffensive jaws, manage, by first moistening the paper, to perforate it very quickly.

We have reached our antepenultimate stage – Samé, where we are to leave our horses. The station is well kept; the rest-house very spacious (three rooms, as usual; the centre one thoroughly airy; a veranda outside). We left Islam and its influence behind at the last station. The village chief (Samé, I think, is his name) came to meet us in a very long, very shabby frock-coat, with a khaki cap, khaki breeches, black leggings, and hobnailed shoes. The whole sight of him ineffably ugly and ludicrous. A large foolishly good-humoured face, and a moustache *à la Kaiser*; but he has shaved it under his nose and kept only the ends. We saw him again later on, but then his bare feet projected from blue and white pyjama trousers. He presented us with a pineapple.

There were beautiful large butterflies again in the neighbourhood of the *marigots*; but, alas! I had nothing to catch them with.

Bounguéré, 29 April

One stage less to do – one of the longest and least interesting of the whole journey too; but, all the same, half-way there there was a narrow strip of big forest to cross that was very fine. The curious thing is that it is not a strip that only follows the bottom of the valley, as usual, but one that stretches right up to the top of the hill. Marvellous denseness of the vegetation. Disappearance of the cicindelas, with the single exception of the smallest species – the one that is so difficult to catch; and, even so, I am not sure that it is the same. Some novelties in the vegetable world; in particular, a bush with spikes of little green trumpet-shaped flowers, and a fine red and yellow lily – rather vulgar, however, and, like the amaryllis we have been seeing lately, in not very 'good taste'. The size and bearing of a martagon lily.

Yoko, 30 April

A fairly short stage. Left not much before six o'clock. Arrived at eleven. Nothing very new on the road. A tree with big yellow flowers – a kind of bignonia; leaves like a sephora; inhabited by a little weevil; I collected its larva in the pulp of the calyx.

Very dilapidated rest-house; the roof was broken in, and, what was worse, half the building was being used by a native trader to dry rubber in (black Congo rubber). A horrible smell of latrines. The huts that were given to the porters had fallen to pieces. And we were also astonished that the administrator, M.B., chief of the sub-division, did not come to meet us. He turned up a little later, however, with a pipe in his mouth. All was explained. It was the end of the month. There was an excessive amount of administrative work. The real station hut had been burnt down three weeks ago. They had had to fall back on the building which had previously been given to the trader. As for the porters, there were huts for them in the village. We were expected to lunch with Father X., a Belgian, who was on his way to N'Gaoundéré.

1 May

My little Dindiki's death has cast a gloom over me. This morning, when I opened the basket where I shut him up every evening, I was astonished to find him for the first time in exactly the same place and position in which I had left him overnight. It was abnormal for a little nocturnal animal not to have stirred all night. I tried to take him, as my habit was, but he would not suffer himself to be touched and bit as hard as he could – a thing he never did as a rule. He was obviously uneasy, and was looking for something (and had been for several days) which it made me unhappy not to be able to give him – bark, herb, or fruit. He was terribly constipated, and for the last fortnight it had been more and more difficult to feed him; he tried one new thing after another; then, for a few days, ate almost nothing; then suddenly, last night, gobbled up a large quantity of rice; and no doubt I was wrong to let him. His stomach was swollen, his eyes sunken; the expression of his little face, which I knew so well, on which I could so clearly read the signs of pleasure, desire, annoyance, and even of amusement, of mischief . . . the mere look of his eyes told me he was lost. One could see he must be suffering. When I put him on the ground, he dragged himself along on one side, almost lying down. I was very anxious; but before getting to the stage, it was impossible to give him the oil enema, which I should have given him sooner, but which would not have saved his life. The absurd thing was that I had very little notion whether what I gave him to eat – stewed fruit, jam, tree gum, cicindelas – would have a laxative effect, or, on the contrary, a constipating. I wanted advice. As we stopped near a stream on one occasion, I caught sight of a big tree which had been slashed and was weeping tears of sap like stearin; I took Dindiki up to it; he began by flinging himself upon it greedily, and then turned quickly away as if he had been seized with a sudden disgust. Marc took him into his *tipoye* – that is, Dindiki had got into it and refused to get out, biting savagely, as he had never done before, at anyone who tried to dislodge him. Marc soon came to tell me that he was worse. As soon as we got to the stage, we gave him a warm oil enema. Then I arranged him in Reï Bouba's basket, with a towel wrapped round him, after which we got into the cars that had been sent to meet us from Yaoundé. When, after a moment, I opened the basket, which I had taken into the car with me, Dindiki's heart had stopped beating.

I tried for nearly a whole hour, I think, to revive him by artificial respiration, as I had done at Ginglëï. But what was the use? . . . Even if I had succeeded, I should not have cured the root of the evil. It was with consternation and revolt that I saw my constant companion – my companion of every moment – leave me in this way. It may appear monstrous, but I felt that I understood, as I never had before, what it may be for a mother to lose a very young child – the ruin of a whole edifice of projects and the feeling of interrupted carnal contact. And there was even something almost superstitious added as well: Dindiki was my familiar demon.

On the last day, this little creature who was so affectionate – or, at any rate, so sensitive to caresses – began to detest me. One felt that there was unconsciously working in him an obscure intelligence that *knew* the right cure. Dindiki was angry at being constantly stopped by me when he set out to find the salutary bark or herb. And yet in his last moments, with a charmingly awkward gesture, he put his little arm up above his head, so as to have his arm-pit caressed.

The last stage was one of the longest we have ever done, but one of the finest. Rain surprised us before we got to Matsa. The station is quite close to an immense grey granite rock, of the strangest appearance. The cars arrived shortly after we did. So we went on at once, just taking time enough to attend to Dindiki, pay our porters, and have a scanty meal.

I thought the road from Matsa to N'Ghila (?), where we are sleeping tonight, one of the most beautiful we have seen. It goes through a forest that reminded me of the finest parts of the forest in the region of Bangui. And, indeed, this luxuriance enraptured me even more than the first time I came into contact with tropical vegetation.

The road must have been beautiful indeed to distract me from reading my mail, which was brought me by courier from Yaoundé.

There was a flood of newspapers and reviews in which the extraordinary and somewhat vain controversy as to *'poésie pure'* is being thrashed out. Glad to be out of Paris. I am not sure whether I should have been able to resist joining in the fray, if only to support Souday, who talks of the whole matter in the most apposite way. What does Abbé Brémond mean? To teach us how to write verse? . . . How to appreciate it? . . . His *'ut musica poesis'* is as fatal to poetry as Horace's *'ut pictura'*. And why can he not see that poetry is essentially untranslatable because of its rhythm and sonority, without going so far as to say that rhythm and sonority are all-sufficient?

Gautier never declared that

La fille de Minos et de Pasiphaé

was 'the finest line in the French language', as some people say. He protested that 'that jackanapes of a Racine' had never written another tolerable line – which is really not the same thing.

It was to be expected that these foolish arguments would be produced as a pendant to the cubists' 'pure painting'. On the other hand, who would deny that there is an unanalysable element of subtle harmony in poetry? Only philistines who are insensible to this harmony – like the celebrated novelist (whose latest work is coming out in *L'Illustration*) who thinks he is quoting Baudelaire when he says:

Là tout est ordre et beauté,[6]

without noticing the cacophony of 'tou tes tordre.' . . .

For the rest, it is easy enough for Souday to admire an atheist's poetry; but the abbé may only do so by having recourse to subterfuge; and, in my opinion, the whole of this flattering theory of his comes merely from a desire to set his conscience at rest: the meaning of this poem is of no importance; we need only listen to its melody – that is true prayer!

And while Abbé Brémond piously disintellectualizes poetry, music, by a deplorable antithesis, tends to clog itself with the signification he refuses to verse . . . Symphonic poems, with explanations in the programme! This it is that makes me flee from concerts. The confusion of styles!

I learn from a few slating articles that *Les Faux-Monnayeurs* has at last come out.

2 May

Rose early, urged out of doors by the fine weather, which I positively *felt* before I saw the heavens – admirable in their blue serenity. An almost full moon was still queen of a sky that was paling in the dawn. The quality of the air was extraordinary – soft, warm, caressing, light, of an incomparable suavity . . . Round the great trees, drowned in mists the sun was beginning to dissipate, floated strange perfumes. Soft, flexible vegetation, rich with hidden strength. Groups of trees, so fine, so great, so noble, that one said to oneself: 'This is what I have come to see!' Songs of birds. Chirping of insects. My heart was flooded with a kind of obscure and complex adoration. But was it the exotic vegetation that filled me with admiration? . . . Was it not rather – above all – the spring itself?

Left N'Ghila about eight o'clock. Shortly after, we went through a piece of admirable forest. Indolent spread of the foliage – grace of the creepers – solemnity of the great trees, darting upwards to such extraordinary heights – beauty of the mere light! I had wanted to go on ahead, but the other lorry, with Marc in it, was in front. We had

---

6. Baudelaire's line is: *'Tout n'est qu'ordre et beauté.'*

decided to sleep at the station, on the Sanaga, and put off arriving at Yaoundé for another day, in order to spend a little more time in the forest. One of the natives was put to sit on the step of the first lorry and told to keep a lookout to see whether we were following, and to stop the chauffeur at my first signal. Moreover, young Pierre (the brother of that lazy scamp Madoua, who has taken Adoum's place since Maroua) was sitting at the back of the lorry, with orders to see that the fragile objects, such as the cinema stand, etc., did not shake about too much, so that he had his face towards me.

So when we were crossing a particularly attractive *marigot*, I made the signals that had been agreed upon, for them to stop. All in vain! We sounded our horn; we shouted, and even, when they got to the next hill, the native sitting on the step of my car rushed off in pursuit of them. But the little idiot, though he saw our wild attempts, continued to smile without budging; so that the first lorry continued to gain on us – we did not meet again till we got to the station. Marc, believing in the lookout's lying assertions that my car was following, kept waiting for my signal – whilst *I* was plunging alone into an enchanting thicket.

Silence, traversed by the songs of mysterious birds. Flowers of gigantic plants; one of them, extraordinarily hairy – or, rather, bristling with spikes – was covered with bunches of orange fruit, like large hirsute grapes. It was sad seeing all this without Marc. I am incapable of enjoying anything by myself.

I found Marc at the station, furious and disappointed. We stormed at Pierre and his brother, through whose carelessness and stupidity we have missed our last farewell to the forest. It was out of pure charity that we brought them with us, so as to help them on their way to Yaoundé. We have refused to take them any farther. These two are the wretched products of a large town (Yaoundé); they are thieves, liars, and hypocrites, and would justify the irritation certain colonists feel against the blacks. But that is just it – they are *not* the natural products of the country. It is contact with our civilization that has spoilt them.

This is the last day. Our journey is over. Perhaps I shall never see the virgin forest again. It never looked more beautiful, and we passed by like travellers in a hurry to reach their goal, when this was the goal. Oh! if I could see it again, if only for a moment! We are only twenty-five kilometres away from it. The car would take us back in less than an hour . . . Alas! the car has got to leave at once. At any rate, we have telegraphed to Yaoundé to tell the one that is coming to fetch us tomorrow to get here early enough to allow of our making this excursion backwards.

The savanna round the station recalls the surroundings of Fort Archambault. The station itself is an outpost of civilization. It is a place where there arrives, by an excellent road, a great abundance of merchandise for the north. Went down to the banks of the Sanaga. At my approach great quantities of grey-brown butterflies rose from the moist sandy shore and circled round me; there were not hundreds of them, but thousands. And farther on I again saw the enormous butterfly that I had caught at Carnot. It has very long wings, like a dragonfly's – black, striped with light blue – and a very voluminous, saffron-coloured abdomen. It is much the biggest butterfly I have seen in Equatorial Africa.

There are waterfalls and rapids above the station.

3 May

The sky this morning was completely overcast. Impossible to photograph. Useless to go back. Went straight on to Yaoundé.

This morning we were brought some fish on the end of a reed; they looked like carp, with hippopotamus snouts.

Every morning one sets about extracting one's hookworms. At the fourth, which by that time is probably about as big as a grain of rice, one takes a glass of cognac, for one feels as if one were going to give up the ghost.

Some of them leave deep holes behind, which have to be watered with iodine. Other tiny ones, which have not had time to grow big and heavy, flee before the pin or scalpel, and if one does not make haste, burrow deeper and deeper into one's flesh. They are often the most difficult ones to extract. If one leaves them, they become enormous, pullulate, turn into a colony. Soon there is nothing for it but to cut one's toe off.

3–6 May

Back to civilization. The forest which the railway passes through is marvellously beautiful. We travelled very comfortably in a luggage van with our boys and all our paraphernalia. But I don't care about noting things any more.

Douala, 7 May

What a hotel! The most repellent of rest-houses is better than this. And what white people! Ugly . . . stupid . . . vulgar . . . As for me, who am always afraid of disturbing other people – other people's thoughts, other people's rest, other people's prayers – such want of consideration fills me first of all with amazement and then with indignation. But I end by saying to myself that if these people disturb us, it is unwittingly; for as they themselves neither meditate, nor read, nor pray – and sleep the sleep of brutes – they are never disturbed by anything. I should like to write a *Praise of Discretion*.

We have to make arrangements to send our boys back to their homes. Two hundred francs from Douala to Matadi. After that I don't know. Besides this, there is owing to them nearly three months' wages. With four hundred francs and the ticket to Matadi as well, I hope they will not be held up for want of money. But I am terrified at the idea that they may be robbed of it, or gamble it away; and we agreed that they were to hand it over to M.M. until the day they leave (the 15th). But when we got on board the *Asie*, where they came to see us off, I caught them in the act of investing in an umbrella apiece, at the price of thirty-five francs. I arrived just in time to stop them.

14 May

It is all over. We have looped the loop. The ship has weighed anchor and Mount Cameroon is disappearing slowly into the fog.

I have given the steward a frightful little animal to take charge of; I bought it last night at Douala – a civet, I think.

This morning, at breakfast, the bishop of Yaoundé came and sat beside me. I ordered some ham without reflecting that it was Friday; so that after that I didn't dare speak to the bishop.

*

There are some children on board – from eleven to fourteen years old. The eldest, who is by far the most affected of the ▮▮▮ declared at one of the little girls that when he grew up, ▮▮▮ intended to be a 'literary critic or else pick up cigarette ends in the street. All or nothing. No medium. That's my motto.' I was hidden in a corner of the saloon, sheltered behind a number of *L'Illustration*, and listened to them indefatigably. How difficult it is to be natural at that age – for a white at any rate! One's single idea is to astonish other people – to make a show.

A little later I came across the same boy, leaning against the bulwarks, with a companion rather younger than himself; they were talking to a Swede.

'We French detest other nations – all of us French . . . don't we, George? . . . Yes, it's a peculiar thing about the French that they can't endure other nations . . . Unless we allow that they have qualities – Oh! then, if we allow them qualities, we do it *thoroughly*.' (This last remark obviously made for the sake of his interlocutor, who looked very much amused – and no wonder.)

'I call a musician,' he said too to the little girl, 'a person who understands what he plays. I don't call a person a musician who bangs on the piano just like people kicking niggers.' And, as he added, with an air of authority, that they should 'be put an end to' – not the niggers, perhaps, and certainly not the people who kick them, but the bad musicians – the little girl exclaimed indignantly:

'But then who will play for us to dance?'